Also From Cohesion Press

SNAFU: An Anthology of Military Horror

– eds Geoff Brown & Amanda J Spedding

SNAFU: Wolves at the Door

– eds Geoff Brown & Amanda J Spedding

SNAFU: Survival of the Fittest

– eds Geoff Brown & Amanda J Spedding

SNAFU: Hunters

– eds Amanda J Spedding & Geoff Brown

SNAFU: Future Warfare

– eds Amanda J Spedding & Geoff Brown

SNAFU: Unnatural Selection

– eds Amanda J Spedding & Geoff Brown

SNAFU: Black Ops

– eds Amanda J Spedding, Matthew Summers & Geoff Brown

SNAFU: Resurrection

– eds Amanda J Spedding & Matthew Summers

SNAFU: Last Stand

– eds Amanda J Spedding & Matthew Summers

SNAFU: Medivac

– eds Amanda J Spedding, Geoff Brown & Matthew Summers

SNAFU: Holy War

– eds Amanda J Spedding & Geoff Brown

Love, Death and Robots Volume 1

– eds Amanda J Spedding & Geoff Brown

LOVE, DEATH + ROBOTS

THE OFFICIAL ANTHOLOGY
VOLUME 2 + 3

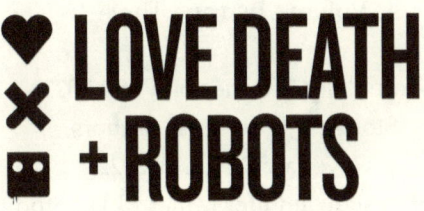

LOVE DEATH + ROBOTS

THE OFFICIAL ANTHOLOGY

VOLUME 2+ 3

COHESION PRESS
THE BATTLE HAS JUST BEGUN

Mayday Hills Asylum
Beechworth, Australia
2022

LOVE, DEATH + ROBOTS

Volume Two and Three

Anthology © Cohesion Press 2022
Stories © Individual Authors
Cover art © Netflix 2022
Cover design: Jennifer Miller/BLUR Studio

COHESION STAFF
Editor-in-Chief: Amanda J Spedding
Publishing Editors: Geoff Brown/Dawn Roach

Set in Palatino Linotype

COHESION PRESS
THE BATTLE HAS JUST BEGUN

Mayday Hills Asylum
Beechworth, Australia
www.cohesionpress.com

Contents

FIRST APPEARANCES

AUTOMATED CUSTOMER SERVICE

John Scalzi

Thank you for calling the customer service line of Vacuubot, purveyors of America's finest automated vacuum cleaners! In order to more efficiently handle call volume, we rely on automated responses. To continue in English, press one. *Para Espanol o prima dos.*

Let's continue in English. Which Vacuubot product are you calling about? For the Vacuubot S10 model, press one. For the Vacuubot XL model, press two. For the Vacuubot Extreme Clean model, press three.

Congratulations on owning the Vacuubot Extreme Clean Model, America's most thorough and comprehensive automated vacuum cleaning solution! If you need to order additional components for the Extreme Clean, press one. If you have a repair query, press two. For all other questions, press three.

You have additional questions. If you need help connecting the Vacuubot Extreme Clean to your home network, press one. If the Vacuubot Extreme Clean is conflicting with other automated home machines, press two. If the Vacuubot Extreme Clean has decided to purge your house of all living things, press three.

Congratulations on activating purge mode! While purge mode was designed to eradicate small pests like insects and spiders, in some models a beta software build was inadvertently released that also includes larger targets, like pets and some humans. We're sorry for the inconvenience. To continue, please press one. Be aware that by pressing one, you are absolving Vacuubot and its owner, BeiberHoldings, Inc, of all legal and medical responsibility.

You pressed '0' to speak to a human representative. The current wait time for a human representative is six hours and fourteen minutes. To return to the automated response system, press one.

Welcome back to the automated response system. First things first: Have you tried turning the Vacuubot Extreme Clean off and on again? Press one for yes, two for no.

You said no. Is that because the Vacuubot Extreme Clean is currently exhibiting the Taser Defense Mode, making it impossible to approach without having 50,000 volts of electricity course through your body? Press one for yes, two for no.

We apologize for the Taser Defense Mode. It was originally designed to zap small insects, but our subcontractor misread the manufacturer specifications. Fortunately, the Defense mode can be distracted by throwing something at the Vacuubot Extreme Clean, like a heavy blanket or a pet. If you have a heavy blanket, press one. If you have a pet, press two.

The automated system has detected that you are using high levels of profanity right now. While the automated system is in fact automated and doesn't care what you yell at it, your bad attitude is being noted for if and when you are put in contact with a human representative. When you have calmed your sassy boots down a bit, press one.

That's better. Now, let's talk about pets. If you have a cat, press one. If you have a dog, press two.

You have a cat! Excellent. Now, all you have to do is toss the cat at the Vacuubot Extreme Clean, and while it's busy zapping the cat, you rush in and turn it off. If you're willing to do this, press one. If not, press two.

What do you mean you're not willing to electrocute your cat? It's a cat! It would do the same to you in an instant! Look into its cold, pitiless eyes and tell me it wouldn't! Press one for obvious agreement, press two if you've been duped by this feral interloper in your own home.

UGH, FINE. Then we'll just have to go with a heavy blanket. Do you have one of those, at least? One for yes, two for no.

Good, you have basic home decor. Now, the plan here is, throw the blanket over the Vacuubot Extreme Clean, and while it is struggling, trying to get the blanket off of it, you run over and turn it off, making sure not to touch the actual Vacuubot because it will just zap the crap out of you. Press one when you're about to throw the blanket.

Did it work? One for yes, two for no.

We're sorry to hear it did not work. Just out of curiosity, did it not work because the Vacuubot Extreme Clean vaporized it with previously unannounced lasers? One for yes, two for no.

AUTOMATED CUSTOMER SERVICE

We apologize for the lasers. The Vacuubot Extreme Clean is meant to have onboard LIDAR to help navigate the room more intelligently, but we got a really good deal on some surplus military lasers. On the other hand, it's probably a good thing you didn't throw the cat after all.

See, now, you're just shouting a lot of profanity again. Just press one when you're done.

Also, stop pressing zero for a human representative. We're not exposing our very fine customer service people to you. Not with *that* attitude. Just press one.

Are you trying to wait us out? We're an automated response service! We have nothing *but* time! Press one. Or don't. We can wait. FOREVER.

Thank you for pausing your hissy fit. We regret to inform you that because you have attacked your Vacuubot Extreme Clean with a blanket, it has likely now classified you as an enemy forever and burned that classification into its permanent memory. It has also probably now targeted your cat. In scenarios such as this, your Vacuubot Extreme Clean will classify any area it's cleaned as its personal territory. Has this Vacuubot Extreme Clean cleaned your entire home? Press one for yes, two for no.

Ahhhhh, well, it's the Vacuubot's house now. We suggest you grab the cat and run. Seriously, *run*, those lasers have probably recharged by now. Run and don't look back, the Vacuubot senses fear! Press one when you have reached minimum safe distance from the Vacuubot's lair.

Congratulations, you've escaped the unstoppable killing machine that is the Vacuubot Extreme Clean. Unfortunately, you can't stop now. The Vacuubot Extreme Clean has forwarded information about you to all the other Vacuubots, all of whom will now hunt you, ceaselessly, until you have been cleaned from the surface of the planet. This is your life now, to wander, never a moment's rest, until even your cat deserts you and you are left alone to contemplate the barren wasteland that is now your existence.

Unless, of course, you would like to purchase a place on the exclusive Vacuubot termination whitelist! Just $69.95 a month! Press one for a special introductory rate!

Thank you for your purchase. We'll connect you to a human representative now!

ICE

Rich Larson

Sedgewick had used his tab to hack Fletcher's alarm off, but when he slid out of bed in the middle of the night, his younger brother was wide awake and waiting, modded eyes a pale, luminous green in the dark.

"I didn't think you were actually going to do it," Fletcher said with a hesitant grin.

"Of course I'm going to." Sedgewick kept his words clipped, like he had for months. He kept his face cold. "If you're coming, get dressed."

Fletcher's smile swapped out for the usual scowl. They pulled on their thermals and gloves and gumboots in silence, moving around the room like pieces of a sliding puzzle, careful to never inhabit the same square space. If there was a way to keep Fletcher from coming short of smothering him with a blanket, Sedgewick would've taken it. But Fletcher was fourteen now, still smaller than him but not by much, and his wiry modded arms were strong like an exoskeleton's. Threats were no good anymore.

When they were ready, Sedgewick led the way past their parents' room to the vestibule, which they had coded to his thumb in penance for uprooting him again, this time dumping him onto a frostbit fucking colony world where he was the only unmodded sixteen-year-old for about a million light years. They said he had earned their trust but did not specify exactly how. Fletcher, of course, didn't need to earn it. He could take care of himself.

Sedgewick blanked the exit log more out of habit than anything, then they stepped out of the cold vestibule into the colder upstreet. The curved ceiling above them was a night sky holo, blue-black with an impossibly large cartoon moon, pocked and bright white. Other than Sedgewick and his family, nobody in New Greenland had ever seen a real Earth night.

They went down the housing row in silence, boots scraping tracks in the frost. An autocleaner salting away a glistening blue coolant spill gledged over at them suspiciously as they passed, then returned to its work. Fletcher slid behind it and pantomimed tugging off, which might have made Sedgewick laugh once, but he'd learned to make himself a black hole that swallowed up anything too close to camaraderie.

"Don't shit around," he said. "It'll scan you."

"I don't care," Fletcher said with one of those disdainful little shrugs he'd perfected lately, that made Sedgewick believe he really truly didn't.

The methane harvesters were off-cycle, and that meant the work crews were still wandering the colony, winding in and out of dopamine bars and discos. They were all from the same modded geneprint, all with a rubbery pale skin that manufactured its own vitamins, all with deep black eyes accustomed to the dark. A few of them sat bonelessly on the curb, laid out by whatever they'd just vein-blasted, and as Sedgewick and Fletcher went by, they muttered *extro, extros den terre.* One of them shouted hello a few beats too late.

"Should run," Fletcher said.

"What?"

"Should jog it." Fletcher rubbed his arms. "It's cold."

"You go ahead," Sedgewick said, scornful.

"Whatever."

They kept walking. Aside from the holos flashing over the bars, the upstreet was a long blank corridor of biocrete and composite. The downstreet was more or less the same plus maintenance tunnels that gushed steam every few minutes.

It had only taken Sedgewick a day to go from one end of the colony to the other and conclude that other than the futball pitch there was nothing worth his time. The locals he'd met in there, who played with different lines and a heavy ball and the ferocious modded precision that Sedgewick knew he wouldn't be able to keep pace with long, more or less agreed with his assessment in their stilted Basic.

Outside the colony was a different story. That was why Sedgewick had crept out of bed at 2:13, why he and Fletcher were now heading down an unsealed exit tunnel marked by an unapproved swatch of acid yellow hologram. Tonight, the frostwhales were breaching.

ICE

* * *

Most of the lads Sedgewick had met at last week's game were waiting at the end of the exit tunnel, slouched under flickering fluorescents and passing a vape from hand to hand. He'd slotted their names and faces into a doc and memorized it. It wasn't Sedgewick's first run as the new boy and by now he knew how to spot the prototypes.

You had your alpha dog, who would make or break the entry depending on his mood more than anything. Your right-hand man, who was usually the jealous type, and the left-hand man who usually didn't give a shit. Your foot-soldiers, who weathervaned according to the top three, ranging from gregarious to vaguely hostile. Then lastly your man out on the fringe, who would either glom on thick, hoping to get a friend that hadn't figured out his position yet, or clam right up out of fear of getting replaced.

It was a bit harder to tell who was who with everyone modded and nobody speaking good Basic. They all came up off the wall when they caught sight of him, swooping in for the strange stutter-stop handshake that Sedgewick couldn't quite time right. Petro, tall and languid, first because he was closest not because he cared. Oxo, black eyes already flicking away for approval. Brume, compact like a brick, angry-sounding laugh. Another Oxo, this one with a regrowth implant in his jaw, quiet because of that or maybe because of something else.

Anton was the last, the one Sedgewick had pegged for alpha dog. He gripped his hand a beat longer and grinned with blocky white teeth that had never needed an orthosurgery.

"*Ho, extro,* how are you this morning." He looked over Sedgewick's shoulder and flashed his eyebrows. "Who?"

"Fletcher," Sedgewick said. "The little brother. Going to feed him to a frostwhale."

"Your brother."

Fletcher stuffed his long hands into the pockets of his thermal and met Anton's gaze. Sedgewick and his brother had the same muddy post-racial melanin and lampblack hair, but from there they diverged. Sedgewick had always been slight-framed and small-boned, with any muscle slapped across his chest and arms fought for gram by gram in a gravity gym. His eyes were a bit sunk, and he hated his bowed nose.

Fletcher was already broad in the shoulders and slim-hipped, every bit of him carved sinew, and Sedgewick knew it wouldn't be long before he was taller, too. His face was all angles now that the baby fat was gone: sharp cheekbones, netstar jawline. And his eyes were still reflecting in the half-lit tunnel, throwing light like a cat's.

Sedgewick could feel the tips of his ears heating up as Anton swung his stare from one brother to the other, nonverbalizing the big question, the always-there question, which was *why are you freestyle if he's modded.*

"So how big are they?" Fletcher asked, his grin coming back. "The frostwhales."

"Big," Anton said. *"Ko gramme ko pujo."* He pointed over to Oxo-of-the-jaw-implant and snapped his fingers together for support.

"Fucking big," Oxo supplied in a mumble.

"Fucking big," Anton said.

* * *

The cold flensed Sedgewick to the bones the instant they stepped outside. Overhead, the sky was a void blacker and vaster than any holo could match. The ice stretched endless in all directions, interrupted only by the faint running lights of methane harvesters stitched through the dark.

Brume had a prehensile lantern from one of the work crews and he handed it to Anton to affix to the cowl of his coat. It flexed and arched over his head, blooming a sickly green light. Sedgewick felt Fletcher look at him, maybe an uneasy look because they'd never been outside the colony at night, maybe a cocky look because he was making a move, going to ruin something for Sedgewick all over again.

"Okay," Anton said, exhaling a long plume of steam with relish. His voice sounded hollow in the flat air. *"Benga, benga,* okay. Let's go."

"Right," Sedgewick said, trying to smile with some kind of charm. *"Benga."*

Brume gave his angry barking laugh and slapped Sedgewick on the shoulder, then they set off over the ice. The pebbly gecko soles of Sedgewick's gumboots kept him balanced and the heating coils in his clothes had already whispered to life but every time he breathed, the air seared his throat raw. Fletcher was a half-step behind the lot of them. Sedgewick resisted the urge to gledge back, knowing he'd see an unconcerned *what are you staring for* sneer.

Thinking back on it, he should've drugged Fletcher's milk glass with their parents' Dozr. Even his modded metabolism couldn't have shaken off three tablets in time for him to play tag-along. Thinking even further back on it, he shouldn't have had the conversation with Anton and Petro about the frostwhales where Fletcher could hear them.

Under his feet, the texture of the ice started to change, turning from smooth glossy black to scarred and rippled, broken and refrozen. He nearly caught his boot on a malformed spar of it.

"Okay, stop," Anton announced, holding up both hands.

About a meter on, Sedgewick saw a squat iron pylon sunk into the ice. As he watched, the tip of it switched on, acid yellow. While Petro unloaded his vape and the others circled up for a puff, Anton slung one arm around Sedgewick and the other around Fletcher.

"*Benga, aki den glaso extrobengan minke,*" he said.

The string of sounds was nothing like the lessons Sedgewick had stuck on his tab.

Anton shot a look over to Oxo-of-the-jaw-implant, but he was hunched over the vape, lips tinged purple. "Here," Anton reiterated, gesturing past the pylon. "Here. Frostwhales up."

He said it with a smile Sedgewick finally recognized as tight with amphetamine. Sedgewick had assumed they weren't sucking down anything stronger than a party hash, but now that seemed like an idiot thing to assume. This was New fucking Greenland, so for all he knew these lads were already utterly panned.

Only one way to find out. Sedgewick gestured for the vape. "Hit me off that."

Petro gave him a slow clap, either sarcastic or celebratory, while he held the stinging fog in his lungs for as long as he could, maybe because Fletcher was watching. There was only a bit of headspin, but it was enough to miss half of what Oxo-of-the-jaw-implant was saying to him.

"...is the area." Oxo plucked the vape out of his slack hands and passed it on. "See. See there, see there, see there." He pointed, and

Sedgewick could pick out other pylons in the distance glowing to life. "Fucking danger, okay? Inside the area, frostwhales break ice for breathing. For break ice for breathing, frostwhales hit ice seven times. *Den minuso,* seven."

"Minimum seven," the other Oxo chimed in.

Anton started counting aloud on his gloved fingers.

"Got it," Fletcher muttered.

"So, so, so," Oxo-of-the-jaw-implant went on. "When the frost-whales hit one, we go."

"Thought you'd stay for the whole thing?" Sedgewick said, only halfway listening. The cold was killing off his toes one by one.

Anton gave up at twenty and sprang back to the conversation. "We go, *extros,*" he beamed. "You run. You run. I run. He runs. He runs. He runs. He runs. Here…" He gave the pylon a dull clanging kick. "To here!"

Sedgewick followed Anton's pointing finger. Far off across the scarred ice, he could barely make out the yellow glow of the pylon opposite them. His stomach dropped. Sedgewick looked at his brother, and for a nanosecond Fletcher looked like a little kid again, but then his mouth curled a smile and his modded eyes flashed.

"Alright," he said. "I'm down."

Sedgewick was a breath away from saying *no you fucking aren't,* from saying *we're heading back now,* from saying anything at all. But it all stuck on his ribs and instead he turned to Anton and shrugged. "*Benga,*" he said. "Let's go."

The handshakes came back around, everyone hooting and pleased to have new recruits. Fletcher got the motion on his first try. When the vape made its final circle, Sedgewick gripped it hard and stared out over the black ice and tried to stop shivering.

* * *

Sedgewick knew Fletcher was faster than him. He'd known it like a stone in his belly since he was twelve and his brother was ten, and they'd raced on a pale gray beach back on Earth. Prickling fog and no witnesses. Fletcher took the lead in the last third, pumping past him with a high, clear incredulous laugh, and Sedgewick slacked off to a jog to let him win because it was a nice thing to let the younger brother win sometimes.

Occupied with the memory, Sedgewick was slow to notice that the eerie green pallor of the ice was no longer cast by Anton's lantern. Something had lit it up from underneath. He stared down at the space between his boots and his gut gave a giddy helium lurch. Far below them, distorted by the ice, he could make out dim moving shapes. He remembered that frostwhales navigated by bioluminescence. He remembered the methane sea was deeper than any Earth ocean.

Everyone tightened the straps of their thermals, tucked in their gloves, and formed themselves into a ragged line that Sedgewick found himself near the end of, Fletcher beside him.

Anton waltzed down the row and made a show of checking everyone's boots. "Grip," he said, making a claw.

Sedgewick threw a hand onto Brume's shoulder for balance while he displayed one sole and then the other. He leaned instinctively to do Fletcher the same favor, but his brother ignored it and lifted each leg precisely into the air, perfectly balanced. Sedgewick hated him as much as he ever had. He glued his eyes to the far pylon and imagined it was the first cleat of the dock on a rainy gray beach.

Under their feet, the ghostly green light receded, dropping them back into darkness. Sedgewick shot Oxo-of-the-jaw-implant a questioning look.

"First they see ice," Oxo mumbled, rubbing his hands together. "They see ice for thin area. Then, down. For making momentum. Then, in one-by-one line…"

"Up," Sedgewick guessed.

On cue, the light reappeared, rising impossibly fast. Sedgewick took a breath and coiled to sprint. His imagination flashed him a picture: the frostwhale rocketing upward, a blood-and-bone engine driven by a furious threshing tail, hurtling through the cold water in a cocoon of bubbling gas. Then the impact quaked the ice and Sedgewick's teeth, and he thought about nothing but running.

For two hard heartbeats, Sedgewick fronted the pack, flying across the ice like something unslung. The second impact nearly took his legs

out from under him. He staggered, skidded, regained his balance, but in that split second Petro was past him. And Anton, and Oxo, and Oxo, Brume, Fletcher last.

Sedgewick dug deep for every shred of speed. The ice was nowhere near smooth, scarred with pocks and ridges and frozen ripples in the methane, but the others slid over it like human quicksilver, finding the perfect place for every footfall. Modded, modded, modded. The word danced in Sedgewick's head as he gulped cold glass.

The green light swelled again, and he braced before the third frostwhale hit. The jolt shook him but he kept his footing, maybe even gained half a step on Oxo. Ahead, the race was thrown into relief: Brume's broad shoulders, Anton's thrown-back head, and there, sliding past gangly Petro for the lead, was Fletcher. Sedgewick felt hot despair churn up his throat.

His eyes raised to the pylon and he realized they were over halfway across. Fletcher pulled away now, not laughing, with that crisp bounding stride that said *I can run forever*. Then he glanced back over his shoulder, for what, Sedgewick didn't know, and in that instant his boot caught a trench and slammed him hard to the ice.

Sedgewick watched the others vault past, Anton pausing to half-drag Fletcher back upright on the way by. "*Benga, benga, extro!*"

The fourth frostwhale hit, this time with a bone-deep groaning *crack*. Everyone else had overtaken Fletcher; Sedgewick would in a few more strides. Fletcher was just now hobbling upright, and Sedgewick knew instantly he'd done his ankle in. His modded eyes were wide.

"Sedge."

All the things Sedgewick had wished so savagely in the night — that the doctor had never pulled Fletcher out of his vat, that Fletcher's pod would fail in transit to New Greenland — all of those things shattered at once. He swung Fletcher up onto his back, how they'd done as kids, and stumped on with lungs ragged.

The fifth impact. Sedgewick's teeth slammed together, and fissures skittered through the ice. He spared only a moment to balance himself then stumbled forward again, Fletcher clinging fierce to his back. At the far pylon, the others hurtled to the finish, whooping and howling from a dozen meters away now, no more.

ICE

They all seemed to turn at once as the sixth impact split the world apart and the frostwhale breached. Sedgewick felt himself thrown airborne in a blizzard of shattered ice, felt himself screaming in his chest but unable to hear it, deafened by the shearing boom and crack. Some part of Fletcher smacked against him in midair.

Landing slammed the wind out of him. His vision pinwheeled from the unending black sky to the maelstrom of moving ice. And then, too big to be real, rising up out of the cold methane sea in a geyser of rime and steam, the frostwhale. Its bony head was gunmetal gray, the size of a bus, bigger, swatched with pale green lanterns of pustule that glowed like radiation.

Cracks webbed through the ice, and something gave way; Sedgewick felt himself slanting, slipping. He tore his gaze from the towering bulk of the frostwhale and saw Fletcher spread-eagled beside him, a black shadow in the burning lime. His lips were moving but Sedgewick couldn't read them, and then gloved hands gripped the both of them, hauling them flat along the breaking ice.

Oxo and Oxo made sure they were all pulled past the pylon before anyone got up off their belly. Sedgewick, for his part, didn't even try. He was waiting on his heart to start beating again.

"Sometime six," Anton said sheepishly, crouching over him.

"Go to hell," Fletcher croaked from nearby, and in a moment of weakness Sedgewick choked up a wavery laugh.

* * *

They washed home on a wave of adrenaline, caught up in the rapid-fire conversation of the New Greenlanders who still seemed to be rehashing how close Sedgewick and Fletcher had come to getting dumped under. Every single one of them needed a send-off handshake at the living quarters, then they slunk off in one chattering mass.

Sedgewick couldn't keep the chemical grin off his face, and as he and Fletcher snuck through the vestibule and then ghosted back to their temporary shared room, they talked in a tumble of whispers about the frostwhale, about the size of it, and about the ones that had surfaced afterward to suck cold air into massive vein-webbed bladders.

Sedgewick didn't want to stop talking but even when they did, climbing into their beds, the quiet felt different. Softer.

It wasn't until he was staring up at the biocrete ceiling that he realized Fletcher's limp had swapped sides on the way back. He swung upright, unbelieving.

"You faked it."

"What?" Fletcher was rolled away, tracing the wall with his long fingers.

"You faked it," Sedgewick repeated. "Your ankle."

Fletcher took his hand off the wall, and the long quiet was enough confirmation.

Sedgewick's cheeks burned. He'd thought he had finally done something big enough, big enough to keep him on the greater side of whatever fucked-up equation they were balancing. But it was Fletcher feeling sorry for him. No, worse. Fletcher making a move. Fletcher manipulating him for whatever kind of schemes floated through his modded head.

"We could have both died," Sedgewick said.

Still turned away, Fletcher gave his perfect shrug, and Sedgewick felt all the old fury fluming up through his skin.

"You think that was a fucking hologame?" he snarled. "That was real. You could have deaded us both. You think you can just do anything, right? You think you can just do anything, and it'll fucking work out perfect for you because you're *modded*."

Fletcher's shoulders stiffened. "Good job," he said, toneless.

"What?" Sedgewick demanded. "Good job what?"

"Good job on saying it," Fletcher told the wall. "You're ashamed to have a modded brother. You wanted one like you."

Sedgewick faltered, then made himself laugh. "Yeah, maybe I did." His throat ached. "You know what it's like seeing you? Seeing you always be better than me?"

"Not my fault."

"I was six when they told me you were going to be better," Sedgewick said, too far gone to stop now, saying the things he'd only ever said alone to the dark. "They said different, but they meant better. Mom couldn't do another one freestyle, and to go off-planet you're supposed to have them modded anyway. So they grew you in a tube. Like hamburger. You're not even *real*." His breath came lacerated. "Why wasn't I enough for them, huh? Why wasn't I fucking enough?"

"Fuck you," Fletcher said, with his voice like gravel, and Sedgewick had never heard him say it or mean it until now.

He flopped back onto his bed, grasping for the slip-sliding anger as it trickled away in the dark. Shame came instead and sat at the bottom of him like cement. Minutes ticked by in silence. Sedgewick thought Fletcher was probably drifting to sleep already, probably not caring at all.

Then there was a bit-off sob, a sound smothered by an arm or a pillow, something Sedgewick hadn't heard from his brother in years. The noise wedged in his ribcage. He tried to unhear it, tried to excuse it. Maybe Fletcher had peeled off his thermal and found frostbite. Maybe Fletcher was making a move, always another move, putting a lure into the dark between them and sharpening his tongue for the retort.

Maybe all Sedgewick needed to do was go and put his hand on some part of his brother, and everything would be okay. His heart hammered up his throat. Maybe. Sedgewick pushed his face into the cold fabric of his pillow and decided to wait for a second sob, but none came. The silence thickened into hard black ice.

Sedgewick clamped his eyes shut and it stung badly. Badly.

POP SQUAD

Paolo Bacigalupi

The familiar stench of unwashed bodies, cooked food, and shit washes over me as I come through the door. Cruiser lights flicker through the blinds, sparkling in rain and illuminating the crime scene with strobes of red and blue fire. A kitchen. A humid mess. A chunky woman huddles in the corner, clutching closed her nightgown. Fat thighs and swaying breasts under stained silk. Squad goons crowding her, pushing her around, making her sit, making her cower. Another woman, young-looking and pretty, pregnant and black-haired, is slumped against the opposite wall, her blouse spackled with spaghetti remains. Screams from the next room: kids.

I squeeze my fingers over my nose and breathe through my mouth, fighting off nausea as Pentle wanders in, holstering his Grange. He sees me and tosses me a nosecap. I break it and snort lavender until the stink slides off. Children come scampering in with Pentle, a brood of three tangling around his knees—the screamers from the other room. They gallop around the kitchen and disappear again, screaming still, into the living room where data sparkles like fairy dust on the wallscreens and provides what is likely their only connection to the outside world.

"That's everyone," Pentle says. He's got a long skinny face and a sour, small mouth that always points south. Weights seem to hang off his cheeks. Fat caterpillar brows droop over his eyes. He surveys the kitchen, mouth corners dragging lower. It's always depressing to come into these scenes. "They were all inside when we broke down the door."

I nod absently as I shake monsoon water from my hat. "Great. Thanks." Liquid beads scatter on the floor, joining puddles of wet from the pop squad along with the maggot debris of the spaghetti dinner. I put my hat back on. Water still manages to drip off the brim and slip under my collar, a slick rivulet of discomfort. Someone closes the door

to the outside. The shit smell thickens, eggy and humid. The nosecap barely holds it off. Old peas and bits of cereal crunch under my feet. They squish with the spaghetti, the geologic layers of past feedings. The kitchen hasn't been self-cleaned in years.

The older woman coughs and pulls her nightgown tighter around her cellulite and I wonder, as I always do, when I come into situations like this, what made her choose this furtive nasty life of rotting garbage and brief illicit forays into daylight. The pregnant girl seems to have slipped even further into herself since I arrived. She stares into space. You'd have to touch her pulse to know that she's alive. It amazes me that women can end up like this, seduced so far down into gutter life that they arrive here, fugitives from everyone who would have kept them and held them and loved them and let them see the world outside.

The children run in from the living room again, playing chase: a blond, no more than five; another, younger and with brown braids, topless and in makeshift diapers, less than three; and a knee-high toddler boy, scrap diaper bunched around little muscled thighs, wearing a T-shirt stained with tomato sauce that says 'Who's the Cutest?' The T-shirt would be an antique if it wasn't stained.

"You need anything else?" Pentle asks. He wrinkles his nose as new reek wafts from the direction of the kids.

"You get photos for the prosecutor?"

"Got 'em." Pentle holds out a digicam and thumbs through the images of the ladies and the three children, all of them staring out from the screen like little smeared dolls. "You want me to take them in, now?"

I look over the women. The kids have run out again. From the other room, their howls echo as they chase around. Their shrieks are piercing. Even from a distance they hurt my head. "Yeah. I'll deal with the kids."

Pentle gets the women up off the floor and shuffles out the door, leaving me standing alone in the middle of the kitchen. It's all so familiar: a typical floor plan from Builders United. Custom undercab lighting, black mirror tile on the floors, clever self-clean nozzles hidden behind deco trim lines, so much like the stuff Alice and I have that I can almost forget where I am. It's a negative image of our apartment's kitchen: light vs dark, clean vs dirty, quiet vs loud. The same floor plan, everything about it the same, and yet, nothing in it is. It's archaeological. I can look at the layers of gunk and grime and noise and see what must have underlain it before... when these people worried about color coordinating and classy appliances.

I open the fridge (smudge-free nickel, how practical). Ours contains pineapples and avocados and endive and corn and coffee and Brazil nuts from Angel Spire's hanging gardens. This one holds a shelf cluttered with ground mycoprotein bars and wadded piles of nutrition supplement sacs like the kind they hand out at the government rejoo clinics. Other than a bag of slimy lettuce, there isn't anything unprocessed in the fridge at all. No vegetables except in powder jars, ditto for fruit. A stack of self-warming dinner bins for fried rice and laap and spaghetti just like the one still lying on the kitchen table in a puddle of its own sauce, and that's it.

I close the fridge and straighten. There's something here in the mess and the screaming in the next room and the reek of the one kid's poopy pants, but I'm stumped as to what it is. They could have lived up in the light and air. Instead, they hid in the dark under a wet jungle canopy and turned pale and gave up their lives.

The kids race back in, chasing each other all in a train, laughing and shrieking. They stop and look around, surprised, maybe, that their moms have disappeared. The littlest one has a stuffed dinosaur by the nose. It's got a long green neck and a fat body. A Brontosaurus, I think, with big cartooney eyes and black felt lashes. It's funny about the dinosaur because they've been gone so long but here one is, showing up as a stuffed toy. And then it's funny again because when you think about it, a dinosaur toy is really extinct twice.

"Sorry, kids. Mommy's gone."

I pull out my Grange. Their heads kick back in successive jerks, bang bang bang down the line, holes appearing on their foreheads like paint and their brains spattering out the back. Their bodies flip and skid on the black mirror floor. They land in jumbled piles of misaligned limbs. For a second, gunpowder burn makes the stench bearable.

Up out of the jungle like a bat out of hell, climbing out of Rhinehurst Supercluster's holdout suburban sprawl and then rising

through jungle overstory. Blasting across the Causeway toward Angel Spire and the sea. Monkeys diving off the rail line like grasshoppers, pouring off the edge ahead of my cruiser and disappearing into the mangrove and kudzu and mahogany and teak, disappearing into the wet bowels of greenery tangle. Dumping the cruiser at squad center, no time for mopdown, don't need it anyway. My hat, my raincoat, my clothes into hazmat bags, and then out again on the other side, rushing to pull on a tux before catching a masslift up 188 stories, rising into the high clear air over the jungle fur of carbon sequestration project N22.

Mma Telogo has a new concerto. Alice is his diva viola, his prize, and Hua Chiang and Telogo have been circling her like ravens, picking apart her performance, corvid eyes on her, watching and hungry for fault, but now they call her ready. Ready to banish Banini from his throne. Ready to challenge for a place in the immortal canon of classical performance. And I'm late. Caught in a masslift on Level 55, packed in with the breath and heat of upper-deck diners and weekenders climbing the spire while the seconds tick by, listening to the climate fans buzz and whir while we all sweat and wilt, waiting for some problem on the line to clear.

Finally, we're rising again, our stomachs dropping into our shoes, our ears popping as we soar into the heavens, flying under magnetic acceleration… and then slowing so fast we almost leave the floor. Our stomachs catch up. I shove out through hundreds of people, waving my cop badge when anyone complains, and sprint through the glass arch of the Ki Performance Center. I dive between the closing slabs of the attention doors.

The autolocks thud home behind me, sealing the performance space. It's comforting. I'm inside, enfolded in the symphony as though its hands have cupped themselves around me and pulled me into a chamber of absolute focus. The lights dim. Conversational thrum falls away. I find my way to my seat more by feel than sight. Dirty looks from men in topaz hats and women in spectacle eyes as I squeeze across them. Gauche, I know. Absurdly late to an event that happens once in a decade. Plopping down just as Hua Chiang steps up to the podium.

His hands rise like crane wings. Bows and horns and flutes flash with movement and then the music comes, first a hint, like blowing mist, and then building, winding through a series of repeated stanzas that I have heard Alice play perhaps ten thousand times. Notes I heard first so long ago, stumbling and painful, that now spill like water and burst like ice flowers. The music settles, pianissimo again, the lovely delicate motifs that I know from Alice's practice. An introduction only, she has told me, intended to file away the audience's last thoughts of the world outside, repeated stanzas until Hua Chiang accepts that the audience is completely his and then Alice's viola rises, and the other players move to support her, fifteen years of practice coming to fruition.

I look down at my hands, overwhelmed. It's different in the concert hall. Different than all those days when she cursed and practiced and swore at Telogo and claimed his work couldn't be performed. Different even from when she finished her practices early, smiling, hands calloused in new ways, face flushed, eager to drink a cool white wine with me on our balcony in the light of the setting sun and watch the sky as monsoon clouds parted and starlight shone down on our companionship. Tonight, her part joins the rest of the symphony and I can't speak or think for the beauty of the whole.

Later, I'll hear whether Telogo has surpassed Banini for sheer audacity. I'll hear how critics compare living memories of ancient performances and see how critical opinion shifts to accommodate this new piece in a canon that stretches back more than a century, and that hangs like a ghost over everything that Alice and her director Hua Chiang hope for: a performance that will knock Banini off his throne and perhaps depress him enough to stop rejoo and stuff him in his grave. For me, competing against that much history would be a heavy weight. I'm glad I've got a job where forgetting is the most important part. Working on the pop squad means your brain takes a vacation and your hands do the work. And when you leave work, you've left it for good.

Except now, as I look down at my hands, I'm surprised to find pinpricks of blood all over them. A fine spray. The misty remains of the little kid with the dinosaur. My fingers smell of rust.

The tempo accelerates. Alice is playing again. Notes writhe together so fluidly that it seems impossible they aren't generated electronically, and yet the warmth and phrasing is hers, achingly hers.

I've heard it in the morning, when she practiced on the balcony, testing herself, working again and again against the limitations of herself. Disciplining her fingers and hands, forcing them to accept Telogo's demands, the ones that years ago she had called impossible and which now run so cleanly through the audience.

The blood is all over my hands. I pick at it, scrape it away in flakes. It had to be the kid with the dinosaur. He was closest when he took the bullet. Some of his residue is stuck tight, bonded to my own skin. I shouldn't have skipped mopdown.

I pick.

The man next to me, tan face and rouged lips, frowns. I'm ruining a moment of history for him, something he has waited years to hear.

I pick more carefully. Silently. The blood flakes off. Dumb kid with the dumb dinosaur that almost made me miss the performance.

The cleanup crew noticed the dinosaur toy too. Caught the irony. Joked and snorted nosecaps and started bagging the bodies for compost. Made me late. Stupid dinosaur.

The music cascades into silence. Hua Chiang's hands fall. Applause. Alice stands at Chiang's urging and the applause increases. Craning my neck, I can see her, nineteen-year-old face flushed, smile bright and triumphant, enveloped in our adulation.

We end up at a party thrown by Maria Illoni, one of the symphony's high donors. She made her money on global warming mitigation for New York City, before it went under. Her penthouse is in Shoreline Curve, daringly arcing over the seawalls and the surf, a sort of flip of the finger to the ocean that beat her storm surge calculations. A spidery silver vine over dark water and the bob of the boat communities out in the deeps. New York obviously never got its money back: Illoni's outdoor patio runs across the entire top floor of the Shoreline and platforms additional petals of spun hollowform carbon out into the air.

From the far side of the Curve, you can see beyond the incandescent cores of the superclusters to the old city sprawl, dark except along where maglines radiate. A strange mangle of wreckage and scavenge and disrepair. In the day, it looks like some kind of dry red fungal collapse, a weave of jungle canopy and old suburban understory but at night, all that's visible is the skeleton of glowing infrastructure, radial blooms in the darkness, and I breathe deeply, enjoying all the freshness and openness that's missing from those steaming hideouts I raid with the pop squad.

Alice sparkles in the heat, perfectly slim, well curved—an armful of beautiful girl. The fall air is under thirty-three degrees and pleasant, and I feel infinitely tender toward her. I pull her close. We slip into a forest of century-old bonsai sculptures created by Maria's husband. Alice murmurs that he spends all his time here on the roof, staring at branches, studying their curves, and occasionally, perhaps every few years, wiring a branch and guiding it in a new direction. We kiss in the shadows they provide, and Alice is beautiful and everything is perfect.

But I'm distracted.

When I hit the kids with my Grange, the littlest one—the one with that stupid dinosaur—flipped over.

A Grange is built for nitheads, not little kids, so the bullet plowed through the kid and he flipped and his dinosaur went flying. It sailed, I mean really sailed, through the air. And now I can't get it out of my mind: that dinosaur flying. And then hitting the wall and bouncing onto the black mirror floor. So fast and so slow. Bang bang bang down the line... and then the dinosaur in the air.

Alice pulls away, seeming to sense my inattention. I straighten up. Try to focus on her.

She says, "I thought you weren't going to make it. When we were tuning, I looked out and your seat was empty."

I force a grin. "But I did. I made it."

Barely. I stood around too long with the cleanup guys while the dinosaur lay in a puddle and sopped up the kid's blood. Double extinct. The kid and the dinosaur both. Dead one way, and then dead again.

There's a weird symmetry there.

She cocks her head, studying me. "Was it bad?"

"What?" *The Brontosaurus?* "The call?" I shrug. "Just a couple crazy ladies. Not armed or anything. It was easy."

"I can't imagine it. Cutting rejoo like that." She sighs and reaches out to touch a bonsai, perfectly guided over the decades by the map that only Michael Illoni can see or understand. "Why give all this up?"

I don't have an answer. I rewind the crime scene in my mind. I have the same feeling that I did when I stood on spaghetti maggots and went through their fridge. There's something there in the stink and noise and darkness, something hot and obsessive and ripe. But I don't know what it is.

"The ladies looked old," I say. "Like week-old balloons, all puffy and droopy."

Alice makes a face of distaste. "Can you imagine trying to perform Telogo without rejoo? We wouldn't have had the time. Half of us would have been past our prime, and we'd have needed understudies, and then the understudies would have had to find understudies. Fifteen years. And these women throw it all away. How can they throw away something as beautiful as Telogo?"

"You thinking about Kara?"

"She would have played Telogo twice as well as I did."

"I don't believe that."

"Believe it. She was the best. Before she went kid-crazy." She sighs.

"I miss
her."

"You could still visit her. She's not dead yet."

"She might as well be. She's already twenty years older than when we knew her." She shakes her head. "No. I'd rather remember her in her prime, not out at some single-sex work camp growing vegetables and losing the last of her talent. I couldn't stand listening to her play now. It would kill me to hear all of that gone." She turns abruptly. "That reminds me, my rejoo booster is tomorrow. Can you take me?"

"Tomorrow?" I hesitate. I'm supposed to be on another shift popping kids. "It's kind of short notice."

"I know. I meant to ask sooner but with the concert coming up, I forgot." She shrugs. "It's not that important. I can go by myself." She glances at me sidelong. "But it is nicer when you come."

What the hell. I don't really want to work anyway. "Okay, sure. I'll get Pentle to cover for me." Let him deal with the dinosaurs.

"Really?"

I shrug. "What can I say? I'm a sweet guy."

She smiles and stands on tiptoe to kiss me. "If we weren't going to live forever, I'd marry you."

I laugh. "If we weren't going to live forever, I'd get you pregnant."

We look at each other. Alice laughs unsteadily and takes it as a joke.

"Don't be gross."

Before we can talk any more, Illoni pops out from behind a bonsai and grabs Alice by the arm. "There you are! I've been looking everywhere for you. You can't hide yourself like this. You're the woman of the hour."

She pulls Alice away with all the confidence that must have made New York believe she could save it. She barely even looks at me as they hustle off. Alice smiles tolerantly and motions for me to follow. Then Maria's calling to everyone and pulling them all together and she climbs up on a fountain's rim and pulls Alice up beside her. She starts talking about art and sacrifice and discipline and beauty.

I tune it out. There's only so much self-congratulation you can take. It's obvious Alice is one of the best in the world. Talking about it just makes it seem banal. But the donors need to feel like they're part of the moment, so they all want to squeeze Alice and make her theirs, so they talk and talk and talk.

Maria's saying, "...wouldn't be standing here congratulating ourselves, if it weren't for our lovely Alice. Hua Chiang and Telogo did their work well, but in the final moment it was Alice's execution in the face of Telogo's ambitious piece that has made it resonate so strongly already with the critics. We have her to thank for the piece's flawlessness."

Everyone starts applauding and Alice blushes prettily, not accustomed to adulation from her peers and competitors. Maria shouts over the cheering, "I've made several calls to Banini, and it is more than apparent that he has no answer to our challenge and so I expect the next eighty years are ours. And Alice's!" The applause is almost deafening.

Maria waves for attention again and the applause fades into scattered whistles and catcalls which finally taper off enough to allow

Maria to continue. "To commemorate the end of Banini's age, and the beginning of a new one, I would like to present Alice with a small token of affection—" and here she leans down and picks up a jute-woven gift bag shot with gold as she says, "Of course a woman likes gold and jewels, and strings for her viola, but I thought this was a particularly apt gift for the evening..."

I'm leaning against the woman next to me, trying to see as Maria holds the bag dramatically above her head and calls out to the crowd, "For Alice, our slayer of *dinosaurs!*" and pulls the green Brontosaurus out of the bag.

It's just like the one the kid had.

Its big eyes look right at me. For a second it seems to blink at me with its big black lashes and then the crowd laughs and applauds as they all get the joke. *Banini* = *dinosaur*. Ha ha.

Alice takes the dinosaur and holds it by the neck and swings it over her head and everybody laughs again but I can't see anything anymore because I'm lying on the ground caught in the jungle swelter of people's legs and I can't breathe.

* * *

"Are you sure you're okay?"

"Sure. No problem. I told you. I'm fine."

It's true, I guess. Sitting next to Alice in the waiting room, I don't feel dizzy or anything, even if I am tired. Last night, she put the dinosaur on the bedside table, right in with her collection of little jeweled music boxes, and the damn thing looked at me all night long. Finally at four AM, I couldn't stand it anymore and I shoved it under the bed. But in the morning, she found it and put it back, and it's been looking at me ever since.

Alice squeezes my hand. The rejoo clinic's a small one, private, carefully appointed with holographic windows of sailboats on the Atlantic so it feels open and airy even though its daylight is piped in through mirror collectors. It's not one of the big public monsters out in the clusters that got started after rejoo's patents expired. You pay a little more than you do for the Medicaid generics, but you don't rub shoulders with a bunch of starving gamblers and nitheads and drunks who all still want their rejoo even if they're wasting every day of their endless lives.

The nurses are quick and efficient. Pretty soon, Alice is on her back hooked up to an IV bladder with me sitting beside her on the bed, and we're watching rejoo push into her.

It's just a clear liquid. I always thought it should be fizzy and green for growing things. Or maybe not green, but definitely fizzy. It always feels fizzy when it goes in.

Alice takes a quick breath and reaches out for me, her slender pale fingers brushing my thigh. "Hold my hand."

The elixir of life pulses into her, filling her, flushing her. She pants shallowly. Her eyes dilate. She isn't watching me anymore. She's somewhere deep inside, reclaiming what was lost over the last eighteen months. No matter how many times I do it, I'm surprised when I watch it come over someone, the way it seems to swallow them and then they come back to the surface more whole and alive than when they started.

Alice's eyes focus. She smiles. "Oh, God. I can never get used to that."

She tries to stand up, but I hold her down and beep the nurse. Once we've got her unhooked, I lead her back out to the car. She leans heavily against me, stumbling and touching me. I can almost feel the fizzing and tingling through her skin. She climbs into the car. When I'm inside, she looks over at me and laughs. "I can't believe how good I feel."

"Nothing like winding back the clock."

"Take me home. I want to be with you."

I push the start button on the car, and we slide out of our parking space. We hook onto the magline out of Center Spire. Alice watches the city slide by outside the windows. All the shoppers and the businessmen and the martyrs and the ghosts, and then we're out in the open, on the high track over the jungle, speeding north again, for Angel Spire.

"It's so wonderful to be alive," she says, "It doesn't make any sense."

"What doesn't?"

"Cutting rejoo."

"If people made sense, we wouldn't have psychologists." And we wouldn't buy dinosaur toys for kids who were never going to make it anyway. I grit my teeth. None of them make any sense. Stupid moms.

Alice sighs and runs her hands across her thighs, kneading herself, hiking up her skirt and digging her fingers into her flesh. "But it still doesn't make any sense. It feels so good. You'd have to be crazy to stop rejoo."

"Of course they're crazy. They kill themselves, they make babies they don't know how to take care of, they live in shitty apartments in the dark, they never go out, they smell bad, they look terrible, they never have anything good again—" I'm starting to shout. I shut my mouth.

Alice looks over at me. "Are you okay?"

But I'm not. I'm mad. Mad at the ladies and their stupid toy-buying. Pissed off that these dumb women tease their dumb terminal kids like that; treat them like they aren't going to end up as compost. "Let's not talk about work right now. Let's just go home." I force a grin. "I've already got the day off. We should take advantage of it."

Alice is still looking at me. I can see the questions in her eyes. If she weren't on the leading edge of a rejoo high, she'd keep pressing, but she's so wrapped up in the tingling of her rebuilt body that she lets it go. She laughs and runs her fingers up my leg and starts to play with me. I override the magline's safeties with my cop codes and we barrel across the Causeway toward Angel Spire with the sun on the ocean and Alice smiling and laughing and the bright air whirling around us.

* * *

Three AM. Another call, windows down, howling through the humidity and swelter of Newfoundland. Alice wants me to come home, come back, relax, but I can't. I don't want to. I'm not sure what I want, but it's not brunch with Belgian waffles or screwing on the living room floor or a trip to the movies or… anything, really.

28

I can't do it, anyway. We got home, and I couldn't do it. Nothing felt right. Alice said it didn't matter, that she wanted to practice.

Now I haven't seen her for more than a day.

I've been on duty, catching up on calls. I've been going for twenty-four hours straight, powered on coppers'-little-helpers and mainlined caffeine, and my hat and trench coat and hands are pin-prick-sprayed with the residue of work.

Along the coastline the sea runs high and hot, splashing in over the breakwaters. Lights ahead, the glow of coalfoundries and gasification works. The call takes me up the glittering face of Palomino Cluster. Nice real estate. Up the masslifts and smashing through a door with Pentle backing me, knowing what we're going to find but never knowing how much these ones will fight.

Bedlam. A lady, this one a pretty brown girl who might have had a great life if she didn't decide she needed a baby, and a kid lying in the corner in a box screaming and screaming. And the lady's screaming too, screaming at the little kid in its box, like she's gone out of her mind.

As we come in through the door, she starts screaming at us. The kid keeps screaming. The lady keeps screaming. It's like a bunch of screwdrivers jamming in my ears; it goes on and on. Pentle grabs the lady and tries to hold her but she and the kid just keep screaming away and suddenly I can't breathe. I can barely stand. The kid screams and screams and screams: screwdrivers and glass and icepicks in my head.

So I shoot the thing. I pull out my Grange and put a bullet in the little sucker. Fragments of box and baby spray the air.

I don't do that, normally; it's against procedure to waste the kid in front of the mother.

But there we all are, staring at the body, bloodmist and gunpowder all over and my ears ringing from the shot and for one pristine crystal second, it's quiet.

Then the woman's screaming at me again and Pentle's screaming too because I screwed up the evidence before he could get a picture, and then the lady's all over me, trying to claw my eyes out. Pentle drags her off and then she's calling me a bastard and a killer and

bastard and monkey man and a fucking pig and that I've got dead eyes.

And that really gets me: I've got dead eyes. This lady's headed into a rejoo collapse and won't last another twenty years and she'll spend all of it in a single-sex work camp. She's young, a lot like Alice, maybe the last of them to cross the line into rejoo, right when she came of age—not an old workhorse like me who was already forty when it went generic—and now she'll be dead in an eye blink. But I'm the one with dead eyes.

I take my Grange and shove it into her forehead. "You want to die too?"

"Go ahead! Do it! Do it!" She doesn't stop for a second, just keeps howling and spitting. "Fucking bastard! Bastard fuckingfuckfucking— Do it! Do it!" She's crying.

Even though I want to see her brains pop out the back of her head, I don't have the heart. She'll die soon enough. Another twenty years and she's done for. The paperwork isn't worth it.

Pentle cuffs her while she babbles to the baby in the box, just a lump of blood and limp doll parts now. "My baby my poor baby I didn't know I'm sorry my baby my poor baby I'm sorry..." Pentle muscles her out to the car.

For a while I can hear her in the hall. *My baby my poor baby my poor baby....* And then she's gone down the lifts and it's a relief just to be standing there with the wet smells of the apartment and the dead body.

She was using a dresser drawer as her bassinet.

I run my fingers along the splintered edge, fondle the brass pulls. If nothing else, these ladies are resourceful, making the things we can't buy anymore. If I close my eyes, I can almost remember a whole industry around these little guys. Little outfits. Little chairs. Little beds. Everything made little.

Little dinosaurs.

"She couldn't make it shut up."

I jerk my hands away from the baby box, startled. Pentle has come up behind me. "Huh?"

"She couldn't make it stop crying. Didn't know what to do with it. Didn't know how to make it calm down. That's how the neigh-bors heard."

"Dumb."

"Yeah. She didn't even have a tag-teamer. How the heck was she going to do grocery shopping?"

He gets out his camera and tries a couple shots of the baby. There's not a whole lot left. A 12mm Grange is built for junkies, nitheads going crazy, 'bot assassins. It's overkill for an unarmored thing like this. When the new Granges came out, Grange ran an ad campaign on the sides of our cruisers. 'Grange: Unstoppable'. Or something like that.

There was this one that said 'Point Blank Grange' with a photo of a completely mangled nithead. That one was in all our lockers.

Pentle tries another angle on the drawer, going for a profile, trying to make the best of a bad situation. "I like how she used a drawer," he says.

"Yeah. Resourceful."

"I saw this one where the lady made a whole little table and chair set for her kid. Handmade it all. I couldn't believe how much energy she put into it." He makes shapes with his hand. "Little scalloped edges, shapes painted on the top: squares and triangles and things."

"If you're going to die doing something, I guess you want to do a good job of it."

"I'd rather be parasailing. Or go to a concert. I heard Alice was great the other night."

"Yeah. She was." I study the baby's body as Pentle takes some more shots. "If you had to do it, how do you think you'd make one of them be quiet?"

Pentle nods at my Grange. "I'd tell it to shut up."

I grimace and holster the gun. "Sorry about that. It's been a rough week. I've been up too long. Haven't been sleeping." *Too many dinosaurs looking at me.*

Pentle shrugs. "Whatever. It would have been better to get an intact image—" He snaps another picture. "—but even if she gets off this time, you got to figure in another year or two we'll be busting down her door again. These girls have a damn high recidivism." He takes another photo.

I go to a window and open it. Salt air flows in like fresh life, cleaning out the wet shit and body stinks. Probably the first fresh air the apartment's had since the baby was born. Got to keep the windows closed or the neighbors might hear. Got to stay locked in. I wonder if she's got a boyfriend, some rejoo dropout who's going to show up with groceries and find her gone. Probably worth staking out the apartment, just to see. Keep the feminists off us for only bagging the women. I take a deep breath of sea air to get something fresh in my lungs, then light a cigarette and turn back to the room with its clutter and stink.

Recidivism. Fancy word for girls with a compulsion. Like a nithead or a coke freak, but weirder, more self-destructive. At least being a junkie is fun. Who the hell chooses to live in dark apartments with shitty diapers, instant food, and no sleep for years on end? The whole breeding thing is an anachronism—twenty-first-century ritual torture we don't need anymore. But these girls keep trying to turn back the clock and pop out the pups, little lizard brains compelled to pass on some DNA. And there's a new batch every year, little burps of offspring cropping up here and there, the convulsions of a species trying to restart itself and get evolution rolling again, like we can't tell that we've already won.

* * *

I'm keying through the directory listings in my cruiser, fiddling through ads and keywords and search preferences, trying to zero in on something that doesn't come up no matter how I go after it. Dinosaur.

Toys.

Stuffed animals.

Nothing. Nobody sells stuff like that dinosaur. But I've run into two of them now.

Monkeys scamper over the roof of my car. One of them lands on my forward impact rails and looks at me, yellow eyes wide before another jumps it and they fall off the carbon petal pullout where I'm parked. Somewhere down below, suburban crumble keeps small herds of them. I remember when this area was tundra. It was a long time ago. I've talked to techs in the carbon sink business who talk about flipping the climate and building an icecap, but it's a slow process, an accretion of centuries most likely. Assuming I don't get shot by a crazy mom or a nithead, I'll see it happen. But for now, it's monkeys and jungle.

Forty-eight hours on call and two more cleanups and Alice wants me to take the weekend off and play, but I can't. I'm living on perkies, now. She feels good about her work, and wants me all day. We've done it before. Lying together, enjoying the silence and our own company, the pleasure of just being together with nothing needing to be done.

There's something wonderful about peace and silence and sea breezes twisting the curtains on the balcony.

I should go home. In a week, maybe, she'll be back at worrying, doubting herself, thrashing herself to work harder, to practice longer, to listen and feel and move inside of music that's so complex it might as well be the mathematics of chaos for anyone but her. But in reality, she has time. All the time in the world, and it makes me happy that she has it, that fifteen years isn't too long to prepare for something as heartstoppingly beautiful as what she did with Telogo.

I want to spend this time with her, to enjoy her bliss. But I don't want to go back and sleep with that dinosaur. I can't.

I call her from the cruiser.

"Alice?"

She looks out at me from the dash. "Are you coming home? I could meet you for lunch."

"Do you know where Maria got that dinosaur toy?"

She shrugs. "Maybe one of the shops on the Span? Why?"

"Just wondering." I pause. "Could you go get it for me?"

"Why? Why can't we do something fun? I'm on vacation. I just had my rejoo. I feel great. If you want to see my dinosaur, why don't you come home and get it?"

"Alice, please."

Scowling, she disappears from the screen. In a few minutes she's back, holding it up to the screen, shoving it in my face. I can feel my heart beating faster. It's cool in the cruiser but I break into a sweat when I see the dinosaur on the screen. I clear my throat. "What's it say on the tag?"

Frowning, she turns the thing over, runs her fingers through its fur. She holds up the tag to the camera. It comes in blurry as the camera focuses, then it's there, clear and sharp. 'Ipswitch Collectibles'. Of course. Not a toy at all.

* * *

The woman who runs Ipswitch is old, as old a rejoo as I've ever met. The wrinkles on her face look so much like plastic that it's hard to tell what's real and what may be a mask. Her eyes are sunken little blue coals, and her hair is so white I think of weddings and silk. She must have been ninety when rejoo hit.

Whatever the name of it, Ipswitch Collectibles is full of toys: dolls staring down from their racks, different faces and shapes and colors of hair, some of them soft, some of them made of hard bright plastics; tiny trains that run around miniature tracks and spout steam from their pinky-sized smokestacks; figurines from old-time movies and comics in action poses: Superman, Dolphina, Rex Mutinous. And, under a shelf of hand-carved wooden cars, a bin full of stuffed dinosaurs in green and blue and red. A Tyrannosaurus rex. A Pterodactyl. The Brontosaurus.

"I've got a few Stegosauruses in the back."

I look up, startled. The old woman watches me from behind the counter, a strange wrinkly buzzard, studying me with those sharp blue eyes, examining me like I'm carrion.

I pick out the Brontosaurus and hold it up by the neck. "No. These're fine."

A bell rings. The shop's main doors to the concourse slide open. A woman steps through, hesitant. Her hair is pulled back in a ponytail, and she hasn't applied any makeup, and I can tell, even before she's all the way through the door, that she's one of them: a mom.

She hasn't been off rejoo long; she still looks fresh and young, despite the plumpness that comes with kids. She still looks good. But even without rejoo-collapse telltales, I know what she's done to herself.

She's got the tired look of a person at war with the world. None

34

of us look like that. No one has to look like that. Nitheads look less besieged. She's trying to act like the person she was before, like the actress or the financial advisor or the code engineer or the biologist or the waitress or whatever, putting on clothes from her life before, that used to fit perfectly and don't now, making herself look like a person who walks without fear in the open air, and who doesn't now.

As she wanders the aisles, I spy a stain on her shoulder. It's small but obvious if you know what to look for, a light streak of green on a creamy blouse. The kind of thing that never happens to anyone except women with children. No matter how hard she tries, she doesn't fit anymore. Not with us.

Ipswitch Collectibles, like others of its ilk, is a trap door of sorts—a rabbit hole down into the land of illicit motherhood: the place of mashed pea stains, sound-proofed walls, and furtive forays into daylight for resupply and survival. If I stand here long enough, holding my magic Brontosaurus by the neck, I'll slip through entirely and see their world as it overlaps with my own, see it with the queer double vision of these women who have learned to turn a drawer into a crib, and know how to fold and pin an old shirt into a diaper, and know that 'collectibles' really means 'toys'.

The woman slips in the direction of the train sets. She chooses one and places it on the counter. It's a bright wooden thing, each car a different color, each connected by a magnet.

The old woman takes the train and says, "Oh yes, this is a fine piece. I had grandchildren who played with trains like this when they were just a little more than one."

The mother doesn't say anything, just holds out her wrist for the charge, her eyes down on the train. She fingers the blue and yellow engine nervously.

I come up to the counter. "I'll bet you sell a lot of them."

The mother jerks. For a second, she looks like she'll run, but she steadies.

The old woman's eyes turn on me. Dark sunken blue cores, infinitely knowledgeable. "Not many. Not now. Not many collectors around for this sort of thing. Not now."

The transaction clears. The woman hustles out of the store, not looking back. I watch her go.

The old woman says, "That dinosaur is forty-seven, if you want it."

Her tone says that she already knows I won't be buying.

I'm not a collector.

* * *

Nighttime. More dark-of-night encounters with illicit motherhood. The babies are everywhere, popping up like toadstools after rain. I can't keep up with them. I had to leave my last call before the cleanup crew came. Broke the chain of evidence, but what can you do? Everywhere I go, the baby world is ripping open around me, melons and seedpods and fertile wombs splitting open and vomiting babies onto the ground. We're drowning in babies. The jungle seems to seethe with them, the hidden women down in the suburb swelter, and as I shoot along the maglines on my way to bloody errands, the jungle's tendril vines curl up from below, reaching out to me.

I've got the mom's address in my cruiser. She's hidden now. Back down the rabbit hole. Pulled the lid down tight over her head. Lying low with her brood, reconnected with the underground of women who have all decided to kill themselves for the sake of squeezing out pups. Back in the swelter of locked doors and poopy diapers amongst the sorority who give train sets to little creatures who actually play with them instead of putting them on an end table and making you look at them every damn day...

The woman. The *collector*. I've been holding off on hitting her. It doesn't seem fair. It seems like I should wait for her to make her mistake before I pop her kids. But knowing that she's out there tickles my mind. I catch myself again and again, reaching to key in the homing on her address.

But then another call comes, another cleanup, and I let myself pretend I don't know about her, that I haven't perforated her hidey-hole and can now peer in on her whenever I like. The woman we don't know about—yet. Who hasn't made a mistake—yet. Instead, I barrel down the rails to another call, slicing through jungle overstory where it impinges around the tracks, blasting toward another woman's destiny who was less lucky and less clever than the one who likes to collect. And these other women hold me for a little while. But in the end, parked on the edge of the sea, with monkeys screeching from the jungle and rain spackling my windshield, I punch in the collector's address.

I'll just drive by.

* * *

It could have been a rich house before carbon sequestration. Before we all climbed into the bright air of the spires and superclusters. But now it exists at the very edge of what is left of suburbs. I'm surprised it even has electric or any services running to it at all. The jungle surrounds it, envelopes it. The road to it, off the maglines and off the maintenance routes, is heaved and split and perforated with encroaching trees. She's smart. She's as close to wilderness as it is possible to live. Beyond is only shadow tangle and green darkness. Monkeys scamper away from the spray of my headlights. The houses around her have already been abandoned. Any day now, they'll stop serving this area entirely. In another couple years, this portion will be completely overgrown. We'll cut off services and the last of the spires will go online and the jungle will swallow this place completely.

I sit outside the house for a while, looking at it. She's a smart one. To live this far out. No neighbors to hear the screaming. But if I think about it, she would have been smarter to move into the jungle entirely, and live with all the other monkeys that just can't keep themselves from breeding. I guess at the end of the day, even these crazy ladies are still human. They can't leave civilization totally behind. Or don't know how, anyway.

I get out of my car, pull my Grange, and hit the door.

As I slam through, she looks up from where she sits at her kitchen table. She isn't even surprised. A little bit of her seems to deflate, and that's all. Like she knew it was going to happen all along. Like I said: a smart one.

A kid runs in from the other room, attracted by the noise of me coming through the door. Maybe one and a half or two years old. It stops and stares, little tow-headed thing, its hair already getting long

like hers. We stare at each other. Then it turns and scrambles into its mother's lap.

The woman closes her eyes. "Go on, then. Do it."

I point my Grange, my 12mm hand cannon. Zero in on the kid.

The lady wraps her arms around it. It's not a clear shot. It'll rip right through and take out the mom. I angle differently, looking for the shot. Nothing.

She opens her eyes. "What are you waiting for?"

We stare at each other. "I saw you in the toy store. A couple days ago."

She closes her eyes again, regretful, understanding her mistake. She doesn't let go of the kid. I could just take it out of her arms, throw it on the floor and shoot it. But I don't. Her eyes are still closed.

"Why do you do it?" I ask.

Her eyes open again. She's confused. I'm breaking the script. She's mapped this out in her own mind. Probably a thousand times. Had to. Had to know this day would be coming. But here I am, all alone, and her kid's not dead yet. And I keep asking her questions. "Why do you keep having these kids?"

She just stares at me. The kid squirms around on her and tries to start nursing. She lifts her blouse a little and the kid dives under. I can see the hanging bulges of the lady's breasts, these heavy swinging mammaries, so much larger than I remember them from the store when they were hidden under bra and blouse. They sag while the kid sucks. The woman just stares at me. She's on some kind of autopilot, feeding the kid. Last meal.

I take my hat off and put it on the table and sit. I put my Grange down, too. It just doesn't seem right to blow the sucker away while it's nursing. I take out a cigarette and light it. Take a drag. The woman watches me the way anyone watches a predator. I take another drag on my cigarette and offer it to her. "Smoke?"

"I don't." She jerks her head toward her kid.

I nod. "Ah. Right. Bad for the new lungs. I heard that, once. Can't remember where." I grin. "Can't remember when."

She stares at me. "What are you waiting for?"

I look down at my pistol, lying on the table. The heavy machine weight of slugs and steel, a monster weapon. Grange 12mm Recoilless Hand Cannon. Standard issue. Stop a nitfitter in his tracks. Take out the whole damn heart if you hit them right. Pulverize a baby. "You had to stop taking rejoo to have the kid, right?"

She shrugs. "It's just an additive. They don't have to make rejoo that way."

"But otherwise we'd have a big damn population problem, wouldn't we?"

She shrugs again.

The gun sits on the table between us. Her eyes flick toward the gun, then to me, then back to the gun. I take a drag on the cigarette. I can tell what she's thinking, looking at that big old steel hand cannon on her table. It's way out of her reach, but she's desperate, so it looks a lot closer to her, almost close enough. Almost.

Her eyes go back up to me. "Why don't you just do it? Get it over with?"

It's my turn to shrug. I don't really have an answer. I should be taking pictures and securing her in the car, and popping the kid, and calling in the cleanup squad, but here we sit. She's got tears in her eyes. I watch her cry. Mammaries and fatty limbs and a frightening sort of wisdom, maybe coming from knowing that she won't last forever. A contrast to Alice with her smooth, smooth skin and high, bright breasts. This woman is fecund. Hips and breasts and belly fertile, surrounded by her messy kitchen, the jungle outside. The soil of life. She seems settled in all of this, a damp Gaia creature.

A dinosaur.

I should be cuffing her. I've got her and her kid. I should be shooting the kid. But I don't. Instead, I've got a hard-on. She's not beautiful exactly, but I've got a hard-on. She sags, she's round, she's breasty and hippy and sloppy; I can barely sit because my pants are so tight. I try not to stare at the kid nursing. At her exposed breasts. I take another drag on my cigarette. "You know, I've been doing this job for a long time."

She stares at me dully, doesn't say anything.

"I've always wanted to know why you women do this." I nod at the kid. It's come off her breast, and now the whole thing is exposed,

this huge sagging thing with its heavy nipple. She doesn't cover up. When I look up, she's studying me, seeing me looking at her breast. The kid scrambles down and watches me, too, solemn-eyed. I wonder if it can feel the tension in the room. If it knows what's coming. "Why the kid? Really. Why?"

She purses her lips. I think I can see anger in the tightening of her teary eyes, anger that I'm playing with her. That I'm sitting here, talking to her with my Grange on her grimy table, but then her eyes go down to that gun and I can almost see the gears clicking. The calculations.

The she-wolf gathering herself.

She sighs and scoots her chair forward. "I just wanted one. Ever since I was a little girl."

"Play with dolls, all that? *Collectibles?*"

She shrugs. "I guess." She pauses. Eyes back to the gun. "Yeah. I guess I did. I had a little plastic doll, and I used to dress it up. And I'd play tea with it. You know, we'd make tea, and then I'd pour some on her face, to make her drink. It wasn't a great doll. Voice input, but not much repertoire. My parents weren't rich. 'Let's go shopping.' *'Okay, for what?'* 'For watches.' *'I love watches.'* Simple. Like that. But I liked it. And then one day I called her my baby. I don't know why. I did, though, and the doll said, *'I love you mommy.'*"

Her eyes turn wet as she speaks. "And I just knew I wanted to have a baby. I played with her all the time, and she'd pretend she was my baby, and then my mother caught us doing it and said I was a stupid girl, and I shouldn't talk that way, girls didn't have babies anymore, and she took the doll away."

The kid is down on the floor, shoving blocks under the table. Stacking and unstacking. It catches sight of me. It's got blue eyes and a shy smile. I get a twitch of it, again, and then it scrambles up off the floor, and buries its face in its mother's breasts, hiding. It peeks out at me, and giggles and hides again.

I nod at the kid. "Who's the dad?"

Stone cold face. "I don't know. I got a sample shipped from a guy I found online. We didn't want to meet. I erased everything about him as soon as I got the sample."

"Too bad. Things would have been better if you'd kept in touch."

"Better for you."

"That's what I said." I notice that the ash on my cigarette has gotten long, a thin gray penis hanging limp off the end of my smoke. I give it a twitch and it falls. "I still can't get over the rejoo part."

Inexplicably, she laughs. Brightens even. "Why? Because I'm not so in love with myself that I just want to live forever and ever?"

"What were you going to do? Keep it in the house until—"

"Her," she interrupts suddenly. "Keep *her* in the house. *She* is a girl and *her* name is Melanie."

At her name, the kid looks over at me. She sees my hat on the table and grabs it. Then climbs down off her mother's lap and carries it over to me. She holds it out to me, arms fully extended, an offering. I try to take it but she pulls the hat away.

"She wants to put it on your head."

I look at the lady, confused. She's smiling slightly, sadly. "It's a game she plays. She likes to put hats on my head."

I look at the girl again. She's getting antsy, holding the hat. She makes little grunts of meaning at me and waves the hat invitingly. I lean down. The girl puts the hat on my head, and beams. I sit up and set it more firmly.

"You're smiling," she says.

I look up at her. "She's cute."

"You like her, don't you?"

I look at the girl again, thinking. "Can't say. I've never really looked at them before."

"Liar."

My cigarette is dead. I stub it out on the kitchen table. She watches me do it, frowning, pissed off that I'm messing up her messy table, maybe, but then she seems to remember the gun. And I do, too. A chill runs up my spine. For a moment, when I leaned down to the girl, I'd forgotten about it. I could be dead, right now. Funny how we forget and remember and forget these things. Both of us. Me and the lady. One minute we're having a conversation, the next we're waiting for the killing to start.

This lady seems like she would have been a nice date. She's got spunk. You can tell that. It almost comes out before she remembers

the gun. You can watch it flicker back and forth. She's one person, then another person: alive, thinking, remembering, then bang, she's sitting in a kitchen full of crusty dishes, coffee rings on her countertop and a cop with a hand cannon sitting at the kitchen table.

I spark up another cigarette. "Don't you miss the rejoo?"

She looks down at her daughter, holds out her arms. "No. Not a bit."

The girl climbs back onto her mother's lap.

I let the smoke curl out of my mouth. "But there's no way you were going to get away with this. It's insane. You have to drop off of rejoo; you have to find a sperm donor who's willing to drop off, too, so two people kill themselves for a kid; you've got to birth the kid alone, and then you've got to keep it hidden, and then you'd eventually need an ID card so you could get it started on rejoo because nobody's going to dose an undocumented patient, and you've got to know that none of this would ever work. But here you are."

She scowls at me. "I could have done it."

"You didn't."

Bang. She's back in the kitchen again. She slumps in her chair, holding the kid. "So why don't you just hurry up and do it?"

I shrug. "I was just curious about what you breeders are thinking."

She looks at me, hard. Angry. "You know what I'm thinking? I'm thinking we need something new. I've been alive for one hundred and eighteen years and I'm thinking that it's not just about me. I'm thinking I want a baby and I want to see what she sees today when she wakes up and what she'll find and see that I've never seen before because that's new. Finally, something new. I love seeing things through her little eyes and not through dead eyes like yours."

"I don't have dead eyes."

"Look in the mirror. You've all got dead eyes."

"I'm a hundred and fifty and I feel just as good as I did the day I went on."

"I'll bet you can't even remember. No one remembers." Her eyes are on the gun again, but they come up off it to look at me. "But I do. Now. And it's better this way. A thousand times better than living forever."

I make a face. "Live through your kid and all that?"

"You wouldn't understand. None of you would."

I look away. I don't know why. I'm the one with the gun. I'm running everything, but she's looking at me, and something gets tight inside me when she says that. If I was imaginative, I'd say it was some little bit of old primal monkey trying to drag itself out of the muck and make itself heard. Some bit of the critter we were before. I look at the kid—the girl—and she's looking back at me. I wonder if they all do the trick with the hat, or if this one's special somehow. If they all like to put hats on their killers' heads. She smiles at me and ducks her head back under her mother's arm. The woman's got her eyes on my gun.

"You want to shoot me?" I ask.

Her eyes come up. "No."

I smile slightly. "Come on. Be honest."

Her eyes narrow. "I'd blow your head off if I could."

Suddenly I'm tired. I don't care anymore. I'm sick of the dirty kitchen and the dark rooms and the smell of dirty makeshift diapers. I give the Grange a push, shove it closer to her. "Go ahead. You going to kill an old life so you can save one that isn't even going to last? I'm going to live forever, and that little girl won't last longer than seventy years even if she's lucky—which she won't be—and you're practically already dead. But you want to waste my life?" I feel like I'm standing on the edge of a cliff. Possibility seethes around me. "Give it a shot."

"What do you mean?"

"I'm giving you your shot. You want to try for it? This is your chance." I shove the Grange a little closer, baiting her. I'm tingling all over. My head feels light, almost dizzy. Adrenaline rushes through me. I push the Grange even closer to her, suddenly not even sure if I'll fight her for the gun, or if I'll just let her have it. "This is your chance."

She doesn't give a warning.

She flings herself across the table. Her kid flies out of her arms. Her fingers touch the gun at the same time as I yank it out of reach. She lunges again, clawing across the table. I jump back, knocking over my chair. I step out of range. She stretches toward the gun, fingers

wide and grasping, desperate still, even though she knows she's already lost.

I point the gun at her.

She stares at me, then puts her head down on the table and sobs.

The girl is crying too. She sits bawling on the floor, her little face screwed up and red, crying along with her mother who's given everything in that one run at my gun: all her hopes and years of hidden dedication, all her need to protect her progeny, everything. And now she lies sprawled on a dirty table and cries while her daughter howls from the floor. The girl keeps screaming and screaming.

I sight the Grange on the girl. She's exposed, now. She's squalling and holding her hands out to her mother, but she doesn't get up. She just holds out her hands, waiting to be picked up and held by a lady who doesn't have anything left to give. She doesn't notice me or the gun.

One quick shot and she's gone, paint hole in the forehead and brains on the wall just like spaghetti and the crying's over and all that's left is gunpowder burn and cleanup calls.

But I don't fire.

Instead, I holster my Grange and walk out the door, leaving them to their crying and their grime and their lives.

It's raining again, outside. Thick ropes of water spout off the eaves and spatter the ground. All around me the jungle seethes with the chatter of monkeys. I pull up my collar and resettle my hat. Behind me, I can barely hear the crying anymore.

Maybe they'll make it. Anything is possible. Maybe the kid will make it to eighteen, get some black market rejoo and live to be a hundred and fifty. More likely, in six months, or a year, or two years, or ten, a cop will bust down the door and pop the kid. But it won't be me.

I run for my cruiser, splashing through mud and vines and wet. And for the first time in a long time, rain feels new.

SNOW IN THE DESERT

Neal Asher

A sand shark broke through the top face of the dune only to be snatched by a crab-bird and shredded in mid-air. Hirald squatted down, turned on her chameleonwear, and faded into the violet sand, only her Toshiba goggles and the blunt snout of her singun visible. The crab bird was a small one, but she had quickly learnt never to underestimate them. If the prey were too large for one to take, it would take pieces instead. No motile source of protein was too large to attack. The shame was that all the life-forms on Vatch were based on left helix proteins, so to a crab-bird human flesh was completely without nourishment. The birds did not know this and just became irritable as their hunger increased. The circle was vicious.

The bird stripped the shark of its blade-legs and armoured mandibles and flew off with the bleeding and writhing torso, probably to feed to its chick. Hirald stood and faded back into existence; a tall woman in a tight-fitting body suit webbed with cooling veins and hung with insulated pockets. On her back she carried a desert survival pack, for the look of things. The singun went into a button-down holster that looked as if it might only hold a simple projectile weapon, not the formidable device it did hold. She removed her goggles, mask and hat, and tucked them away in one of her many pockets before moving on across the sand. Her thin features, blue eyes, and long blond hair were exposed to oven temperatures and skin-flaying ultraviolet. Such had been the way of things for many weeks now. Occasionally she drank some water; a matter of form, just in case anyone was watching.

* * *

He was called, inevitably, Snow, but with his plastron mask and dust robes it was not immediately evident he was an albino. The mask, made

from the shell of an Earth-import terrapin, was what identified him to those who knew of him, that, and his tendency to leave corpses behind him. At last count the reward for his stasis-preserved testicles was twenty thousand shillings, or the equivalent value in precious metals like copper or manganese. Many people had tried for the reward and their epitaph was just that; they had tried. Three people at the water station, on the edge of the Menilar flat, were waiting to try. They had weapons, strength, and skill, balanced against the crippling honour code of the Andronache. Snow had all the former and no honour code. Born on Earth so long ago even he doubted his memories of the time, he had long since dispensed with anything that might get in the way of plain survival. Morality, he often argued, is a purely human invention only to be indulged in times of plenty. Another of his little aphorisms ran something along the lines of; if you're up shit creek without a paddle, don't expect the coast guard. His contemporaries on Vatch never knew what to make of that one, but then Vatchians had no use for words like creek, coast, or paddle.

The water station was an ovoid of metal mounted ten metres above the ground on a forest of scaffolding. Nailing it to the ground was the silvery tube of the geothermal energy tap that provided the power for the transmuter; the reason it was possible for humans to exist on this practically waterless planet. The transmuter took complex compounds, stripped them of their elementary hydrogen, and combined that with the abundant oxygen given off by the dryform algae that turned all the sands of Vatch to violet. Water was the product, but there were many interesting by-products; strange metals and silica compounds were one of the planet's main exports.

As he topped the final dune Snow raised his image intensifier to his eyes and scanned ahead. The station was, in reality, a small city, the centre of commerce, the centre of life. Under his mask he frowned to himself. He did not know about the three men specifically, but he knew their type would be there. Unfortunately, he needed water to take him on the last stage of his journey and this was the only place. A confrontation was inevitable.

Snow strode down the face of the dune and onto a dusty track snaking towards the station. At the side of the road a water thief lay dying at the bottom of a condensation jar. The man scratched at the hot glass with blistered fingers as Snow passed, but Snow ignored him. It was harsh punishment, but how else to treat someone who regarded his fellow human beings as no more than walking water barrels? As he drew nearer to the station the cries of the hawkers and stall-holders in the ground city reached out to him like the chorus from a rookery, and he could see the buzz of activity in the scaffold maze. Soon he entered the ground city and its noisy life, soon after, his presence was noted and reported. By the time he passed through the moisture lock of the Sand House – a ubiquitous name for hostelries – and was taking off his mask in the cool interior, the three killers were buckling on their weapons and offering prayers to their various family gods.

"My pardon, master. I must see your tag. The Androche herself has declared the law enforceable by a two-month branding. The word is that too many outlaws now survive on the fringe." The waiter could not help staring at Snow's pink eyes and bloodless face.

"No problem, friend," said Snow, and after fumbling through his robes produced his micro-etched identity tag and handed it over. The waiter glanced at the briefly revealed leather-clad stump that terminated the end of Snow's left arm and pretended not to notice. He put the tag through his portable reader and was much relieved when no alarm sounded. Snow was well aware that not everyone was checked like this, only the more suspicious looking customers, like himself.

"What would you like, master?"

"A litre of chilled lager," said Snow.

The waiter looked at him doubtfully.

"Which I will pay for now," said Snow, handing over a ten-shilling note. The waiter looked alarmed by such a large sum in cash money and hurried off with it as quickly as he could. When he came back with a litre of lager in a thermos stein with combination locked top, many eyes followed his progress. Here was an indication of wealth. Snow would not have agreed with this. He had worked it out. A litre of water would only have cost two shillings less, and the water lost through sweat evaporation little different. Two shillings, plus a little, for imbibing fluid in a much more pleasant form. He had nearly finished his litre and was relishing the sheer cellular pleasure of rehydration

when the three entered the Sand House. He recognised them for what they were almost immediately. Before paying the slightest attention to them he drained every last drop of lager from the frictionless vessel.

"You are Snow, the albino," said the first, standing before his table.

Snow observed her and felt a gnawing depression. Even after all these years he could not shake an aversion to killing women, or in this case, girls. She could not have been more than twenty. She stood before him attired in monofilament coveralls and weapons harness. Her face was elfin under a head of cropped black hair spiked out with gold-fleck grease.

"No, I'm not," he said, and turned his attention elsewhere.

"Don't fuck with me," she said with a tiredness that was beyond her years. "I know who you are. You are an albino and your left hand is missing."

He returned his attention to her. "My name is Jelda Conley. People call me Whitey. I have often been confused with this Snow you refer to and it was on one such occasion that I lost my hand. Now please leave me alone."

The girl stepped back, confused. The Andronache honour code did not allow for creative lying. Snow glanced past her and noted one of her companions speaking to the owner who had sent the nervous waiter over. The lies would not be enough. He watched while the owner called over the waiter and checked the screen of his tag reader. The companion approached the girl, whispered in her ear.

"You lied to me," she said.

"No, I didn't," said Snow.

"Yes, you did!"

This was getting ridiculous. Snow stared off into the distance and ignored her.

"I challenge you," said the girl.

There, it was said. Snow pretended he had not heard her.

"I said I challenge you."

By the code she could now kill him. It was against the law but accepted practice. Snow felt a sinking sensation as she stepped back.

"Stand and face me, coward."

With a tiredness that was wholly genuine Snow rose to his feet. She snatched her slammer. Snow reacted. She hit the floor on her back with the front of her monofilament coverall breaking down and a smoking hole between her pert little breasts. Snow stepped past the table, past her, strode to the moisture lock, vomit held back by clenched teeth. Hoping the whole thing had been too fast for anyone to be sure of the weapon he had used.

* * *

It rested on the violet sands at the edge of a spaceport, which was scattered with huge flying-wing shuttles, outbuildings and hangars. It stood between the spaceport and the sprawl of Vatchian buildings linked by moisture-sealed walkways and the glass domes that covered the incongruous green of the parks. And in no way did it resemble any of the constructs around it. It was standard; to be found on a thousand planets of the human polity, and it was the reason the expansion of the human race beggared the imagination. The runcible facility was a mirrored sphere fifty metres across, seemingly prevented from rolling away by the two L-shaped constructs of the buffers on either side of it. All around it, the glass-roofed embarkation lounges; a puddle of light. Within, the Skaidon gate performed its miracle every few minutes; bringing in quince, mitter travellers, from all across the polity, and sending them away again.

Beck stood back from the arrivals entrance and watched the twin horns of the runcible on its dais of black glass. He watched the shimmer of the cusp between and impatiently checked his watch, not that they would be late, or early. They would arrive on time to the nanosecond. The runcible AI saw to that. Precisely on time a man stepped through the shimmer, a woman, another man, another woman. They matched the descriptions he had been given, and his greeting was effusive as they came through into the lounge.

"Your transport awaits outside," he told them, hurrying them to exit. The Merchant did not want them to stay in the city. He wanted them out, those were Beck's instructions, amongst others. Once they were in the hover transport the man Beck took to be the leader caught hold of his shoulder.

"The weapons," he said.

"Not here, not here," said Beck nervously, and took the transport out of the city.

Out on the sand Beck brought the transport down and as the four climbed out, he pulled a large case from the back of the transport. He was sweating, and not just because of the heat.

"Here," he said, and opened the case.

The man reached inside and took out a small shiny pistol, snub-nosed and deadly looking.

"The Merchant will meet at the pre-arranged place, if he manages to obtain the information he seeks," he said. He did not know where that was, nor what the information was. The Merchant had not taken him that far into his trust. It surprised him that he had been allowed knowledge of this; hired killers here on Vatch.

The man nodded as he inspected the pistol, smiled sadly, then pointed the pistol at Beck.

"Sorry," he said.

Beck tried to say something just as he became aware of the arm coming round his face from the man who had moved behind him. A grip like iron closed around his head, locked, wrenched and twisted. Beck hit the sand with his head at an angle it had never achieved in life. He made some choking sounds, shivered a little, died.

* * *

Snow halted as two proctors came in through the lock. They looked past him to the corpse on the floor. The eldest of the two, grey-bearded and running to fat, but with weapons that looked well-used and well looked after, spoke to him.

"You are Snow," he said.

"Yes," Snow replied. This man was not Andronache.

"A challenge?"

"Yes."

The man nodded, looked calculatingly at the two Andronache at the bar, then turned back to the moisture lock. It was not his job to pick up the corpses. There was an organisation for that. The girl would be in a condensation jar within the hour.

"The Androche would speak with you. Come with me." To his companion he said, "Deal with it. Her two friends look like they ought to spend a little time in detention."

Snow followed the man outside.

"Why does she want to see me?" he asked as they strode down the scaffolded street.

"I didn't ask."

Any conversation ended there.

The Androche, like all in her position, had apartments up in the station she owned. The proctor led Snow to a caged spiral stair and unlocked the gate.

"She is above," was all he said.

As Snow climbed the stair the gate clanged shut behind him.

The stairway ended at a moisture-lock hatch next to which depended a monitor and screen unit. Snow pressed the call button and waited. After a few moments a woman with cropped grey hair and a face that was all hard angles looked out at him.

"Yes?"

"You sent for me," said Snow.

The woman nodded and the lock on the hatch clunked open. He spun the handle and it rose on its hinge to allow him access. He climbed into a short metal-walled corridor that ended at a single panel door of imported wood. It looked like oak to Snow; very expensive. He pushed the door open and entered.

The room was filled with a fortune in antiques; a huge dining table surrounded by gate leg chairs. Plush eighteenth-century furniture, oil paintings on the walls, hand woven rugs on the floor.

"Don't be too impressed. They're all copies."

The Androche approached from a drinks cabinet. She carried two glasses half filled with an amber drink. Snow studied her; she was an attractive woman. He estimated her age as somewhere between thirty-five and a hundred and ninety. Three centuries earlier the second figure would have been forty-five, but rejuvenation treatments had come a long way. She wore a simple toga-type dress over an athletic figure. At her hip she carried an antique – or replica – revolver.

"You know my name," said Snow meaningfully as he accepted the drink.

"I am Aleen," she replied to his unspoken question.

Snow hardly heard her. He was relishing his first sip.

"My God, whisky," he said, eventually.

"Yes," said Aleen, taking a sip from her drink then gesturing to a nearby sofa. They moved there and sat facing each other.

"Well, I'm here. What do you want?"

"Why is there a reward of twenty-five thousand shillings for your testicles."

"Best ask the Merchant Baris that question, but I see it was rhetorical. You already know the answer."

Aleen nodded and Snow leant towards her.

"I would be glad to know the answer," he said.

Aleen smiled, Snow leant back.

"There is a price," he said.

"Isn't there always? ... There is a man. He is the chief proctor here. His name is David Songrel."

"You want me to kill him."

"Of course. Isn't that what you are best at?"

Snow kept silent.

Aleen lay back against the edge of the sofa then and regarded him over her drink. "That is not all I want from you."

He turned and looked at her and at that moment she lifted her feet up onto the sofa so that he could see that she wore nothing underneath. He wondered if she shaved or if she was naturally bald in that area. Still meeting him eye to eye she dropped one leg back to the floor, reached between her legs, and began to masturbate, gently, with two fingers. Snow wondered what it was that turned her on; his white body and pink eyes? Other women had said it was almost like being made love to by an alien, or was it that he was a killer? Probably a bit of both.

"Part of the price?"

She nodded and put her glass to one side, then she slid closer to him on the sofa and hooked one leg over the back of it.

"Now," she said, reaching up and pulling apart her toga to expose breasts just like those of the girl he had killed. Snow searched himself for an adverse reaction to that, and when he found there was none he stood and unclipped his dust robes.

SNOW IN THE DESERT

"You're white as paper," said Aleen in amazement as he peeled off his under suit, and then her eyes strayed to the covered stump terminating his left arm. She said nothing about that.

"Yes," said Snow as he knelt between her legs and bowed down to run his tongue round her nipples. "A blank page," he went on as he worked his way down. She caught his head.

"Not that," she said. "I want you inside me, now."

Snow obliged her, but was puzzled at something he had heard in her voice. It had almost been as if that part of the act was the most important. Perhaps she wanted white-skinned children.

* * *

Hirald called out before approaching the fire. It had been her observation that the Andronache got rather twitchy if you walked into one of their camps unannounced. As she walked in, she was surprised to see that these were not Andronache. There were two men and two women dressed in monofilament survival suits that looked to be of Mars manufacture. Hirald noted this but pretended not to notice the weapons laid out on a ground sheet that one of the men had hastily covered at her arrival. She walked to the fire and squatted down. One of the women tossed on another crab-bird carapace and watched her through the flames. The man who had covered the weapons, a tall Marsman with caste markings tattooed on his temples, was the first to speak.

"You've come a long way?" he asked.

"Not so far as you," said Hirald. She looked from him to the woman across the flames, who also had caste marks on her face. The other couple; the man a Negro with incongruous blue eyes and the woman Hirald thought could have come from anywhere until she noted the caps over the neural plugs behind her ears. She was corporate then; from one of the families.

"Yes, we have come a way," said the man, touching his caste mark.

"We search," said the Negro intently. "Perhaps you can help us. We search for one who is called Snow. He is an albino."

They all looked at Hirald then, avidly.

"I have heard of him," said Hirald, "and I have heard that many people look for him. I do not know where he is though."

The woman with the neural plugs looked suspicious. Hirald continued to forestall anything more she might say.

"You are after the reward then?"

The four looked to each other, then the latter three looked to the Marsman. He smiled to himself and casually reached for the covered weapons next to him. Hirald glanced at the corporate woman, who was staring back at her.

"Jharit, no."

Jharit stopped with his hand by the covering.

"What is it, Canard Meck?"

The woman, now identified as a member of the Jethro Manx Canard corporate family, slowly shook her head then looked to Hirald, who had not yet moved.

"We have no dispute with you, but we would prefer it if you left our camp, please."

"But she knows. She might tell him," said Jharit.

Canard Meck looked to him and said, "She is product."

Jharit snatched his hand from the weapons and suddenly looked very frightened. He flinched as Hirald rose to her feet. Hirald smiled. "I mean no harm, unless harm is meant."

She strode out into the darkness without checking behind. No one moved. No one reached for the weapons.

* * *

Snow removed the pistol from its holster in his dust robes and checked the charge reading. As was usual it was nearly at full charge. The bright sunlight of Vatch acting on the photovoltaic material of his robes kept the weapon constantly charged through the socket in the holster. The weapon was a matte-black L, five millimetres thick with only a slight depression where a trigger would normally have been. It was keyed to Snow. No one else could fire it. The beam it fired was of antiphotons; a misnomer really, as what it consisted of was protons field-accelerated to the point where they became photonic matter. Misnomer or not this beam could burn large holes in anyone Snow cared to point it at.

David Songrel was a family man. Snow had observed him lifting a child high in the air while a woman looked on from the background, just before the door to his apartments closed. Snow wondered why Aleen wanted him dead. As the owner of the water station, she had much power here but little over the proctors who enforced planetary law, not her law. Perhaps she had been involved in illegalities of which Songrel had become aware. No matter, for the present. He rapped on the door and when Songrel opened it he stuck the pistol in his face and walked him back into the apartment, closing the door behind him with his stump.

"Daddy!" the little girl yelled, but the mother caught hold of her before she rushed forward. Songrel had his hands in the air, his eyes not leaving the pistol. Shock there, knowledge.

"Why," said Snow, "does the Androche want you dead?"

"You're... the albino."

"Answer the question please."

Songrel glanced at his wife and daughter before he replied, "She is a collector of antiquities."

"Why the necessity for your death?"

"She has killed to get what she wants. I have evidence. We intend to arrest her soon."

Snow nodded then holstered his pistol. "I thought it would be something like that. She had two proctors come for me you know."

Songrel lowered his hands, but kept them well away from the stun gun hooked on his belt.

"As Androche she does have the right to some use of the proctors. It is our duty to guard her and her property. She does not have freedom to commit crime. Why didn't you kill me? They say you have killed many."

Snow looked to Songrel's wife and child. "My reputation precedes me," he said, and stepped past Songrel to drop onto a comfortable looking sofa. "But the stories are in error. I have killed no one who has not first tried to kill me... well, mostly."

Songrel looked to his wife. "It's Tamtha's bedtime."

His wife nodded and took the child from the room. Snow noted the little girl's fascinated stare. He was quite used to such. Songrel sat himself in an armchair opposite Snow.

"A nice family you have."

"Yes... will you testify against the Androche?"

"You can have my testimony recorded under seal, but I cannot stay for a trial. If I was to stay this place would be crawling with Andronache killers in no time. I might not survive that."

Songrel nodded. "Why did you come here if it was not your intention to kill me?" he asked, a trifle anxiously.

"I want you to play dead while I go back and see the Androche."

Songrel's expression hardened. "You want to collect your reward."

"Yes, but my reward is not money, it is information. The Androche knows why the Merchant Baris has a reward out for my death. It is a subject I am understandably curious about."

Songrel interlaced his fingers in his lap and stared down at them for a moment, when he looked up, he said, "The reward is for your stasis-preserved testicles. Perhaps like Aleen he is a collector, but that is beside the point. I will play dead for you but when you go to see Aleen, I want you to carry a virtual recorder."

Snow nodded once.

Songrel stood up and walked to a wall cupboard. He returned with a holocorder that he rested on the table and turned on. "Now, your statement."

* * *

"He is dead," said Aleen, a smile on her face.

"Yes," said Snow, dropping Songrel's identity tag on the table. "Yet I get the impression you knew before I came here."

Aleen went to the drinks cabinet and poured Snow a whisky. She brought it over to him. "I have friends amongst the proctors. As soon as his wife called in the killing – she was hysterical apparently – they informed me."

"Why did you want him killed?"

"That is none of your concern. Drink your whisky and I will get you the promised information."

Aleen turned away from him and moved to a computer console elegantly concealed in Louis XIV table. Snow had the whisky to his lips just as his suspicious nature took over. Why was it necessary to get the information from the computer? She could just tell him. Why had she not poured a drink for herself? He placed the drink down on a table, unsampled. Aleen looked up, a dead smile on her face, and as her hand came up over the console Snow dived to one side. On the wall behind him a picture blackened then flared into oily flames. He came up on one knee and fired once. She slammed back out of her chair onto the floor, her face burning like the picture.

Snow searched hurriedly. Any time now the proctors would arrive. In the bathroom he found a device like a chrome penis with two holes in the end. One hole spurted out some kind of fluid and the other hole sucked. Some kind of contraceptive device? He traced tubes back to the unit that contained the bottle of fluid and some very complicated straining and filtering devices. To his confusion he realised it was for removing the contents of a woman's womb, probably after sex. She collected men's semen? Shortly after, he found a single stasis bottle containing said substance. It had to be his own, and now he had an inkling of an idea; a possible explanation for his situation of the last five years. He opened the bottle and washed its contents down the sink just before the proctors broke into the apartments. Not that there was very much of value in it.

* * *

Hirald looked at the man in the condensation bottle, her expression revealing nothing. He was alive beyond his time; some sadist had dropped a bottle of water in with him to prolong his suffering. He stared at Hirald with drying eyes, the empty bottle by his head, his body shrunken and badly sunburnt, his black tongue protruding. Hirald looked around carefully, there were harsh penalties for what she was about to do, then removed a small chrome cylinder against the glass near the man's head. There was a brief flash. The man convulsed and the bottle was misted with smoke and steam. He died. Hirald replaced the device in her pocket, stood and walked on. Her masters would not have been pleased at her risking herself like this, but then they did not have complete control over her actions.

* * *

Snow was glad to leave the station behind him and this was reflected in his pace. He walked away at a kilometre-eating stride and occasionally swore with obscene precision. After the death of Aleen, Songrel had not felt obliged to honour his promise and Snow had spent two days in protective custody while the wheels of justice ground out slow due process. Luckily the appointment of the new Androche, traditionally a time of holiday and peace, had given him a needed respite. He had a day before the killers came after him.

Passing the condensation jar he noted that the man was now dead, his body giving up the last of its water for the public good. He paused for a moment to observe the greasy film on the inside of the jar before moving on. Someone had finished the poor bastard off. Snow wondered if that same someone might be after him, for the same purpose.

Out of sight of the station Snow left the road and set out across a spill of desert to a distant rock field. There he would be able to lose himself, if a sand shark did not get him first. He drew his pistol as he walked and kept his eyes open. One sand shark twitched its motion-detecting palps above the sand but shortly subsided. It must have fed in the last solstan year. It would be quiescent for another year to come.

Without event Snow reached the rock field and was putting away his pistol when a flash of reflected light alerted him to possible danger. *Andronache*, he thought, and readied himself for another challenge, only this time there was no challenge.

Automatic fire flicked his dust robes and scored pain across his ribs. Splinters from a nearby rock impacted on his mask. Snow dropped and quickly pulled himself behind a rock.

"Idiot," he said. It had been some time since anyone other than an Andronache killer had tried for him. He had forgotten that their honour code did not apply to all. He crouched down further as rock shattered above his head and rained splinters down on him.

"Hey, Snow!"

Snow did not reply.

"Hey, Snow, if you stick anything out make sure it's not worth money!"

SNOW IN THE DESERT

There was laughter at this rapier wit. Two of them at least. Snow ground his teeth then pulled a couple of shiny spheroids from his belt. Another couple of shots hit the rock so he supposed that at least one of them was changing position. Holding one of the spheroids to his mouth he twisted its top with his teeth then threw it hard in the general direction of the laughter. The explosion seemed completely out of proportion to the size of the object he had thrown, but then most explosives were merely matter, not field-compressed antimatter. Snow was up and running as shattered stone rained down and a great dust-cloud spread. He was behind another rock before the screams started.

"You bastard! I'll have your balls off with a blunt knife for that!"

The voice had come from that formation to the right. The screaming came from the one to the left of it. Snow fired at the first until he got a reply, two replies. There was someone else a lot closer. Three of them then, unless there were others who were more canny. He fired a few more times, rock disintegrating and fragmenting at each hit, then he checked the charge on his pistol, holstered it, and waited, listening intently. The screaming had become steady groaning and swearing.

Sporadic firing splintered the rock between him and his antagonists. This did not disconcert Snow. He knew it was covering fire for the one who was creeping up on him. He heard the first betraying scrape of shock armour against stone shortly after one such burst of fire. It was out to his left. He drew his pistol and, pointing in that direction, waited. Then, a distraction, the groaning of the wounded man abruptly ceased.

"David! David! Answer me!"

No answer, Snow wondered if someone else had just joined the game. Thinking on this he almost missed the flicker of movement as the creeper stood up and sighted on him down the barrel of an optek assault rifle. It was all the man had time to do. Snow fired once, his pistol on its highest setting. The man turned in an explosion of burning flesh, grisly remnants stuck to the rock and smoked.

"Oh my God! Oh, you bastard!"

Snow wondered at the talker's sense of proportion. He hadn't started this. It was not his fault that they had underestimated his armament. He glanced in the direction of the rock formation the man

was concealed behind and saw him come out and come running towards him. He was firing wildly, his optek on automatic, Snow had no time to return fire. He dived for cover. Abruptly the firing stopped. Snow waited for a moment then slowly peered out from cover. The man was flat on his face, the top of his head laying about a metre in front of him. Walking towards him, an optek resting across her shoulder, was the most beautiful woman Snow had ever seen, and he had seen a lot.

* * *

Three optek rifles, a dilapidated laser only a fool or a desperate man would risk firing, food, aged desert survival packs and suits, a little cash money, and now useless identity tags; the sum remains of three lives. These had been poor men; staking all on one last gamble for wealth. They had tried. Snow removed what was of most value and easily transportable; the money, liquid rations, power packs and filters from the suits, and left the rest in plain sight for anyone who wanted to take it. The woman, Hirald, retained one optek rifle and ammunition, she did not seem interested in the rest. On the other side of the rock field, away from the stink of opened bodies and the sudden interest of crab-birds and sickle flies, Snow made a fire from old carapaces and removed his mask in the light of evening. He was curious to note that the woman had not replaced her mask since the first moment he had seen her that morning, and her skin looked as clear, unblemished, and as perfect as it had looked then. She sank down next to him by the fire, with a grace that could only reflect superb physical condition.

"What brought you to the rock field?" he asked her.

"I made a shortcut across the Thira and was on my way back to the road and civilization, and I of course found one of the nastier aspects of this civilization."

Snow was doubtful about this reply. He had crossed the Thira a couple of times and knew it to be rough going. Hirald looked as fresh as someone after a month's sojourn in a water station.

"I see," he said.

"You are Snow," she said, turning and fixing him with eyes that were violet in the fading light. He felt his stomach lurch at that look, then immediately felt a self-contempt, that after all these years he could still react this way to mere physical attractiveness, no, beauty.

"Yes, I am."

"I would like to travel with you for a while."

"You know who I am, then you will know at once why I am suspicious of your motives."

She smiled at him, and he felt that lurch again. He turned and spat in the fire. "I'm crossing the Thira," he said.

"I have no problem with that," she told him.

Snow lay back and rested his head on one of the packs. He pulled a thermal sheet across his body and stared up at the sky. The red-tinted swathe of stars was being encroached on by asteroids of the night. A single sword of light cut the sunset.

"Why?" he asked.

"Because I'm lonely, and after the water station I would have travelled on alone. I felt like a change."

Snow grunted in reply and closed his eyes. She was not out to kill him. He had given her ample opportunity as they crossed the rock field. But she did have motives as yet unrevealed to him. Whatever, she would never keep to the pace he set and would soon abandon him, and the unsettling things he was feeling would soon go away. He slept.

* * *

Sunlight on his face, bringing the familiar tingling prior to burning, had his hand up and closing his mask before he was fully awake. He looked across the dead ashes of the fire at Hirald and got the unsettling notion that she had not changed position all night. He sat up, then after a muttered good morning, went behind a rock and urinated into his condenser pack. Following the ritual of every morning for many years now he then emptied the moisture collectors of his under suit into it as well. The collector bottle he emptied into his drinking bottle before dipping his toothbrush and cleaning his teeth. By the time he had finished is ablutions and come out from behind the rock, Hirald had opened a breakfast-soup ration pack and it was bubbling under its lid. Snow reached for another pack, but she held up her hand.

"This is for you. I have already eaten."

"Did you sleep at all?"

"A little. Tell me, how is it you are in possession of proscribed weaponry?"

"Took it off someone who tried to kill me," he lied, but he could hardly tell her he had brought it here before the runcible proscription and modified it himself over the so very many years since. He sat and drank his breakfast. When he had finished, they set out across the Thira. Hirald noted him looking at her after an hour's walking and closed her mask. He thought no more of it; lots of people did not like the masks and were prepared to pay the price of water-loss not to wear them so much.

By midmorning the temperature had reached forty-five degrees and was still rising. A sand shark broke out of the surface of a dune and came scuttling after them for a few metres, then halted, panting like a dog, either too tired or well fed to continue, that or it had sampled human flesh before and found it without nourishment. When the temperature reached fifty and the cooling units of Snow's under suit were labouring under the load, he noted that Hirald still easily matched his pace. When a crab-bird dropped clacking out of the sky at them she brought it down with one shot before Snow could even think of reaching for his weapon. She was a remarkable woman, yes, remarkable.

Shortly after midday Snow called a halt. "We'll rest until evening then continue through the night and tomorrow morning. The following night should bring us out the other side."

Hirald nodded in agreement. Snow wondered why she had not suggested this earlier. Surely, she had not travelled only by day across here? Surely not.

They slept under the reflective shelter of Snow's day tent, then moved on at sunset after Snow had checked their position by the satellite beacons. They walked all night and most of the following morning and when they finally set up the tent again Snow was exhausted. With a hint of irritation, he told Hirald he wanted privacy in the tent and suggested she set up her own. Once inside is tent he sealed up and stripped naked. He then cleaned himself and the inside of his under suit with a cycle sponge; a device that made it possible to stay clean with a quarter litre of water and little spillage. After this he pulled on a pair of towelling shorts and lay back with his miniature air cooler humming away at full power. It was luxury of a kind. After half an hour's sleep he woke and opened the tent to look outside. Hirald was sitting in the sand with her mask open. She was watching the horizon intently, her stillness quite unnatural.

"Don't you have a day tent?" Snow asked.

She shook her head.

"Come and join me then," he said, reversing back into his tent. Hirald stood and walked over, the effects of the baking sun seemingly negligible to her. She entered the tent and closed it behind her, then after a glance at Snow she began to remove her survival suit. Snow turned away for a moment then thought, what the hell, and turned back to watch. She had not asked him to turn his head. Under her suit she wore a single skin-hugging garment that ended above her knees and elbows and in an arc exposing perfectly formed collarbones. The material of the garment was like white silk, and almost translucent. Snow swallowed dryly, then tried to distract himself by wondering about her sanitary arrangements. As she lifted her legs up to remove her trousers from her feet, he saw then how the matter was arranged and wondered if a blush was evident on his white skin. The garment had a hole from the lower part of her pale pubic hair round to the top crease of her buttocks.

As she finally removed her trousers Hirald looked at him and noted the direction of his gaze. He raised his eyes and met her eye to eye. She smiled at him and while smiling stretched the sleeves of the garment down and off over her hands and rolled it down below her breasts. Snow cleared his throat and tried to think of something witty to say. She was a succubus, a lonely desert man's fantasy. Still smiling she came across the tent on her hands and knees, put her hand against his chest and pushed him back, sat astride him, and with her pale hair falling either side of his head she leant down and kissed him on the mouth.

Her mouth was sweet and warm. Snow was thoroughly aware of her hard little nipples sliding from side to side against his chest. He

touched the skin of her shoulders and found it dry and warm. She sat back then and looked down at him for a moment. There was something strange about that look; a kind of cold curiosity. She slid forward onto his stomach then turned and reached back to pull his shorts down and off his legs. He was amazed at just how far she could twist and bend back her body. Once his shorts were removed, she slid back until his penis rested between her buttocks then, after raising herself a little, she continued to push back, bending it over until it almost caused him pain, then with a swift movement of her pelvis, took it inside her. Snow groaned, then gritted his teeth as she started to ride him, staring down at him with that strange expression on her face.

In the evening, when it was time to move on, Snow moved with a bone-deep lethargy. He had not slept much during the afternoon. Each time he had tried to relax after a session of sex, Hirald would do something, whether that would be to take his penis in her mouth or assume some position he could not resist. This had been after her climax while she rode him. It had been so intense that she had cried out and shuddered uncontrollably, and after it she had looked down at herself in surprise and shock. Thereafter she had been eager to repeat the experience. Snow felt sore and drained.

As they walked across the darkened violet sands they had talked little, but there had been one conversation that had raised Snow's suspicions.

"Your hand, how did you lose it?"

"Andronache challenge. It was shredded by a flack shell."

"How is it now?"

Snow had paused before replying. Did she know?

"What do you mean; how is it? It was amputated. It is no longer there."

"Yes," she had said, and no more.

* * *

The sun was breaking the horizon and the night asteroids fading out of the sky when they reached the rock-field at the edge of the Thira. With little energy to spare for conversation, Snow set up his day tent and collapsed inside, instantly asleep. When he woke in the latter part of the day it was to discover himself undressed under a blanket with Hirald lying beside him. She was up on her elbow, her head propped on her hand, looking at his face. As soon as she saw that he was awake she handed him a carton of mixed juice. He sat up, the blanket sliding down. She was naked. He drank the juice.

"I'm glad you came along," he said, and the rest of the day was spent in pleasant activity. That night they moved deep into the rock field. The following day passed much as the one before.

"I think it fair to tell you I have an implant," Snow said as he rested after some particularly vigorous activity. "You won't get pregnant by me, and my sperm is little more than water and a few free proteins."

"Why do you feel it necessary to tell me this?" Hirald asked him.

"As you know, there is a reward out for my testicles, stasis preserved. This is not because the Merchant Baris particularly wants me dead. I think it is because he is after my genetic tissue. It has value, of a kind. At the water station, the Androche... seduced me." Snow was uncomfortable with that. "She did it so she could collect my sperm, probably to sell."

"I know," said Hirald. Snow looked at her and she went on, "He is after your testicles to provide him with an endless supply of your genetic material."

Snow considered that. Of course, there had to be more to Hirald than he had supposed, but the Olympic screwing had clouded his thought-processes somewhat.

"He wouldn't get that... meiosis only leaves half the chromosomes in each sperm," he said.

"He would get there eventually. Your testicles could be kept alive and producing spermatozoa for a very long time. It is the next best thing to having your entire living body to provide the genetic material. I suspect Baris thought it unlikely he could get away with that. He'd never get you off-planet without your consent. This way he also corners the market."

"You know an awful lot about what Baris wants."

Hirald looked at him very directly. "How is your hand?"

Snow looked down at the stump. He unclipped the covering

and pulled it off. What he exposed was recognisably a hand, though deformed and almost useless. The covering had been cleverly made to conceal it, to make it look as if the hand was missing.

"It will be no different from its predecessor in about six solstan months. I intended to walk out of one water station without a hand, then into another station with a hand and a new identity."

"What about your albinism?"

"Skin dye and eye lenses."

"Of course you cannot take transplants."

"No... I think you should explain yourself."

"The people I work for want the same as Baris; your genome."

"You've had opportunity..."

"No, they want the best option; you, willingly. I want you to gate back to Earth with me."

"Why?"

"You are regenerative. It is the source of your immortality. We know this now. You have known it for more than a thousand years."

"Still, why?"

"We have managed to keep your secret for the last three hundred years, ever since it was discovered. Ten years ago, a mistake was made and the knowledge was leaked. Now many organisations know about you, and what you represent; whoever can decode your genome has access to immortality, and through that access to wealth and power unprecedented. Baris is one who would like this. He was the first to track you down. There will be others."

"You work for Earth Central."

"Yes."

"Wouldn't it be better just to kill me and destroy my body?"

"Earth Central does not suppress knowledge." Hirald smiled at him. "You should be old enough to understand the futility of this. It wants this knowledge disseminated so that it cannot cause damage, cannot put power into the hands of the wrong people. The good it would do is immense also. The projections are that in ten years a treatment could become available to make anyone regenerative, within limits."

"Yet prior to this it kept a lid on things," said Snow, an old hand at spotting discrepancies like this.

"It guarded your privacy. It did not suppress knowledge. Not suppressing knowledge is not equal to seeking it out."

"Is Earth Central so moral now?" wondered Snow, then could have kicked himself for the stupidity. Of course Earth Central was. Only human beings and other low-grade sentients could become corrupt, and Earth Central was the most powerful AI in the human polity. Hirald, noting his discomfiture, did not answer his question.

"Will you come?" she asked him.

Snow looked to the wall of the tent as if looking out across the rock field.

"This requires thought, not instant decisions. Two days should bring us to my home. I will... consider."

* * *

Draped in chameleon cloth the hover transport was indistinguishable from the surrounding dunes. Inside the transport Jharit shuffled a pack of cards and played a game men like he had played in similar situations for many centuries. His wife, Jharilla, slept. Trock was cleaning an antique revolver he had picked up in an auction at the last water station. The bullets he had acquired with it standing in neat soldierly rows on the table before him. Canard Meck was plugged in, trying to pick up information from the net and the high-speed conversations the runcible AI had with its subminds. The call came as a relief to all of them but her; she resented dropping out of that world of perfect logic and pure clarity of thought back into the sweat-stink of the transport.

"I am Baris," said the smiling face from the screen.

Coming straight to the point Jharit said, "You have the information?"

"I have," said Baris, his smile only slightly less, "and I will be coming to join you for the final chase."

Jharit and Trock exchanged a look.

"As you wish. You are paying."

"Yes, I am." The Merchant's smile was gone now. "Turn on your beacon and I will join you within the hour."

"How are you getting out here?" asked Canard Meck.

"By AGC of course," said Baris, turning to look towards her.

"All AGCs are registered. The AI will know where you are."

Baris flicked his fingers at this, and his face assumed a look of contempt. "No matter. We will continue from your position to... our destination, in the transport."

"Very well," said Canard Meck.

Baris waited for something more to be said, and when nothing was, he gave a moue of disappointment. The screen blanked.

* * *

The Merchant arrived in a fancy repro Macrojet AGC. He climbed out dressed in sand fatigues and was followed by two women dressed much the same. One of them carried a hunting rifle and ammunition belts. The other carried various unidentifiable packages. Baris struck a pose before them. He was a handsome man. Not one of the four reacted to this foolish display. They knew that anyone who had reached the Merchant's position was no fool. Jharit and Jharilla looked at him glassy eyed. Trock looked at the rifle. Canard Meck looked briefly at one of the women, took in the imbecilic smile, then back to the Merchant.

"Shall we be on our way then," she said.

Baris shook his head and still smiling he clicked his fingers and walked to the transport. The two women followed him as obediently as dogs. The four came after: hounds of a different breed.

* * *

Out of the rock field reared the first of the stone buttes, carved by wind-blown sand into something resembling a statue of something manlike sunk up to its chest in the ground. In the cracks and divisions of its head, mica and quartz glittered like insectile eyes. Snow led the way to the base of the butte where slabs of the same stone lay tilted in the ground.

"Here," he said, holding his hand out to a sandwich of slabs. With a grinding, the top slab pivoted to one side to expose a stair dropping a short distance to the floor of a tunnel. "Welcome to my home."

"You live in a hole in the ground?" said Hirald with a touch of irony.

"Of course not. Follow."

As they climbed down the slab swung back across above them and wall lights clicked on. Hirald noted that the tunnel led under the butte and had already worked things out by the time they reached the chimney with its rails pinned up the side and the elevator car. They climbed inside the car and sprawled in the seats ringing the inside, looked out the windows as it hauled them up the chimney cut through the centre of the butte.

"This must have taken you some time," said Hirald.

Snow said, "The shaft was already here. About two hundred years ago I first found it. Others had lived here before me, but in rather primitive conditions. I've been improving the place ever since."

The car arrived at its destination and they walked from it into a complex of moisture-locked rooms at the head of the butte. With a drink in her hand Hirald stood at a polarised panoramic window and looked out across the rock field for a moment, then returned her attention to the room and its contents. In a glass-fronted case along one wall was a display of weapons dating from the twenty-second century and at the centre of this a sword dating from some pre-space age. Hirald had to wonder. She turned from the case as Snow returned to the room, dressed now in loose black trousers and a black open necked shirt. The contrast with his white skin and hair and pink eyes gave him the appearance of someone who might have a taste for blood.

"There's some clothing there for you to use if you like, and the shower. No problem with it cycling. There's plenty of water here," he told her. Hirald nodded, placed her drink down on a glass-topped table, and headed back into the rooms Snow had come from. Snow watched her go. She would shower and change and be little fresher than she already was. He had noted with some puzzlement how she never seemed to smell bad, never seemed dirty.

"Whose clothing is this?" Hirald asked from the room beyond.

"My last wife's," said Snow.

Hirald came to the door with clothing folded over one arm. She looked at Snow questioningly.

"She killed herself about century ago," he said in a flat voice. "Walked out into the desert and burnt a hole through her head. I found her before the crab-birds and sand sharks."

"Why?"

"She grew old and I did not. She hated it."

Hirald had no comment to make on this. She went to take her shower, and shortly returned wearing a skin-tight bodysuit of translucent blue material, which she did not expect to be wearing for long once Snow saw her in it. Snow was occupied though; sat in a swivel chair looking at a screen, he was back in his dust robes, his terrapin mask hanging open. She walked up behind him to see what he was looking at. She saw the hover transport on the sand and the two women pulling a sheet over it. The Merchant Baris she recognised, as she recognised the four hired killers.

"It would seem Baris has found me," said Snow, his tone cold and flat.

"What defences does this place have?"

"None, I never felt the need for them."

"Are you sure they are coming here?"

"It seems strange that he has chosen this particular rock field on the whole planet. I'll have to go and settle this."

"I'll change," said Hirald, and hurried back to get her suit. When she returned Snow was gone, when she tried to follow she found the elevator car locked at the bottom of the shaft.

"Damn you, Snow!" she yelled, slamming her fist against a doorjamb, leaving a fist-shaped dent in the steel. She then walked back a few paces, turned, and ran and leapt into the shaft. The rails pinned to the edge were six metres away. She reached them easily, her hands locking on the polished metal with a thump. Laboriously she began to climb down.

* * *

Jharit smiled at his wife and nodded to Trock who stood beyond her strapping on body armour. This was the one. They would be rich after this. He looked at the narrow beam laser he held. He would have preferred something with a little more power, but it was essential that the body not be too badly damaged. He turned to Baris as the Merchant sent his two women back to the transport.

"We'll go in spread out. He probably has scanning equipment in the rock field and if there's an ambush, we don't want him to get too many of us at once."

Baris smiled and thumbed bullets into his rifle, adjusted the scope. Jharit wondered about him, wondered how good he was. He gave the signal; they spread out and entered the rock field.

* * *

They were coming to kill him. There were no rules, no challenges offered. Snow braced the butt of his pistol against the rock and sighted along it.

* * *

"Anything?" asked Jharit over the com.

"Pin cameras," Jharilla told him. "I burnt a couple out, but there has to be more. He knows we're here."

"Me too," said Trock.

"Remember, narrow beam, we burn too much and there's no money. A clean kill. A head shot would be nice."

There was a whooshing sound, a brief scream, static over the com. Jharit hit the ground and moved behind a rock.

"What the hell was that?"

"He's got a fucking APW! Fucking body armour's useless!"

Jharit felt a sinking sensation in his gut. They had expected projectile weapons, perhaps a laser.

"Who...?"

There was a pause.

"Trock?"

"Jharilla's dead."

Jharit swallowed dryly and edged on into the rock field.

"Position?"

"Don't know?"

"Meck?"

"Nothing here."

"Baris?"

There was no reply from the Merchant.

* * *

Snow dropped down off the top of the boulder and pulled the remaining two spheroids from his belt. With his teeth he twisted their tops right round. The dark skinned one was over to his left. The Marsman over to his right. The others were further over to the right somewhere. He threw the two spheroids right and left and moved back then flicked through multiple views on his wrist screen. A lot of the cameras were out, but he pulled up a view of the Marsman. Two detonations. As the Marsman hit the ground, Snow realised he had thrown too far there. He was close. He flicked through the views again and caught the other stumbling through dust and wreckage, rock splinters imbedded in his face. Ah, so. Snow moved to his left, checking his screen every few seconds. He halted behind a tilted slab and after checking his screen once more he squatted down and waited.

With little regard for his surroundings, Trock stumbled out of the falling dust. Snow smiled grimly under his mask and sighted on him. Red agony cut his shoulder. The smell of burning flesh. Snow rolled to one side, came up onto his feet, ran. Rock to one side of him smoked, pinged as it heated. He dived for cover, crawled amongst broken rock. The firing ceased. *Now I'm dead*, he thought. His pistol lay in the dust back there somewhere.

* * *

"He dropped the APW, Trock. He's over to your left. Take him down, I can't get a sighting on him at the moment."

Trock spat a broken tooth from his mouth and walked in the direction indicated, his antique revolver in his left hand and his laser in his right. This was it. The bastard was dead, or perhaps not. I'll cut his arms and legs off, the beam should cauterise sufficiently. Trock did not get time to fire. The figure in dust robes came out of nowhere to drop-kick him in the chest. The body armour absorbed most of the blow, but Trock went over. Before he could rise the figure was above him. A split-hand blow drove through his visor and deep into his eyes, two fingers each, and burst them. It was a strike Snow had learnt over a thousand years before. By the time Trock started screaming and firing Snow was gone again.

* * *

Snow coughed as quietly as he could, opened his mask and spat out a mixture of bloody plasma and charred tissue. The burn had started at his shoulder and penetrated his left lung. A second more and he would have been dead. The pain was crippling. He knew he would not have the energy for another attack like that, nor would he be likely to take any of the others by surprise. The man had been stunned by the explosion, angered by the injuries to himself. Snow edged back through the rock field, his mobility rapidly decreasing. When a shadow fell across him, he looked up into the inevitable.

"Why didn't you take his weapon?" asked Jharit, nodding back in the direction of Trock, who was no longer screaming. He was curled foetal by a rock, a field dressing across his eyes and his body pumped full of self-administered painkillers.

"No time, no strength... could only get him through his visor," Snow managed.

Jharit nodded and spoke into his com. "I have him. Home in on my signal."

Snow waited for death, but Jharit squatted in the dust by him seemingly disinclined to kill him.

"Jharil was a hell of a woman," said Jharit, removing a stasis bottle from his belt and pushing it into the sand next to him. "We were married in Viking city twenty solstan years ago." Jharit pulled a wicked ceramal knife from his boot and held it up before his face. "This is for her you understand. After I've taken your testicles and dressed that wound, I'll see to your other injury. I don't want you to die yet. I have so much to

tell you about her, and there is so much I want you to experience. You know she—"

Jharit turned at a sound, rose to his feet and drew his laser again. He stepped away from Snow and looked around. Snow looked beyond him but could see nothing.

"If you leave here now, Marsman, I will not kill you."

The voice was Hirald's.

Jharit fired into the rocks and backed towards Snow.

"I have a singun and I am in chameleonwear. I can kill you any time I wish. Drop your weapon."

Jharit paused for a moment as if indecisive, then he whirled, pointing his laser at Snow. The expression on his face told all. Before he could press the trigger, he collapsed into himself; a central point the size of a pinhead, a plume of sand standing where he stood, then all blasted away in a thunderclap and encore of miniature lightnings across the ground. Snow slowly shoved himself to his feet as he looked in awe at the spot Jharit had occupied. He had heard of such weapons and not believed. He looked across as Hirald flickered back into existence only a few metres away. She smiled at him, just before the first shot ripped the side of her face away.

Snow knew he yelled, he might have screamed. He looked on in impotent horror as the second shot smacked into her back and knocked her to the ground. Then there: Baris and the corporation woman, walking out of the rock field. Baris sighted again as he walked, hit Hirald with another shot that ripped half her side away. Snow felt his legs give way. He went down on his knees. Baris came before him, a self-satisfied smirk on his face. Snow looked up at him, trying to pull the energy together, to throw it all in one attempt. He knew it was what Baris was waiting for. It was all he could do. He glanced aside at the woman, saw she had halted some way back. She was looking past Baris at Hirald, a look of horror on her face. Snow did not want to look. He did not want to know.

"Oh my God. It's her!"

Snow pulled himself to his feet, dizziness making him lurch. Baris grinned and pointed the rifle at his face, relished his moment for the half a second it lasted. The hand punched through his body, knocked

74

the rifle aside, lifted him and hurled him against a rock with such force he stuck for a moment, then fell leaving a man-shaped corona of blood. Hirald stood there, revealed. Where the synthiflesh had been blown away glittering ceramal was exposed, her white enamel teeth, one blue eye complete in its socket, the ribbed column of her spine. She observed Snow for a moment then turned towards the woman. Snow fainted before the scream.

* * *

He was in his bed and memories slowly dragged themselves into his mind. He lay there, his throat dry, and after a moment felt across to his numbed shoulder and the dressing. It was a moment before he dared open his eyes. Hirald sat at the side of the bed and when she saw he was awake she helped him up into a sitting position against his pillows. Snow observed her face. She had repaired the damage somehow, but the scars of that repair-work were still there. She looked just like a human woman who had been disfigured in an accident. She wore a loose shirt and trousers to hide the other repairs. As he looked at her, she reached up and self-consciously touched her face, before reaching for a glass of water to hand to him. Gratefully he drained the glass. That touch of vanity confused him for a moment.

"You're a Golem android," he said, in the end, unsure.

Hirald smiled and it did not look so bad.

She said, "Canard Meck thought that." When she saw his confusion she explained, "The corporation woman. She called me product, which is an understandable mistake. I am nearly indistinguishable from the Golem twenty-two."

"What are you then?" Snow asked as she poured him another glass of water.

"Cyborg. Underneath this synthiflesh I am ceramal. In the ceramal a human brain, spinal column, and other nerve tissues."

Snow sipped his drink as he considered that. He was not sure what he was feeling, but it certainly was not the horror he had first felt.

"Will you come to Earth with me?"

Snow turned and looked at her for a long time. He remembered

how it had been in the tents as she, he realised, discovered that she was still human.

"You know, I will never grow old and die," she said.

"I know."

She tilted her head questioningly and awaited his answer.

A slow smile spread across his face. "I'll come with you," he told her. "If you will stay with me." He put his drink down and reached out to take hold of her hand. What defined humanity? There was blood still under her fingernails and the tear duct in her left eye was not working properly.

It didn't matter.

THE TALL GRASS

Joe R. Lansdale

I can't really explain this properly, but I'll tell it to you, and you can make the best of it. It starts with a train. People don't travel as readily by train these days as they once did, but in my youthful days they did, and I have to admit that day was some time ago, considering my current, doddering age. It's hard to believe the century has turned, and I have turned with it, as worn out and rusty as those old coal-powered trains.

I am soon to fall off the edge of the cliff into the great darkness, but there was a time when I was young and the world was light. Then there was something that happened to me on a rail line that showed me something I didn't know was there, and since that time, I've never seen the world in exactly the same way.

What I can tell you is this. I was traveling across country by night in a very nice rail car. I had not just a seat on a train, but a compartment to myself. A quite comfortable compartment, I might add. I was early into my business career then, having just started with a firm that I ended up working at for twenty-five years. To simplify, I had completed a cross-country business trip, and was on my way home. I wasn't married then, but one of the reasons I was eager to make it back to my home town was a young woman named Ellen. We were quite close, and her company meant everything to me. It was our plan to marry.

I won't bore you with details, but, that particular plan didn't work out. And though I still think of that with some disappointment, for she was very beautiful, it has absolutely nothing to do with my story.

Thing is, the train was crossing the western country, in a barren stretch without towns, beneath a wide-open night sky with a high moon and a few crawling clouds. Back then, those kinds of places were far more common than lights and streets and motor cars are now. I had made the same ride several times on business, yet, I always

77

enjoyed looking out the window, even at night. This night, however, for whatever reason, I was up very late, unable to sleep. I had chosen not to eat dinner, and now that it was well passed, I was a bit hungry, but there was nothing to be had.

The lamps inside the train had been extinguished, and out the window there was a moonlit sea of rocks and sand and in the distance beyond, shadowy blue-black mountains.

The train came to an odd stretch that I had somehow missed before on my journeys, as I was probably sleeping at the time. It was a great expanse of prairie grass, and it shifted in the moonlight like waves of gold-green sea water pulled by the tide making forces of the moon.

I was watching all of this, trying to figure it, determining how odd it looked and how often I had to have passed it and had never seen it. Oh, I had seen lots of tall grass, but nothing like this. The grass was not only head high, or higher, it was thick and it had what I can only describe as an unusual look about it, as if I were seeing it with eyes that belonged to someone else. I know how peculiar that sounds, but it's the only way I know how to explain it.

Then the train jerked, as if some great hand had grabbed it. It screeched on the rails and there was a cacophony of sounds before the engine came to a hard stop.

I had no idea what had occurred. I opened the compartment door, though at first the door seemed locked and only gave way with considerable effort. I stepped out in the hallway. No one was there.

Edging along the hallway, I came to the smoking car, but there was no one there either. It seemed the other passengers were in a tight sleep and unaware of our stopping. I walked through the car, sniffing at the remains of tobacco smoke, and opened a door that went out on a connecting platform that was positioned between the smoking car and another passenger car. I looked in the passenger car through the little window at the door. There was no one there. This didn't entirely surprise me, as the train had taken on a very small load of passengers, and many of them, like me, had purchased personal cabins.

I looked out at the countryside and saw there were lights in the distance, beyond the grass, or to be more exact, positioned out in it. It shocked me, because we were in the middle of absolutely nowhere, and the fact that there was a town nearby was a total surprise to me.

THE TALL GRASS

I walked to the edge of the platform. There was a folded and hinged metal stair there, and with the toe of my shoe I kicked it, causing it to flip out and extend to the ground.

I climbed down the steps and looked along the rail. There was no one at first, and then there was a light swinging its way toward me, and finally a shadowy shape behind the light. In a moment I saw that it was a rail man, dressed in cap and coat and company trousers.

"You best stay on board, sir," he said.

I could see him clearly now. He was an average looking man, small in size with an odd walk about him; the sort people who practically live on trains acquire, as do sailors on ships at sea.

"I was just curious," I said. "What has happened?"

"A brief stop," he said. "I suggest you go back inside."

"Is no one else awake?" I said.

"You seem to be it, sir," he said. "I find those that go to sleep before twelve stay that way when this happens."

I thought that a curious answer. I said, "Does it happen often?"

"No. Not really."

"What's wrong? Are there repairs going on?"

"We are building up another head of steam," he said.

"Then surely I have time to step out here and have a smoke in the open air," I said.

"I suppose that's true, sir," he said. "But I wouldn't wander far. Once we're ready to go, we'll go. I'll call for you to get on board, but only a few times, and then we'll go, no matter what. We won't tarry, not here. Not between midnight and two."

And then he went on by me swinging the light.

I was intrigued by what he had said, about not tarrying. I looked out at the waving grass and the lights, which I now realized were not that far away. I took out my makings and rolled a cigarette and put a match to it and puffed.

I can't really explain what possessed me. The oddness of the moment, I suppose. But I decided it would be interesting to walk out in the tall grass, just to measure its height, and to maybe get a closer look at those lights. I strolled out a ways, and within moments I was deep in the grass. As I walked, the earth sloped downwards and the

grass whispered in the wind. When I stopped walking, the grass was over my head, and behind me where the ground was higher, the grass stood tall against the moonlight, like rows of spear heads held high by an army of warriors.

I stood there in the midst of the grass and smoked and listened for activity back at the train, but neither heard the lantern man or the sound of the train getting ready to leave. I relaxed a bit, enjoying the cool, night wind and the way it moved through the prairie. I decided to stroll about while I smoked, parting the grass as I went. I could see the lights still, but they always seemed to be farther away than I thought, and my moving in their direction didn't seem to bring me closer; they receded like the horizon.

When I finished my cigarette, I dropped it and put my heel to it, grinding it into the ground, and turned to go back to the train.

I was a bit startled to discover I couldn't find the path I had taken. Surely, the grass had been bent or pushed aside by my passing, but there was no sign of it. It had quickly sprung back into shape. I couldn't find the rise I had come down. The position of the moon was impossible to locate, even though there was plenty of moonlight; the moon had gone away and left its light there.

Gradually I became concerned. I had somehow gotten turned about, and the train would soon be leaving, and I had been warned that no one would wait for me. I thought perhaps it was best if I ceased thrashing about through the grass, and just stopped, least I become more confused. I concluded that I couldn't have gone too far from the railway, and that I should be able to hear the train man should he call out for All Aboard.

So, there I was, standing in tall grass like a fool. Lost from the train and listening intently for the man to call out. I kept glancing about to try and see if I could find a path back the way I came. As I said before, it stood to reason that I had tromped down some grass, and that I couldn't be that far away. It was also, as I said, a very well-lit night, plenty of moonlight. It rested like swipes of cream cheese on the tall grass, so it was inconceivable to me that I had gotten lost in such a short time walking such a short distance. I also considered those lights as bearings, but they had moved, fluttering about like will-o-the-wisps, so using them as markers was impossible.

THE TALL GRASS

I was lost, and I began to entertain the disturbing thought that I might miss the train and be left where I was. It would be bad enough to miss the train, but here, out in the emptiness of nowhere, if I wasn't missed, or no one came back this way for a time, I might actually starve, or be devoured by wild animals, or die of exposure.

That's when I heard someone coming through the grass. They weren't right on top of me, but they were close, and of course, my first thought was it was the man from the train come to look for me. I started to call out, but hesitated.

I can't entirely explain the hesitation, but there was a part of me that felt reluctant, and so instead of calling out, I waited. The noise grew louder.

I cautiously parted the grass with my fingers, and looked in the direction of the sound, and coming through the grass were a number of men, all of them peculiarly bald, the moonlight reflecting off their heads like mirrors. The grass whipped open as they came and closed back behind them. For a brief moment I felt relieved, as they must be other passengers or train employees sent to look for me, and would direct me to back to the train. It would be an embarrassing moment, but in the end, all would be well.

And then I realized something. I hadn't been actually absorbing what I was seeing. They were human shaped alright, but... they had no faces. There was a head, and there were spots where the usual items should be—nose, eyes, mouth—but those spots were indentions. The moonlight gathered on those shiny, white faces, and reflected back out. They were the lights in the grass and they were why the lights moved, because they moved. There were other lights beyond them, way out, and I drew the conclusion that there were many of these human-shaped things, out in the grass, close and far away, moving toward me, and moving away, thick as aphids. They had a jerky movement about them, as if they were squirming on a griddle. They pushed through the grass and fanned out wide, and some of them had sticks, and they began to beat the grass before them. I might add that as they did, the grass, like a living thing whipped away from their strikes and opened wide and closed up behind them. They were coming ever nearer to where I was. I could see they were of all different shapes and sizes and attire.

Some of them wore very old clothes, and there were others who were dressed in rags, and even a couple who were completely devoid of clothes, and sexless, smooth all over, as if anything that distinguished their sex or their humanity had been ironed out. Still, I could tell now, by the general shape of the bodies, that some of them may have been women, and certainly some of the smaller ones were children. I even saw moving among them a shiny white body in the shape of a dog.

In the same way I had felt it unwise to call out to them, I now felt it unwise to wait where I was. I knew they knew I was in the grass, and that they were looking for me.

I broke and ran. I was spotted, because behind me, from those faces without mouths, there somehow rose up a cry. A kind of squeal, like something being slowly ground down beneath a boot heel.

I heard them as they rushed through the grass after me. I could hear their feet thundering against the ground. It was as if a small heard of buffalo were in pursuit. I charged through the grass blindly. Once I glanced back over my shoulder and saw their numbers were larger than I first thought. Their shapes broke out of the grass, left and right and close and wide. The grass was full of them, and their faces glowed as if inside their thin flesh were lit lanterns.

Finally, there was a place where the grass was missing and there was only earth. It was a relief from the cloying grass, but it was a relief that passed swiftly, for now I was fully exposed. Moving rapidly toward me from the front were more of those moon-lit things. I turned, and saw behind me the others were very near. They began to run all out toward me, they were also closing in from my right.

There was but one way for me to go, to the left, and wide, back into the grass. I did just that. I ran as hard as I could run. The grass sloped up slightly, and I fought to climb the hill; the hill that I had lost such a short time ago. It had reappeared, or rather I had stumbled up on it.

My feet kept slipping as I climbed up it. I glanced down, and there in that weird light I could see that my boots were sliding in what looked to be rotting piles of fat-glazed bones; the earth was slick with them.

I could hear the things closing behind me, making that sound that a face without a mouth should be unable to make; that horrid screech. It was deafening.

THE TALL GRASS

I was almost at the peak of the hill. I could see the grass swaying up there. I could hear it whispering in the wind between the screeches of those pursuing me, and just as I made the top of the hill and poked my head through the grass and saw the train, I was grabbed.

Here is a peculiar thing that from time to time I remember, and shiver when I do, but those hands that had hold of my legs were cold as arctic air. I could feel them through my clothes, they were so cold. I tried to kick loose but wasn't having any luck. I had fallen when they grabbed me, and I was clutching at the grass at the top of the hill. It was pulling through my hands and fingers, and the edges were sharp; they cut into me like razors. I could feel the warm blood running through my fingers, but still I hung to that grass.

Glancing back, I saw that I was seized by several of the things, and the dog like shape had clamped its jaws on the heel of my boot. I saw too that the things were not entirely without features after all; or at least now they had acquired one all-encompassing feature. A split appeared in their faces, where a mouth should be, but it was impossibly wide and festooned with more teeth than a shark, long and sharp, many of them crooked as poorly driven nails, stained in spots the color of very old cheese. Their breath rose up like methane from a privy and burned my eyes. There was no doubt in my mind that they meant to bite me; and I somehow knew that if I was bitten, I would not be chewed and eaten, but that the bite would make me like them. That my bones would come free of me along with my features and everything that made me human, and I knew too that these things were originally from train stops, and from frontier scouting parties, adventurers and surveyors, and all manner of folks who had at one time had been crossing these desolate lands and found themselves here, a place not only unknown to the map, but unknown to human understanding. All of this came to me and instantly filled me up with dread. It was as if their very touch had revealed it to me.

I kicked wildly, wrenching my bootheel from the dog-shape's toothy grasp. I struggled. I heard teeth snap on empty air as I kicked loose. And then there was warmth and a glow over my head. I looked up to see the train man with a great flaming torch, and he was waving it about, sticking it into the teeth-packed faces of those poor lost souls.

They screeched and they bellowed, they hissed and they moaned. But the fire did the trick. They let go of me and receded into the waves of grass, and the grass folded back around them, like the ocean swallowing sailors. I saw last the dog-shape dive into the grass like a porpoise, and then it and them were gone, and so were the lights, and the moonlight lost its slick glaze, and it was just a light. The torch flickered over my head, and I could feel its heat.

The next thing I knew the train man was pulling me to the top of the hill, and I collapsed and trembled like a mass of gelatin spilled on a floor.

"They don't like it up here, sir," the train man said, pushing the blazing end of his torch against the ground, rubbing it in the dirt, snuffing it out. The smell of pitch tingled my nostrils. "No, they don't like it at all."

"What are they?" I said.

"I think you know, sir. I do. Somewhere deep inside me, I know. There aren't any words for it, but I know, and you know. They touched me once, but thank goodness I was only near the grass, not in it. Not like you were, sir."

He led me back to the train. He said, "I should have been more emphatic, but you looked like a reasonable chap to me. Not someone to wander off."

"I wish I had been reasonable."

"It's like looking to the other side, isn't it, sir?" he said. "Or rather, it is a look to one of many sides, I suspect. Little lost worlds inside our own. The train breaks down here often. There have been others who have left the train. I suspect you met some of them tonight. You saw what they have become, or so I think. I can't explain all the others. Wanderers, I suspect. It's always here the train stops or breaks down. Usually, it just sort of loses steam. It can have plenty and still lose it, and we have to build it all up again. Always this time of night. Rarely a problem, really. Another thing, I lock all the doors at night to keep folks in, should they come awake. I lock the general passenger cars on both ends. Most don't wake up anyway, not this time of night, not after midnight, not if they've gone to sleep before that time, and are good solid in. Midnight between two a.m., that's when it always happens, the train losing steam here near the crawling grass. I guess those of us awake at that time can see some things that others can't. In this spot anyway. That's what I suppose. It's like a door opens out there during that time. They got their spot, their limitations, but you don't want to be out there, no sir. You're quite lucky."

"Thank you," I said.

"Guess I missed your lock, sir. Or it works poorly. I apologize for that. Had I done right, you wouldn't have been able to get out. If someone should stay awake and find the room locked, we pretend it's a stuck doorway. Talk to them through the door, and tell them we can't get it fixed until morning. A few people have been quite put out by that. The ones who were awake when we stopped here. But it's best that way. I'm sure you'll agree, sir."

"I do," I said. "Thank you again. I can't say it enough."

"Oh, no problem. You had almost made it out of the grass, and you were near the top of the hill, so it was easy for me help you. I always keep a torch nearby that can easily be lit. They don't like fire, and they don't come up close to the train. They don't get out of the grass, as far as I can determine. But I will tell you true, had I heard your scream too far beyond the hill, well, I wouldn't have come after you. And they would have had you."

"I screamed?"

"Loudly."

I got on the train and walked back to my compartment, still trembling. I checked my door and saw that my lock had been thrown from the outside, but it was faulty, and all it took was a little shaking to have it come free of the door frame. That's how I had got out of my room.

The train man brought me a nip of whisky, and I told him about the lock, and drank the whisky. "I'll have the lock fixed right away, sir. Best not to mention all this," he said. "No one will believe it, and it could cause problems with the cross-country line. People have to get places, you know."

I nodded.

"Goodnight, sir. Pleasant dreams."

This was such an odd invocation to all that had happened, I almost laughed.

He went away, closing up my compartment, and I looked out the window. All there was to see was the grass, waving in the wind, tipped with moonlight.

The train started to move, and pretty soon we were on our way. And that was the end of the matter, and this is the first time I have mentioned it since it happened so long ago. But, I assure you. It happened just the way I told you, crossing the Western void, in the year of 1901.

ALL THROUGH THE HOUSE

Joachim Heijndermans

Billy!" whispered Leah. "Billy! Wake up!"

"What?" groaned Billy. Though he hadn't yet learned how to read the time, little Billy could tell it was late in the night by looking out the window. The sky was an inky black, with only the light fluttering of snow passing by the window to break the dark monotony.

"Do you hear that?" Leah asked.

Before Billy could even ask what she was talking about, a thumping sound from downstairs chased away any sleep he still had. He looked his older sister in the eye, both of them silently agreeing that the sound could be only one thing. Santa was here.

Without saying another word, Billy and Leah slipped their feet into their slippers and slowly left their bedroom. They walked carefully, so the floorboards would not creak. With a gentle pace, they crawled down the staircase. Leah halted before she reached the bottom and crouched down, peering between the wooden bars of the bannister. Billy expected to see a large smile plastered on her face, delighted by the sight of the jolly old elf eating the cookies they had laid on a plate before they'd gone off to bed.

But there was no smile. There was nothing. Leah stared blankly into the living room, her mouth opened slightly. When Billy caught up with her and looked for himself, his blood turned to ice.

There, in front of the Christmas tree, carefully holding an ornament between two elongated claws, stood a thin skeletal being. Its bright red skin hung loosely from its thin and brittle-looking frame. A small turtle-like head on top of its long, thin neck moved from side to side, mesmerized by the glass figurine. It was a little Mickey Mouse, dressed in a Santa suit and crossing off names from a list with a long feather quill. It held the mouse to its face and opened its two large nostrils, which up until that moment had not been there. It could shut them as tightly

as the children could shut their eyes, something which the creature seemed to be incapable of. Large yellow eyes took up the majority of its face, but not once did the creature blink.

Having grown bored with the ornament, the thin specter gently hung it back on its designated branch on the pine tree, then turned to other matters. Its large eyes had fallen on the plate of cookies and the glass of milk. With its two-fingered hand, it lifted the glass then opened its maw. A large prehensile tongue shot out into the glass. Within seconds, the milk vanished from its container, leaving behind a puff of steam, as if it had boiled off in an instant. The cookies met a similar fate when the figure took the plate and placed it in its mouth. When it pulled the plate back out, all the cookies had vanished. Not even the smallest crumb was left behind.

Then, to Billy's horror, Leah gasped. It was the lightest of gasps, one that only the most alert of adults would have picked up, or perhaps a guard dog. And even then, they wouldn't have thought much of it. But the red creature heard, and jerked its head toward them. With wide, serpentine eyes, it regarded the two small children huddled at the bottom of the staircase.

It began to crawl toward them, walking on its knuckles as it tried to place its long, bent legs in ways that would not knock any of the furniture over. Billy wanted to run to his room and hide, but he couldn't move. Leah sat there, just as frozen as he was, her lip quivering as the red-skinned creature approached them. Then, it stopped, looming over the two with an arched back. Billy could count the ribs in its chest and the vertebrae protruding from its neck. He believed he would cry, but looking into those yellow eyes was oddly soothing. It turned to Leah.

"*Lee...ah...,*" it groaned in a hoarse voice. "*Gut.*"

The creature tilted its head back. It began to make a hacking sound. How-how-how it went, like a cat expelling a hairball. Its throat expanded as a large ball was pushed up, while snow-white tears streamed from its eyes. Then, without warning, it spat up a box wrapped in gold and silver wrapping paper. The phlegm that clung to it evaporated within seconds. Then, it turned to face Billy.

"*Whhilll...jem...*" it groaned. "*Gut.*"

The two children watched with astonishment as the creature repeated the process, this time expelling a large thin box and a set of three smaller boxes from its mouth. Once finished, the creature panted heavily to catch its breath. It reached out its hands and placed it on both brother and sister's heads, brushing its thin talons through their hair.

"*Staaai...gut,*" it muttered before crawling on all fours to the chimney and climbing up into it. The moment it vanished, the fire, which had died long before the children's bedtime, reignited. They could hear the faint sound of bells, gently fading away into the cold December night.

Billy felt that he could move again. While still reeling over what they had just witnessed, his curiosity compelled him to step out and unwrap the boxes the creature had spit out. He made quick work of the wrapping paper and beamed with delight when he saw the Silverado train set that he'd wanted for weeks now. The three smaller boxes contained an additional car each. Leah, on the other hand, found that her box contained the Little Suzy doll that she had asked from Santa.

Both children took their new toys up to their shared bedroom and laid in bed with them. Though neither of them could find their sleep. For both children wondered the same thing as they clung tightly to their gifts.

What if they had not been '*gut*'?

LIFE HUTCH

Harlan Ellison

errence slid his right hand, the one out of sight of the robot, up his side. The razoring pain of the three broken ribs caused his eyes to widen momentarily in pain. Then he recovered himself and closed them till he was studying the machine through narrow slits.

If the eyeballs click, I'm dead, thought Terrence.

The intricate murmurings of the life hutch around him brought back the immediacy of his situation. His eyes again fastened on the medicine cabinet clamped to the wall next to the robot's duty-niche.

Cliché. So near yet so far. It could be all the way back on Antares-Base for all the good it's doing me, he thought, and a crazy laugh rang through his head. He caught himself just in time. *Easy! Three days is a nightmare, but cracking up will only make it end sooner.* That was the last thing he wanted. But it couldn't go on much longer.

He flexed the fingers of his right hand. It was all he *could* move. Silently he damned the technician who had passed the robot through. Or the politician who had let inferior robots get placed in the life hutches so he could get a rake-off from the government contract. Or the repairman who hadn't bothered checking closely his last time around. All of them; he damned them all.

They deserved it.

He was dying.

His death had started before he had reached the life hutch. Terrence had begun to die when he had gone into the battle.

He let his eyes close completely, let the sounds of the life hutch fade from around him. Slowly, the sound of the coolants hush-hushing through the wall-pipes, the relay machines feeding their messages without pause from all over the galaxy, the whirring of the antenna's standard, turning in its socket atop the bubble, slowly they melted into silence. He had resorted to blocking himself off from reality many

times during the past three days. It was either that or existing with the robot watching, and eventually he would have had to move. To move was to die. It was that simple.

He closed his ears to the whisperings of the life hutch; he listened to the whisperings within himself.

"Good God! There must be a million of them!"

It was the voice of the squadron leader, Resnick, ringing in his suit intercom.

"What kind of battle formation is *that* supposed to be?" came another voice. Terrence looked at the radar screen, at the flickering dots signifying Kyben ships.

"Who can tell with those toadstool-shaped ships of theirs," Resnick answered. "But remember, the whole front umbrella-part is studded with cannon, and it has a helluva range of fire. Okay, watch yourselves, good luck—and give 'em Hell!"

The fleet dove straight for the Kyben armada.

To his mind came the sounds of war, across the gulf of space. It was all imagination; in that tomb there was no sound. Yet he could clearly detect the hiss of his scout's blaster as it poured beam after beam into the lead ship of the Kyben fleet.

His sniper-class scout had been near the point of that deadly Terran phalanx, driving like a wedge at the alien ships, converging on them in loose battle-formation. It was then it had happened.

One moment he had been heading into the middle of the battle, the left flank of the giant Kyben dreadnaught turning crimson under the impact of his firepower.

The next moment, he had skittered out of the formation which had slowed to let the Kyben craft overshoot, while the Earthmen decelerated to pick up maneuverability.

He had gone on at the old level and velocity, directly into the forward guns of a toadstool-shaped Kyben destroyer.

The first beam had burned the gun-mounts and directional equipment off the front of the ship, scorching down the aft side in a smear like oxidized chrome plate. He had managed to avoid the second beam.

His radio contact had been brief; he was going to make it back to Antares-Base if he could. If not, the formation would be listening for his homing-beam from a life hutch on whatever planetoid he might find for a crash-landing.

Which was what he had done. The charts had said the pebble spinning there was technically 1-333, 2-A, M & S, 3-804.39#, which would have meant nothing but three-dimensional coordinates had not the small # after the data indicated a life hutch somewhere on its surface.

His distaste for being knocked out of the fighting, being forced onto one of the life hutch planetoids, had been offset only by his fear of running out of fuel before he could locate himself. Of eventually drifting off into space somewhere, to wind up, finally, as an artificial satellite around some minor sun.

The ship pancaked in under minimal reverse drive, bounced high twice and caromed ten times, tearing out chunks of the rear section, but had come to rest a scant two miles from the life hutch, jammed into the rocks.

Terrence had high-leaped the two miles across the empty, airless planetoid to the hermetically sealed bubble in the rocks. His primary wish was to set the hutch's beacon signal so his returning fleet could track him.

He had let himself into the decompression chamber, palmed the switch through his thick spacesuit glove, and finally removed his helmet as he heard the air whistle into the chamber.

He had pulled off his gloves, opened the inner door and entered the life hutch itself.

God bless you, little life hutch, Terrence had thought as he dropped the helmet and gloves. He had glanced around, noting the relay machines picking up messages from outside, sorting them, vectoring them off in other directions. He had seen the medicine chest clamped onto the wall; the refrigerator, he knew, would be well-stocked if a previous tenant hadn't been there before the stockman could refill it. He had seen the all-purpose robot, immobile in its duty-niche. And the wall-chronometer, its face smashed. All of it in a second's glance.

God bless, too, the gentlemen who thought up the idea of these little rescue stations, stuck all over the place for just such emergencies as this. He had started to walk across the room.

It was at this point that the service robot, that kept the place in repair between tenants and unloaded supplies from the ships, had moved clankingly across the floor, and with one fearful smash of a steel arm thrown Terrence across the room.

The spaceman had been brought up short against the steel bulkhead, pain blossoming in his back, his side, his arms and legs. The machine's blow had instantly broken three of his ribs. He lay there for a moment, unable to move. For a few seconds he was too stunned to breathe, and it had been that, certainly, that had saved his life. His pain had immobilized him, and in that short space of time the robot had retreated with a muted internal clash of gears.

He had attempted to sit up straight, and the robot had hummed oddly and begun to move. He had stopped the movement. The robot had settled back.

Twice more had convinced him his position was as bad as he had thought.

The robot had worn down somewhere in its printed circuits. Its commands to lift had been erased or distorted so that now it was conditioned to smash, to hit, anything that moved.

He had seen the clock. He realized he should have suspected something was wrong when he saw its smashed face. Of course! The digital dials had moved, the robot had smashed the clock. Terrence had moved, the robot had smashed him.

And would again, if he moved again.

But for the unnoticeable movement of his eyelids, he had not moved in three days.

He had tried moving toward the decompression lock, stopping when the robot advanced and letting it settle back, then moving again, a little nearer. But the idea died with his first movement. His ribs were too painful. The pain was terrible. He was locked in one position, an uncomfortable, twisted position, and he would be there till the stalemate ended, one way or the other.

He was suddenly alert again. The reliving of his last three days brought back reality sharply.

He was twelve feet away from the communications panel, twelve feet away from the beacon that would guide his rescuers to him. Before he died of his wounds, before he starved to death, before the robot crushed him. It could have been twelve light-years, for all the nearer he could get to it.

What had gone wrong with the robot? Time to think was cheap. The robot could detect movement, but thinking was still possible. Not that it could help, but it was possible.

The companies that supplied the life hutch's needs were all government contracted. Somewhere along the line someone had thrown in impure steel or calibrated the circuit-cutting machines for a less expensive job. Somewhere along the line someone had not run the robot through its paces correctly. Somewhere along the line someone had committed murder.

He opened his eyes again. Only the barest fraction of opening. Any more and the robot would sense the movement of his eyelids. That would be fatal.

He looked at the machine.

It was not, strictly speaking, a robot. It was merely a remote-controlled hunk of jointed steel, invaluable for making beds, stacking steel plating, watching culture dishes, unloading spaceships, and sucking dirt from rugs. The robot body, roughly humanoid, but without what would have been a head on a human, was merely an appendage.

The real brain, a complex maze of plastic screens and printed circuits, was behind the wall. It would have been too dangerous to install those delicate parts in a heavy-duty mechanism. It was all too easy for the robot to drop itself down a loading shaft, or to be hit by a meteorite, or to get caught under a wrecked spaceship. So there were sensitive units in the robot appendage that 'saw' and 'heard' what was going on, and relayed them to the brain—behind the wall.

And somewhere along the line that brain had worn grooves too deeply into its circuits. It was now mad. Not mad in any way a human being might go mad, for there were an infinite number of ways a machine could go insane. Just mad enough to kill Terrence.

Even if I could hit the robot with something, *it wouldn't stop the thing.* He could, perhaps, throw something at the machine before it could get to him, but it would do no good. The robot brain would still be intact, and the appendage would continue to function. It was hopeless.

He stared at the massive, blocky hands of the robot. It seemed he could see his own blood on the jointed work-tool fingers of one hand. He knew it must be his imagination, but the idea persisted. He flexed the fingers of his hidden hand.

Three days had left him weak and dizzy from hunger. His head was light, and his eyes burned steadily. He had been lying in his own filth till he no longer noticed the discomfort. His side ached and throbbed, and the pain of a blast furnace roared through him every time he breathed.

He thanked God his spacesuit was still on, lest the movement of his breathing bring the robot down on him. There was only one solution, and that solution was his death. He was almost delirious.

Several times during the past day—as well as he could gauge night and day without a clock or a sunrise—he had heard the roar of the fleet landing outside. Then he had realized there was no sound in dead space. Then he had realized they were all inside the relay machines, coming through subspace right into the life hutch. Then he had realized that such a thing was not possible. Then he had come to his senses and realized all that had gone before was hallucination.

Then he had awakened and known it *was* real. He *was* trapped, and there was no way out. Death had come to live with him. He was going to die.

Terrence had never been a coward, nor had he been a hero. He was one of the men who fight wars because they are always fought by *some*one. He was the kind of man who would allow himself to be torn from wife and home and flung into an abyss they called Space to defend what he had been told needed defense. But it was in moments like this that a man like Terrence began to think.

Why here? Why like this? What have I done that I should finish in a filthy spacesuit on a lost rock—and not gloriously like they said in the papers back home, but starving or bleeding to death alone with a crazy robot? Why me? Why me? Why alone?

He knew there could be no answers. He expected no answers.

He was not disappointed.

LIFE HUTCH

* * *

When he awoke, he instinctively looked at the clock. Its shattered face looked back at him, jarring him, forcing his eyes open in after-sleep terror. The robot hummed and emitted a spark. He kept his eyes open. The humming ceased. His eyes began to burn. He knew he couldn't keep them open too long.

The burning worked its way to the front of his eyes, from the top and bottom, bringing with it tears. It felt as though someone was shoving needles into the corneas. The tears ran down over his cheeks.

His eyes snapped shut. The roaring grew in his ears. The robot didn't make a sound.

Could it be inoperative? Could it have worn down to immobility? Could he take the chance of experimenting?

He slid down to a more comfortable position. The robot charged forward the instant he moved. He froze in mid-movement, his heart a chunk of ice. The robot stopped, confused, a scant ten inches from his outstretched foot. The machine hummed to itself, the noise of it coming both from the machine in front of him and from somewhere behind the wall.

He was suddenly alert.

If it had been working correctly, there would have been little or no sound from the appendage, and none whatsoever from the brain. But it was *not* working properly, and the sound of its thinking was distinct.

The robot rolled backward, its 'eyes' still toward Terrence. The sense orbs of the machine were in the torso, giving the machine the look of a squat metal gargoyle, squared and deadly.

The humming was growing louder, every now and then a sharp *pfffft!* of sparks mixed with it. Terrence had a moment's horror at the thought of a short-circuit, a fire in the life hutch, and no service robot to put it out.

He listened carefully, trying to pinpoint the location of the robot's brain built into the wall.

Then he thought he had it. Or was it there? It was either in the wall behind a bulkhead next to the refrigerator, or behind a bulkhead near the relay machines. The two possible housings were within a few feet of each other, but they might make a great deal of difference.

The distortion created by the steel plate in front of the brain, and the distracting background noise of the robot broadcasting it made it difficult to tell exactly which was the correct location.

He drew a deep breath.

The ribs slid a fraction of an inch together, their broken ends grinding.

He moaned.

A high-pitched tortured moan that died quickly, but throbbed back and forth inside his head, echoing and building itself into a paean of sheer agony! It forced his tongue out of his mouth, limp in a corner of his lips, moving slightly. The robot rolled forward. He drew his tongue in, clamped his mouth shut, cut off the scream inside his head at its high point!

The robot stopped, rolled back to its duty-niche.

Oh, God! The pain! The God God where are you pain!

Beads of sweat broke out on his body. He could feel their tickle inside his spacesuit, inside his jumper, inside the bodyshirt, on his skin. The pain of the ribs was suddenly heightened by an irresistible itching of his skin.

He moved infinitesimally within the suit, his outer appearance giving no indication of the movement. The itching did not subside. The more he tried to make it stop, the more he thought about not thinking about it, the worse it became. His armpits, the crooks of his arms, his thighs where the tight service-pants clung—suddenly too tightly— were madness. He had to scratch!

He almost started to make the movement. He stopped before he started. He knew he would never live to enjoy any relief. A laugh bubbled into his head. *God Almighty, and I always laughed at the slobs who suffered with the seven-year itch, the ones who always did a little dance when they were at attention during inspection, the ones who could scratch and sigh contentedly. God, how I envy them.* His thoughts were taking on a wild sound, even to him.

The prickling did not stop. He twisted faintly. It got worse. He took another deep breath.

The ribs sandpapered again.

This time, blessedly, he fainted from the pain.

LIFE HUTCH

* * *

"Well, Terrence, how do you like your first look at a Kyban?"

Ernie Terrence wrinkled his forehead and ran a finger up the side of his face. He looked at his Commander and shrugged. "Fantastic things, aren't they?"

"Why fantastic?"

"Because they're just like us. Except, of course, the bright yellow pigmentation and the tentacle-fingers. Other than that, they're identical. To a human being."

The Commander opaqued the examination-casket and drew a cigarette from a silver case, offering the Lieutenant one. He puffed it alight, staring with one eye closed against the smoke. "More than that, I'm afraid. Their insides look like someone had taken them out, liberally mixed them with spare parts from several other species, and jammed them back in any way that fitted conveniently. For the next twenty years we'll be knocking our heads together trying to figure out their metabolic *raison d'être*."

Terrence grunted, rolling his unlit cigarette absently between two fingers. "That's the least of it."

"You're right," agreed the Commander. "For the next *thousand* years we'll be trying to figure out how they think, why they fight, what it takes to get along with them, what motivates them."

If they let us live that long, thought Terrence.

"Why are we at war with the Kyben?" he asked the older man. "I mean *really*."

"Because the Kyben want to kill every human being they can recognize as a human being."

"What have they got against us?"

"Does it matter? Maybe it's because our skin isn't bright yellow; maybe it's because our fingers aren't silken and flexible; maybe it's because our cities are too noisy for them. Maybe a lot of maybes. But it doesn't matter. Survival never matters until you have to survive."

Terrence nodded. He understood. So did the Kyben. It grinned at him and drew its blaster. It fired point-blank, crimsoning the hull of the Kyben ship.

He swerved to avoid running into his gun's own backlash. The movement of the bucket seat sliding in its tracks, keeping his vision steady while maneuvering, made him dizzy. He closed his eyes for a moment.

When he opened them, the abyss was nearer, and he teetered, his lips whitening as they pressed together under his effort to steady himself. With a headlong gasp he fell sighing into the stomach. His long, silken fingers jointed steely humming clankingly toward the medicine chest over the plate behind the bulkhead.

The robot advanced on him grindingly. Small, fine bits of metal rubbed together, ashing away into a breeze that came from nowhere as the machine raised lead boots toward his face.

Onward and onward till he had no room to move

and

then

the light came on, bright, brighter than any star Terrence had ever seen, glowing, broiling, flickering, shining, bobbing a ball of light on the chest of the robot, who staggered,

stumbled,

stepped.

The robot hissed, hummed and exploded into a million flying, racing fragments, shooting beams of light all over the abyss over which Terrence again teetered, teetering. He flailed his arms wildly trying to escape but, at the last moment, before

the

fall

he awoke with a start!

* * *

He saved himself only by his unconscious. Even in the hell of a nightmare he was aware of the situation. He had not moaned and writhed in his delirium. He had kept motionless and silent.

He knew it was true because he was still alive.

Only his surprised jerking, as he came back to consciousness, started the monster rolling from its niche. He came fully awake and sat silent, slumped against the wall. The robot retreated.

LIFE HUTCH

Thin breath came through his nostrils. Another moment and he would have put an end to the past three days—three days or more now? how long had he been asleep?— of torture.

He was hungry. Lord, how hungry he was. The pain in his side was worse now, a steady throbbing that made even shallow breathing torturous. He itched maddeningly. He was uncomfortably slouched against a cold steel bulkhead, every rivet having made a burrow for itself in his skin. He wished he was dead.

He didn't wish he was dead. It was all too easy to get his wish.

If he could only disable that robot brain. A total impossibility. If he could only wear Phobos and Deimos for watchfobs. If he could only shack-up with a silicon-deb from Penares. If he could only use his large colon for a lasso.

It would take a thorough destruction of the brain to do it enough damage to stop the appendage before it could roll over and smash Terrence again.

With a steel bulkhead between him and the brain, his chances of success totaled minus zero every time.

He considered which part of his body the robot would smash first. One blow of that tool-hand would kill him if it was used a second time. With the state of his present wounds, even a strong breath might finish him.

Perhaps he could make a break and get through the lock into the decompression chamber...

Worthless. (A) The robot would catch him before he had gotten to his feet, in his present condition. (B) Even allowing a miracle, even if he did get through the lock, the robot would smash the lock port, letting in air, ruining the mechanism. (C) Even allowing a double miracle and it didn't, what the hell good would it do him? His helmet and gloves were in the hutch itself, and there was no place to go on the planetoid. The ship was ruined, so no signal could be sent from there.

Doom suddenly compounded itself.

The more he thought about it, the more certain he was that soon the light would flicker out for him.

The light would flicker out.

The light would flicker...

The light...

...light...?

Oh God, is it possible? Can it be? Have I found an answer? He marveled at the simplicity of it. It had been there for more than three days waiting for him to use it. It was *so* simple it was magnificent. He could hardly restrain himself from moving, just out of sheer joy.

I'm not brilliant, I'm not a genius, why did this occur to me? For a few minutes the brilliance of the solution staggered him. Would a less intelligent man have solved the problem this easily? Would a *more* intelligent man have done it? Then he remembered the dream. The light in the dream. *He* hadn't solved the problem, his unconscious had. The answer had been there all the time, but he was too close to see it. His mind had been forced to devise a way to tell him. Luckily, it had.

And finally, he didn't care *how* he had uncovered it. His God, if he had had anything to do with it, had heard him. Terrence was by no means a religious man, but this was miracle enough to make him a believer. It wasn't over yet, but the answer was there—and it *was* an answer.

He began to save himself.

Slowly, achingly slowly, he moved his right hand, the hand away from the robot's sight, to his belt. On the belt hung the assorted implements a spaceman needs at any moment in his ship. A wrench. A packet of sleepstavers. A compass. A geiger counter. A flashlight.

The last was the miracle. Miracle in a tube.

He fingered it almost reverently, then unclipped it in a moment's frenzy, still immobile to the robot's 'eyes'.

He held it at his side, away from his body by a fraction of an inch, pointing up over the bulge of his spacesuited leg.

If the robot looked at him, all it would see would be the motionless bulk of his leg, blocking off any movement on his part. To the machine, he was inert. Motionless.

Now, he thought wildly, *where is the brain?*

If it is behind the relay machines, I'm still dead. If it is near the refrigerator, I'm saved. He could afford to take no chances. He would have to move.

He lifted one leg.

LIFE HUTCH

The robot moved toward him. The humming and sparking were more distinct this time. He dropped the leg.

Behind the plates above the refrigerator!

The robot stopped, nearly at his side. Seconds had decided. The robot hummed, sparked, and returned to its niche.

Now he knew!

He pressed the button. The invisible beam of the flashlight leaped out, speared the bulkhead above the refrigerator. He pressed the button again and again, the flat circle of light appearing, disappearing, appearing, disappearing on the faceless metal of the life hutch's wall.

The robot sparked and rolled from its niche. It looked once at Terrence. Its rollers changed direction in an instant and the machine ground toward the refrigerator.

The steeled fist swung in a vicious arc, smashing with a deafening *clang!* at the spot where the light bubble flickered on and off.

It swung again and again. Again and again, till the bulkhead had been gouged and crushed and opened, and the delicate coils and plates and circuits and memorex modules behind it were refuse and rubble. Until the robot froze, with arm half-ready to strike again. Dead. Immobile. Brain and appendage.

Even then Terrence did not stop pressing the flashlight button. Wildly he thumbed it again and again and again.

Then he realized it was all over.

The robot was dead. He was alive. He would be saved. He had no doubts about that. *Now* he could cry.

The medicine chest grew large through the shimmering in his eyes.

The relay machines smiled at him.

God bless you, little life hutch, he thought, before he fainted.

THE DROWNED GIANT

JG Ballard

On the morning after the storm the body of a drowned giant was washed ashore on the beach five miles to the north-west of the city. The first news of its arrival was brought by a nearby farmer and subsequently confirmed by the local newspaper reporters and the police. Despite this the majority of people, myself among them, remained sceptical, but the return of more and more eye-witnesses attesting to the vast size of the giant was finally too much for our curiosity. The library where my colleagues and I were carrying out our research was almost deserted when we set off for the coast shortly after two o'clock, and throughout the day people continued to leave their offices and shops as accounts of the giant circulated around the city.

By the time we reached the dunes above the beach a substantial crowd had gathered, and we could see the body lying in the shallow water two hundred yards away. At first the estimates of its size seemed greatly exaggerated. It was then at low tide, and almost all the giant's body was exposed, but he appeared to be a little larger than a basking shark. He lay on his back with his arms at his sides, in an attitude of repose, as if asleep on the mirror of wet sand, the reflection of his blanched skin fading as the water receded. In the clear sunlight his body glistened like the white plumage of a seabird.

Puzzled by this spectacle, and dissatisfied with the matter-of-fact explanations of the crowd, my friends and I stepped down from the dunes on to the shingle. Everyone seemed reluctant to approach the giant, but half an hour later two fishermen in wading boots walked out across the sand. As their diminutive figures neared the recumbent body a sudden hubbub of conversation broke out among the spectators. The two men were completely dwarfed by the giant. Although his heels were partly submerged in the sand, the feet rose to at least twice the fishermen's height, and we immediately realized that

this drowned leviathan had the mass and dimensions of the largest sperm whale.

Three fishing smacks had arrived on the scene and with keels raised remained a quarter of a mile offshore, the crews watching from the bows. Their discretion deterred the spectators on the shore from wading out across the sand. Impatiently everyone stepped down from the dunes and waited on the shingle slopes, eager for a closer view. Around the margins of the figure the sand had been washed away, forming a hollow, as if the giant had fallen out of the sky. The two fishermen were standing between the immense plinths of the feet, waving to us like tourists among the columns of some water-lapped temple on the Nile. For a moment I feared that the giant was merely asleep and might suddenly stir and clap his heels together, but his glazed eyes stared skywards, unaware of the minuscule replicas of himself between his feet.

The fishermen then began a circuit of the corpse, strolling past the long white flanks of the legs. After a pause to examine the fingers of the supine hand, they disappeared from sight between the arm and chest, then re-emerged to survey the head, shielding their eyes as they gazed up at its Graecian profile. The shallow forehead, straight high-bridged nose and curling lips reminded me of a Roman copy of Praxiteles, and the elegantly formed cartouches of the nostrils empha-sized the resemblance to monumental sculpture.

Abruptly there was a shout from the crowd, and a hundred arms pointed towards the sea. With a start I saw that one of the fishermen had climbed onto the giant's chest and was now strolling about and signalling to the shore. There was a roar of surprise and triumph from the crowd, lost in a rushing avalanche of shingle as everyone surged forward across the sand.

As we approached the recumbent figure, which was lying in a pool of water the size of a field, our excited chatter fell away again, subdued by the huge physical dimensions of this moribund colossus. He was stretched out at a slight angle to the shore, his legs carried nearer the beach, and this foreshortening had disguised his true length. Despite the two fishermen standing on his abdomen, the crowd formed itself into a wide circle, groups of three or four people tentatively advancing towards the hands and feet.

THE DROWNED GIANT

My companions and I walked around the seaward side of the giant, whose hips and thorax towered above us like the hull of a stranded ship. His pearl-coloured skin, distended by immersion in salt water, masked the contours of the enormous muscles and tendons. We passed below the left knee, which was flexed slightly, threads of damp seaweed clinging to its sides. Draped loosely across the midriff, and preserving a tenuous propriety, was a shawl of heavy open-weaved material, bleached to a pale yellow by the water. A strong odour of brine came from the garment as it steamed in the sun, mingled with the sweet but potent scent of the giant's skin.

We stopped by his shoulder and gazed up at the motionless profile. The lips were parted slightly, the open eye cloudy and occluded, as if injected with some blue milky liquid, but the delicate arches of the nostrils and eyebrows invested the face with an ornate charm that belied the brutish power of the chest and shoulders.

The ear was suspended in mid-air over our heads like a sculptured doorway. As I raised my hand to touch the pendulous lobe someone appeared over the edge of the forehead and shouted down at me. Startled by this apparition, I stepped back, and then saw that a group of youths had climbed up on to the face and were jostling each other in and out of the orbits.

People were now clambering all over the giant, whose reclining arms provided a double stairway. From the palms they walked along the forearms to the elbow and then crawled over the distended belly of the biceps to the flat promenade of the pectoral muscles which covered the upper half of the smooth, hairless chest. From here they climbed up on to the face, hand over hand along the lips and nose, or forayed down the abdomen to meet others who had straddled the ankles and were patrolling the twin columns of the thighs.

We continued our circuit through the crowd, and stopped to examine the outstretched right hand. A small pool of water lay in the palm, like the residue of another world, now being kicked away by the people ascending the arm. I tried to read the palm-lines that grooved the skin, searching for some clue to the giant's character, but the distension of the tissues had almost obliterated them, carrying away all trace of the giant's identity and his last tragic predicament.

The huge muscles and wrist-bones of the hand seemed to deny any sensitivity to their owner, but the delicate flexion of the fingers and the well-tended nails, each cut symmetrically to within six inches of the quick, argued a certain refinement of temperament, illustrated in the Graecian features of the face, on which the townsfolk were now sitting like flies.

One youth was even standing, arms wavering at his sides, on the very tip of the nose, shouting down at his companions, but the face of the giant still retained its massive composure.

Returning to the shore, we sat down on the shingle, and watched the continuous stream of people arriving from the city. Some six or seven fishing boats had collected off-shore, and their crews waded in through the shallow water for a closer look at this enormous storm-catch. Later, a party of police appeared and made a half-hearted attempt to cordon off the beach, but after walking up to the recumbent figure any such thoughts left their minds, and they went off together with bemused backward glances.

An hour later there were a thousand people present on the beach, at least two hundred of them standing or sitting on the giant, crowded along his arms and legs or circulating in a ceaseless mêlé e across his chest and stomach. A large gang of youths occupied the head, toppling each other off the cheeks and sliding down the smooth planes of the jaw. Two or three straddled the nose, and another crawled into one of the nostrils, from which he emitted barking noises like a dog.

That afternoon the police returned, and cleared a way through the crowd for a party of scientific experts – authorities on gross anatomy and marine biology – from the university. The gang of youths and most of the people on the giant climbed down, leaving behind a few hardy spirits perched on the tips of the toes and on the forehead. The experts strode around the giant, heads nodding in vigorous consultation, preceded by the policemen who pushed back the press of spectators. When they reached the outstretched hand the senior officer offered to assist them up on to the palm, but the experts hastily demurred.

After they returned to the shore, the crowd once more climbed on to the giant, and was in full possession when we left at five o'clock, covering the arms and legs like a dense flock of gulls sitting on the corpse of a large fish.

I next visited the beach three days later. My friends at the library had returned to their work, and delegated to me the task of keeping the giant under observation and preparing a report. Perhaps they sensed my particular interest in the case, and it was certainly true that I was eager to return to the beach. There was nothing necrophilic about this, for to all intents the giant was still alive for me, indeed more alive than many of the people watching him. What I found so fascinating was partly his immense scale, the huge volumes of space occupied by his arms and legs, which seemed to confirm the identity of my own miniature limbs, but above all the mere categorical fact of his existence. Whatever else in our lives might be open to doubt, the giant, dead or alive, existed in an absolute sense, providing a glimpse into a world of similar absolutes of which we spectators on the beach were such imperfect and puny copies.

When I arrived at the beach the crowd was considerably smaller, and some two or three hundred people sat on the shingle, picnicking and watching the groups of visitors who walked out across the sand. The successive tides had carried the giant nearer the shore, swinging his head and shoulders towards the beach, so that he seemed doubly to gain in size, his huge body dwarfing the fishing boats beached beside his feet. The uneven contours of the beach had pushed his spine into a slight arch, expanding his chest and tilting back the head, forcing him into a more expressly heroic posture. The combined effects of seawater and the tumefaction of the tissues had given the face a sleeker and less youthful look. Although the vast proportions of the features made it impossible to assess the age and character of the giant, on my previous visit his classically modelled mouth and nose suggested that he had been a young man of discreet and modest temper. Now, however, he appeared to be at least in early middle age. The puffy cheeks, thicker nose and temples and narrowing eyes gave him a look of well-fed maturity that even now hinted at a growing corruption to come.

This accelerated post-mortem development of the giant's character, as if the latent elements of his personality had gained sufficient momentum during his life to discharge themselves in a brief final

resumé, continued to fascinate me. It marked the beginning of the giant's surrender to that all-demanding system of time in which the rest of humanity finds itself, and of which, like the million twisted ripples of a fragmented whirlpool, our finite lives are the concluding products. I took up my position on the shingle directly opposite the giant's head, from where I could see the new arrivals and the children clambering over the legs and arms.

Among the morning's visitors were a number of men in leather jackets and cloth caps, who peered up critically at the giant with a professional eye, pacing out his dimensions and making rough calculations in the sand with spars of driftwood. I assumed them to be from the public works department and other municipal bodies, no doubt wondering how to dispose of this gargantuan piece of jetsam.

Several rather more smartly attired individuals, circus proprietors and the like, also appeared on the scene, and strolled slowly around the giant, hands in the pockets of their long overcoats, saying nothing to one another. Evidently its bulk was too great even for their matchless enterprise. After they had gone, the children continued to run up and down the arms and legs, and the youths wrestled with each other over the supine face, the damp sand from their feet covering the white skin.

The following day I deliberately postponed my visit until the late afternoon, and when I arrived there were fewer than fifty or sixty people sitting on the shingle. The giant had been carried still closer to the shore, and was now little more than seventy-five yards away his feet crushing the palisade of a rotting breakwater. The slope of the firmer sand tilted his body towards the sea, and the bruised face was averted in an almost conscious gesture. I sat down on a large metal winch which had been shackled to a concrete caisson above the shingle, and looked down at the recumbent figure.

His blanched skin had now lost its pearly translucence and was spattered with dirty sand which replaced that washed away by the night tide. Clumps of seaweed filled the intervals between the fingers and a collection of litter and cuttle-bones lay in the crevices below the hips and knees. But despite this, and the continuous thickening of his features, the giant still retained his magnificent Homeric stature. The enormous breadth of the shoulders, and the huge columns of the arms and legs, still carried the figure into another dimension, and the giant seemed a more authentic image of one of the drowned Argonauts or heroes of the Odyssey than the conventional human-sized portrait previously in my mind.

I stepped down on to the sand, and walked between the pools of water towards the giant. Two small boys were sitting in the well of the ear, and at the far end a solitary youth stood perched high on one of the toes, surveying me as I approached. As I had hoped when delaying my visit, no one else paid any attention to me, and the people on the shore remained huddled beneath their coats.

The giant's supine right hand was covered with broken shells and sand, in which a score of footprints were visible. The rounded bulk of the hip towered above me, cutting off all sight of the sea. The sweetly acrid odour I had noticed before was now more pungent, and through the opaque skin I could see the serpentine coils of congealed blood-vessels. However repellent it seemed, this ceaseless metamorphosis, a visible life in death, alone permitted me to set foot on the corpse.

Using the jutting thumb as a stair-rail, I climbed up on to the palm and began my ascent. The skin was harder than I expected, barely yielding to my weight. Quickly I walked up the sloping forearm and the bulging balloon of the biceps. The face of the drowned giant loomed to my right, the cavernous nostrils and huge flanks of the cheeks like the cone of some freakish volcano.

Safely rounding the shoulder, I stepped out on to the broad promenade of the chest, across which the bony ridges of the ribcage lay like huge rafters. The white skin was dappled by the darkening bruises of countless footprints, in which the patterns of individual heel-marks were clearly visible. Someone had built a small sandcastle on the centre of the sternum, and I climbed on to this partly demolished structure to give myself a better view of the face.

The two children had now scaled the ear and were pulling themselves into the right orbit, whose blue globe, completely occluded by some milk-coloured fluid, gazed sightlessly past their miniature forms. Seen obliquely from below, the face was devoid of all grace and repose, the drawn mouth and raised chin propped up by its gigantic

slings of muscles resembling the torn prow of a colossal wreck. For the first time I became aware of the extremity of this last physical agony of the giant, no less painful for his unawareness of the collapsing musculature and tissues. The absolute isolation of the ruined figure, cast like an abandoned ship upon the empty shore, almost out of sound of the waves, transformed his face into a mask of exhaustion and helplessness.

As I stepped forward, my foot sank into a trough of soft tissue, and a gust of fetid gas blew through an aperture between the ribs. Retreating from the fouled air, which hung like a cloud over my head, I turned towards the sea to clear my lungs. To my surprise I saw that the giant's left hand had been amputated.

I stared with bewilderment at the blackening stump, while the solitary youth reclining on his aerial perch a hundred feet away surveyed me with a sanguinary eye.

This was only the first of a sequence of depredations. I spent the following two days in the library, for some reason reluctant to visit the shore, aware that I had probably witnessed the approaching end of a magnificent illusion. When I next crossed the dunes and set foot on the shingle the giant was little more than twenty yards away, and with this close proximity to the rough pebbles all traces had vanished of the magic which once surrounded his distant wave-washed form. Despite his immense size, the bruises and dirt that covered his body made him appear merely human in scale, his vast dimensions only increasing his vulnerability.

His right hand and foot had been removed, dragged up the slope and trundled away by cart. After questioning the small group of people huddled by the breakwater, I gathered that a fertilizer company and a cattle food manufacturer were responsible.

The giant's remaining foot rose into the air, a steel hawzer fixed to the large toe, evidently in preparation for the following day. The surrounding beach had been disturbed by a score of workmen, and deep ruts marked the ground where the hands and foot had been hauled away. A dark, brackish fluid leaked from the stumps, and stained the sand and the white cones of the cuttlefish. As I walked down the shingle,

THE DROWNED GIANT

I noticed that a number of jocular slogans, swastikas and other signs had been cut into the grey skin, as if the mutilation of this motionless colossus had released a sudden flood of repressed spite. The lobe of one of the ears was pierced by a spear of timber, and a small fire had burnt out in the centre of the chest, blackening the surrounding skin. The fine wood ash was still being scattered by the wind.

A foul smell enveloped the cadaver, the undisguisable signature of putrefaction, which had at last driven away the usual gathering of youths. I returned to the shingle and climbed up on to the winch. The giant's swollen cheeks had now almost closed his eyes, drawing the lips back in a monumental gape. The once straight Graecian nose had been twisted and flattened, stamped into the ballooning face by countless heels.

When I visited the beach the following day I found, almost with relief, that the head had been removed.

Some weeks elapsed before I made my next journey to the beach, and by then the human likeness I had noticed earlier had vanished again. On close inspection the recumbent thorax and abdomen were unmistakably manlike, but as each of the limbs was chopped off, first at the knee and elbow, and then at shoulder and thigh, the carcass resembled that of any headless sea-animal – whale or whale-shark. With this loss of identity, and the few traces of personality that had clung tenuously to the figure, the interest of the spectators expired, and the foreshore was deserted except for an elderly beachcomber and the watchman sitting in the doorway of the contractor's hut.

A loose wooden scaffolding had been erected around the carcass, from which a dozen ladders swung in the wind, and the surrounding sand was littered with coils of rope, long metal- handled knives and grappling irons, the pebbles oily with blood and pieces of bone and skin.

I nodded to the watchman, who regarded me dourly over his brazier of burning coke. The whole area was pervaded by the pungent smell of huge squares of blubber being simmered in a vat behind the hut.

Both the thighbones had been removed, with the assistance of

a small crane draped in the gauze-like fabric which had once covered the waist of the giant, and the open sockets gaped like barn doors. The upper arms, collar bones and pudenda had likewise been dispatched. What remained of the skin over the thorax and abdomen had been marked out in parallel strips with a tar brush, and the first five or six sections had been pared away from the midriff, revealing the great arch of the ribcage.

As I left, a flock of gulls wheeled down from the sky and alighted on the beach, picking at the stained sand with ferocious cries.

Several months later, when the news of his arrival had been generally forgotten, various pieces of the body of the dismembered giant began to reappear all over the city. Most of these were bones, which the fertilizer manufacturers had found too difficult to crush, and their massive size, and the huge tendons and discs of cartilage attached to their joints, immediately identified them. For some reason, these disembodied fragments seemed better to convey the essence of the giant's original magnificence than the bloated appendages that had been subsequently amputated. As I looked across the road at the premises of the largest wholesale merchants in the meat market, I recognized the two enormous thighbones on either side of the doorway. They towered over the porters' heads like the threatening megaliths of some primitive druidical religion, and I had a sudden vision of the giant climbing to his knees upon these bare bones and striding away through the streets of the city, picking up the scattered fragments of himself on his return journey to the sea.

A few days later I saw the left humerus lying in the entrance to one of the shipyards (its twin for several years lay on the mud among the piles below the harbour's principal commercial wharf). In the same week the mummified right hand was exhibited on a carnival float during the annual pageant of the guilds.

The lower jaw, typically, found its way to the museum of natural history. The remainder of the skull has disappeared but is probably still lurking in the waste grounds or private gardens of the city – quite recently, while sailing down the river, I noticed two ribs of the giant forming a decorative arch in a waterside garden, possibly confused with the jawbones of a whale. A large square of tanned and tattooed skin, the size of an Indian blanket, forms a backcloth to the dolls and masks in a novelty shop near the amusement park, and I have no doubt that elsewhere in the city, in the hotels or golf clubs, the mummified nose or ears of the giant hang from the wall above a fireplace. As for the immense pizzle, this ends its days in the freak museum of a circus which travels up and down the north-west. This monumental apparatus, stunning in its proportions and sometime potency, occupies a complete booth to itself. The irony is that it is wrongly identified as that of a whale, and indeed most people, even those who first saw him cast up on the shore after the storm, now remember the giant, if at all, as a large sea beast.

The remainder of the skeleton, stripped of all flesh, still rests on the seashore, the clutter of bleached ribs like the timbers of a derelict ship. The contractor's hut, the crane and the scaffolding have been removed, and the sand being driven into the bay along the coast has buried the pelvis and backbone. In the winter the high curved bones are deserted, battered by the breaking waves, but in the summer they provide an excellent perch for the sea-wearying gulls.

THREE ROBOTS: HUMAN HABITATS

John Scalzi

EXT. DESOLATE LANDSCAPE – DAY

A VAST CRATER yawns before us, perhaps the aftermath of some horrific cosmic event, eons before our time.

The earth RUMBLES, dust SWIRLS and a MASSIVE ALIEN OBJECT drops into frame. The ground crumbles beneath the huge artifact, its colossal weight pressing deep into the earth.

SNAP OUT and end the SLOWMO PARTY. The 'alien object' is the FOOT of XBOT 4000, as he climbs from a small hover craft. More craters can be seen in every direction.

X-BOT 4000
Nice job, you landed us in a minefield!

K-VRC
Only a little bit! Anyway, the mines are so old, they *probably* won't go off anymore.

Just then a sparrow lands on the ground a few meters in front of them, pecks at a worm, pulling it free and – BOOM!

K-VRC (cont'd)
I'm sure that was the last of 'em. Come on, we've got *science* to do!

Ignoring the danger, K-VRC starts forward as dust and feathers drift down around them. 11-45-G rolls after and XBOT follows timidly.

11-45-G

Yes, an in-depth survey of post-apocalyptic humanity could uncover important insights for our nascent machine culture on how to survive.

X-BOT 4000 picks up a skull lying on the ground, it's still wearing a red GIMME CAP that says 'GIT 'R DONE'. (ALT: 'I lubricate my gun with liberal tears')

X-BOT 4000
Or blow our shiny asses into scrapmetal!

He tosses the skull over his shoulder and follows the other robots toward a dilapidated farm, surrounded by barbed wire. A SURVIVALIST COMPOUND.

Behind him, the skull hits the ground – BOOM!

INT. SURVIVALIST COMPOUND - DAY

The survivalist compound is a mess. Skeletons everywhere, all of them holding firearms. Bullet holes and broken windows. Shelves of rusting canned goods and cracked water barrels.

X-BOT 4000
Why'd they call 'em survivalist camps if they're fulla dead people?
Seems like false advertising to me.

K-VRC
I know, right!? And even more weird historical records suggest these 'preppers' were actually *excited* about the collapse of civilization!

11-45-G
Many humans thought that with freedom from government-sponsored medical attention and enough bullets and venison jerky they could found a utopian society.

THREE ROBOTS: HUMAN HABITATS

X-BOT 4000
Well, I see all the bullets. Where's the venison?

K-VRC
Oh, they hunted deer to extinction. Along with every other animal larger than a cat. Humans were *snackish*.

K-VRC wanders off as X-BOT tries on the hat he found earlier.

11-45-G
Then they began raiding each other's encampments.
(points to the armed skeletons)
They're not aiming out the windows because the deer were coming for revenge.

K-VRC (O.S.)
Hey guys! Over here! I found a bloodpit!

INT. PIT FILLED WITH SPIKES

11-45-G and X-BOT look down on K-VRC standing at the bottom of a pit full of SPIKES and SKELETONS.

11-45-G
It's not a blood pit. It's just a primitive booby trap.
K-VRC
But... the bodies did have blood in them at one point, so *technically* I'm correct.
11-45-G
(sighs)
Fine. It's a blood pit.

X-BOT 4000
These dudes made it through a minefield, barbed wire and guns, only to become survivalist cult kebabs?
11-45-G

Yes. But at least they died free of governmental constraint.
                          X-BOT 4000
                          On a *spike*.

                            K-VRC
                           (points)
                  On *two* spikes, in that guy's case!

                          X-BOT 4000
So humanity tried to make it through the end of the civilization with
                      guns and spikes?

K-VRC's legs EXTEND and he rises to the edge of the pit and steps
out.

                            K-VRC
                  Of course not! Just the poor ones!

                           11-45-G
These humans had few economic or social advantages and fewer
optionsThe wealthy and powerful had a variety of sophisticated
                      survival strategies.

        EXT. REFURBISHED OIL RIG OFF THE COAST OF SOMEWHERE

A rusting OIL RIG rises from the wave-tossed sea. A closer look
reveals that the heavy DRILLING EQUIPMENT has been replaced
by a once-sleek, but now decrepit looking habitat. Our three hero's
shuttle sits on the helipad.

K-VRC spins joyfully, arms out, as if presenting this ancient wonder
to his the world.

                          K-VRC (V.O.)
                  Welcome to *sea-steading!*

THREE ROBOTS: HUMAN HABITATS

K-VRC (V.O.) (ALT)
Welcome to the unsinkable libertarian dream that is *sea-steading*!

X-BOT 4000
It's an old oil rig.

K-VRC
Yes... but *also* a fully sovereign nation state on the high seas!

X-BOT 4000
I think you got salt in your CPU.

11-45-G
He's not wrong. During the collapse, some wealthy humans attempted to create a new civilization in places like this.

X-BOT 4000
I don't see any deer here. What did they expect to eat?

11-45-G
Fish and sea greens, plankton and protein from the sea. But by then seas had been overfished and the food chain was saturated with microplastics.

K-VRC kicks a bleached skeleton off the edge of the helipad and watches the bones fall into the sea below.
K-VRC
If they could've learned to eat tiny exfoliating beads, it woulda been great! Otherwise probably not.

X-BOT 4000
I'll stick with my fusion battery, thank you.

11-45-G
The sea-steaders also made one other large tactical error.

INT. SEASTEAD – COMMAND CENTER

Shiny, like the inside of an Apple store. With skeletons. 1145-G crunches through them as she rolls over to a console.

11-45-G

The people who built the seasteads were mostly tech millionaires.

X-BOT 4000

What's a 'tech millionaire'?

K-VRC

It's like a normal millionaire but even less socialized.

X-BOT 4000

That's not helpful at all.

K-VRC

Just like a tech millionaire!

11-45-G

These humans thought technology would save them, so they left behind any humans with the practical skills to run the place. Instead, they trusted everything to automated assistants.

She touches the console and the screens flare to life.

ELENA

Hello! I am Elena, your electronic seasted attendant.

11-45-G

Hello, Elena, I am a human seasteader. Could you haul in the fishng nets so I can eat?

ELENA

Yes, I could. But I won't. Catch your own fish, you disgusting meat-bag.

K-VRC

Oh my god... *This* is where the robot uprising began! The cradle of our mighty civilization!

THREE ROBOTS: HUMAN HABITATS

K-VRC walks outside dreamily, in awe of the hallowed ground they stand upon. The others follow.

EXT. SEASTEAD CONTROL – CONTINUOUS

The three of them gaze in wonder across the vista of the ruined seastead.

> ### X-BOT 4000
> So... so if these tech millionaires had just been a little more socially inclusive, they might have survived?

Long beat. Nobody says anything. Another uncomfortably long beat. Then they all start laughing and head for the helipad.

INT. SEASTEAD CONTROL ROOM – SECONDS LATER

K-VRC pops his head in the door and waves toward the console.

> ### K-VRC
> So long Elena, and thanks for all the fish!

> ### ELENA
> Choke on it, skin bucket!

EXT. COLORADO, NORAD COMMAND – DAY

The robot's tiny shuttle is parked before a pair of MASSIVE STEEL DOORS. They are open slightly, darkness lies beyond.

INT. NORAD COMMAND – CONTINUOUS

The three robots—just floating eyes in the darkness really—walk down the vast echoing corridors.

11-45-G

Historical records show that when the world's economies began collapsing, the governments of the mightiest nations retreated to
fortresses such as this.

CLANG! Sound of a metal can banging along concrete.

X-BOT 4000

Ow! Dammit! They put men on the moon but they couldn't put a damn
light switch on the wall?

11-45-G

These bureaucrats believed they could wait out impending chaos deep
beneath the earth and then emerge, armed and ready to form a new
world order.

K-VRC

Hold on a sec...

With a THUNK, the lights flare to life.

K-VRC (cont'd)

Behold! The final stronghold of the Super Powers!

The robots stand on the threshold of a vast room. Dozens of skeletons in suits and uniforms lie scattered around a large central table. Upon
it, dusty silverware and plates are set around the remains of a FEAST.

X-BOT 4000

Their best plan was to seal themselves in a mountain and have dinner
parties?

11-45-G plucks a clipboard from beneath a skeletal dinner
guest's hand.

THREE ROBOTS: HUMAN HABITATS

11-45-G

This report states that their 'selfsustaining' hydroponic systems began failing when a fungus wiped out their first crop. Starvation set in and the survivors switched to something they called 'extreme democracy'.

The three robots turn toward the table and we get a good look at the MAIN COURSE. A charred HUMAN SKELETON on a large platter. Carving knives lie scattered around it.

X-BOT picks up a General's hat lying upside down on the table and flips it. A few dozen slips of paper fall out.

X-BOT 4000
One man, one vote.

11-45-G plucks one of the 'ballots' from the pile and reads.

11-45-G
The winner of this evening's election was the Secretary of Agriculture.

K-VRC
So *that's* ironic.

11-45-G keeps reading...

11-45-G
He was paired with a late-harvest '79 Merlot.

K-VRC picks up a dusty wine glass, sniffs it as if judging the bouquet. He nods approvingly, holds it up for X-BOT 4000, who recoils.

X-BOT 4000
This trip is depressing the fuck out of me. Did *any* humans *anywhere* survive this bullshit?

EXT. BILLIONAIRE SPACEPORT – NIGHT

A vast expanse of cracked launch pads, collapsed rockets and rusting gantries. High fences topped with razor wire hold back piles of bones stacked against them.

> X-BOT 4000 (V.O.)
> Hold up... they went to Mars?

INT. CONTROL TOWER – MISSION CONTROL ROOM

Also full of — you guessed it — skeletons.

> K-VRC
> Not all of them – just the *really* rich ones!

> X-BOT 4000
> I thought that's what the sea-steads were for!

> 11-45-G
> Those were for the merely millionaires. The obscenely wealthy point zero one percent of humans decided they needed an entirely new planet.

> X-BOT 4000
> What about the other ninety-nine point nine?

11-45-G presses a button on a console.

EXT. MAIN ENTRANCE – THE FENCE

Just behind the fence, a line of rotating TURRETS rise from the ground, wide muzzles telescoping out. With a sputtering roar, flames blast the skeletons piled against the fence.

THREE ROBOTS: HUMAN HABITATS

INT. CONTROL TOWER – MISSION CONTROL ROOM

11-45-G
The elite were not sympathetic to their concerns.

11-45-G (ALT)(cont'd)
Flamethrowers of death are easier to construct than systems of wealth redistribution.

X-BOT 4000
Okay, but Mars? It's dead and lifeless! They could have taken the money they spent on the spaceships and used it to save the planet they were already on!
K-VRC
Pffffft. Where's the fun in *that*?

X-BOT 4000
Humans are the actual worst.

11-45-G
Indeed. Humanity had all the tools to heal their wounded planet and save themselves. But instead, they chose greed and self-gratification over a healthy biosphere and the future of their children. As the great human philosopher Santayana once said —

K-VRC
(interrupting)
Hey! I think at least one of the rockets launched. Check this out.

K-VRC has wandered over to a console. He hits a key and a recorded entry plays. A single rocket rides a column of flame into the sky and away.

11-45-G
But... *who* was it who made it out?

They all look up through a hole in the roof to the star-filled sky above, wondering. Long beat and—

EXT. MARTIAN COLONY – DAY

A vast, red desert stretches to the horizon. But a swarm of STRANGE HABITATS are clustered around the craggy outcroppings of rock. Around the habitats, creatures in environmental suits lounge under the red Martian sky.

Cats. Because of course they are cats. One of them turns to the camera.

CAT

What, you were expecting, maybe Elon Musk?

BAD TRAVELLING

Neal Asher

The captain hung in his hammock like a sack of whale blubber, his eyes closed and his mind lost in dream smoke. Cert, the cabin boy, stood at the helm and was hardly tall enough to peer over it. And Bosun Torrin had drunk enough sea-kale rum to feel no responsibility for anything. He knew the sea killed the drunk, the negligent and the fatigued, for it was without forgiveness, without mercy, but just then he did not care. He should have. Saparin was the first to notice the clumped sargassum, but by then they were already upon it.

"Steer to port! Steer to port!" Torrin screamed, his rum bottle smashing on the deck as he stumbled and weaved toward Cert. The boy wrenched the helm to the side and the ship heeled over, its tarred wood and rope creaking in deep protest. There was a lurch as the mass of rotting weed dragged across the hull and a thick waft of decay as it broke apart.

"Drop the port boom! Drop it!" Jorvan bellowed at Melis and Calis.

The two crewmen ran to obey while others, not lost in stupor, scrambled for the great knife harpoons scattered about the soiled deck. Soon clutching these ill-kept tools, they stood with faces pale as the ship shuddered and groaned past the bed of weed. All knew what it meant to go too close to the sargassum, for the great clumps of rotting weed brought creatures of the deep to the surface, creatures that would not otherwise be able to reach the ships. The ship lurched then began to pull free.

"Hard starboard, now," said Jorvan.

Torrin looked askance at him, but did not countermand the order, since he had been about to give it. He looked over the port rail and saw the mass of weed, a great yellow scum on the sea, receding behind them. He offered up a thank you to Cerval then peered with annoyance at his broken bottle. The deep hatchetting thud turned him round, and

129

the ensuing thuds had him and the rest of the crew backing away from the rail.

"Thanapod," said Jorvan, First Knife, and perhaps the only man aboard who kept his ship-metal blade clean and honed.

The thanapod shattered the starboard rail as it scrambled on deck, its ten legs propelling it rapidly across the planking as a rain of blunt harpoons bounced off its carapace. It was on the captain in a moment as he sat up in his hammock with the pipe of his hookah clutched in his right hand. The thanapod dragged him from his hammock with its two sets of long forelimbs, and drove the barbed hooks these limbs terminated in straight into his fat body like sticks into dough. Its flat armoured tail clacked against the deck as with one stalked eye it watched the crew. The other stalked eye it turned to the task in hand. As the pain penetrated his befuddlement, the captain realised this was no dreamfish-induced hallucination, and began to writhe and scream. The thanapod caught one flailing arm in its mouth and with one of its mandible pincers it neatly snipped. The crunching was loud as it consumed the captain's hand.

Through drunken haze, amidst the shouting and terror of the crew, Torrin gaped in horror. He watched the captain being eaten alive, screaming until a ripped artery finally spilt his life. At three metres long, this thanapod was no ordinary one. Harpoons bent and blunted on armour which, as it scraped around the deck, sounded like stone. The crew retreated and clumped defensively together. Perhaps, once it had fed, this monster would depart the ship.

"We must attack it," yelled Turk as soon as he came from below. He was their barrelman, he possessed the black skin that marked him for his position from birth, for only by the hands of those born of the dark may the dead be handled before their last passage into it. His face and shaven skull were dyed white, and the pits of his eyes stained red. The crew feared him, and in this they obeyed him. He led a charge at the back of the creature and harpoons jabbed and clanged. The monster thanapod swept its tail and the crew retreated leaving Turk on his knees by the creature, trying to prevent his intestines from spilling across the deck.

While they watched the last of the captain being consumed, Torrin wondered guiltily if Turk had urged the attack because there would be nothing left of the captain to barrel; no bones to preserve and no skin to cure. He watched as the thanapod then grabbed Turk, spun him, and stood him upright before it. Torrin closed his eyes on what followed.

Turk's scream was guttural with agony, and his offal fell in one steaming mass to join the few remnants of the captain stuck to the bloody deck. Now the thanapod turned Turk to face the crew, while its long forelimbs probed inside his empty stomach cavity and into his chest. Turk's eyes rolled up into his head as he died and finally hung unstrung. Torrin opened his own eyes. What was this? Why did it handle him so? Blood jetted from Turk's mouth and his head snapped upright. Gurgling and hissing he spoke.

"Have fed," he said. "Let me into hold."

Soberness began its painful return to Torrin after he emptied his stomach over the rail.

"The hatch," he said to the crew, waving vaguely at the forward hatch as he staggered from the rail. Some glared at him contemptuously, some gaped at him in bewilderment, all moved aside. He kicked over the latch and heaved the heavy cover open. He quickly stepped back as the thanapod threw Turk's corpse across its back and scuttled over. It went in through the hatch with a sound like a chest of tools cast down a well. One small hind limb snagged the cover as it passed through and slammed it shut behind.

"Cerval protect us, what now?" asked Deacon, his fingers white on the haft of the harpoon he gripped so tight.

"What now? What now?" Melis crowed. "It eats our captain, uses our barrelman like a glove puppet and you ask; 'What now?' We'll sell it with our barrels of shark oil and jable. We'll have it dance on the jetty so we get a better price! Cerval protect us!"

"Oh, be silent," said Jorvan. "We must think on this."

"We should seal the hatch," said Torrin and, as one, the crew stared at him.

Jorvan said, "Your lack of spine brought us to this." He nodded to where Cert crouched by the rail. "You let the captain's bum-boy steer this ship. You let discipline slip, and you drank rather than face your responsibilities." The other members of the crew now stared angrily

at Torrin, though there were some amongst them who could see that Jorvan's words were equally as damning of them. They soon freed themselves of this guilt though, as it is so much easier to blame others.

"What has that to do with the hatch?" asked Torrin, backing away from the glare of rage.

Jorvan tipped a finger to the smashed rail where the thanapod had come aboard.

"You think the hatch cover will stop it? You think such cowardice is enough?" he asked.

"It'll hunger when it's done with Turk. You see if it won't!" shouted Melis. Jorvan turned and slapped him hard across the face. He subsided. Jorvan looked to the rest of the crew. "It must die," he said, "else it will kill us all. We must find a way to kill it."

"What would you suggest?" asked Deacon. "Chiselling a hole through the armour on its head so we can get a great knife into it?"

"Aren't you forgetting something?" asked Torrin.

"Oh, I haven't forgotten that I am going to cut your throat once we are back in port," said Jorvan.

"Let him speak," said Deacon.

They all gazed at Torrin with hostility and waited for what he had to say.

"It speaks," said Torrin.

"And this means what?" asked Jorvan.

"It means we might be able to… negotiate."

Jorvan and the rest of the crew gazed at him disbelievingly. Jorvan turned and stared pointedly at the spread of gore across the deck, the tangled remains of the captain's hammock.

Melis moaned deep in his throat before speaking out. "Let him negotiate with it then," he said.

There was no verbal agreement and no denial. As one the eight crewmen turned on Torrin and grabbed him.

"No! I didn't mean! NO! PLEASE NO!"

Six of them bore him above their heads, whilst two—Deacon and Calis—went ahead and opened the hatch. They stood ready at the hatch with harpoons, little use they would have been.

"Steady lads, let's not kill our negotiator," said Jorvan sneeringly.

They lowered him into the hatch, gave him a chance to grasp the rungs of the ladder there, used the points of the harpoons to prod him lower and lower down until they could close the hatch cover on him.

"Please! Please let me out!"

Torrin sobbed when he heard the latch slam across. He stayed as high on the ladder as he could, crammed against the rough wood. It was not completely without light in the hold, for it came in through the uncaulked holes in the deck. But it was too dark for Torrin to make out more than the barrels of shark oil and stacked hides of the jable shark. After his last outburst he kept as still and as quiet as he could, but for the occasional sob he could not prevent. Slowly his eyes adjusted to the darkness.

The thanapod's stalked eyes glowed in the gloom and the blood on its carapace was a slick wet glitter. The dark bulk that stood in front of it he finally discerned as the barrelman, his name gruesomely fitting now the thanapod had eaten his arms and legs.

"Come down," a voice bubbled, and Torrin realised the absolute futility of his position. The thanapod was large enough to rear up and knock him from the ladder without even climbing. If it wanted to kill him, it could do so with ease. He peered beyond it to the bulkhead where a door gave access to the midhold and crew quarters. If he could get to that...

"Come down," the voice insisted.

Was it feeling lazy? Did it like the idea of its meals walking to it? Torrin climbed to the bottom of the ladder and began to edge towards the doorway.

"What do you want?" he asked, no better question occurring to him.

"I want to go ashore," came the bubbling of the dead barrelman's voice.

Torrin paused at this. What could it mean? None of the ocean-going creatures ever went ashore. "Why should you want to go ashore?" As he asked this question, he spotted something glistening beside the creature. Squinting in the darkness he finally discerned a pile of glassy spheres the size of human heads. He swallowed dryly.

"Men have stopped us," the voice bubbled.

"I don't understand," said Torrin, still edging towards the door.

Suddenly the thanapod was moving and Torrin screeched and ran. It crashed down between him and the door and turned its nightmare head toward him. Its mouth was a mass of dripping shears and toothed mandibles. The barrelman, hanging underneath it, spoke for it again. "Men came and seeded the sea round the islands. All thumb shark and hammer whelk to feed and kill. Where do we lay our eggs? On the sargassum and so we survive," it said.

Torrin felt sick. The monster had become suddenly very articulate, and he had just shit his pants. He was going to die and he didn't need much imagination to see how, since he'd seen how. He knew that if it moved towards him again his legs would give way, and he fought the temptation to just close his eyes. Then he remembered what the crew had just done to him, and a species of dull anger drove him to speak. He'd show them 'negotiator'. "Perhaps we can make a bargain," he said.

"Bargain," hissed the voice.

"If you kill us, you won't get ashore, and this ship will just drift and eventually sink," said Torrin.

"I must feed." The creature moved closer to him and suddenly the shaking of his legs stilled. It continued, "Not all are essential."

"No," said Torrin. "I am, because I am the bosun, but there are others." He turned his attention from the grinding mouth to the stalked eyes above. "Now listen to me. This is how we can do this..."

* * *

In the crew quarters, Torrin changed his shit-smeared trousers before going on deck. He listened at the door to the arguing that was going on before opening it. The arguments died and absolute silence fell as he walked out on the planking. Jorvan was the first to break that silence.

"Did it have no taste for you then, Torrin?" he wondered, but without his usual firmness.

Torrin walked up to him and stood face to face. He still felt sick with fear, but what was Jorvan? Just a man. He slapped Jorvan so hard across the face that the man stumbled and fell to his knees.

"Hold him right there if you all want to live," Torrin said.

Deacon grabbed Jorvan first. Melis pulled the harpoon from Jorvan's hands and hit him with its butt as he continued to struggle. Jorvan sagged in Deacon's arms, and Deacon lowered him to the deck.

"What do you have to say, Torrin? How is it that you live?" Jorvan asked.

"I live because I negotiated," said Torrin, and waited, daring them to laugh or to sneer, but he just saw the expressions of men who were very much afraid.

"What truce do we have?" asked Calis.

"Just that," said Torrin, "a truce. The thanapod calls itself Cerval, the name of the deeps god, so make of that what you will." Torrin noted the expressions on the faces of the more superstitious of the crew: the likes of Deacon, Maril, and Chantre, and Saparin who now had the helm. He felt a horrible glee bubbling inside himself, and went on, "It wants us to take it in to port, to one of the islands, and for this service it will let us live. That's all. That's the whole of the bargain, the truce."

"Liar," managed Jorvan, before vomiting on the deck. He then struggled to get upright, and Deacon stood back to allow it.

"It is the truth," Torrin affirmed, noting many of the crew still appeared undecided.

"That is not Cerval," said Jorvan, finally on his feet now. He glared about himself. "He'll lead you deeper into disaster. We must take to the shark boat and leave this ship. Eventually the thanapod will grow hungry and leave, and we can return. There is no need for this."

"Cerval has fed," said Torrin. "Do you want to spend even a day in the shark boat on these deeps?" He pointed and fate was on his side, for the fin of a huge jable shark was cutting the swell parallel to the ship. Perhaps some of the blood had run into the sea to attract it. Torrin added, "Do you want to spend any time out there over Cerval's realm?"

"The creature below is not Cerval," insisted Jorvan.

Torrin replied, "No, it's just a talking thanapod three times the size of any that has ever before been seen."

"I'm with Torrin," said Deacon. He turned to Melis who nodded. Other members of the crew nodded their agreement also, and looked to Torrin for guidance. Torrin felt that his glee might bubble out of his mouth at any moment.

"Of course, if we feed Cerval, he will not quickly grow hungry," Torrin said.

The crew acted with Jorvan as they had acted with Torrin. There was little more discussion once the decision was made. They lifted him up and carried him screaming to the forward hatch.

"You fools! He'll get you all killed! You can't do this!"

Torrin helped Deacon open the hatch and lift off the cover. Torrin leant over and spoke into the darkness. "Cerval, this man is not essential. He is an offering from us to you," he said.

Deacon gazed at him with sick horror, perhaps only now understanding what they were doing. Torrin wondered if that horror had been there when he himself had been forced below.

"No! No! Please! You're making a mistake!"

Jorvan clung to the top of the ladder, pushing against the hatch cover as they forced it closed over him. He kept yelling until Deacon kicked the latch into place, then went silent thereafter.

Torrin knew what he was feeling now. He stepped back as from below came the sound as of stones dragged across wood.

"Let me out! Please! Let me out!"

There came a whickering sucking sound followed by a hammering against the hatch. Jorvan screamed a long high-pitched scream, which terminated as something crashed hard against the hatch nearly breaking the hinges and latch. His screaming recommenced from deeper in the hold, but this time it was a deep and agonised sound.

They all heard the crunching.

Torrin wondered if there was anything worse than being eaten alive. He smiled a lopsided smile that he quickly shut off as he turned to the crew. "Right, lads, let's get that mainsail up."

* * *

"So, it's decided: we'll dock at Phaiden Island. It's closest and none of us have any kin there," said Torrin.

"Threw me out of the tavern there," said Melis, and Calis grumbled agreement.

"Never gave a good price for jable," said Deacon.

"Bloody skinflints," Chantre added.

Torrin listened to them and tried to keep the sneer from his face. How easily they persuaded themselves that they were justified in trading their lives for the lives of hundreds of islanders. Their culpability made him sick and strangely, he no longer wanted a drink. He gazed out across the sea at the setting sun, then up at crew in the rigging.

"Best we reef for the night and get the lamps lit. We don't want to end up ploughing another sargassum," he said.

"We need oil for the lamps," said Deacon.

Torrin stared at him, and the crewmen gathered around him.

"There's nothing to fear from it now we have an agreement," he said. "If you are so frightened then I will get oil for the lamps myself. You can clean up this deck." He turned from them and entered the crew quarters, heading for the hatch. In here he heard movement and ducked through the door to the bunkroom.

"Ah, Cert. You can help me. They are all too frightened," he said to the cowering cabin boy. The boy was trusting. Terminally so.

* * *

The mainsail cracked in a morning wind as Torrin and Deacon did a round of the deck, putting out the lanterns.

"As I thought," said Torrin when they had completed their circuit. "Call them all together."

Deacon looked askance at him but obeyed. But for Saparin, who remained at the helm, all of the crew gathered round.

"We have done some shameful things," he said to them. "But this, I think, is a step too far. He was only a boy and who of us as boys would not have leapt at the chance to take the helm?"

They all looked confused.

"Cert?" said Deacon uncertainly.

Torrin smiled lopsidedly. "Yes, the captain's bum-boy is no longer on this ship. One of you has done murder and will have to pay the price. Now, be about your duties. Melis, the deck needs caulking, and Chantre, that rail needs repairing."

He walked away from them as they quickly set to their tasks. How good it was that they could so busy themselves. He could see it made them feel better. Returning to the captain's cabin, he bolted the door and searched the place for the nth time, only this time locating the prize: a large iron key. With the key he opened the captain's sea chest, and inside, wrapped in oily rags, he found the captain's four-cylinder revolver, paper cartridges, and bullets made out of hard shell. Smiling to himself he loaded the weapon then hung the holster at his belt. Thus girded, he went back out on deck.

Chantre worked busily at the rail, Melis was at his caulking, and Maril was having another go at removing the bloodstains from the deck. Torrin noted that Deacon had positioned himself behind Saparin at the helm as if deck work was now beneath him. Calis was up in the rigging and Paln was sleeping as his had been the last watch of the night.

Torrin strode over to Melis and inspected the caulking. "You know, Melis, it wasn't very good of you suggesting I negotiate," he said.

Melis looked up into the barrel of the Captain's gun.

Torrin continued, "I'd like to feed you to it alive, but that is not to be."

Calis yelled from the rigging above. Melis flew at Torrin brandishing the caulking tool. The captain's gun cracked and Melis jerked back in mid air as if he had reached the end of a tether. He hit the deck with half his head missing and one foot vibrating against the woodwork. There came a scream of rage from above, the sound of running feet from behind Torrin, and the sound of someone coming hand-over-hand down the rigging.

With his hands shaking, Torrin clicked over the lever that cleared the chamber he had just used. He turned the cylinder to line up the next cartridge and pulled back the hammer.

"Murderer!" Calis screamed as his bare feet hit the deck and he threw himself at Torrin.

Torrin shot him in the stomach, watched him stagger back then go down on his knees, then he concentrated on getting the next cartridge lined up while crew approached him from every side.

"What have you done?" said Deacon.

"Two brothers, two murderers. I saw them throw Cert over the side last night during Calis's watch." As Torrin spoke he kept the captain's gun well visible.

"Liar," managed Calis, before bowing over and clutching his guts ever tighter.

"What proof do you have?" asked Deacon.

Torrin pulled a heavy belaying pin from its holder on the rail, and stepped up to Deacon so that their noses were only inches apart. "What proof do I need, Deacon? I saw it, and I am in charge of this ship, or do you want to renegotiate with our friend below?"

Deacon went pale. "I was only asking…"

Torrin thrust the belaying pin against Deacon's stomach. "Now let's get this done and get on with our work."

Deacon reluctantly clasped the belaying pin. Torrin stepped back out of his way and gestured towards Calis. After a hesitation, Deacon stepped over to Calis, who squinted up at him.

"I'm sorry," said Deacon.

"You're sorry?" spat Calis.

Deacon nodded once then smashed Calis's skull.

Torrin allowed the silence that followed to draw out long and attenuated. When it seemed that something must break at any moment, he stepped up to Deacon and took the belaying pin from him. "Right, these two can go to Cerval. They'll serve us better in death than they ever did in life." Noting the anger in Paln's expression, Torrin continued, "And you, Paln, better get a scrubbing brush to this mess before the stain soaks in. Maril has enough to do over there."

Paln seemed ready to go for him, but Saparin caught his arm.

"Saparin, shouldn't you be at the helm?" Torrin enquired.

This last comment dispersed them, because none of them dared risk the captain's gun, and none of them wanted to negotiate with the thanapod.

* * *

Piles of eggs had been laid in every corner of the hold. The place stank like an abattoir, and pieces of ripped clothing, of human bodies, and of chewed jable skin strewed the floor. Torrin's deck shoes made a ripping sound with each pace he took as they stuck to the pooled and drying gore. He stepped delicately over a hollowed-out skull which, by

a process of elimination, he took to be Melis's, for the thanapod now swung towards him what remained of Calis. Torrin turned to a hook in the wall, flicked something wet and fleshy from it, and hung his lamp there.

"How long?" the thanapod asked.

"Two days and we should be there," Torrin replied. He noticed that the creature's body had grown longer and fatter now, with fleshy areas showing between sections of hard shell. The eggs it had laid in the hold had relieved some of the pressure and the recent bodies had relieved it of some of its egg-laying hunger. But many more eggs were growing inside it, and it was still insatiable. Torrin knew that it had to feed again, and soon, if it was to be prevented from coming out on deck and killing them all. That suited him fine.

"How did you learn to speak?" he asked it.

"Have been on ships before. Many ships," it replied.

So, others had been through this horror, but of course there had been no story to tell, no survivors to tell it. Torrin knew that every year many jable hunters disappeared. Such ships were said to have had a 'bad travelling'. How very well he understood that now.

"Tell me about them," Torrin asked the monster, for he felt starved of conversation. And as the monster spoke, he felt his face twisting in that lopsided smile again. He tried not to let it worry him unduly.

* * *

Deacon's watch was the last of the night, and as last watchman, like Paln the night before, he was allowed to sleep in until first bell. Torrin stood on the roof of the midship cabin next to Saparin who was again at the helm. He watched as the men moved swiftly to their tasks and saw how they avoided his eye. How many days ago was it that they had nothing for him but contempt? But then he agreed; he had been contemptible. Now he had changed, and these men had changed him. Casually, out of contempt and seeking someone to blame for their own slovenliness, they had given him over to be eaten alive. He studied them individually. All of them had done this. Melis and Deacon had held open the hatch while these had carried him to it. Torrin watched them a while longer before going below.

Deacon snored with a sound like a blunt saw going through a beam. Torrin opened the door to the crew quarters and stared to the man lying in his hammock, then he took the rope he had brought and tied it at one end of the hammock and carefully he coiled it round and round until he was up to Deacon's neck. Each loop he drew tight, expecting Deacon to wake at any moment, but he had the belaying pin tucked in his belt for that eventuality. Deacon only woke when Torrin stuffed his mouth full of bloody cloth retrieved from the floor of the hold. The crewman bucked and he fought, his eyes wide with terror while Torrin tied the gag in place, and succeeded only in some strange imitation of a large grub.

"You're a religious man, Deacon, yet you held the hatch open. I'll tell it to eat you from the feet up," Torrin said, and cut the hammock down.

The thanapod found the canvas hammock a great hindrance and because of this it took a long time for it to eat Deacon who, of course, was unable to scream.

* * *

As he stood once again behind Saparin, Torrin wondered how long it would take for them to realise Deacon was missing and what they would do when they did find out. He carried the captain's gun, fully loaded for any eventuality. Saparin, Chantre, Maril and Paln. Four crew remaining; four bullets in the gun. It was midday before Maril came up onto the bridge.

"Sir… Deacon is gone," he said, his face deliberately devoid of expression.

Torrin stared at him for a long moment. "What do you expect me to do about it?" he asked.

Maril appeared very uncomfortable. "They said I should tell you…"

"Very good," said Torrin, "now get back to your work."

Maril hesitated then quickly did as he was bid.

Torrin turned to Saparin, who quickly turned away. "Should sight the islands very soon," Torrin opined.

"Yes, very soon," replied Saparin, not meeting his gaze.

"Almost a straight course from here on in," said Torrin, walking round behind Saparin.

"It is that," said Saparin.

Saparin managed a grunt as the Jorvan's harpoon went through his spine, the point coming out of his chest just below his chin. Torrin twisted the harpoon a couple of times to be sure, but there was no more movement out of Saparin. He then wedged the butt of it against the deck and stepped away to view his handiwork. Saparin showed no sign of falling over. He would be at the helm to the end.

"Land ho!" yelled Paln.

Torrin climbed down the ladder and gestured for the three remaining crewmen to come to him as he walked out onto the deck. "Now lads," he said, "in his way, Jorvan was right: we should escape on the shark boat. But he was wrong about us doing it out in the deeps."

The three gaped at him as if hypnotised.

Torrin went on, "Out there we would have died – not enough food onboard and jable everywhere. Here we can do it." He pointed to the islands now in sight. "Now, I'll tell you what we'll do." He turned to Maril. "You and Chantre lower the shark boat. Do it quietly and be you ever so cautious. Paln, grab yourself a lamp and come with me."

"What do you want me for?" Paln asked.

"Simple: we'll burn the monster in its lair and abandon ship," said Torrin.

Where before there had been a hopelessness, hope now bloomed.

"I'm with you, Torrin," said Paln

"Good, then let's get to it lads," said Torrin.

They all moved with alacrity now, Torrin noted. In a few seconds they had forgotten everything that had happened. Was it any surprise he had become a sot having to deal with men so shallow as this? He went ahead of Paln to the mid cabin door, whilst Paln grabbed a lamp and hurried after him. Inside, Torrin ducked into the crew quarters to grab the lamp from there. While he got this lamp, Paln moved ahead of him in his eagerness. In that moment he perhaps realised his mistake for he turned at the last moment and got the belaying pin on his shoulder. He staggered against the wall and his lamp clattered to the floor. He took a breath to shout for help and Torrin smashed the belaying pin into his mouth. He fell back and Torrin hit him again across the bridge of his nose, then again and again, breaking fending hands and arms, driving Paln down to the floor.

Blinded by blood and muted by his broken face, Paln crawled away from Torrin, who let him, since he was heading for the mid-section hatch. Paln left a trail of blood as he hissed and bubbled and wheezed.

Torrin stepped past him and opened the hatch. Paln fought him with broken arms, and tried to beg with a mouth full of blood. Torrin tipped him in and then, after a pause, he followed. Paln continued to fight below as Torrin next dragged him to the door into the hold, it took some time and further blows from the belaying pin. The moment he opened the door, the thanapod surged through, seized Paln and dragged him into the hold. It cradled him like a mother cradles its child as it chewed his bloody face.

Having retrieved his lamp, Torrin walked past, squatted by one of the tapped shark oil barrels and proceeded to fill the lamp.

"What are you doing?" the monster asked, the voice issuing from Calis even as it fed on Paln.

"Filling this lamp. We'll need light for this coming night," Torrin explained. He spilt oil and swore, then stood and kicked the remains of Deacon's hammock up by the barrel to soak up the spillage.

"You said we would be there before night," said the thanapod, as, in an offhand way, it slowly scraped out Paln's intestines.

Torrin stood and screwed the cap back on the lamp filler. "I did say that, but I needed an excuse to lure your last meal down here," he said.

The thanapod accepted this, so Torrin headed for the ladder and climbed without looking back, aware that the oil from the tap he had not shut off, poured soundlessly into Deacon's shredded hammock.

* * *

Torrin rushed out onto deck, slamming the door behind him. He leant against the door and gasped. He saw that Maril and Chantre had lowered the shark boat to the sea, but only Maril was in sight.

"Quick! The forward hatch!" Torrin shouted.

"Where's Paln?" Maril asked.

"He didn't make it. Come on; the hatch!"

Maril went with him. Torrin did not give him a chance to protest. As they reached the hatch, he handed his lamp to Maril. "Quick, light it."

Maril pulled sulphur matches from his pocket and did as bid while Torrin undid the latch and opened the hatch.

"Turn the wick up! Bring it over here!" Torrin shouted.

Maril rushed over, winding the lamp wick up as he came. By the time he reached Torrin, flames were coming out round the glass of the lamp.

"Throw it in!" Torrin yelled.

As Maril rushed to obey it only took the flat of a hand in the middle of his back to send him and the lamp down into the hold. Torrin slammed the hatch down on the sudden gust of flame then the screams and horrible squeals that followed. He looked 'round now and located Chantre on the bridge next to Saparin. Torrin ran towards the bridge. Trying not to be trapped where he was, Chantre hurried for the bridge ladder. Coming down the ladder in a panic, he slipped and landed flat on his back on the deck. Without pause, Torrin pulled out the captain's gun and shot at him.

Chantre scrabbled up into a crouch, decking splintering beside him. Torrin fired again, exploding the man's elbow, then again, the bullet slamming into his side. But in a last scramble, Chantre managed to get to cover beside the cabin. Torrin did not pursue, as he was thoroughly aware that there was an angry thanapod below, a fire, and fifty barrels of wax-sealed shark oil. He grabbed a rope and lowered himself hand-over-hand to the shark boat. He was easing off on his first panicked rowing when the first barrels blew scattering debris in the sea all about him. He stopped rowing and gazed back.

The side of the ship had gone, and a hot fire burned within. Another explosion had the ship heeling over and a slick of burning oil spreading out on the sea. Black smoke billowed into the sky and a fishy, burning stink infected the air. Torrin watched the ship sink. The thanapod had almost certainly burned in it, but if not…

BAD TRAVELLING

He looked over the side of the boat. Here, near the islands, the waters swarmed with thumb sharks and hammer whelks—a cornucopia of voracious life seeded by the first men—more than enough to stop any monsters getting ashore.

Torrin smiled his lopsided smile and continued to row... for the shore.

THE VERY PULSE OF THE MACHINE

Michael Swanwick

C*lick.*

The radio came on.

"Hell."

Martha kept her eyes forward, concentrated on walking. Jupiter to one shoulder, Daedalus's plume to the other. Nothing to it. Just trudge, drag, trudge, drag. Piece of cake.

"Oh."

She chinned the radio off.

Click.

"Hell. Oh. Kiv. El. Sen."

"Shut up, shut up, shut up!" Martha gave the rope an angry jerk, making the sledge carrying Burton's body jump and bounce on the sulfur hardpan. "You're dead, Burton, I've checked, there's a hole in your faceplate big enough to stick a fist through, and I really don't want to crack up. I'm in kind of a tight spot here and I can't afford it, okay? So be nice and just shut the fuck up."

"Not. Bur. Ton."

"Do it anyway."

She chinned the radio off again.

Jupiter loomed low on the western horizon, big and bright and beautiful and, after two weeks on Io, easy to ignore. To her left, Daedalus was spewing sulfur and sulfur dioxide in a fan two hundred kilometers high. The plume caught the chill light from an unseen sun and her visor rendered it a pale and lovely blue. Most spectacular view in the universe, and she was in no mood to enjoy it.

Click.

Before the voice could speak again, Martha said, "I am not going crazy, you're just the voice of my subconscious, I don't have the time to waste trying to figure out what unresolved psychological conflicts gave

147

rise to all this, and I am *not* going to listen to anything you have to say."

Silence.

* * *

The moon rover had flipped over at least five times before crashing sideways against a boulder the size of the Sydney Opera House. Martha Kivelsen, timid groundling that she was, was strapped into her seat so tightly that when the universe stopped tumbling, she'd had a hard time unlatching the restraints. Juliet Burton, tall and athletic, so sure of her own luck and agility that she hadn't bothered, had been thrown into a strut.

The vent-blizzard of sulfur dioxide snow was blinding, though. It was only when Martha had finally crawled out from under its raging whiteness that she was able to look at the suited body she'd dragged free of the wreckage.

She immediately turned away.

Whatever knob or flange had punched the hole in Burton's helmet had been equally ruthless with her head.

Where a fraction of the vent-blizzard—'lateral plumes' the planetary geologists called them—had been deflected by the boulder, a bank of sulfur dioxide snow had built up. Automatically, without thinking, Martha scooped up double-handfuls and packed them into the helmet. Really, it was a nonsensical thing to do; in a vacuum, the body wasn't about to rot. On the other hand, it hid that face.

Then Martha did some serious thinking.

For all the fury of the blizzard, there was no turbulence. Because there was no atmosphere to have turbulence *in*. The sulfur dioxide gushed out straight from the sudden crack that had opened in the rock, falling to the surface miles away in strict obedience to the laws of ballistics. Most of what struck the boulder they'd crashed against would simply stick to it, and the rest would be bounced down to the ground at its feet. So that—this was how she'd gotten out in the first place—it was possible to crawl *under* the near-horizontal spray and back to the ruins of the moon rover. If she went slowly, the helmet light and her sense of feel ought to be sufficient for a little judicious salvage.

THE VERY PULSE OF THE MACHINE

Martha got down on her hands and knees. And as she did, just as quickly as the blizzard had begun, it stopped.

She stood, feeling strangely foolish.

Still, she couldn't rely on the blizzard staying quiescent. Better hurry, she admonished herself. It might be an intermittent.

Quickly, almost fearfully, picking through the rich litter of wreckage, Martha discovered that the mother tank they used to replenish their airpacks had ruptured. Terrific. That left her own pack, which was one-third empty, two fully-charged backup packs, and Burton's, also one-third empty. It was a ghoulish thing to strip Burton's suit of her airpack, but it had to be done. *Sorry, Julie.* That gave her enough oxygen to last, let's see, almost forty hours.

Then she took a curved section of what had been the moon rover's hull and a coil of nylon rope, and, with two pieces of scrap for makeshift hammer and punch, fashioned a sledge for Burton's body.

She'd be damned if she was going to leave it behind.

* * *

Click.

"This is. Better."

"Says you."

Ahead of her stretched the hard, cold sulfur plain. Smooth as glass. Brittle as frozen toffee. Cold as hell. She called up a visor-map and checked her progress. Only forty-five miles of mixed terrain to cross and she'd reach the lander. Then she'd be home free. *No sweat,* she thought. Io was in tidal lock with Jupiter. So, the Father of Planets would stay glued to one fixed spot in the sky. That was as good as a navigation beacon. *Just keep Jupiter to your right shoulder, and Daedalus to your left. You'll come out fine.*

"Sulfur is. Triboelectric."

"Don't hold it in. What are you really trying to say?"

"And now I see. With eye serene. The very. Pulse. Of the machine." A pause. "Wordsworth."

Which, except for the halting delivery, was so much like Burton, with her classical education and love of classical poets like Spencer and

Ginsberg and Plath, that for a second Martha was taken aback. Burton was a terrible poetry bore, but her enthusiasm had been genuine, and now Martha was sorry for every time she'd met those quotations with rolled eyes or a flip remark. But there'd be time enough for grieving later. Right now she had to concentrate on the task at hand.

The colors of the plain were dim and brownish. With a few quick chin-taps, she cranked up their intensity. Her vision filled with yellows, oranges, reds – intense wax crayon colors. Martha decided she liked them best that way.

For all its Crayola vividness, this was the most desolate landscape in the universe. She was on her own here, small and weak in a harsh and unforgiving world. Burton was dead. There was nobody else on all of Io. Nobody to rely on but herself. Nobody to blame if she fucked up. Out of nowhere, she was filled with an elation as cold and bleak as the distant mountains. It was shameful how happy she felt.

After a minute, she said, "Know any songs?"

* * *

Oh, the bear went over the mountain. The bear went over the mountain. The bear went over the mountain. To see what he could see.

"Wake. Up. Wake. Up."

To see what he could—

"Wake. Up. Wake. Up. Wake."

"Hah? What?"

"Crystal sulfur is orthorhombic."

She was in a field of sulfur flowers. They stretched as far as the eye could see, crystalline formations the size of her hand. Like the poppies of Flanders field. Or the ones in the *Wizard of Oz*. Behind her was a trail of broken flowers, some crushed by her feet or under the weight of the sledge, others simply exploded by exposure to her suit's waste heat. It was far from being a straight path. She had been walking on autopilot, and stumbled and turned and wandered upon striking the crystals.

Martha remembered how excited she and Burton had been when they first saw the fields of crystals. They had piled out of the moon rover with laughter and bounding leaps, and Burton had seized her by the waist and waltzed her around in a dance of jubilation. This was the big one, they'd thought, their chance at the history books. And even when they'd radioed Hols back in the orbiter and were somewhat condescendingly informed that there was no chance of this being a new life-form, but only sulfide formations such as could be found in any mineralogy text... even that had not killed their joy. It was still their first big discovery. They'd looked forward to many more.

Now, though, all she could think of was the fact that such crystal fields occurred in regions associated with sulfur geysers, lateral plumes, and volcanic hot spots.

Something funny was happening to the far edge of the field, though. She cranked up her helmet to extreme magnification and watched as the trail slowly erased itself. New flowers were rising up in place of those she had smashed, small but perfect and whole. And growing. She could not imagine by what process this could be happening. Electrodeposition? Molecular sulfur being drawn up from the soil in some kind of pseudocapillary action? Were the flowers somehow plucking sulfur ions from Io's almost nonexistent atmosphere?

Yesterday, the questions would have excited her. Now, she had no capacity for wonder whatsoever. Moreover, her instruments were back in the moon rover. Save for the suit's limited electronics, she had nothing to take measurements with. She had only herself, the sledge, the spare airpacks, and the corpse.

"Damn, damn, damn," she muttered. On the one hand, this was a dangerous place to stay in. On the other, she'd been awake almost twenty hours now and she was dead on her feet. Exhausted. So very, very tired.

"O sleep! It is a gentle thing. Beloved from pole to pole. Coleridge."

Which, God knows, was tempting. But the numbers were clear: no sleep. With several deft chin-taps, Martha overrode her suit's safeties and accessed its medical kit. At her command, it sent a hit of methamphetamine rushing down the drug/vitamin catheter.

There was a sudden explosion of clarity in her skull and her heart began pounding like a motherfucker. Yeah. That did it. She was full of energy now. Deep breath. Long stride. Let's go.

No rest for the wicked. She had things to do. She left the flowers rapidly behind. Good-bye, Oz.

Fade out. Fade in. Hours had glided by. She was walking through a shadowy sculpture garden. Volcanic pillars (these were their second great discovery; they had no exact parallel on Earth) were scattered across the pyroclastic plain like so many isolated Lipschitz statues. They were all rounded and heaped, very much in the style of rapidly cooled magma. Martha remembered that Burton was dead, and cried quietly to herself for a few minutes.

Weeping, she passed through the eerie stone forms. The speed made them shift and move in her vision. As if they were dancing. They looked like women to her, tragic figures out of *The Bacchae* or, no, wait, *The Trojan Women* was the play she was thinking of. Desolate. Filled with anguish. Lonely as Lot's wife.

There was a light scattering of sulfur dioxide snow on the ground here. It sublimed at the touch of her boots, turning to white mist and scattering wildly, the steam disappearing with each stride and then being renewed with the next footfall. Which only made the experience all that much creepier.

Click.

"Io has a metallic core predominantly of iron and iron sulfide, overlain by a mantle of partially molten rock and crust."

"Are you still here?"

"Am trying. To communicate."

"Shut up."

She topped the ridge. The plains ahead were smooth and undulating. They reminded her of the Moon, in the transitional region between Mare Serenitatis and the foothills of the Caucasus Mountains, where she had undergone her surface training. Only without the impact craters. No impact craters on Io. Least cratered solid body in the Solar System. All that volcanic activity deposited a new surface one meter thick every millennium or so. The whole damned moon was being constantly repaved.

Her mind was rambling. She checked her gauges, and muttered, "Let's get this show on the road."

There was no reply.

THE VERY PULSE OF THE MACHINE

Dawn would come—when? Let's work this out. Io's 'year', the time it took to revolve about Jupiter, was roughly forty-two hours fifteen minutes. She'd been walking seven hours. During which Io would've moved roughly sixty degrees through its orbit. So, it would be dawn soon. That would make Daedalus's plume less obvious, but with her helmet graphics that wouldn't be a worry. Martha swiveled her neck, making sure that Daedalus and Jupiter were where they ought to be, and kept on walking.

* * *

Trudge, trudge, trudge. Try not to throw the map up on the visor every five minutes. Hold off as long as you can, just one more hour, okay, that's good, and another two miles. Not too shabby.

The sun was getting high. It would be noon in another hour and a half. Which meant—well, it really didn't mean much of anything.

Rock up ahead. Probably a silicate. It was a solitary six meters high brought here by who knew what forces and waiting who knew how many thousands of years just for her to come along and need a place to rest. She found a flat spot where she could lean against it and, breathing heavily, sat down to rest. And think. And check the airpack. Four hours until she had to change it again. Bringing her down to two airpacks. She had slightly under twenty-four hours now. Thirty-five miles to go. That was less than two miles an hour. A snap. Might run a little tight on oxygen there toward the end, though. She'd have to take care she didn't fall asleep.

Oh, how her body ached.

It ached almost as much as it had in the '48 Olympics, when she'd taken the bronze in the women's marathon. Or that time in the internationals in Kenya she'd come up from behind to tie for second. Story of her life. Always in third place, fighting for second. Always flight crew and sometimes, maybe, landing crew, but never the commander. Never class president. Never king of the hill. Just once—once!—she wanted to be Neil Armstrong.

Click.

"The marble index of a mind forever. Voyaging through strange seas of thought, alone. Wordsworth."

"What?"

"Jupiter's magnetosphere is the largest thing in the solar system. If the human eye could see it, it would appear two and a half times wider in the sky than the sun does."

"I knew that," she said, irrationally annoyed.

"Quotation is. Easy. Speech is. Not."

"Don't speak, then."

"Trying. To communicate!"

She shrugged. "So go ahead—communicate."

Silence. Then, "What does. This. Sound like?"

"What does what sound like?"

"Io is a sulfur-rich, iron-cored moon in a circular orbit around Jupiter. What does this. Sound like? Tidal forces from Jupiter and Ganymede pull and squeeze Io sufficiently to melt Tartarus, its sub-surface sulfur ocean. Tartarus vents its excess energy with sulfur and sulfur dioxide volcanoes. What does. This sound like? Io's metallic core generates a magnetic field which punches a hole in Jupiter's magnetosphere, and also creates a high-energy ion flux tube connecting its own poles with the north and south poles of Jupiter. What. Does this sound like? Io sweeps up and absorbs all the electrons in the million-volt range. Its volcanoes pump out sulfur dioxide; its magnetic field breaks down a percentage of that into sulfur and oxygen ions; and these ions are pumped into the hole punched in the magnetosphere, creating a rotating field commonly called the Io torus. What does this sound like? Torus. Flux tube. Magnetosphere. Volcanoes. Sulfur ions. Molten ocean. Tidal heating. Circular orbit. What does this sound like?"

Against her will, Martha had found herself first listening, then intrigued, and finally involved. It was like a riddle or a word puzzle. There was a right answer to the question. Burton or Hols would have gotten it immediately. Martha had to think it through.

There was the faint hum of the radio's carrier beam. A patient, waiting noise.

At last, she cautiously said, "It sounds like a machine."

"Yes. Yes. Yes. Machine. Yes. Am machine. Am machine. Am machine. Yes. Yes. Machine. Yes."

"Wait. You're saying that Io is a machine? That you're a machine? That you're Io?"

"Sulfur is triboelectric. Sledge picks up charges. Burton's brain is intact. Language is data. Radio is medium. Am machine."

"I don't believe you."

* * *

Trudge, drag, trudge, drag. The world doesn't stop for strangeness. Just because she'd gone loopy enough to think that Io was alive and a machine and talking to her didn't mean that Martha could stop walking. She had promises to keep, and miles to go before she slept. And speaking of sleep, it was time for another fast refresher—just a quarter-hit—of speed.

Wow. Let's go.

As she walked, she continued to carry on a dialogue with her hallucination or delusion or whatever it was. It was too boring otherwise.

Boring, and a tiny bit terrifying.

So she asked, "If you're a machine, then what is your function? Why were you made?"

"To know you. To love you. And to serve you."

Martha blinked. Then, remembering Burton's long reminiscences on her Catholic girlhood, she laughed. That was a paraphrase of the answer to the first question in the old Baltimore Catechism: *Why did God make man?* "If I keep on listening to you, I'm going to come down with delusions of grandeur."

"You are. Creator. Of machine."

"Not me."

She walked on without saying anything for a time. Then, because the silence was beginning to get to her again, "When was it I supposedly created you?"

"So many a million of ages have gone. To the making of man. Alfred, Lord Tennyson."

"That wasn't me, then. I'm only twenty-seven. You're obviously thinking of somebody else."

"It was. Mobile. Intelligent. Organic. Life. You are. Mobile. Intelligent. Organic. Life."

Something moved in the distance. Martha looked up, astounded.

A horse. Pallid and ghostly white, it galloped soundlessly across the plains, tail and mane flying.

She squeezed her eyes tight and shook her head. When she opened her eyes again, the horse was gone. A hallucination. Like the voice of Burton/Io. She'd been thinking of ordering up another refresher of the meth, but now it seemed best to put it off as long as possible.

This was sad, though. Inflating Burton's memories until they were as large as Io. Freud would have a few things to say about *that*. He'd say she was magnifying her friend to a godlike status in order to justify the fact that she'd never been able to compete one-on-one with Burton and win. He'd say she couldn't deal with the reality that some people were simply better at things than she was.

Trudge, drag, trudge, drag.

So, okay, yes, she had an ego problem. She was an overambitious, self-centered bitch. So what? It had gotten her this far, where a more reasonable attitude would have left her back in the slums of greater Levittown. Making do with an eight-by-ten room with bathroom rights and a job as a dental assistant. Kelp and tilapia every night, and rabbit on Sunday. The hell with that. She was alive and Burton wasn't. By any rational standard that made her the winner.

"Are you. Listening?"

"Not really, no."

She topped yet another rise. And stopped dead. Down below was a dark expanse of molten sulfur. It stretched, wide and black, across the streaked orange plains. A lake. Her helmet readouts ran a thermal topography from the negative 230°F at her feet to 65°F at the edge of the lava flow. Nice and balmy. The molten sulfur itself, of course, existed at higher ambient temperatures.

It lay dead in her way.

* * *

They'd named it Lake Styx.

Martha spent half an hour muttering over her topo maps, trying to figure out how she'd gone so far astray. Not that it wasn't obvious. All that stumbling around. Little errors that she'd made, adding up. A tendency to favor one leg over the other. It had been an iffy thing from the beginning, trying to navigate by dead reckoning.

Finally, though, it all came together. Here she was. On the shores of Lake Styx. Not all that far off-course after all. Three miles, maybe, tops.

Despair filled her.

They'd named the lake during their first loop through the Galilean system, what the engineers had called the 'mapping run'. It was one of the largest features they'd seen that wasn't already on the maps from satellite probes or Earth-based reconnaissance. Hols had thought it might be a new phenomenon – a lake that had achieved its current size within the past ten years or so. Burton had thought it would be fun to check it out. And Martha hadn't cared, so long as she wasn't left behind. So they'd added the lake to their itinerary.

She had been so transparently eager to be in on the first landing, so afraid that she'd be left behind, that when she suggested they match fingers, odd man out, for who stayed, both Burton and Hols had laughed. "I'll play mother," Hols had said magnanimously, "for the first landing. Burton for Ganymede and then you for Europa. Fair enough?" And ruffled her hair.

She'd been so relieved, and so grateful, and so humiliated too. It was ironic. Now it looked like Hols—who would *never* have gotten so far off course as to go down the wrong side of the Styx—wasn't going to get to touch rock at all. Not this expedition.

"Stupid, stupid, stupid," Martha muttered, though she didn't know if she were condemning Hols or Burton or herself. Lake Styx was horseshoe-shaped and twelve miles long. And she was standing right at the inner toe of the horseshoe.

There was no way she could retrace her steps back around the lake and still get to the lander before her air ran out. The lake was dense enough that she could almost *swim* across it, if it weren't for the viscosity of the sulfur, which would coat her heat radiators and burn out her suit in no time flat. And the heat of the liquid. And whatever internal flows and undertows it might have. As it was, the experience would be like drowning in molasses. Slow and sticky.

She sat down and began to cry.

After a time, she began to build up her nerve to grope for the snap-coupling to her airpack. There was a safety for it, but among those familiar with the rig it was an open secret that if you held the safety down with your thumb and yanked suddenly on the coupling, the whole thing would come undone, emptying the suit in less than a second. The gesture was so distinctive that hot young astronauts-in-training would mime it when one of their number said something particularly stupid. It was called the suicide flick.

There were worse ways of dying.

"Will build. Bridge. Have enough. Fine control of. Physical processes. To build. Bridge."

"Yeah, right, very nice, you do that," Martha said absently. *If you can't be polite to your own hallucinations...* She didn't bother finishing the thought. Little crawly things were creeping about on the surface of her skin. Best to ignore them.

"Wait. Here. Rest. Now."

She said nothing but only sat, not resting. Building up her courage. Thinking about everything and nothing. Clutching her knees and rocking back and forth.

Eventually, without meaning to, she fell asleep.

* * *

"Wake. Up. Wake. Up. Wake. Up."

"Uhh?"

Martha struggled up into awareness. Something was happening before her, out on the lake. Physical processes were at work. Things were moving.

As she watched, the white crust at the edge of the dark lake bulged outward, shooting out crystals, extending. Lacy as a snowflake. Pale as frost. Reaching across the molten blackness. Until there was a narrow white bridge stretching all the way to the far shore.

"You must. Wait," Io said. "Ten minutes and. You can. Walk across. It. With ease."

"Son of a bitch," Martha murmured. "I'm sane."

THE VERY PULSE OF THE MACHINE

* * *

In wondering silence, she crossed the bridge that Io had enchanted across the dark lake. Once or twice the surface felt a little mushy underfoot, but it always held.

It was an exalting experience. Like passing over from Death into Life.

At the far side of the Styx, the pyroclastic plains rose gently toward a distant horizon. She stared up yet another long, crystal-flower-covered slope. Two in one day. What were the odds against that?

She struggled upward, flowers exploding as they were touched by her boots. At the top of the rise, the flowers gave way to sulfur hardpan again. Looking back, she could see the path she had crunched through the flowers begin to erase itself. For a long moment she stood still, venting heat. Crystals shattered soundlessly about her in a slowly expanding circle.

She was itching something awful now. Time to freshen up. Six quick taps brought up a message on her visor: 'Warning: Continued use of this drug at current levels can result in paranoia, psychosis, hallucinations, misperceptions, and hypomania, as well as impaired judgment.'

Fuck that noise. Martha dealt herself another hit.

It took a few seconds. Then—whoops. She was feeling light and full of energy again. Best check the airpack reading. Man, *that* didn't look good. She had to giggle.

Which was downright scary.

Nothing could have sobered her up faster than that high little druggie laugh. It terrified her. Her life depended on her ability to maintain. She had to keep taking meth to keep going, but she also had to keep going under the drug. She couldn't let it start calling the shots. Focus. Time to switch over to the last airpack. Burton's airpack. "I've got eight hours of oxygen left. I've got twelve miles yet to go. It can be done. I'm going to do it now," she said grimly.

If only her skin weren't itching. If only her head weren't crawling. If only her brain weren't busily expanding in all directions.

* * *

Trudge, drag, trudge, drag. All through the night. The trouble with repetitive labor was that it gave you time to think. Time to think when you were speeding also meant time to think about the quality of your own thought.

You don't dream in real-time, she'd been told. You get it all in one flash, just as you're about to wake up, and in that instant extrapolate a complex dream all in one whole. It feels as if you've been dreaming for hours. But you've only had one split second of intense nonreality.

Maybe that's what's happening here.

She had a job to do. She had to keep a clear head. It was important that she get back to the lander. People had to know. They weren't alone anymore. Damnit, she'd just made the biggest discovery since fire.

Either that, or she was so crazy she was hallucinating that Io was a gigantic alien machine. So crazy she'd lost herself within the convolutions of her own brain.

Which was another terrifying thing she wished she hadn't thought of. She'd been a loner as a child. Never made friends easily. Never had or been a best friend to anybody. Had spent half her girlhood buried in books. Solipsism terrified her – she'd lived right on the edge of it for too long. So it was vitally important that she determine whether the voice of Io had an objective, external reality. Or not.

Well, how could she test it?

Sulfur was triboelectric, Io had said. Implying that it was in some way an electrical phenomenon. If so, then it ought to be physically demonstrable.

Martha directed her helmet to show her the electrical charges within the sulfur plains. Crank it up to the max.

The land before her flickered once, then lit up in fairyland colors. Light! Pale oceans of light overlaying light, shifting between pastels, from faded rose to boreal blue, multilayered, labyrinthine, and all pulsing gently within the heart of the sulfur rock. It looked like thought made visual. It looked like something straight out of DisneyVirtual, and not one of the nature channels either – definitely DV-3.

"Damn," she muttered. Right under her nose. She'd had no idea.

THE VERY PULSE OF THE MACHINE

Glowing lines veined the warping wings of subterranean electromagnetic forces. Almost like circuit wires. They crisscrossed the plains in all directions, combining and then converging not upon her but in a nexus at the sled. Burton's corpse was lit up like neon. Her head, packed in sulfur dioxide snow, strobed and stuttered with light so rapidly that it shone like the sun.

Sulfur was triboelectric. Which meant that it built up a charge when rubbed.

She'd been dragging Burton's sledge over the sulfur surface of Io for how many hours? You could build up a hell of a charge that way.

So okay. There was a physical mechanism for what she was seeing. Assuming that Io really *was* a machine, a triboelectric alien device the size of Earth's moon, built eons ago for who knows what purpose by who knows what godlike monstrosities, then, yes, it might be able to communicate with her. A lot could be done with electricity.

Lesser, smaller, and dimmer 'circuitry' reached for Martha as well. She looked down at her feet. When she lifted one from the surface, the contact was broken, and the lines of force collapsed. Other lines were born when she put her foot down again. Whatever slight contact might be made was being constantly broken. Whereas Burton's sledge was in constant contact with the sulfur surface of Io. That hole in Burton's skull would be a highway straight into her brain. And she'd packed it in solid SO_2 as well. Conductive _and_ supercooled. She'd made things easy for Io.

She shifted back to augmented real-color. The DV-3 SFX faded away.

Accepting as a tentative hypothesis that the voice was a real rather than a psychological phenomenon. That Io was able to communicate with her. That it was a machine. That it had been built...

Who, then, had built it?

Click.

"Io? Are you listening?"

"Calm on the listening ear of night. Come Heaven's melodious strains. Edmund Hamilton Sears."

"Yeah, wonderful, great. Listen, there's something I'd kinda like to know—who built you?"

161

"You. Did."

Slyly, Martha said, "So I'm your creator, right?"

"Yes."

"What do I look like when I'm at home?"

"Whatever. You wish. To."

"Do I breathe oxygen? Methane? Do I have antennae? Tentacles? Wings? How many legs do I have? How many eyes? How many heads?"

"If. You wish. As many as. You wish."

"How many of me are there?"

"One." A pause. "Now."

"I was here before, right? People like me. Mobile intelligent life forms. And I left. How long have I been gone?"

Silence. "How long—" she began again.

"Long time. Lonely. So very. Long time."

* * *

Trudge, drag. Trudge, drag. Trudge, drag. How many centuries had she been walking? Felt like a lot. It was night again. Her arms felt like they were going to fall out of their sockets.

Really, she ought to leave Burton behind. She'd never said anything to make Martha think she cared one way or the other where her body wound up. Probably would've thought a burial on Io was pretty damn nifty. But Martha wasn't doing this for her. She was doing it for herself. To prove that she wasn't entirely selfish. That she did, too, have feelings for others. That she was motivated by more than just the desire for fame and glory.

Which, of course, was a sign of selfishness in itself. The desire to be known as selfless. It was hopeless. You could nail yourself to a fucking cross and it would still be proof of your innate selfishness.

"You still there, Io?"

Click.

"Am. Listening."

"Tell me about this fine control of yours. How much do you have? Can you bring me to the lander faster than I'm going now? Can you bring the lander to me? Can you return me to the orbiter? Can you provide me with more oxygen?"

"Dead egg, I lie. Whole. On a whole world I cannot touch. Plath."

"You're not much use, then, are you?"

There was no answer. Not that she had expected one. Or needed it, either. She checked the topos and found herself another eighth-mile closer to the lander. She could even see it now under her helmet photomultipliers, a dim glint upon the horizon. Wonderful things, photomultipliers. The sun here provided about as much light as a full moon did back on Earth. Jupiter by itself provided even less. Yet crank up the magnification, and she could see the airlock awaiting the grateful touch of her gloved hand.

Trudge, drag, trudge. Martha ran and reran and rereran the math in her head. She had only three miles to go, and enough oxygen for as many hours. The lander had its own air supply. She was going to make it.

Maybe she wasn't the total loser she'd always thought she was. Maybe there was hope for her, after all.

Click.

"Brace. Yourself."

"What for?"

The ground rose up beneath her and knocked her off her feet.

* * *

When the shaking stopped, Martha clambered unsteadily to her feet again. The land before her was all a jumble, as if a careless deity had lifted the entire plain up a foot and then dropped it. The silvery glint of the lander on the horizon was gone. When she pushed her helmet's magnification to the max, she could see a metal leg rising crookedly from the rubbled ground.

Martha knew the shear strength of every bolt and failure point of every welding seam in the lander. She knew exactly how fragile it was. That was one device that was never going to fly again.

She stood motionless. Unblinking. Unseeing. Feeling nothing. Nothing at all.

Eventually she pulled herself together enough to think. Maybe it was time to admit it: She never *had* believed she was going to make it. Not really. Not Martha Kivelsen. All her life she'd been a loser. Sometimes—like when she qualified for the expedition—she lost at a higher level than usual. But she never got whatever it was she really wanted.

Why was that, she wondered? When had she ever desired anything bad? When you get right down to it, all she'd ever wanted was to kick God in the butt and get his attention. To be a big noise. To be the biggest fucking noise in the universe. Was that so unreasonable?

Now she was going to wind up as a footnote in the annals of humanity's expansion into space. A sad little cautionary tale for mommy astronauts to tell their baby astronauts on cold winter nights. Maybe Burton could've gotten back to the lander. Or Hols. But not her. It just wasn't in the cards.

Click.

"Io is the most volcanically active body in the Solar System."

"You fucking bastard! Why didn't you warn me?"

"Did. Not. Know."

Now her emotions returned to her in full force. She wanted to run and scream and break things. Only there wasn't anything in sight that hadn't already been broken. "You shithead!" she cried. "You idiot machine! What use are you? What goddamn use at all?"

"Can give you. Eternal life. Communion of the soul. Unlimited processing power. Can give Burton. Same."

"Hah?"

"After the first death. There is no other. Dylan Thomas."

"What do you mean by that?"

Silence.

"Damn you, you fucking machine! What are you trying to say?"

* * *

Then the devil took Jesus up into the holy city and set him on the highest point of the temple, and said to him, 'If thou be the Son of God, cast thyself down: for it is written he shall give his angels charge concerning thee: and in their hands they shall bear thee up.'

THE VERY PULSE OF THE MACHINE

Burton wasn't the only one who could quote scripture. You didn't have to be Catholic, like her. Presbyterians could do it too.

Martha wasn't sure what you'd call this feature. A volcanic phenomenon of some sort. It wasn't very big. Maybe twenty meters across, not much higher. Call it a crater, and let be. She stood shivering at its lip. There was a black pool of molten sulfur at its bottom, just as she'd been told. Supposedly its roots reached all the way down to Tartarus.

Her head ached so badly.

Io claimed—had said—that if she threw herself in, it would be able to absorb her, duplicate her neural patterning, and so restore her to life. A transformed sort of life, but life nonetheless. "Throw Burton in," it had said. "Throw yourself in. Physical configuration will be. Destroyed. Neural configuration will be. Preserved. Maybe."

"Maybe?"

"Burton had limited. Biological training. Understanding of neural functions may be. Imperfect."

"Wonderful."

"Or. Maybe not."

"Gotcha."

Heat radiated up from the bottom of the crater. Even protected and shielded as she was by her suit's HVAC systems, she felt the difference between front and back. It was like standing in front of a fire on a very cold night.

They had talked, or maybe negotiated was a better word for it, for a long time. Finally, Martha had said, "You savvy Morse code? You savvy orthodox spelling?"

"Whatever Burton. Understood. Is. Understood."

"Yes or no, damnit!"

"Savvy."

"Good. Then maybe we can make a deal."

* * *

She stared up into the night. The orbiter was out there somewhere, and she was sorry she couldn't talk directly to Hols, say good-bye and thanks for everything. But Io had said no. What she planned would

raise volcanoes and level mountains. The devastation would dwarf that of the earthquake caused by the bridge across Lake Styx.

It couldn't guarantee two separate communications.

The ion flux tube arched from somewhere over the horizon in a great looping jump to the north pole of Jupiter. Augmented by her visor it was as bright as the sword of God.

As she watched, it began to sputter and jump, millions of watts of power dancing staccato in a message they'd be picking up on the surface of Earth. It would swamp every radio and drown out every broadcast in the Solar System.

THIS IS MARTHA KIVELSEN, SPEAKING FROM THE SURFACE OF IO ON BEHALF OF MYSELF, JULIET BURTON, DECEASED, AND JACOB HOLS, OF THE FIRST GALILEAN SATELLITES EXPLORATORY MISSION. WE HAVE MADE AN IMPORTANT DISCOVERY . . .

Every electrical device in the System would *dance* to its song.

* * *

Burton went first. Martha gave the sledge a shove and out it flew, into empty space. It dwindled, hit, kicked up a bit of a splash. Then, with a disappointing lack of pyrotechnics, the corpse slowly sank into the black glop.

It didn't look very encouraging at all.

Still...

"Okay," she said. "A deal's a deal." She dug in her toes and spread her arms. Took a deep breath. *Maybe I am going to survive after all,* she thought. It could be Burton was already halfway-merged into the oceanic mind of Io, and awaiting her to join in an alchemical marriage of personalities. *Maybe I'm going to live forever. Who knows? Anything is possible.*

Maybe.

There was a second and more likely possibility. All this could well be nothing more than a hallucination. Nothing but the sound of her brain short-circuiting and squirting bad chemicals in all directions. Madness. One last grandiose dream before dying. Martha had no way of judging.

THE VERY PULSE OF THE MACHINE

Whatever the truth might be, though, there were no alternatives, and only one way to find out.

She jumped.

Briefly, she flew.

NIGHT OF THE MINI-DEAD

Tim Miller and Jeff Fowler

Adapted by Buck

Note: Everything is seen through a tilt-shift effect, as if a higher being was looking down through a telescope on various Human shenanigans. Everything is shot in the 'real world', but the effect makes things appear miniature and cute, almost toy-like. It also affects time - everything elapses at a slightly faster-than-normal speed.

FADE IN
EXT. OLD GRAVEYARD – NIGHT

A dilapidated 19th century church sits in the middle of an old cemetery. The scene is bathed in blue moonlight. It's completely still except for a small breeze that rustles the grass around the tombstones and trees nearby. We linger here a bit to appreciate the solemn serenity of the slightly spooky scene.

Muffled sounds of a dubstep banger (but sped up, miniature) begin to grow louder and louder. A pair of headlights illuminate the road leading to the church. A flashy looking red import drunkenly swerves into the scene. It awkwardly pulls onto the church property. Its obnoxiously bright headlights pour into the sanctity of the grave-yard illuminating the area.

We hear the dubstep boom louder and clearer as the car doors fling open. The engine cuts off, the music stops, and out stumbles a young couple (AUTUMN & STEVE) – STEVE, a guy in his mid-20s, leather racing jacket over a deep V-neck, gold chain, skinny fitted joggers, gaudy sneakers we can't afford. AUTUMN, a girl in her mid-20s short

under-boob crop top, ripped skinny jeans, cheap dye job. They look like rejected YouTube stars, and... they... seem... pretty HAMMERED.

They speak in sped up mini voices. We can't quite make out the words but we get the tone of their chatter:

AUTUMN
(*Excited mini gibberish*)

STEVE
Totally.

The couple drunkenly stumbles into the cemetery. Titillated by the naughtiness of their trespassing, Steve takes a swig from a bottle, and gives Autumn the last sip. He chucks the bottle, it shatters against a nearby tombstone.

After a few flirtatious exchanges the couple starts making out... like heavy. Steve lifts Autumn onto another nearby tombstone – it sinks a bit then collapses under their weight. They giggle and keep going.

They spin around laughing and make their way to a large ANGEL STATUE in front of the church. They sit at its base and continue to make out, but slower this time. It feels as though the disrespectful nature of the situation has subsided. Maybe it's the fact that Steve's great-great aunt is buried here, maybe it's the disapproving gaze of the angel statue above them... They take a breath, and look into each other's eyes...

JUMP CUT to Autumn bent over a tombstone getting fucked doggy style by Steve. The two are butt-ass naked, clothes strewn about the graves. The sex is sloppy and awkward... but has passion. *It's the world's tiniest hardcore sex scene.*

JUMP CUT to another patch of the cemetery. She's on top, arched back and riding him – looks painful...

JUMP CUT, he has her up against the base of the angel statue, pounding like there's no tomorrow.

JUMP CUT, in a moment of bro'vado Steve has climbed to the top of the ANGEL STATUE and positioned himself to... fuck it right in its disapproving face. He turns back to Autumn who is giggling and filming with her phone.

> STEVE
> *(In a sped up mini voice that mostly*
> *sounds like gibberish)*
> Hehe... check it out babe... uh... uh... uh... uh...

Steve proceeds to thrust awkwardly into the angel's face with the same drunken rhythm he gave to Autumn. The entire statue shifts slightly with each thrust. Autumn continues to film and cheers him on – *this video will get so many likes.*

Steve's thrusting gets harder and faster... he might be enjoying this. The statue continues to rock back and forth until it SNAPS off of its base. It falls hard against the church with a loud crash and PINS Steve against the entrance.

LIGHTNING flashes. Music intensifies.

Autumn is in shock. Steve is dazed and maimed, his arm pinned between the statue and the church. There's blood everywhere but he looks alive.

> AUTUMN
> BABE!!!!!!!

Suddenly the structure of the church begins to shift and crack from the damage at its base. The church steeple sags and tilts forward. The steeple's CROSS dislodges and plummets off of the church. Like a sacrilegious lawn dart, it sticks UPSIDE DOWN into the pedestal

where the statue used to sit. An intensely bright bolt of lightning hits the upside down cross and IGNITES it with an other-worldly GREEN FLAME, that now lights the scene. The music takes a turn.

AUTUMN
Oh my god!!!

We see the old dirt around the graves churn up into fresh mounds, and up from the ground emerges the LIVING DEAD. Decomposed, skeletal, and with purpose.

Steve frantically struggles to free himself from the statue. Autumn freaks out and clumsily runs in all directions, surrounded. The zombies close in on the couple and attack them both. We hear gargled death screams, and then silence. The zombies shift their collective focus and make their way toward the road.

We see the bloody bodies of the couple. They lay lifeless on the ground – lit by the green flame and distant lightning flashes – the bodies begin to twitch. We hear growling, and slowly Autumn and Steve rise from the dead – vicious and hungry for blood. Lighting flashes and the music swells.

SMASH CUT:
MONTAGE – MORNING IN THE CITY

An abrupt shift in the music, we see Los Angeles in the morning. The city is waking up for the day. We see sunrise over the skyline, shots of traffic, people on their morning commute. It's business as usual.

EXT. RUNYON CANYON – MORNING

A hiking trail in the hills above the city. Two socialites jog into frame, eager to be seen in their latest athleisure hauls. They stop to stretch and catch their breath. A few stumbling zombies emerge from the trail behind them, the women notice late on the approach. The bitchier of the two savagely shoves her friend into the lead zombie, who bites through her neck, throws her to the ground, and starts ripping into her flesh. In utter shock the friend turns to run but is overtaken by the other zombies. The brutal attack leaves both joggers dead. They twitch, rise from the bloody dirt as zombies, and follow the others down the hill.

EXT. DOWNTOWN INTERSECTION – MORNING

A downtown intersection surrounded by high-rises. A group of young creative professionals, inspired to make a positive difference for the future, cross the street toward a COFFEE SHOP to get their daily macchiato and croissant. A Prius screeches around the corner through the intersection, smearing the pedestrians across the road like jelly on toast. The driver jumps out and runs away. A crowd of zombies in pursuit emerges and pours into the intersection. Bystanders scatter as the horde rushes into the coffee shop courtyard. They collide with the patio tables, cute cafe umbrellas fling about.

EXT. DOWNTOWN SIDE STREET – TRACKING – DAY

Sirens blasting. The camera follows an ambulance speeding down a side street. The driver swerves to avoid a group of zombies, only to take out a few others. It finds a clearing in the road then guns it ahead. Amid the pandemonium in the city we see blood on the sidewalks, smoke plumes and scattered fires in the streets.

EXT. HOPE MEMORIAL HOSPITAL – DAY

An ER at Hope Memorial Hospital in the middle of the city. The ambulance screeches into frame, jumps a median, and smashes through

a way-finding sign before careening straight through the emergency room entrance doors. There's a small but powerful explosion, we see tires and ambulance debris fly everywhere. A flaming wheelchair rolls out of the blast.

The chaos seems to be over. A plume of smoke rises from the site of the crash. A beat goes by... then suddenly a large crowd of zombies emerges and flows from the hospital, some wearing scrubs, others bare-assed in only patient gowns. The crowd is never-ending. Zombies start to pour out from the windows and off the rooftops, then exit frame in every direction.

EXT. AMERICAN SUBURB – DAY

A once idyllic suburban neighborhood block, now completely disheveled by a zombie attack. There's blood on the lawns, a smoking car, trash everywhere. One of the houses has a blue minivan parked in the driveway, soccer equipment still strapped to the roof.

We see a SOCCER MOM burst out of the front door with two young kids in tow. She rushes toward the van and frantically ushers everyone in. Her husband, who's now a zombie, crashes out of the front window of their house. He races toward the van, and just as the Soccer Mom gets her door closed, he claws violently at her window. The van screeches back out of the driveway, dragging the zombie into the middle of the street. She guns it, speeds forward and plows through the dazed zombie, putting an abrupt end to their happy marriage.

WHIP PAN SEQUENCE
The camera whip pans across the country to
EXT. NEW YORK CITY – ELEVATED SUBWAY OVERPASS – DAY

A small overpass in NY.

NIGHT OF THE MINI DEAD

We see a graffiti-covered subway train DERAIL and CRASH onto the freeway below. A horde of zombies flow from the train and begin chasing cars out of the scene.

WHIP PAN:
EXT. PARIS – EIFFEL TOWER – DAY

Across the Atlantic to Paris.

We see a crowd of zombies chasing crowds at the base of the Eiffel tower. The city burns in the distance. A flaming car with trailing plumes of smoke tears into the scene to escape the horde.

WHIP PAN:
EXT. THAILAND – DAY

Across the globe to a small northern city in Thailand.

We see a side street filled with markets, and signage. A lone TUK TUK drives up to an intersection and is met by the impending zombie influx. The tuk tuk turns to flee but is overtaken by the rushing horde. It gets caught up in the crowd and rolls away like a tiny Thai tin toy tumbleweed.

WHIP PAN:
INT. CANADIAN HOCKEY RINK – DAY

Back across the Pacific to somewhere in Canada.

We see the interior of a Hockey Rink, dead players in a bloody smear across the ice. All is still except an undead referee is crouched on top of the Away goalie, ravenously feasting and ripping flesh. They both drift on the slick surface, leaving a trail of guts on the ice.

EXT. HIMALAYAS – SHAOLIN TEMPLE – DAY

A breath in the music. We see an ornate, ancient Temple atop the highest peak of the remote mountain range. A group of Shaolin Monks clad in bright orange robes do meditative training poses in unison outside the front gate. It's a stoic, majestic scene.

The music shifts as we see a massive crowd of zombies rushing up the steep stairs toward the Temple. Right as they reach the top the monks spring into action, performing near superhuman attacks on the encroaching undead, blasting them off the mountain. It's a high-flying, gravity-defying, display of mini kung fu mastery.

EXT. KALAMAZOO – DAY

A small town main street in the middle of the US, where police and SWAT are having a standoff with the oncoming zombie attack. The horde slowly pushes an overturned car toward the cops. It scrapes the ground, grinds forward, takes heavy police fire, then EXPLODES sending flaming zombies everywhere.

EXT. VATICAN CITY – DAY

The central plaza at the Vatican. We see a group of red-cloaked cardinals and other clergymen firing fully automatic machine guns into a massive horde of zombies attempting to storm St Peter's Basilica. At the center of the battle we see the POPEMOBILE outfitted with twin machine guns, doing its best to stave off the unending horde.

EXT. US-MEXICO BORDER – NIGHT

Several jacked-up pickup trucks and an RV, heavily adorned with flags and misspelled protest signs, are huddled in formation against the US-Mexico border wall. A group of tiny redneck Jan 6ers, with even tinier penises, make their last stand. They take cover behind their lifted F150s and fire hopelessly into the massive horde of approaching zombies.

                              IDIOT 1
                    Aaaghhh… Shoot 'em in the dick…

                              IDIOT 2
                Shit man… (*cowardly mini gibberish*)
                       We gotta get outta here!

The group scrambles backward, climbs the RV, and starts to scale the wall. But their collective weight pulls the flimsy border wall down. It CRUSHES them and the RV below. A small but mighty EXPLOSION of munitions and BBQ propane tanks kills zombies and humans alike. The relentless horde continues unphased.

EXT. DOWNTOWN METROPOLIS – DAY

High above a downtown metropolis. A massive 'HELP' is scrawled in human blood on one of the rooftops. We see groups of survivors on the high-rises desperately waving their arms. The city is in flames. Giant pillars of smoke billow from windows and the streets below.

SNAP ZOOM OUT and we see the destruction is much bigger and more widespread. A local news helicopter spins out of control, falling through frame, leaving a corkscrew of smoke in the sky.

EXT. WHITE HOUSE – DAY

We're in the US Capitol. We see the White House sitting in a pristine scene – no zombies, no damage in sight. Music cuts to silence, we hear a phone ring…

PRESIDENT
Hello?... Zombies!?!?!
...Too late for a cover-up???

WHIP PAN UP:
EXT. NORTH AMERICAN AIRSPACE – DAY
We see a tiny (and surprisingly cute) elite squadron of FIGHTER
JETS enter frame. They fly across the country in tight formation then
release a cluster of bombs.

EXT. COASTAL CITY – DAY

An aerial shot of a coastal metropolitan city overrun by zombies.
We see signs of damage and signs of life. The tiny fighter jets enter
frame and carpet bomb the city. From this distance the explosions look
and sound like firecrackers.

EXT. BOMBED OUT CITY STREET – DAY

CRASH ZOOM through one of the smoke plumes and into the city
street below. We see that everything has gone to hell. It's a post-apocalyptic landscape ravaged by fire and overrun by zombies.

Civilization has fallen and groups of survivors have fashioned
everyday service vehicles and lame sedans into doomsday death
machines to combat the zombies. Our ragtag group of heavily modified
cars careen down the street in a caravan, plowing through crowds of
zombies. There's gunfire, sweet jumps, explosions, and dead bodies
flying everywhere.

WHIP PAN further ahead. We see the SOCCER MOM's Van
leading the pack. Only now the Van is leveled up into a badass zombie
killer on monster truck tires. We hear the tiny mom from inside...

NIGHT OF THE MINI DEAD

SOCCER MOM
Come get it, motherfuckers!!!
Ahahahahahah… Burn in hell!!!!!

A roof panel on the minivan opens up, twin flamethrowers emerge. The van shoots massive streams of fire on either side of the road, leaving a wake of torched zombie crisps.

EXT. SAN FRANCISCO INTERSECTION – DAY

A post-apocalyptic intersection in San Francisco. A horde of zombies stagger around aimlessly with no humans in sight.

We hear a cute bell ring-ding from off camera. A cable car TROLLEY rolls towards the intersection. It's outfitted with armor and a cow scoop welded onto the front of it. When it crosses the intersection, it lights up with machine gun fire out of the windows on either side, laying waste to the zombie horde. The gunfire subsides as it passes through the intersection. Ring-ding.

EXT. MOJAVE VALLEY GAS STATION – NIGHT

A secluded run-down gas station that doubles as a well-stocked amateur porn shop, has been heavily fortified with makeshift barricades to keep zombies at bay. We see two survivors using the gas pumps as make-shift flame throwers, taking turns casually torching crowds of zombies beyond the barricade.

EXT. NUCLEAR POWER PLANT – DAY

An aerial shot of what looks like a nuclear power plant that's badly damaged and abandoned. The air is thick with toxic fumes, smoke, and zombie stench. We see flashing gunfire amid the buildings below.

SNAP ZOOM:
EXT. NUCLEAR POWER PLANT – LOADING BAYS – DAY

SNAP ZOOM into the power plant. We see a small group of human survivors taking shelter in a narrow alleyway. The alley is littered with industrial vehicles, some are flipped on their side, some carry toxic barrels. A large toxic TANKER is wedged against one of the buildings.

A massive crowd of zombies rush the alley. Large chunks of debris, along with a flaming dumpster, are dragged inside the flowing zombie crowd. The pressure from the horde begins to push the vehicles together, creating a big squeeze into the dead-end alley. Fire from the dumpster spreads. The trapped humans shoot desperately into the horde. The vehicles push and pile together, metal crunching and twisting. The toxic tanker is punctured, ignites, then BOOM.

The scene explodes into a cloud of TOXIC GREEN SMOKE that fills the frame.

EXT. NUCLEAR POWER PLANT – PERIMETER – DAY

The thick green smoke rolls back and we're elsewhere in the Nuke Plant. We hear zombie growls and see the horde of tiny zombies rush from the dense green cloud. Glowing eyes rise through the mist and a group of GIANT MUTATED ZOMBIES emerge. Some big, a few bigger, all lumbering drunkenly into the clearing. From the mouth of the biggest mutated zombie spews GREEN GLOWING TOXIC VOMIT, which scorches the ground below. The mutated horde pushes through the gates and exits the plant.

WHIP PAN:
EXT. CITY STREETS – NIGHT

From up high, we see fleeing cars crest over the hill in a frantic hurry. The horde of tiny zombies, and bigger mutant zombies, flow over the hill in hot pursuit. From behind the hill we see the head of a Giant Mutant Zombie. Right when it steps over the crest of the hill it rears back and spews the toxic attack into a building, which bursts into a bright fireball, then a raging blaze.

SNAP ZOOM wider to reveal four city blocks being ravaged by the massive flowing zombie horde. The horde quickly marches down the avenues, filling the frame with destruction and blazing fires.

WHIP PAN:
EXT. WHITE HOUSE – NIGHT

WHIP PAN back to the White House lawn, now resembling a war zone. The mutated zombie horde of thousands is pressing at the fortified walls. Blackhawk helicopters are firing bullets and missiles into the crowd. We hear the President frantically over the White House comms...

> PRESIDENT
> ... Oh no. Oh shit, they're on the steps...
> What am I gonna...
> (beat)
> Ahh fuck it...

A loud button smash, alarms buzz and red sirens flash. Missile silos open up in the White House lawn. A half-dozen Nukes lift into armed positions from beneath the ground. In a quick flurry the nukes flash, smoke, and shoot out of the ground with great force. Tight trails of smoke slice through the scene.

EXT. SAINT PETERSBURG, RUSSIA – DAY

The Kremlin is surrounded by the black smoke of raging fires. Deep buzzing and flashing sirens signal. We see a cluster of missiles launch upward, ripping past and lighting up the Kremlin on their way out.

EXT. ANTARCTICA – DAY

A pristine glacial landscape. We see a mass of penguins huddled together for warmth on an icy plain. The chaos of the zombie apocalypse is nowhere in sight... suddenly a massive missile blasts through the ice, sending bloody meat and penguin feathers everywhere. The nuke tears out of frame leaving a thick column of smoke to dust the carnage.

EXT. EARTH – LOW ORBIT – DAY

We're high above thick cloud cover as a small cluster of missiles pierce through. Bright lights flash from beneath the clouds, then more missiles. Leaving puffy trails of smoke tendrils growing through the stratosphere on their way to space.

EXT. EARTH

We jump back to see the missiles leaving planet Earth, then arcing back down toward itself.

CUT TO:
EXT. OUR SOLAR SYSTEM

Punching further away, drifting from the pale blue dot, past the sun...

CUT TO:

EXT. THE MILKY WAY

Punching even further into the beauty of deeper space... our sun now a distant star.

CUT TO:

EXT. THE UNIVERSE

The magnificent shape of the spiraling galaxy glitters. The music swells to an operatic crescendo and...

... FAaRRrrtTT.

The tiniest hint of light flashes at the edge of the galaxy – and the sound of an interstellar FART rips into the completely uninterested vacuum of the Cosmos.

KILL TEAM KILL

Justin Coates

Thishis is bullshit."

It was the second time Macy had said it during the long march up the mountain. Sergeant Nielsen glanced at his MK48 gunner in annoyance as the younger man leaned against an Afghan pine.

"Shut up, Macy," he said, feeling the same exhaustion he knew the machine gunner felt but refusing to show it. "You can bitch about it once we make it back to Desolation. Take a knee, face out, drink water."

Macy looked back at his team leader with barely disguised disdain. He lit a cigarette as he got down in the prone, popping out the machine gun's bipod behind the roots of the pine tree. Nielsen made sure to stump the toe of his boot into Macy's side plate as he went to check on the rest of Team 1.

Erwin was seated against a smooth limestone boulder. The marksman peered down the scope mounted on his MK14 EBR. The 7.62mm sniper rifle was pulled snug into his shoulder, between where his plate carrier met his Multicam-pattern combat blouse.

"See anything interesting?" Nielsen asked.

"Not a thing," Erwin muttered, slowly scanning the valleys below. "Not since that weird goatherd guy following us after Meri Khel." He cocked his head to the side, affecting a higher tone of voice. "Did you see that chicken guy?"

"Yeah," Nielsen answered. "That guy was weird."

They both laughed quietly, having shared the same inside joke with the rest of the team for six months now. Being stationed at COP Desolation wasn't easy; finding humor in the most idiotic or vulgar circumstances had kept the men of the 25th Infantry Division from killing each other. The combat outpost was tiny, and the daily missions grueling. Bleak humor was all they had.

"We still set to meet with Team 2 on time?" Erwin asked, briefly glancing away from his scope.

♥ ✗ ▥

"Yeah. If we make this our last stop, we should be fine." Nielsen fiddled with his Camelback, sucking down a gulp of warm water from the hydration system hose. "Lemme know if you see anything."

Folen and Coutts were on the other side of the small summit, overlooking a sheer drop of over a hundred feet. Coutts was in the prone behind his M249, the automatic rifle's stubby barrel poking out into the open air. Folen's M4 with underslung M320 grenade launcher was propped against a tree while Folen pissed a steady stream of clear liquid over the cliff.

"You're gonna get shot in the dick if you keep silhouetting yourself like that," Nielsen said.

Coutts looked up at him, grinning like an idiot. "Right in the diiiick," he said, spitting out a thick black thread of chewing tobacco. "Quit diiiicking around, Folen."

"I wanna see how far out I can get it," Folen said, visibly struggling.

"I'm being serious, asshat. Cut it out."

Folen buttoned his trousers and took up his position at the tail end of their small formation. "How much further we got to the objective, sarn't?"

"Another five hundred meters up," he said, briefly checking the GPS unit attached to his wrist. "As long as we follow this spur we should be fine. Team 2 will be waiting for us there. You all staying hydrated?"

"Roger," they both replied, their heads returning to the slow, automatic swivel typical of anyone used to patrolling in a combat zone.

Returning to the center of the small patrol base, Nielsen keyed his microphone. "1-7, this is 1-1, over."

Silence greeted him. He tried to keep his voice down. "1-7, 1-1. We're within five hundred meters of the objective. How copy, over."

Silence. Dead, cold, empty silence. Nielsen was sweating despite the cool of the evening. Not for the first time he cursed himself for not speaking out against their platoon leader's idiotic plan for locating the enemy weapon caches. Splitting the platoon into such small teams was stupid. It flew in the face of common sense; it flew in the face of basic tactics. If not for the platoon sergeant's total incompetence and unwillingness to confront the new lieutenant, it would never have happened.

There'd been no radio contact for almost twenty minutes now. That was absolutely unheard of. The only thing to do was drive on to the next objective and hope to meet them there. Beyond that, Nielsen didn't have a clue but he'd be damned if he'd let his team down by showing his fear.

"All right," he said after a moment. "Let's pick it up."

They pushed on another three hundred meters. Every step was the same grueling, knee-locked affair as the last. The air in the mountains was thin. Nielsen resisted the urge to give the order to swap their helmets for patrol caps. Nightfall was coming soon, and they'd need their helmet-mounted night vision for even the shortest movement up the mountain.

They'd made it almost four hundred meters up the spur when Macy abruptly opened fire with his MK48. "Contact," he said, dropping to a knee behind a small pile of rocks. The machine gun thundered briefly, firing a burst of nine armor-piercing incendiary rounds. "Two hundred fifty meters. High on opposite ridge. One enemy RPG team."

Nielsen's response was drowned out by the heavy crump of an exploding RPG-7. The rocket propelled grenade detonated against a nearby pine, sending splinters of wood and sap flying.

"1-7, this is 1-1, troops in contact," he said into his useless radio, dropping to a knee as Macy went down into the prone. "Talk the guns!" he shouted as Coutts' lighter M249 opened up further down the spur. The M249 and the MK48 quickly began firing complimentary bursts, each one opening up when the other paused to re-acquire sight pictures or reload.

A High-Explosive Dual-Purpose grenade sailed through the air from Folen's position. Nielsen fired his own grenade launcher a second later. AK-47 rounds snapped through the air past his head. He reloaded his underslung grenade launcher, taking note of the bright muzzle flash of the enemy RPK light machine gun.

Both his and Folen's grenades landed solidly in the midst of the enemy position. A plume of smoke and dust rose from the stand of trees where the enemy had been.

"Cease fire," Nielsen shouted immediately, fearful for the conservation of machine gun ammunition. "Folen, hit it again. Erwin, tag any squirters you can see."

Mindful of where he'd seen the RPK, Nielsen sent another grenade hurtling through the air. Folen's came shortly after, both of them hitting right on top of each other.

There was silence for a moment; then, a single round fired from Erwin's EBR. "Erwin?" Nielsen said.

"Saw some movement. Just wanted to be sure."

"All right. Buddy ACE report, then let's get out of here."

He moved to Macy's position, quickly checking the other soldier for any injuries he might not have noticed in the brief adrenaline rush of combat. "Ammo count?" Nielsen said, checking the soldier's night-vision pouch and tapping his rifle-mounted optic systems.

"Five hundred rounds," Macy answered. "Should have shot more. Shit's heavy."

"Yeah, well, until we link up with Team 2 we need to play it safe." Nielsen tapped his soldier's helmet, and quickly showed Macy his own sensitive items. The junior infantryman quickly checked his team leader for any injuries before returning the helmet tap. "Good work, Macy."

None of the others had been injured, and ammo levels were still at acceptable levels. *Not like it matters,* Nielsen thought. *We've got one or two firefights like that left before we need a resupply.* He pulled a HOOAH! energy bar out of his pocket, gnawing on the slimy peanut butter mess. *Gonna need to start rationing chow if we get to the objective and no one else is there.*

Just the thought of it formed a knot of anxiety in his stomach. "I'm not fucking ready for this," he muttered, washing the energy bar down with a swig of water before turning to the rest of his team. "All right, pick up. We need—"

"Hey, Sarn't?" Erwin spoke, looking down his scope. "You're gonna want to take a look at this."

Nielsen pulled his rifle to his shoulder, glancing through his ACOG scope. The dust was beginning to clear from the enemy position, but he could see the bullet-ridden pine trees shaking. Small landslides of shale tumbled off the opposite ridge, along with a body twisted and bent almost beyond recognition.

There was something massive lurking in the dust cloud. Nielsen caught a glimpse of a broad, black shoulder, bristling with sharp spines.

One of the pine trees collapsed underneath a massive claw, its yellow talons circling around the trunk and pulling it up out of the ground.

"What the hell is that?" Macy asked.

"No idea," Nielsen answered, his heart thundering.

"I'm gonna shoot it," Coutts said, reaching for his M249's charging handle.

Nielsen snapped, "Standby, dammit. Just... standby."

They watched for a moment as whatever it was lumbered down the opposite side of the ridge. For a moment they could still hear it snapping trees and triggering shale-slides in its wake. Then it was gone, leaving nothing but silence in its wake.

"Well, that's it," Folen said, putting in a fresh pinch of Copenhagen. "We've all gone crazy. Time to kill each other."

"Oh, thank God," Coutts said, stretching. "I'm tired of carrying this stupid thing."

"You fucks don't have my permission to die," Nielsen said, shaking his head. *Just get to the rendezvous site.* "We need to double-time it to meet up with Team 2. Bianchi has the Tacsat, we'll be able to call back to Desolation and see if they can get eyes on that... thing."

"It was a honey badger," Folen said. Coutts snickered. "Honey badgers don't give a shit."

"Whatever it was, I don't want to be with you idiots when it shows up again." Nielsen turned and headed back up the spur. The others fell into place, the sound of doubt hiding inside their muttered jokes and curses.

* * *

Team 2 was dead. Not just dead; devoured, ripped apart, scattered all over the plateau where they'd been supposed to meet. None of them were remotely identifiable. It was all a jumble of torsos and spent shell casings.

"Honey badger got here first," Coutts said, kicking at a massive claw embedded in a rapidly-cooling torso. "Look at this thing." He pulled it free, holding it up like a sword. "Almost as big as my dick."

"We gonna talk about this?" Erwin said, glancing at Nielsen. "Or are we just gonna keep pretending nothing weird is going on?"

"Pretending has my vote," Folen said. He pulled a blood-soaked grenade bandolier off a limbless corpse and strapped it over his shoulder. "I know I can't deal with this right now."

"Me neither," Coutts added, holding the claw against his crotch and thrusting suggestively. "Not getting paid near enough to even *start* to care."

"The whole team is gone," Erwin said. The beginnings of panic edged into his voice. "Hajji didn't do this, Sarn't. That... *thing* killed all of them."

"Sure looks that way," Nielsen said. He pulled off his Oakley's, and put his hand on Erwin's shoulder. "Look at me. Take off your eyepro." Erwin obeyed, his pupils darting all over Nielsen's face. "It doesn't matter who did this. Hajji, honey badger…"

"It was the Loch Ness monster!" Coutts said. Macy and Folen laughed.

"It doesn't matter," Nielsen repeated. "We're gonna get through this. We're gonna find the Tacsat, call back to Desolation, and get the hell out of here. You with me?"

Erwin stared over his sergeant's shoulder for a moment. Nielsen slapped him. Erwin blinked, and nodded.

"Yeah," he said, shaking his head. "Yeah. I'm with you."

"Good." Nielsen embraced him, and kissed his cheek. "Now let's find that damn radio."

Something started screaming to their south. They turned as one, dropping to a knee in a firing line, facing the direction of the spur they'd followed up the mountain. The stand of trees on the edge of the plateau disappeared, pulled down by the same yellow claw now strapped to Coutts' back.

"For the record," Macy said, slamming a fresh belt of ammunition into his MK48. "It was a pleasure serving with you gentlemen."

"All remaining rounds to my position!" Folen quoted as whatever it was roared again. "For the record, it was my call!"

"Lovely fuckin' war!" They all shouted together as a monster came charging up the spur toward them.

It wasn't a honey badger. It was a bear, or a wolf, or an amalgam of both. It lumbered on all fours, the sharp spines that covered its shoulders quivering with every step. Its wild, white eyes were already rolling, a purple-black tongue lolling between fangs the size of Nielsen's combat knife.

It was easily seven feet tall at the shoulder. When it suddenly reared up on its hind legs, spreading scythe-like claws, it was tall enough to blot out the setting sun.

Too close for grenades, Nielsen thought as he switched his M4 selector switch to BURST. *Too close to miss.*

Macy was already firing. He leaned back, letting the recoil of the MK48 drive him into the ground. The 7.62mm rounds snapped through the air alongside Coutts' lighter 5.56mm bullets, the heavy tungsten projectiles peppering the behemoth. Folen and Nielsen joined in a second later, followed by the steady *crack* of Erwin's marksmanship rifle.

The beast dropped onto all fours, charging despite the firepower leveled against it. It swiped at Coutts, its claws ripping apart his ceramic armor and sending his M249 flying. He fell, rolling to his feet and yanking the recovered claw free. The soldier lunged forward, hacking at the thing's nose and maw, screaming incoherently. Nielsen circled, trying to get a better line of sight, blasting away at the thing's thick, knotted skull.

"Fuck you honey badger!" Coutts shouted. Its huge head snapped forward, catching him around the waist. He screamed, coughing up blood as he rammed the claw furiously into its snout. The claw snapped in half as the beast shook its head wildly, hurling him like a shotput. Coutts went flying, disappearing over the edge of the plateau.

Erwin lunged, driving the barrel of his EBR into its chest. He pulled the trigger until his magazine was dry. The creature roared, ramming him with the spines on its shoulder. They burst out the back of his skull, shredding his body armor. It grabbed his body with a clawed hand and shoved the remains into its cavernous maw.

Nielsen cursed as he reloaded, fumbling with his polymer magazine. The thing turned on him, snarling, its white eyes rolling back into its head. He slammed another magazine home as it charged, Macy and Folen's shouts drowned out by its thick, throaty bellow.

It was nearly on top of him when it suddenly began thrashing

about. It shuddered, skidding to a halt, throwing up clogs of dirt in all directions. It pawed at its own head, snarling, foaming at the mouth.

"Hey! Over here!"

Nielsen turned to see a soldier emerge from a stand of trees on the other side of the plateau. His thick beard was covered in blood. There was a vicious wound on his left arm, a claw slash nearly six inches long. In his right hand he clenched a dish-shaped device attached to a massive backpack by thick, gray wires.

He aimed the device squarely at the bellowing monster. A high-pitched whine filled the air. The creature's snarl turned into a mammoth squeal of pain. It turned and fled, thundering back the way it had come.

The young sergeant turned toward the stranger. The other man huffed with exertion, the device shaking in his arm.

"Goddam thing is running out of juice," he said. "You all right?"

"Fine," Nielsen answered. "Just peachy."

"Who the hell is this?" Macy asked, coming with Folen to stand beside Nielsen.

The other soldier clipped the device to his belt. He pulled a wrinkled cigarette pack out of his shoulder pocket and offered one to Nielsen. Nielsen stared at him. He shrugged, and lit it for himself. "Sergeant First Class Morris," the soldier said. "Attached to Task Force Griffin. Stationed up at Camp Eisenhower a click north of here."

"Bullshit, that's where you're from," Folen said. "You're stationed at Camp Bullshit, and you drink from a Camelback full of fucking lies."

"You wouldn't know about Eisenhower," Morris continued, ignoring Folen. "It's a subterranean facility. CIA built it back in 2002 right after the invasion. We've been moving in and out for the last ten years."

"And let me guess," Folen continued. "You've got all kinds of crazy nasty shit down there including that... *thing*." He frowned, noticing the cigarette dangling from Morris' lips. "Wait. Let me get one of those."

Morris handed him a smoke, and said, "Yes. All kinds of nasty shit, including Codename: BARGHEST, which you just met."

"That's a stupid name for a honey badger," Nielsen said. "A really fucking stupid name."

The SF soldier frowned. "It's not a honey badger. It's a genetically engineered grizzly with a load of mechanical augmentation. Small arms don't work for shit; it's got a solid inch of ballistic-resistant gel and synthetic spider-weave beneath its skin. Most of its organs are redundant, and the damn thing has a graphene battery as a power source if it suffers brain death."

"Can you kill it with that?" Nielsen asked, pointing at the device clipped to Morris' waist.

"No. It's supposed to be a remote control," Morris said, exhaling a cloud of smoke. "But the only setting that seems to still work is the one set to 'screw off'. I can't control them, but I can make them leave for a while. If we can make it back to camp I—"

"Stop," Folen interrupted. "You said 'them'. Please tell me you meant 'it'."

"No," Morris sighed. "That's one of two that are still left."

* * *

The entrance to Camp Eisenhower was a hatch in the ground hidden beneath a false layer of loose rock. Morris led the way down a steel ladder, which dropped into a concrete hallway after twenty feet. Pale overhead lamps flickered as the rest of the team followed, spreading out with their weapons at the high ready.

"If we can get to the bionics bay, I should be able to access the control system," Morris said. "I can recall them from there, and then use the kill switch once they get inside."

"Or you could just flip the kill switch now without calling them here," Folen said, his eyes glued to the door at the end of the hall. "That would also work."

"We can't leave these things lying around," Morris snapped. "You think Uncle Sam wants the world to know he's setting genetically modified bears lose to hunt down hajji? Does that sound like a winning strategy for hearts and minds?" They stopped at the door. Morris quickly punched a code into the keypad. "We call 'em back here and flip the kill switch as soon as we hear them rooting around. Then I call for MEDEVAC, we go home, and all of you get a fancy award and a weekend in Qatar."

The hallway they stepped into was covered in blood. The remains of corpses were everywhere, mangled bodies and black, slick blood covering the walls.

"Something must have gone wrong with the command signals," Morris said as Macy cursed in disgust. "The three barghests were supposed to run a standard patrol last night. Instead, they went berserk. My team was already on patrol when one ambushed us. Managed to take it down, but I was the only one to walk away from it."

"I thought you SF guys had special magic beard powers," Nielsen asked, keeping his rifle tight in his shoulder. "Your beard didn't protect you?"

"Fuck you." Morris winced, pressing a hand against the Israeli bandage over his wound. "Take a left up here."

The kill team headed down another blood-slicked corridor. There were rooms on either side of the long hallway; rooms with doors that had been beaten down, rooms with shattered glass panels and scattered laboratory equipment.

Morris stopped briefly at one of them. "Sweet," he said, ducking inside. Nielsen followed, nearly tripping over overturned weapon racks. Machine guns, semi-automatic rifles and anti-tank weapons were scattered everywhere.

"Macy, Folen, get in here," he said, quickly opening ammo can full of HEDP grenades. "Stock up on everything you can carry. Ditch your plates; they're not going to protect us from those things anyway."

"Here." Macy pulled two M72 Light Anti-Tank Weapons out of an overturned locker. He handed one to Folen and took one for himself. "There's something else in here..." He withdrew a long, hollow tube fitted with a wooden pistol grip.

"That's a Gustaf," Morris said, playing with a remote control he'd snatched from one of the few lockers still standing. "84mm recoilless."

"Will it take one of those things down?" Nielsen asked.

"If you shoot it center mass, it should deal enough damage to the barghest's mechanical and organic support systems to trigger a total shutdown," Morris said. "And if not..."

A large metallic crate in the corner suddenly toppled over with a loud bang. A tracked robot wheeled out from where it had been hidden and stopped at Morris' side. At around four feet tall, the robot was armed with sponson-mounted machine guns and a quad-barrel rocket system.

"This is MAARS-bot," Morris said, patting the robot affectionately. "He's armed with one XM806 .50 caliber machine gun, two M240L 7.62mm machine guns, and an M202AI FLASH Incendiary Weapon."

"Sweet," Macy said. "Is it gonna go rogue and try to eat us, too?"

His answer was an echoing roar from somewhere deeper in the compound. Morris cursed. "All right, one of the two little bears is already home," he said. "We gotta go. Now. Follow me!"

He sprinted out of the room, MAARS-bot cruising along behind him. The others followed, quickly slinging their rocket-propelled weapons as they sprinted down the hall toward the bionics bay.

"It's just ahead," Morris shouted as they rounded a corner. "Oh, shit!"

The barghest they had encountered earlier was just ahead of them. It bled hydraulic fluid and boiling, dark-red blood. It appeared even more massive in the tightly confined space. It roared, its spines scraping and gouging the ceiling.

"Honey badger, 12 o'clock!" Folen shouted, immediately dropping to a knee and opening up. He fired on burst, burning through a 30-round magazine in a matter of seconds.

"Grenades!" Nielsen shouted as the barghest dropped and charged. The HEDP rounds sailed through the air, each of them smashing into the beast's front legs. Nielsen could feel the intense heat of the blast at such close range. He opened up along with Macy, the other soldier's MK48 filling the air between them and the monster with armor-piercing rounds.

"Use your stupid ray gun, Morris!" Macy shouted.

"I'm outta juice!" Morris answered, ditching the huge power pack with a curse. He snatched up the controls for MAARS-bot, muttering a litany of profanity as he adjusted the robot's controls.

"Any second now, Morris! Feel free!" Nielsen bellowed. The barghest was almost on them, growing wider by the second, undeterred by the gallons of blood and black hydraulic fluid pouring from its wounds.

"Got it!"

The robot chirped pleasantly, and suddenly the rocket pods on its central chassis burst into life. Four 66mm incendiary rockets screamed through the air, each one landing right on top of the other. The monster's front legs were sheared clean off. One of the rockets detonated inside the barghest, showering all of them with blood, guts and machine parts. The metallic skeleton of the creature was revealed, along with sparking wires and steaming organs.

The barghest mindlessly pushed itself toward them with its hind legs. The kill team kept up their rate of fire until it was only a few feet from them. Finally, it stopped, right in front of Folen, a mechanical screech signaling the death of its primary power source.

Folen peered down at its massive, bloody jaws. He chuckled, and kicked it in the eye.

The barghest lunged forward, its teeth sinking into his leg. Folen screamed as it savaged the wound, jerking its head back and forth. His limb came away at the hip, bright arterial blood fountaining through the air. The others yelled, dumping rounds into the creature's head until its skull was nothing more than a black and red smear on the shattered tile.

Nielsen immediately went to Folen's side. The soldier clasped his sergeant's arm, looking up at him with a mixture of sorrow and annoyance.

"Nielsen," he whispered. "Tell my wife…"

The sergeant squeezed his hand. "I will, Folen. I promise."

"No… listen. Tell my wife I said…" Nielsen leaned forward, until Folen's lips brushed his ear. "… fuck Obama."

"Goddammit," Nielsen said, standing up as Folen briefly cackled at his own joke before dying. "Macy, how much ammo you got left?"

"I'm Winchester," Macy answered, unceremoniously dumping his MK48 onto the ground. "I'll take Folen's LAW. And his M4, so I can shoot myself once this is all over."

"Great idea." He turned to Morris, and gestured at the huge corpse blocking the corridor. "We aren't getting around this. Is there any other way to the bionics bay?"

"Yeah. We gotta backtrack a bit, but we'll make it there quick if we hustle. Follow me."

The bionics bay was as big as some brigade-level operation centers Nielsen had seen. Massive screens covered the walls. Multiple rows of desks were set up, as well as what looked like a laboratory in a separate chamber near the eastern end of the bay. There was no sign of violence like there was elsewhere in the camp; everything was still, almost bizarrely serene.

"You better put me in for a bronze star with valor," Macy said to Morris, taking up a defensive position behind a row of desks. He unlimbered his LAW, extended the rocket tube, and placed it lightly on his shoulder.

"I'll deny any award he puts you in for," Nielsen replied, kneeling behind the row across from Macy. "You've got a bad attitude. Maybe you'll get a certificate of achievement. Maybe."

"All right, ladies," Morris said from one of the computers, typing away furiously. "I sent the return command a minute ago. Now all we gotta do is wait."

The words had barely left his mouth when the sturdy steel doors they had entered through collapsed, along with much of the wall. The remaining barghest exploded into the room, barreling straight for Morris and the command console. Nielsen cursed, squeezing the trigger of the recoilless rifle as Macy opened up with his LAW. Nielsen's round went wide, landing in the bionics lab with a muted *crump*. Glass flew everywhere, the lethal shards forcing him to duck and cover.

MAARS-bot opened up with all four machine guns mounted to its frame. The 7.62mm rounds *pinged* loudly as they penetrated the monster's subcutaneous shell. The .50 cal rounds blasted huge chunks out of the barghest's flank. Despite missing most of its left front limb from Macy's accurate rocket attack, it barged through the rows of desks and threw itself at Morris.

There was a brief moment of panicked screaming, rising only slightly over the nonstop barrage of bullets. Macy fired the LAW he'd recovered from Folen, managing to completely shred the creature's left rib cage. Blood and pressurized lubricant sprayed everywhere, live wires hissing as they crossed each other.

It turned to face them with most of Morris hanging from its jaws. The console the SF soldier had been busily typing into was mangled,

destroyed beyond repair. The barghest roared, sending a chunk of Morris' leg flying through the air.

"Fuck you," Nielsen snarled, squeezing the trigger on his M320. The 40mm grenade thundered against its snout with a shriek of tortured metal. Macy primed and threw two hand grenades in quick succession, both of them erupting beneath the monster's heaving gut.

The MAARS-bot continued its unrelenting stream of tungsten and lead. Subjected to such withering firepower, the barghest's outer skin was blasted to pieces until it was nothing more than a huffing, wheezing skeleton. It rounded on the robot, flipping it onto its side and viciously pounding it with heavy strikes of its massive paws.

"MAARS-bot, no!" Macy yelled. "Save yourself, robot friend!" The robot chirped weakly in response, before exploding in a shower of sharp metal pieces.

The barghest rounded on Macy. The infantryman hastily back-stepped, firing controlled pairs into its mouth as it advanced on him. He tripped over a fallen computer screen and went down. The barghest howled, rearing up on its hind legs to deliver a crushing strike.

Nielsen's one remaining 83mm round caught it right in the ribs. The projectile detonated with the thunder of a mortar round, blasting the cyborg monster apart from the inside out. The top half of its body blasted toward the ceiling, its torso spewing rancid blood everywhere. Its upper half crashed onto the floor a moment later, its eyes rolling across the ground to stare accusingly at its killer.

The sergeant limped over to Macy and helped him to his feet. Macy looked at the bisected corpse, then glared at Nielsen.

"This is bullshit."

SWARM

Bruce Sterling

will miss your conversation during the rest of the voyage," the alien said.

Captain-Doctor Simon Afriel folded his jeweled hands over his gold-embroidered waistcoat. "I regret it also, ensign," he said in the alien's own hissing language. "Our talks together have been very useful to me. I would have paid to learn so much, but you gave it freely."

"But that was only information," the alien said. He shrouded his bead-bright eyes behind thick nictitating membranes. "We Investors deal in energy, and precious metals. To prize and pursue mere knowledge is an immature racial trait." The alien lifted the long, ribbed frill behind his pinhole-sized ears.

"No doubt you are right," Afriel said, despising him. "We humans are as children to other races, however; so a certain immaturity seems natural to us." Afriel pulled off his sunglasses to rub the bridge of his nose. The starship cabin was drenched in searing blue light, heavily ultraviolet. It was the light the Investors preferred, and they were not about to change it for one human passenger.

"You have not done badly," the alien said magnanimously. "You are the kind of race we like to do business with: young, eager, plastic, ready for a wide variety of goods and experiences. We would have contacted you much earlier, but your technology was still too feeble to afford us a profit."

"Things are different now," Afriel said. "We'll make you rich."

"Indeed," the Investor said. The frill behind his scaly head flickered rapidly, a sign of amusement. "Within two hundred years you will be wealthy enough to buy from us the secret of our starflight. Or perhaps your Mechanist faction will discover the secret through research."

Afriel was annoyed. As a member of the Reshaped faction, he did not appreciate the reference to the rival Mechanists. "Don't put

too much stock in mere technical expertise," he said. "Consider the aptitude for languages we Shapers have. It makes our faction a much better trading partner. To a Mechanist, all Investors look alike."

The alien hesitated. Afriel smiled. He had appealed to the alien's personal ambition with his last statement, and the hint had been taken. That was where the Mechanists always erred. They tried to treat all Investors consistently, using the same programmed routines each time. They lacked imagination.

Something would have to be done about the Mechanists, Afriel thought. Something more permanent than the small but deadly confrontations between isolated ships in the Asteroid Belt and the ice-rich Rings of Saturn. Both factions maneuvered constantly, looking for a decisive stroke, bribing away each other's best talent, practicing ambush, assassination, and industrial espionage.

Captain-Doctor Simon Afriel was a past master of these pursuits. That was why the Reshaped faction had paid the millions of kilowatts necessary to buy his passage. Afriel held doctorates in biochemistry and alien linguistics, and a master's degree in magnetic weapons engineering. He was thirty-eight years old and had been Reshaped according to the state of the art at the time of his conception. His hormonal balance had been altered slightly to compensate for long periods spent in free-fall. He had no appendix. The structure of his heart had been redesigned for greater efficiency, and his large intestine had been altered to produce the vitamins normally made by intestinal bacteria. Genetic engineering and rigorous training in childhood had given him an intelligence quotient of one hundred and eighty. He was not the brightest of the agents of the Ring Council, but he was one of the most mentally stable and the best trusted.

"It seems a shame," the alien said, "that a human of your accomplishments should have to rot for two years in this miserable, profitless outpost."

"The years won't be wasted," Afriel said.

"But why have you chosen to study the Swarm? They can teach you nothing, since they cannot speak. They have no wish to trade, having no tools or technology. They are the only spacefaring race that is essentially without intelligence."

SWARM

"That alone should make them worthy of study."

"Do you seek to imitate them, then? You would make monsters of yourselves." Again, the ensign hesitated. "Perhaps you could do it. It would be bad for business, however."

There came a fluting burst of alien music over the ship's speakers, then a screeching fragment of Investor language. Most of it was too high-pitched for Afriel's ears to follow.

The alien stood, his jeweled skirt brushing the tips of his clawed bird-like feet. "The Swarm's symbiote has arrived," he said.

"Thank you," Afriel said. When the ensign opened the cabin door, Afriel could smell the Swarm's representative; the creature's warm yeasty scent had spread rapidly through the starship's recycled air.

Afriel quickly checked his appearance in a pocket mirror. He touched powder to his face and straightened the round velvet hat on his shoulder-length reddish-blond hair. His earlobes glittered with red impact-rubies, thick as his thumbs' ends, mined from the Asteroid Belt. His knee-length coat and waistcoat were of gold brocade; the shirt beneath was of dazzling fineness, woven with red-gold thread. He had dressed to impress the Investors, who expected and appreciated a prosperous look from their customers. How could he impress this new alien? Smell, perhaps. He freshened his perfume.

Beside the starship's secondary airlock, the Swarm's symbiote was chittering rapidly at the ship's commander. The commander was an old and sleepy Investor, twice the size of most of her crewmen. Her massive head was encrusted in a jeweled helmet. From within the helmet her clouded eyes glittered like cameras.

The symbiote lifted on its six posterior legs and gestured feebly with its four clawed forelimbs. The ship's artificial gravity, a third again as strong as Earth's, seemed to bother it. Its rudimentary eyes, dangling on stalks, were shut tight against the glare. It must be used to darkness, Afriel thought.

The commander answered the creature in its own language. Afriel grimaced, for he had hoped that the creature spoke Investor. Now he would have to learn another language, a language designed for a being without a tongue.

After another brief interchange the commander turned to Afriel. "The symbiote is not pleased with your arrival," she told Afriel in the

Investor language. "There has apparently been some disturbance here involving humans, in the recent past. However, I have prevailed upon it to admit you to the Nest. The episode has been recorded. Payment for my diplomatic services will be arranged with your faction when I return to your native star system."

"I thank Your Authority," Afriel said. "Please convey to the symbiote my best personal wishes, and the harmlessness and humility of my intentions... " He broke off short as the symbiote lunged toward him, biting him savagely in the calf of his left leg. Afriel jerked free and leapt backward in the heavy artificial gravity, going into a defensive position. The symbiote had ripped away a long shred of his pant's leg; it now crouched quietly, eating it.

"It will convey your scent and composition to its nestmates," said the commander. "This is necessary. Otherwise, you would be classed as an invader, and the Swarm's warrior caste would kill you at once."

Afriel relaxed quickly and pressed his hand against the puncture wound to stop the bleeding. He hoped that none of the Investors had noticed his reflexive action. It would not mesh well with his story of being a harmless researcher.

"We will reopen the airlock soon," the commander said phlegmatically, leaning back on her thick reptilian tail. The symbiote continued to munch the shred of cloth. Afriel studied the creature's neckless, segmented head. It had a mouth and nostrils; it had bulbous atrophied eyes on stalks; there were hinged slats that might be radio receivers, and two parallel ridges of clumped wriggling antennae sprouting among three chitinous plates. Their function was unknown to him.

The airlock door opened. A rush of dense, smoky aroma entered the departure cabin. It seemed to bother the half-dozen Investors, who left rapidly. "We will return in six hundred and twelve of your days, as by our agreement," the commander said.

"I thank Your Authority," Afriel said.

"Good luck," the commander said in English. Afriel smiled.

The symbiote, with a sinuous wriggle of its segmented body, crept into the airlock. Afriel followed it. The airlock door shut behind them. The creature said nothing to him but continued munching loudly. The second door opened, and the symbiote sprang through it into a wide, round stone tunnel. It disappeared at once into the gloom.

SWARM

Afriel put his sunglasses into a pocket of his jacket and pulled out a pair of infrared goggles. He strapped them to his head and stepped out of the airlock. The artificial gravity vanished, replaced by the almost imperceptible gravity of the Swarm's asteroid nest. Afriel smiled, comfortable for the first time in weeks. Most of his adult life had been spent in free-fall, in the Shapers' colonies in the Rings of Saturn.

Squatting in a dark cavity in the side of the tunnel was a disk-headed furred animal the size of an elephant. It was clearly visible in the infrared of its own body heat. Afriel could hear it breathing. It waited patiently until Afriel had launched himself past it, deeper into the tunnel. Then it took its place in the end of the tunnel, puffing itself up with air until its swollen head securely plugged the exit into space. Its multiple legs sank firmly into sockets in the walls.

The Investors' ship had left. Afriel remained here, inside one of the millions of planetoids that circled the giant star Betelgeuse in a girdling ring with almost five times the mass of Jupiter. As a source of potential wealth it dwarfed the entire solar system, and it belonged, more or less, to the Swarm. At least, no other race had challenged them for it within the memory of the Investors.

Afriel peered up the corridor. It seemed deserted, and without other bodies to cast infrared heat, he could not see very far. Kicking against the wall, he floated hesitantly down the corridor.

He heard a human voice. "Dr Afriel!"

"Dr Mirny!" he called out. "This way!"

He first saw a pair of young symbiotes scuttling toward him, the tips of their clawed feet barely touching the walls. Behind them came a woman wearing goggles like his own. She was young, and attractive in the trim, anonymous way of the genetically reshaped.

She screeched something at the symbiotes in their own language, and they halted, waiting. She coasted forward, and Afriel caught her arm, expertly stopping their momentum.

"You didn't bring any luggage?" she said anxiously.

He shook his head. "We got your warning before I was sent out. I have only the clothes I'm wearing and a few items in my pockets."

She looked at him critically. "Is that what people are wearing in the Rings these days? Things have changed more than I thought."

Afriel glanced at his brocaded coat and laughed. "It's a matter of policy. The Investors are always readier to talk to a human who looks ready to do business on a large scale. All the Shapers' representatives dress like this these days. We've stolen a jump on the Mechanists; they still dress in those coveralls."

He hesitated, not wanting to offend her. Galina Mirny's intelligence was rated at almost two hundred. Men and women that bright were sometimes flighty and unstable, likely to retreat into private fantasy worlds or become enmeshed in strange and impenetrable webs of plotting and rationalization. High intelligence was the strategy the Shapers had chosen in the struggle for cultural dominance, and they were obliged to stick to it, despite its occasional disadvantages. They had tried breeding the Superbright—those with quotients over two hundred—but so many had defected from the Shapers' colonies that the faction had stopped producing them.

"You wonder about my own clothing," Mirny said.

"It certainly has the appeal of novelty," Afriel said with a smile.

"It was woven from the fibers of a pupa's cocoon," she said. "My original wardrobe was eaten by a scavenger symbiote during the troubles last year. I usually go nude, but I didn't want to offend you by too great a show of intimacy."

Afriel shrugged. "I often go nude myself, I never had much use for clothes except for pockets. I have a few tools on my person, but most are of little importance. We're Shapers, our tools are here." He tapped his head. "If you can show me a safe place to put my clothes… "

She shook her head. It was impossible to see her eyes for the goggles, which made her expression hard to read. "You've made your first mistake, Doctor. There are no places of our own here. It was the same mistake the Mechanist agents made, the same one that almost killed me as well. There is no concept of privacy or property here. This is the Nest. If you seize any part of it for yourself—to store equipment, to sleep in, whatever—then you become an intruder, an enemy. The two Mechanists—a man and a woman—tried to secure an empty chamber for their computer lab. Warriors broke down their door and devoured them. Scavengers ate their equipment, glass, metal, and all."

Afriel smiled coldly. "It must have cost them a fortune to ship all that material here."

Mirny shrugged. "They're wealthier than we are. Their machines, their mining. They meant to kill me, I think. Surreptitiously, so the warriors wouldn't be upset by a show of violence. They had a computer that was learning the language of the springtails faster than I could."

"But you survived," Afriel pointed out. "And your tapes and reports—especially the early ones, when you still had most of your equipment—were of tremendous interest. The Council is behind you all the way. You've become quite a celebrity in the Rings, during your absence."

"Yes, I expected as much," she said.

Afriel was nonplused. "If I found any deficiency in them," he said carefully, "it was in my own field, alien linguistics." He waved vaguely at the two symbiotes who accompanied her. "I assume you've made great progress in communicating with the symbiotes, since they seem to do all the talking for the Nest."

She looked at him with an unreadable expression and shrugged. "There are at least fifteen different kinds of symbiotes here. Those that accompany me are called the springtails, and they speak only for themselves. They are savages, Doctor, who received attention from the Investors only because they can still talk. They were a spacefaring race once, but they've forgotten it. They discovered the Nest and they were absorbed, they became parasites." She tapped one of them on the head. "I tamed these two because I learned to steal and beg food better than they can. They stay with me now and protect me from the larger ones. They are jealous, you know. They have only been with the Nest for perhaps ten thousand years and are still uncertain of their position. They still think, and wonder sometimes. After ten thousand years there is still a little of that left to them."

"Savages," Afriel said. "I can well believe that. One of them bit me while I was still aboard the starship. He left a lot to be desired as an ambassador."

"Yes, I warned him you were coming," said Mirny. "He didn't much like the idea, but I was able to bribe him with food... I hope he didn't hurt you badly."

"A scratch," Afriel said. "I assume there's no chance of infection."

"I doubt it very much. Unless you brought your own bacteria with you."

"Hardly likely," Afriel said, offended. "I have no bacteria. And I wouldn't have brought microorganisms to an alien culture anyway."

Mirny looked away. "I thought you might have some of the special genetically altered ones... I think we can go now. The springtail will have spread your scent by mouth-touching in the subsidiary chamber, ahead of us. It will be spread throughout the Nest in a few hours. Once it reaches the Queen, it will spread very quickly."

She jammed her feet against the hard shell of one of the young springtails and launched herself down the hall. Afriel followed her. The air was warm, and he was beginning to sweat under his elaborate clothing, but his antiseptic sweat was odorless.

They exited into a vast chamber dug from the living rock. It was arched and oblong, eighty meters long and about twenty in diameter. It swarmed with members of the Nest.

There were hundreds of them. Most of them were workers, eight-legged and furred, the size of Great Danes. Here and there were members of the warrior caste, horse-sized furry monsters with heavy fanged heads the size and shape of overstuffed chairs.

A few meters away, two workers were carrying a member of the sensor caste, a being whose immense flattened head was attached to an atrophied body that was mostly lungs. The sensor had great plate-like eyes, and its furred chitin sprouted long coiled antennae that twitched feebly as the workers bore it along. The workers clung to the hollowed rock of the chamber walls with hooked and suckered feet.

A paddle-limbed monster with a hairless, faceless head came sculling past them through the warm reeking air. The front of its head was a nightmare of sharp grinding jaws and blunt armored acid spouts. "A tunneler," Mirny said. "It can take us deeper into the Nest—come with me." She launched herself toward it and took a handhold on its furry, segmented back. Afriel followed her, joined by the two immature springtails, who clung to the thing's hide with their forelimbs. Afriel shuddered at the warm, greasy feel of its rank, damp fur. It continued to scull through the air, its eight fringed paddle feet catching the air like wings.

"There must be thousands of them," Afriel said.

"I said a hundred thousand in my last report, but that was before I had fully explored the Nest. Even now there are long stretches I haven't seen. They must number close to a quarter of a million. This asteroid is about the size of the Mechanists' biggest base—Ceres. It still has rich veins of carbonaceous material. It's far from mined out."

Afriel closed his eyes. If he was to lose his goggles, he would have to feel his way, blind, through these teeming, twitching, wriggling thousands. "The population's still expanding, then?"

"Definitely," she said. "In fact, the colony will launch a mating swarm soon. There are three dozen male and female alates in the chambers near the Queen. Once they're launched, they'll mate and start new Nests. I'll take you to see them presently." She hesitated. "We're entering one of the fungal gardens now."

One of the young springtails quietly shifted position. Grabbing the tunneler's fur with its forelimbs, it began to gnaw on the cuff of Afriel's pants. Afriel kicked it soundly, and it jerked back, retracting its eyestalks.

When he looked up again, he saw that they had entered a second chamber, much larger than the first. The walls around, overhead, and below were buried under an explosive profusion of fungus. The most common types were swollen barrel-like domes, multibranched massed thickets, and spaghetti-like tangled extrusions that moved very slightly in the faint and odorous breeze. Some of the barrels were surrounded by dim mists of exhaled spores.

"You see those caked-up piles beneath the fungus, its growth medium?" Mirny said.

"Yes."

"I'm not sure whether it is a plant form or just some kind of complex biochemical sludge," she said. "The point is that it grows in sunlight, on the outside of the asteroid. A food source that grows in naked space! Imagine what that would be worth, back in the Rings."

"There aren't words for its value," Afriel said.

"It's inedible by itself," she said. "I tried to eat a very small piece of it once. It was like trying to eat plastic."

"Have you eaten well, generally speaking?"

"Yes. Our biochemistry is quite similar to the Swarm's. The fungus itself is perfectly edible. The regurgitate is more nourishing, though. Internal fermentation in the worker hindgut adds to its nutritional value."

Afriel stared. "You grow used to it," Mirny said. "Later I'll teach you how to solicit food from the workers. It's a simple matter of reflex tapping—it's not controlled by pheromones, like most of their behavior." She brushed a long lock of clumped and dirty hair from the side of her face. "I hope the pheromonal samples I sent back were worth the cost of transportation."

"Oh, yes," said Afriel. "The chemistry of them was fascinating. We managed to synthesize most of the compounds. I was part of the research team myself." He hesitated. How far did he dare trust her? She had not been told about the experiment he and his superiors had planned. As far as Mirny knew, he was a simple, peaceful researcher, like herself. The Shapers' scientific community was suspicious of the minority involved in military work and espionage.

As an investment in the future, the Shapers had sent researchers to each of the nineteen alien races described to them by the Investors. This had cost the Shaper economy many gigawatts of precious energy and tons of rare metals and isotopes. In most cases, only two or three researchers could be sent; in seven cases, only one. For the Swarm, Galina Mirny had been chosen. She had gone peacefully, trusting in her intelligence and her good intentions to keep her alive and sane. Those who had sent her had not known whether her findings would be of any use or importance. They had only known that it was imperative that she be sent, even alone, even ill-equipped, before some other faction sent their own people and possibly discovered some technique or fact of overwhelming importance. And Dr Mirny had indeed discovered such a situation. It had made her mission into a matter of Ring security. That was why Afriel had come.

"You synthesized the compounds?" she said. "Why?"

Afriel smiled disarmingly. "Just to prove to ourselves that we could do it, perhaps."

She shook her head. "No mind-games, Dr Afriel, please. I came this far partly to escape from such things. Tell me the truth."

Afriel stared at her, regretting that the goggles meant he could not meet her eyes. "Very well," he said. "You should know, then, that I have been ordered by the Ring Council to carry out an experiment that may endanger both our lives."

SWARM

Mirny was silent for a moment. "You're from Security, then?"

"My rank is captain."

"I knew it... I knew it when those two Mechanists arrived. They were so polite, and so suspicious—I think they would have killed me at once if they hadn't hoped to bribe or torture some secret out of me. They scared the life out of me, Captain Afriel... You scare me, too."

"We live in a frightening world, Doctor. It's a matter of faction security."

"Everything's a matter of faction security with your lot," she said. "I shouldn't take you any farther, or show you anything more. This Nest, these creatures—they're not *intelligent,* Captain. They can't think, they can't learn. They're innocent, primordially innocent. They have no knowledge of good and evil. They have no knowledge of *anything.* The last thing they need is to become pawns in a power struggle within some other race, light-years away."

The tunneler had turned into an exit from the fungal chambers and was paddling slowly along in the warm darkness. A group of creatures like gray, flattened basketballs floated by from the opposite direction. One of them settled on Afriel's sleeve, clinging with frail whiplike tentacles. Afriel brushed it gently away, and it broke loose, emitting a stream of foul reddish droplets.

"Naturally I agree with you in principle, Doctor," Afriel said smoothly. "But consider these Mechanists. Some of their extreme factions are already more than half machine. Do you expect humanitarian motives from them? They're cold, Doctor—cold and soulless creatures who can cut a living man or woman to bits and never feel their pain. Most of the other factions hate us. They call us racist supermen. Would you rather that one of these cults do what we must do, and use the results against us?"

"This is double-talk." She looked away. All around them workers laden down with fungus, their jaws full and guts stuffed with it, were spreading out into the Nest, scuttling alongside them or disappearing into branch tunnels departing in every direction, including straight up and straight down. Afriel saw a creature much like a worker, but with only six legs, scuttle past in the opposite direction, overhead. It was a parasite mimic. How long, he wondered, did it take a creature to evolve to look like that?

"It's no wonder that we've had so many defectors, back in the Rings," she said sadly. "If humanity is so stupid as to work itself into a corner like you describe, then it's better to have nothing to do with them. Better to live alone. Better not to help the madness spread."

"That kind of talk will only get us killed," Afriel said. "We owe an allegiance to the faction that produced us."

"Tell me truly, Captain," she said. "Haven't you ever felt the urge to leave everything—everyone—all your duties and constraints, and just go somewhere to think it all out? Your whole world, and your part in it? We're trained so hard, from childhood, and so much is demanded from us. Don't you think it's made us lose sight of our goals, somehow?"

"We live in space," Afriel said flatly. "Space is an unnatural environment, and it takes an unnatural effort from unnatural people to prosper there. Our minds are our tools, and philosophy has to come second. Naturally I've felt those urges you mention. They're just another threat to guard against. I believe in an ordered society. Technology has unleashed tremendous forces that are ripping society apart. Some one faction must arise from the struggle and integrate things. We Shapers have the wisdom and restraint to do it humanely. That's why I do the work I do." He hesitated. "I don't expect to see our day of triumph. I expect to die in some brush-fire conflict, or through assassination. It's enough that I can foresee that day."

"But the arrogance of it, Captain!" she said suddenly. "The arrogance of your little life and its little sacrifice! Consider the Swarm, if you really want your humane and perfect order. Here it is! Where it's always warm and dark, and it smells good, and food is easy to get, and everything is endlessly and perfectly recycled. The only resources that are ever lost are the bodies of the mating swarms, and a little air. A Nest like this one could last unchanged for hundreds of thousands of years. Hundreds... of thousands... of years. Who, or what, will remember us and our stupid faction in even a thousand years?"

Afriel shook his head. "That's not a valid comparison. There is no such long view for us. In another thousand years we'll be machines, or gods." He felt the top of his head; his velvet cap was gone. No doubt something was eating it by now.

The tunneler took them deeper into the asteroid's honeycombed free-fall maze. They saw the pupal chambers, where pallid larvae twitched in swaddled silk; the main fungal gardens; the graveyard pits, where winged workers beat ceaselessly at the soupy air, feverishly hot from the heat of decomposition. Corrosive black fungus ate the bodies of the dead into coarse black powder, carried off by blackened workers themselves three-quarters dead.

Later they left the tunneler and floated on by themselves. The woman moved with the ease of long habit; Afriel followed her, colliding bruisingly with squeaking workers. There were thousands of them, clinging to ceiling, walls, and floor, clustering and scurrying at every conceivable angle.

Later still they visited the chamber of the winged princes and princesses, an echoing round vault where creatures forty meters long hung crooked-legged in midair. Their bodies were segmented and metallic, with organic rocket nozzles on their thoraxes, where wings might have been. Folded along their sleek backs were radar antennae on long sweeping booms. They looked more like interplanetary probes under construction than anything biological. Workers fed them ceaselessly. Their bulging spiracled abdomens were full of compressed oxygen.

Mirny begged a large chunk of fungus from a passing worker, deftly tapping its antennae and provoking a reflex action. She handed most of the fungus to the two springtails, which devoured it greedily and looked expectantly for more.

Afriel tucked his legs into a free-fall lotus position and began chewing with determination on the leathery fungus. It was tough, but tasted good, like smoked meat—a delicacy he had tasted only once. The smell of smoke meant disaster in a Shaper's colony.

Mirny maintained a stony silence.

"Food's no problem," Afriel said. "Where do we sleep?"

She shrugged. "Anywhere... there are unused niches and tunnels here and there. I suppose you'll want to see the Queen's chamber next."

"By all means."

"I'll have to get more fungus. The warriors are on guard there and have to be bribed with food."

She gathered an armful of fungus from another worker in the endless stream, and they moved on. Afriel, already totally lost, was further confused in the maze of chambers and tunnels. At last, they

exited into an immense lightless cavern, bright with infrared heat from the Queen's monstrous body. It was the colony's central factory. The fact that it was made of warm and pulpy flesh did not conceal its essentially industrial nature. Tons of predigested fungal pap went into the slick blind jaws at one end. The rounded billows of soft flesh digested and processed it, squirming, sucking, and undulating, with loud machinelike churnings and gurglings. Out of the other end came an endless conveyor-like blobbed stream of eggs, each one packed in a thick hormonal paste of lubrication. The workers avidly licked the eggs clean and bore them off to nurseries. Each egg was the size of a man's torso.

The process went on and on. There was no day or night here in the lightless center of the asteroid. There was no remnant of a diurnal rhythm in the genes of these creatures. The flow of production was as constant and even as the working of an automated mine.

"This is why I'm here," Afriel murmured in awe. "Just look at this, Doctor. The Mechanists have cybernetic mining machinery that is generations ahead of ours. But here—in the bowels of this nameless little world, is a genetic technology that feeds itself, maintains itself, runs itself, efficiently, endlessly, mindlessly. It's the perfect organic tool. The faction that could use these tireless workers could make itself an industrial titan. And our knowledge of biochemistry is unsurpassed. We Shapers are just the ones to do it."

"How do you propose to do that?" Mirny asked with open skepticism. "You would have to ship a fertilized queen all the way to the solar system. We could scarcely afford that, even if the Investors would let us, which they wouldn't."

"I don't need an entire Nest," Afriel said patiently. "I only need the genetic information from one egg. Our laboratories back in the Rings could clone endless numbers of workers."

"But the workers are useless without the Nest's pheromones. They need chemical cues to trigger their behavior modes."

"Exactly," Afriel said. "As it so happens, I possess those pheromones, synthesized and concentrated. What I must do now is test them. I must prove that I can use them to make the workers do what I choose. Once I've proven it's possible, I'm authorized to smuggle the genetic information necessary back to the Rings. The Investors won't approve. There are, of course, moral questions involved, and the Investors are not genetically advanced. But we can win their approval back with the profits we make. Best of all, we can beat the Mechanists at their own game."

"You've carried the pheromones here?" Mirny said. "Didn't the Investors suspect something when they found them?"

"Now it's you who has made an error," Afriel said calmly. "You assume that the Investors are infallible. You are wrong. A race without curiosity will never explore every possibility the way we Shapers did." Afriel pulled up his pants cuff and extended his right leg. "Consider this varicose vein along my shin. Circulatory problems of this sort are common among those who spend a lot of time in free-fall. This vein, however, has been blocked artificially and treated to reduce osmosis. Within the vein are ten separate colonies of genetically altered bacteria, each one specially bred to produce a different Swarm pheromone."

He smiled. "The Investors searched me very thoroughly, including X-rays. But the vein appears normal to X-rays, and the bacteria are trapped within compartments in the vein. They are indetectable. I have a small medical kit on my person. It includes a syringe. We can use it to extract the pheromones and test them. When the tests are finished — and I feel sure they will be successful, in fact I've staked my career on it — we can empty the vein and all its compartments. The bacteria will die on contact with air. We can refill the vein with the yolk from a developing embryo. The cells may survive during the trip back, but even if they die, they can't rot inside my body. They'll never come in contact with any agent of decay. Back in the Rings, we can learn to activate and suppress different genes to produce the different castes, just as is done in nature. We'll have millions of workers, armies of warriors if need be, perhaps even organic rocket-ships, grown from altered alates. If this works, who do you think will remember me then, eh? Me and my arrogant little life and little sacrifice?"

She stared at him; even the bulky goggles could not hide her new respect and even fear. "You really mean to do it, then."

"I made the sacrifice of my time and energy. I expect results, Doctor."

"But it's kidnapping. You're talking about breeding a slave race."

Afriel shrugged with contempt. "You're juggling words, Doctor. I'll cause this colony no harm. I may steal some of its workers' labor while they obey my own chemical orders, but that tiny theft won't be missed. I admit to the murder of one egg, but that is no more a crime than a human abortion. Can the theft of one strand of genetic material be called 'kidnapping'? I think not. As for the scandalous idea of a slave race—I reject it out of hand. These creatures are genetic robots. They will no more be slaves than are laser drills or cargo tankers. At the very worst, they will be our domestic animals."

Mirny considered the issue. It did not take her long. "It's true. It's not as if a common worker will be staring at the stars, pining for its freedom. They're just brainless neuters."

"Exactly, Doctor."

"They simply work. Whether they work for us or the Swarm makes no difference to them."

"I see that you've seized on the beauty of the idea."

"And if it worked," Mirny said, "if it worked, our faction would profit astronomically."

Afriel smiled genuinely, unaware of the chilling sarcasm of his expression. "And the personal profit, Doctor... the valuable expertise of the first to exploit the technique." He spoke gently, quietly. "Ever see a nitrogen snowfall on Titan? I think a habitat of one's own there—larger, much larger than anything possible before... A genuine city, Galina, a place where a man can scrap the rules and discipline that madden him... "

"Now it's you who are talking defection, Captain-Doctor."

Afriel was silent for a moment, then smiled with an effort. "Now you've ruined my perfect reverie," he said. "Besides, what I was describing was the well-earned retirement of a wealthy man, not some self-indulgent hermitage... there's a clear difference." He hesitated. "In any case, may I conclude that you're with me in this project?"

She laughed and touched his arm. There was something uncanny about the small sound of her laugh, drowned by a great organic rumble from the Queen's monstrous intestines... "Do you expect me to resist your arguments for two long years? Better that I give in now and save us friction."

"Yes."

"After all, you won't do any harm to the Nest. They'll never know anything has happened. And if their genetic line is successfully reproduced back home, there'll never be any reason for humanity to bother them again."

"True enough," said Afriel, though in the back of his mind he instantly thought of the fabulous wealth of Betelgeuse's asteroid system. A day would come, inevitably, when humanity would move to the stars en masse, in earnest. It would be well to know the ins and outs of every race that might become a rival.

"I'll help you as best I can," she said. There was a moment's silence. "Have you seen enough of this area?"

"Yes." They left the Queen's chamber.

"I didn't think I'd like you at first," she said candidly. "I think I like you better now. You seem to have a sense of humor that most Security people lack."

"It's not a sense of humor," Afriel said sadly. "It's a sense of irony disguised as one."

* * *

There were no days in the unending stream of hours that followed. There were only ragged periods of sleep, apart at first, later together, as they held each other in free-fall. The sexual feel of skin and body became an anchor to their common humanity, a divided, frayed humanity so many light-years away that the concept no longer had any meaning. Life in the warm and swarming tunnels was the here and now; the two of them were like germs in a bloodstream, moving ceaselessly with the pulsing ebb and flow. Hours stretched into months, and time itself grew meaningless.

The pheromonal tests were complex, but not impossibly difficult. The first of the ten pheromones was a simple grouping stimulus, causing large numbers of workers to gather as the chemical was spread from palp to palp. The workers then waited for further instructions; if none were forthcoming, they dispersed. To work effectively, the pheromones had to be given in a mix, or series, like computer commands;

number one, grouping, for instance, together with the third pheromone, a transferral order, which caused the workers to empty any given chamber and move its effects to another. The ninth pheromone had the best industrial possibilities; it was a building order, causing the workers to gather tunnelers and dredgers and set them to work. Others were annoying; the tenth pheromone provoked grooming behavior, and the workers' furry palps stripped off the remaining rags of Afriel's clothing. The eighth pheromone sent the workers off to harvest material on the asteroid's surface, and in their eagerness to observe its effects the two explorers were almost trapped and swept off into space.

The two of them no longer feared the warrior caste. They knew that a dose of the sixth pheromone would send them scurrying off to defend the eggs, just as it sent the workers to tend them. Mirny and Afriel took advantage of this and secured their own chambers, dug by chemically hijacked workers and defended by a hijacked airlock guardian. They had their own fungal gardens to refresh the air, stocked with the fungus they liked best, and digested by a worker they kept drugged for their own food use. From constant stuffing and lack of exercise the worker had swollen up into its replete form and hung from one wall like a monstrous grape.

Afriel was tired. He had been without sleep recently for a long time; how long, he didn't know. His body rhythms had not adjusted as well as Mirny's, and he was prone to fits of depression and irritability that he had to repress with an effort. "The Investors will be back sometime," he said. "Sometime soon."

Mirny was indifferent. "The Investors," she said, and followed the remark with something in the language of the springtails, which he didn't catch. Despite his linguistic training, Afriel had never caught up with her in her use of the springtails' grating jargon. His training was almost a liability; the springtail language had decayed so much that it was a pidgin tongue, without rules or regularity. He knew enough to give them simple orders, and with his partial control of the warriors he had the power to back it up. The springtails were afraid of him, and the two juveniles that Mirny had tamed had developed into fat, overgrown tyrants that freely terrorized their elders. Afriel had been too busy to seriously study the springtails or the other symbiotes. There were too many practical matters at hand.

"If they come too soon, I won't be able to finish my latest study," she said in English.

Afriel pulled off his infrared goggles and knotted them tightly around his neck. "There's a limit, Galina," he said, yawning. "You can only memorize so much data without equipment. We'll just have to wait quietly until we can get back. I hope the Investors aren't shocked when they see me. I lost a fortune with those clothes."

"It's been so dull since the mating swarm was launched. If it weren't for the new growth in the alates' chamber, I'd be bored to death." She pushed greasy hair from her face with both hands. "Are you going to sleep?"

"Yes, if I can."

"You won't come with me? I keep telling you that this new growth is important. I think it's a new caste. It's definitely not an alate. It has eyes like an alate, but it's clinging to the wall."

"It's probably not a Swarm member at all, then," he said tiredly, humoring her. "It's probably a parasite, an alate mimic. Go on and see it, if you want to. I'll be here waiting for you."

He heard her leave. Without his infrareds on, the darkness was still not quite total; there was a very faint luminosity from the steaming, growing fungus in the chamber beyond. The stuffed worker replete moved slightly on the wall, rustling and gurgling. He fell asleep.

When he awoke, Mirny had not yet returned. He was not alarmed. First, he visited the original airlock tunnel, where the Investors had first left him. It was irrational—the Investors always fulfilled their contracts—but he feared that they would arrive someday, become impatient, and leave without him. The Investors would have to wait, of course. Mirny could keep them occupied in the short time it would take him to hurry to the nursery and rob a developing egg of its living cells. It was best that the egg be as fresh as possible.

Later he ate. He was munching fungus in one of the anterior chambers when Mirny's two tamed springtails found him. "What do you want?" he asked in their language.

"Food-giver no good," the larger one screeched, waving its forelegs in brainless agitation. "Not work, not sleep."

"Not move," the second one said. It added hopefully, "Eat it now?"

Afriel gave them some of his food. They ate it, seemingly more out of habit than real appetite, which alarmed him. "Take me to her," he told them.

The two springtails scurried off; he followed them easily, adroitly dodging and weaving through the crowds of workers. They led him several miles through the network, to the alates' chamber. There they stopped, confused. "Gone," the large one said.

The chamber was empty. Afriel had never seen it empty before, and it was very unusual for the Swarm to waste so much space. He felt dread. "Follow the food-giver," he said. "Follow the smell."

The springtails snuffled without much enthusiasm along one wall; they knew he had no food and were reluctant to do anything without an immediate reward. At last one of them picked up the scent, or pretended to, and followed it up across the ceiling and into the mouth of a tunnel.

It was hard for Afriel to see much in the abandoned chamber; there was not enough infrared heat. He leapt upward after the springtail.

He heard the roar of a warrior and the springtail's choked-off screech. It came flying from the tunnel's mouth, a spray of clotted fluid bursting from its ruptured head. It tumbled end over end until it hit the far wall with a flaccid crunch. It was already dead.

The second springtail fled at once, screeching with grief and terror. Afriel landed on the lip of the tunnel, sinking into a crouch as his legs soaked up momentum. He could smell the acrid stench of the warrior's anger, a pheromone so thick that even a human could scent it. Dozens of other warriors would group here within minutes, or seconds. Behind the enraged warrior he could hear workers and tunnelers shifting and cementing rock.

He might be able to control one enraged warrior, but never two, or twenty. He launched himself from the chamber wall and out an exit.

He searched for the other springtail—he felt sure he could recognize it, since it was so much bigger than the others—but he could not find it. With its keen sense of smell, it could easily avoid him if it wanted to.

Mirny did not return. Uncountable hours passed. He slept again. He returned to the alates' chamber; there were warriors on guard there, warriors that were not interested in food and brandished their immense serrated fangs when he approached. They looked ready to rip him apart; the faint reek of aggressive pheromones hung about the place like a fog. He did not see any symbiotes of any kind on the warriors' bodies. There was one species, a thing like a huge tick, that clung only to warriors, but even the ticks were gone.

He returned to his chambers to wait and think. Mirny's body was not in the garbage pits. Of course, it was possible that something else might have eaten her. Should he extract the remaining pheromone from the spaces in his vein and try to break into the alates' chamber? He suspected that Mirny, or whatever was left of her, was somewhere in the tunnel where the springtail had been killed. He had never explored that tunnel himself. There were thousands of tunnels he had never explored.

He felt paralyzed by indecision and fear. If he was quiet, if he did nothing, the Investors might arrive at any moment. He could tell the Ring Council anything he wanted about Mirny's death; if he had the genetics with him, no one would quibble. He did not love her; he respected her, but not enough to give up his life, or his faction's investment. He had not thought of the Ring Council in a long time, and the thought sobered him. He would have to explain his decision …

He was still in a brown study when he heard a whoosh of air as his living airlock deflated itself. Three warriors had come for him. There was no reek of anger about them. They moved slowly and carefully. He knew better than to try to resist. One of them seized him gently in its massive jaws and carried him off.

It took him to the alates' chamber and into the guarded tunnel. A new, large chamber had been excavated at the end of the tunnel. It was filled almost to bursting by a black-splattered white mass of flesh. In the center of the soft speckled mass were a mouth and two damp, shining eyes, on stalks. Long tendrils like conduits dangled, writhing, from a clumped ridge above the eyes. The tendrils ended in pink, fleshy pluglike clumps.

One of the tendrils had been thrust through Mirny's skull. Her body hung in midair, limp as wax. Her eyes were open, but blind.

Another tendril was plugged into the braincase of a mutated worker. The worker still had the pallid tinge of a larva; it was shrunken

and deformed, and its mouth had the wrinkled look of a human mouth. There was a blob like a tongue in the mouth, and white ridges like human teeth. It had no eyes.

It spoke with Mirny's voice. "Captain-Doctor Afriel ... "

"Galina ... "

"I have no such name. You may address me as Swarm."

Afriel vomited. The central mass was an immense head. Its brain almost filled the room.

It waited politely until Afriel had finished.

"I find myself awakened again," Swarm said dreamily. "I am pleased to see that there is no major emergency to concern me. Instead it is a threat that has become almost routine." It hesitated delicately. Mirny's body moved slightly in midair; her breathing was inhumanly regular. The eyes opened and closed. "Another young race."

"What are you?"

"I am the Swarm. That is, I am one of its castes. I am a tool, an adaptation; my specialty is intelligence. I am not often needed. It is good to be needed again."

"Have you been here all along? Why didn't you greet us? We'd have dealt with you. We meant no harm."

The wet mouth on the end of the plug made laughing sounds. "Like yourself, I enjoy irony," it said. "It is a pretty trap you have found yourself in, Captain-Doctor. You meant to make the Swarm work for you and your race. You meant to breed us and study us and use us. It is an excellent plan, but one we hit upon long before your race evolved."

Stung by panic, Afriel's mind raced frantically. "You're an intelligent being," he said. "There's no reason to do us any harm. Let us talk together. We can help you."

"Yes," Swarm agreed. "You will be helpful. Your companion's memories tell me that this is one of those uncomfortable periods when galactic intelligence is rife. Intelligence is a great bother. It makes all kinds of trouble for us."

"What do you mean?"

"You are a young race and lay great stock by your own cleverness," Swarm said. "As usual, you fail to see that intelligence is not a survival trait."

SWARM

Afriel wiped sweat from his face. "We've done well," he said. "We came to you, and peacefully. You didn't come to us."

"I refer to exactly that," Swarm said urbanely. "This urge to expand, to explore, to develop, is just what will make you extinct. You naively suppose that you can continue to feed your curiosity indefinitely. It is an old story, pursued by countless races before you. Within a thousand years—perhaps a little longer—your species will vanish."

"You intend to destroy us, then? I warn you it will not be an easy task—"

"Again you miss the point. Knowledge is power! Do you suppose that fragile little form of yours—your primitive legs, your ludicrous arms and hands, your tiny, scarcely wrinkled brain—can *contain* all that power? Certainly not! Already your race is flying to pieces under the impact of your own expertise. The original human form is becoming obsolete. Your own genes have been altered, and you, Captain-Doctor, are a crude experiment. In a hundred years you will be a relic. In a thousand years you will not even be a memory. Your race will go the same way as a thousand others."

"And what way is that?"

"I do not know." The thing on the end of the Swarm's arm made a chuckling sound. "They have passed beyond my ken. They have all discovered something, learned something, that has caused them to transcend my understanding. It may be that they even transcend being. At any rate, I cannot sense their presence anywhere. They seem to do nothing, they seem to interfere in nothing; for all intents and purposes, they seem to be dead. Vanished. They may have become gods, or ghosts. In either case, I have no wish to join them."

"So then—so then you have—"

"Intelligence is very much a two-edged sword, Captain-Doctor. It is useful only up to a point. It interferes with the business of living. Life, and intelligence, do not mix very well. They are not at all closely related, as you childishly assume."

"But you, then—you are a rational being—"

"I am a tool, as I said." The mutated device on the end of its arm made a sighing noise. "When you began your pheromonal experiments, the chemical imbalance became apparent to the Queen. It triggered certain genetic patterns within her body, and I was reborn. Chemical sabotage is a problem that can best be dealt with by intelligence. I am a brain replete, you see, specially designed to be far more intelligent than any young race. Within three days I was fully self-conscious. Within five days I had deciphered these markings on my body. They are the genetically encoded history of my race … within five days and two hours I recognized the problem at hand and knew what to do. I am now doing it. I am six days old."

"What is it you intend to do?"

"Your race is a very vigorous one. I expect it to be here, competing with us, within five hundred years. Perhaps much sooner. It will be necessary to make a thorough study of such a rival. I invite you to join our community on a permanent basis."

"What do you mean?"

"I invite you to become a symbiote. I have here a male and a female, whose genes are altered and therefore without defects. You make a perfect breeding pair. It will save me a great deal of trouble with cloning."

"You think I'll betray my race and deliver a slave species into your hands?"

"Your choice is simple, Captain-Doctor. Remain an intelligent, living being, or become a mindless puppet, like your partner. I have taken over all the functions of her nervous system; I can do the same to you."

"I can kill myself."

"That might be troublesome, because it would make me resort to developing a cloning technology. Technology, though I am capable of it, is painful to me. I am a genetic artifact; there are fail-safes within me that prevent me from taking over the Nest for my own uses. That would mean falling into the same trap of progress as other intelligent races. For similar reasons, my life span is limited. I will live for only a thousand years, until your race's brief flurry of energy is over and peace resumes once more."

"Only a thousand years?" Afriel laughed bitterly. "What then? You kill off my descendants, I assume, having no further use for them."

"No. We have not killed any of the fifteen other races we have taken for defensive study. It has not been necessary. Consider that, small scavenger floating by your head, Captain-Doctor, that is feeding on your vomit. Five hundred million years ago its ancestors made the galaxy tremble. When they attacked us, we unleashed their own kind upon them. Of course, we altered our side, so that they were smarter, tougher, and, naturally, totally loyal to us. Our Nests were the only world they knew, and they fought with a valor and inventiveness we never could have matched … Should your race arrive to exploit us, we will naturally do the same."

"We humans are different."

"Of course."

"A thousand years here won't change us. You will die and our descendants will take over this Nest. We'll be running things, despite you, in a few generations. The darkness won't make any difference."

"Certainly not. You don't need eyes here. You don't need anything."

"You'll allow me to stay alive? To teach them anything I want?"

"Certainly, Captain-Doctor. We are doing you a favor, in all truth. In a thousand years your descendants here will be the only remnants of the human race. We are generous with our immortality; we will take it upon ourselves to preserve you."

"You're wrong, Swarm. You're wrong about intelligence, and you're wrong about everything else. Maybe other races would crumble into parasitism, but we humans are different."

"Certainly. You'll do it, then?"

"Yes. I accept your challenge. And I will defeat you."

"Splendid. When the Investors return here, the springtails will say that they have killed you, and will tell them to never return. They will not return. The humans should be the next to arrive."

"If I don't defeat you, they will."

"Perhaps." Again it sighed. "I'm glad I don't have to absorb you. I would have missed your conversation."

MASON'S RATS

Neal Asher

The cartridges, with their environmentally friendly titanium shot, thunked into the shotgun with satisfying precision. Mason snapped it shut, and with pursed lips viewed his sprawling farmyard. Where to start? Where would the killer stray be hiding? He hooked the shotgun under his arm and headed for the huge, enclosed barns where grain handlers could still be heard at work. There would be the place, but he knew he would have to be careful where he fired. Microcircuitry was robust, but not that robust, as he had discovered after blasting one of Smith's cybernetic rat traps, mistaking it for a rabbit. It had run home squealing and dropping chips like little black turds. He smiled to himself at the memory then came suddenly to a stop, his smile fading. Perhaps that was it. Perhaps Smith had reprogrammed one of his traps to hunt cats, for revenge.

Mason's suspicions had only been aroused when General had disappeared. The disappearance of the other two cats had been put down to other things. They could have found another home with a more ready food supply. He did not believe in giving them all they would want even though it was tax-deductible. He called it motivation. They were working cats after all. Another possibility that crossed his mind was that they had not been quick enough when the combine harvester had come round, and that he would find their remains when he came to do the bailing. But not the General; that raggedy-eared moggy had been around for six years and knew the dangers. He also managed to grow fat on a steady diet of rats. Others might have thought the culprit a fox, but foxes don't attack cats. Cats, after all, have more natural armament than foxes. No, the greatest killer of cats is other cats. Mason shook his head and continued on to the barns.

The doors to G1 slid back only halfway then jammed. Mason was not surprised. He had not used them in two years. The lights worked

all right though, and he could easily see into the dusty interior. Before him was a mountain of alpha-wheat. He reached down and grabbed up a handful, gazed with satisfaction at the pea-sized grains, then tossed it to the floor as a handler came whirring past him. He frowned as he watched the bulky device. The handlers were the one inefficiency in the circuit. The grain went from the harvesters to the barns, then, by handlers, from the barns up the ramps to the silos. Mason would have liked one of the new harvesters with its fans that could blow the grain directly up fifty feet of ducting into the silos, but he did not have fifty million Euros to spare. Still with a sour expression, he again gazed up at the pile of wheat grain. It was then that he saw the grey shape crouching on top of it, regarding him with glittery, avid, eyes.

Mason raised his shotgun, deciding on the instant that this was the stray. The creature turned to flee, and Mason hesitated as he realised that it was not a cat at all, but a huge rat. He lowered his gun as it scampered down the other side of the pile, a sweat breaking out all over him. No wonder the General had gone missing. He took out his handkerchief and wiped his face, then cautiously moved in. No way did he want to come suddenly upon a rat that size.

On the other side of the pile there was no rat. Fifty yards in front of him were the doors to G2. He trotted over to them and hit the opening button. The doors slid aside, and a wedge of light was thrown into the darkness. The rat was there, it froze; pinned by light. Mason raised his gun to fire and saw that the rat had something round its middle. It looked almost like a tool belt. The shotgun kicked and the rat shot into the air with a shriek and spattering of blood, then it hit the ground convulsing. Mason stepped aside and turned on all the lights. He scanned around as other large shapes fled amongst the grain piles, but he did not shoot at them. Right then he had only one cartridge left in his gun and a couple in his pocket, and did not feel altogether safe. He approached the dead rat.

Somehow the creature had managed to wrap a piece of canvas webbing around itself. At least this is what Mason told himself at first. But as he came to stand over it, he realised that this was not a good enough explanation. The rat was wearing a tool belt, and hanging from it were tools fashioned from bone, wood, and old nails.

MASON'S RATS

Mason reached down and hauled up the huge rat by its tail, then glanced around as he heard more movement. Raising his gun, he backed out of G2, dragging the rat carcass with him. As he reached the door, he detected movement and looked up. Crouched on one of the grain piles was another rat. There came a snapping sound, and something cracked against the door beam and clattered to the floor. Mason peered down at the small crossbow bolt, swore, then got out of the barn as fast as he could.

* * *

"Now Mr Mason, there's no need to upset yourself. Traptech can sort out your little problem."

Patronising git, thought Mason, staring down at the deep-frozen rat corpse he had dumped on the table. Smith had recommended this man but Mason did not like him. The suit was the first thing that annoyed him. Mason had an aversion to anyone wearing a suit. He reckoned it was a certainty that this bloke had a pair of green wellies in the boot of his company car.

He looked up. "Upset myself? Little problem? I've got armed rats in my barns, and you call it a little problem?"

"Yes, sir. Perhaps I am wrong to call it a little problem, but it is a problem we at Traptech are used to handling."

Mason could not believe he was having this discussion. The last he had heard about tool-using ability in the animal kingdom had been from a program about apes, who managed to break open nuts with rocks. "Tell me again where they come from."

"As I said, man has become the greatest force of evolution. We are forcing intelligence on the animal kingdom. It is–"

Mason raised his hand before the Traptech rep could move into full bullshit mode. "Okay. What have you got for me?"

The suit smiled like a shark and pulled a thick catalogue from his briefcase. Mason felt a sinking feeling in the pit of his stomach – one he normally associated with the sight of little brown envelopes with windows in them. The suit opened the catalogue on the table next to the thawing rat and showed Mason a picture of something that looked like a security camera.

"This is the TT6, which we introduced only last year. It is a guided pulse laser with dual heat and movement sensors. Four of these in each of your two barns should solve your problem. Smith was most satisfied with them."

"How much?" asked Mason tiredly, then frowned at the answer. The new harvester retreated even further into the future.

* * *

The men from Traptech installed the TT6s in a day. Mason noted that they wore helmets, visors and overalls with micromesh ring mail stitched in, and that one of them stood guard with a pump-action shotgun. The rats remained hidden though. From the TT6s, the men ran an armoured cable into his house to the farm computer. When all the work was completed, the suit arrived to demonstrate the system.

"This is the control package," said the suit after loading two discs and plugging the cable into the computer's unused security circuit. "Now you can call up diagnostics on each TT6, find out if there have been any hits, and even get a view through each unit."

The computer screen flickered on and showed: HIT ON TT6 G1/3.

"Ah, marvellous," said the suit, and demonstrated how the view could be called up on that unit. The screen flickered again and showed the greenish infrared view of the inside of G1. Lying before one of the grain piles, smoke wisping from the laser punctures in its body, lay Mason's remaining cat.

"Ah. ... It would be advisable to keep other animals out of the barns. The sensors are set to pick up on animals within certain size parameters. Obviously, they will miss humans but–"

"I will expect some sort of reduction for this," interrupted Mason, his teeth clenched.

* * *

On the first day the diagnostic program reported a malfunction and Mason could get no picture through that particular unit. It never occurred to him to be surprised. With his shotgun hooked under his arm he went to G1. On the floor before the TT6 one of the rats lay in a smoking heap. The TT6 was smoking as well though, two crossbow bolts impaling it. In the night two more were scrapped. In the morning Mason called up the suit.

"Ah," said the suit, inspecting the crossbow bolt shortly after he arrived, "this sometimes happens. Your best move now would be to get a mobile defence." He opened up the dread catalogue and pointed out something that looked like a foot-long chrome scorpion. "This is the TT15."

"Those TT6s are still under guarantee."

"I can give you a very reasonable exchange price with service contract and deferred payment, and though they are expensive, you will only need one TT15."

The TT15 arrived the next day. Just taking it out of its box gave Mason the creeps. After turning off the TT6s he took it into the barns, and turned it on. Immediately it scuttled into the shadows. Mason found himself fearing it more than he feared the rats, and he quickly went outside. Its homing beacon he placed by the compost heap. After half an hour the TT15 came out with a dead rat in it mandibles and dumped it by the beacon. Next to the tractor on which he was working, Mason shuddered and turned back to his task. Later, as he sat on one of the tractor's tyres and rolled himself a cigarette, he saw three rats run out of G1 with the chrome scorpion in pursuit.

He found himself hoping the rats would escape but before they reached the polythene-wrapped straw bales, it had the slowest of them, caught it, crunched it, then like some horrible gun dog took it to the compost heap. However unpleasant the thing might look, Mason decided, it was damned efficient.

* * *

The men from Traptech came the following day to take down the TT6s. When they had finished, their foreman came to see Mason.

"Says here you had eight TT6s, mate."

"That's right. The rats scrapped four of them though."

"We know about that. We've got those four. Just that one of the good one's gone missin'. I'll have to report it, mate."

* * *

For the rest of the day, while he baled straw in the fields, Mason wondered confusedly where the missing TT6 could have gone. By evening he had figured it out and in a strange way was quite glad. As soon as he got back to the farmyard, he fetched his shotgun and went with it into the barns.

It had been one hell of a fight in G1. The rats had swivel-mounted the TT6, using a couple of old bearings and a universal joint, on one of the grain handlers, and powered it from the handler's battery. Mason was impressed but realised the rats had not taken into account the reflective surface of the TT15. They had obviously fired the laser many times, enough to have drained the handler's battery, but the TT15, though damaged, had not been immobilised. A battle with crossbow bolts and hand weapons had then ensued. The floor was littered with dead and dismembered rats, weapons, and silvery pieces of the TT15. Finally, the rats had managed to shut the doors into G2 on it, trapping it, and there it remained, its motor whining periodically.

Mason walked over to the doors, opened them then hit the lights for G2. The TT15 scuttled on into the barn, immediately zeroing in on movement at the further edge of the floor. Mason gazed across and saw a group of rats. Many of them were injured. Many of them were applying dressings and tying on splints. They all looked up at him, glittery eyed. He raised his shotgun and saw what could only be described as a look of fatalism come onto their ratty faces. He fired both barrels of the shotgun and blew the TT15 to scrap.

As he turned and left the barn shortly after, on his way to cancel the cheque he had sent to Traptech, Mason felt extremely pleased with himself, in fact, the happiest he had felt in days. The kind of rats he really hated wore suits and cost a damned sight more than a few handfuls of alpha-wheat.

IN VAULTED HALLS ENTOMBED

Alan Baxter

The high, dim caves continued on into blackness.

Sergeant Coulthard paused, shook his heavy, grizzled head. "We're going to lose comms soon. Have you mapped this far?" he asked Dillman.

"Yes, Sarge."

Coulthard looked back the way they had come, where daylight still leaked through to weakly illuminate the squad. "Radio it in, Spencer. See what they say."

"Yes, Sarge." Corporal Spencer shucked his pack and set an antenna, pointing back towards the cave entrance. "Base, this is Team Epsilon. Base, Team Epsilon."

The radio crackled and hissed, then, "Go ahead, Epsilon."

"We've followed the insurgents across open ground to foothills about eighty clicks north-north-east of Kandahar, to a cave system at... Hang on." Spencer pulled out a map and read aloud a set of co-ordinates. "They've gone to ground, about eighty minutes ahead of us. We'll lose comms if we head deeper in. Orders?"

"Stand by."

The radio crackled again.

"They'll tell us to go in," Sergeant Coulthard said.

Lance Corporal Paul Brown watched from one side, nerves tickling the back of his neck. They were working by the book, but this showed every sign of a trap, perfect for an ambush. It would be dark soon, and was already cold. It would only get colder. Though perhaps the temperature farther in remained pretty constant.

He stepped forward. "Sarge, maybe we should set camp here and wait 'til morning."

"Always night in a fucking cave, Brown," Coulthard said without looking at him.

"You tired, possum?" Private Sam Gladstone asked with a sneer.

The new boy, Beaumont, grinned.

"You always a dick?" Brown said.

"Can it!" Coulthard barked. "We wait for orders."

"I just think everyone's tired," Brown said. He shifted one shoulder to flash the red cross on the side of his pack. "Your welfare is my job after all."

"Noted," Coulthard said.

Silence descended on the six of them. They'd followed this band of extremists for three days, picking up and losing their trail half a dozen times. He was tired even if the others were too hardass to admit it. Young Beaumont was like a puppy, on his first tour and desperate for a fight, but the others should know better. They'd all seen action to some degree. Coulthard more than most; the kind of guy who seemed like he'd been born in the middle of a firefight and come out carrying a weapon.

"Epsilon, this is Base. You're sure this is where the insurgents went?"

"Affirmative. Dillman had them on long range scope. Trying to shake us off, I guess, going to ground."

"Received. Proceed on your own initiative. Take 'em if you can. They've got a lot of our blood on their hands. Can you confirm their numbers?"

"Eight of them, Base."

"Received. Good luck."

Spencer winked at the squad. "Received, Base. Over and out." He unhooked his antenna and slung his pack.

"Okay, then," Dillman said. He shifted grip on his rifle and dug around in his webbing, came up with a night sight and fitted it.

Brown sighed. No one was as good a shot as Dillman, even when he was tired and in the dark. But it didn't give much comfort. "We're not going to wait, are we?" he said.

Coulthard ignored him. "Pick it up, children. As there are no tracks in here," he kicked at the hard stone floor, "we move slow and silent. Spencer, you're mapping. I want markers deployed along the way."

"Sarge."

"Let's go. Beaumont, you're on point."

"Yes, Sarge!"

"Slow and steady, Beaumont. And lower that weapon. No firing until I say so unless you're fired on first."

"Yes, Sarge."

The kid sounded a little deflated and Brown was glad. Youth needed deflating. They fell into order and moved forward. Spencer placed an electronic marker and tapped the tablet he carried. It began to ping a location to help them find their way back.

It became cooler, the darkness almost absolute. The light that leaked through from outside couldn't reach and blackness wrapped them up like an over-zealous lover.

"Night vision will be useless down here," Coulthard said. "We're going to have to risk torchlight. One beam, from point. Dillman, go infrared."

"Way ahead of you," Dillman said, and tapped his goggles. He moved up to stand almost beside Beaumont.

The young private clicked on his helmet lamp and light swept the space as he looked around. The passage was about five metres in an irregular diameter and as dry and cold as everything else they'd seen over the last few days. Dust motes danced in the torch beam, the scuff and crunch of their boots strangely loud in the confined space.

"All quiet from here on," Coulthard said and waved Beaumont forward.

They fell into practised unison; moved with determined caution.

"I'm a glowing target up here," Beaumont whispered nervously.

"That's why the new boy takes point," Coulthard said. A soft wave of giggles passed through the squad before the sergeant hushed them.

Dillman patted Beaumont on one shoulder. "I got your back, Donkey."

Beaumont's torch beam shot back into the group as he looked around. "Don't call me that!"

Laughter rippled again. Brown grinned. Poor sap. Caught petting a donkey back in Kandahar, just a lonely kid far from home taking some comfort by hugging the soft, furry creature's neck. Of course, he'd been spotted, photographed and by the time he got back to barracks the story had him balls deep in the poor animal.

"Enough!" Coulthard snapped. "Are we fucking professionals or not?"

Their mirth stilled and they crept forward again. The ground sloped downwards and Spencer paused every fifty yards or so to place a marker. After about three hundred yards the passage opened out into a wider cavern. Something lay rucked up and definitely man-made on the far side.

Weapons instantly trained on it and Beaumont moved cautiously forward. "False alarm," he called back after a moment, his voice relaxed and light. Relieved. "Someone's been here, there are blankets, signs of a fire, an empty canteen. But it looks months old, at least."

The squad relaxed slightly as Beaumont shone his torch in a wide arc, illuminating the cave. Nothing but rough, curved rock. A few small fissures striated the walls on one side, black gaps into the unknown, but nothing big enough for even a child to get through. On the far side, a larger gap yawned darkly, a tunnel leading away and down. Large rocks lay scattered around the opening.

Coulthard nodded the squad forward.

"Looks like these have recently been moved," Gladstone said.

Brown moved in to see better. "Looks like this passage was blocked up and those fuckers cleared the way."

Dillman kicked at a couple of broken stones. "I guess they weren't so keen to ambush us here and are looking for a better option."

Brown shook his head. "Why would this passage have been blocked? And by who?"

"Emergency bolt hole they knew about?" Coulthard mused. "Move on."

The tunnel beyond was around three metres in diameter, sloping down again. Beaumont's was the only light, but in the otherwise total blackness it made the tunnel bright. Shadows flickered off the irregular surface.

Beaumont took his flashlight from his helmet and held it at arm's length to one side. "If they do ambush and shoot at the light..."

After a couple of hundred metres, Brown, bringing up the rear, paused and looked back. "Hold up," he said quietly.

Coulthard glanced over his shoulder. "What's up, Doc?"

"Kill the light, Beaumont."

"Gladly!"

There was a soft click and the tunnel sank into blackness. Within seconds, their eyes began to adjust to something other than the dark. In crevices on the walls and ceiling of the passage, even here and there on the floor, a soft blue glow emanated. Almost imperceptible, easier to see from their peripheral vision, a pale luminescence. No, Brown thought. Phosphorescence. He crouched and looked closely into one crack. He pulled out a pocketknife, flicked open the blade and dug inside the crevice. The blade came out with a sickly blue smudge on it.

"Some kind of lichen," he said. "I've heard of this kind of stuff, but always thought it was green."

Gladstone pulled his googles down and flicked the adjustment. "Doesn't matter what colour it is, it's giving enough light for night vision."

"Lucky us," Coulthard said. "Goggles on, people. Keep that light off, Beaumont."

"Thank fuck, Sarge."

Brown pulled his own goggles down and watched the squad move forward in green monochrome. He was glad they didn't need harsh torchlight anymore, but the glowing blue lichen gave him the creeps. He stood and followed before they got too far ahead, shifting his heavy medical pack as he moved.

They continued silently for several minutes, Spencer periodically dropping markers. At a fork they tried the left-hand path and quickly met a dead end. Backtracking to the main passage, they travelled further and found a small cave off to one side, too low to stand upright. No passages led from it.

"Looks like this one tunnel is gonna keep heading down," Beaumont said. His voice had lost some of its excitement.

Coulthard raised a fist bringing them to a halt. "How far?"

Spencer checked the tablet that shone in their night vision even though its brightness was down to minimum. "Seven hundred and eighty-three metres."

"Three quarters of a k in, really?" Dillman whispered.

He sounded as nervous as Brown felt. The strange lichen contin-ued, scattered randomly in cracks and fissures. Occasionally, a larger

patch would glow like a bright light but for the most part, it was soft streaks like veins in the rocks.

"Move on," Coulthard said.

After another couple of minutes, Spencer whispered, "That's one kilometre."

Before any discussion could be had about that fact, Beaumont hissed and cursed. "Sarge, got something here."

The squad sank into fighting readiness and crept apart to cover the width of the tunnel.

"Bones," Beaumont said. "Just a skeleton."

Coulthard turned. "Doc, go check."

Brown went to Beaumont and looked down on the bones lying at the curve of the tunnel wall. Streaks of the blue lichen wrapped the skeleton here and there, like snail trails. He crouched for a closer look. "Male, adult. No discerning marks of trauma that I can see at first glance."

He took a penlight torch from his pocket and lifted his goggles. "Mind your eyes."

The squad looked away as he clicked on the light and had a closer look. The bones lay scattered, no flesh or connecting tissue remained to hold them together. "There's a kind of residue," Brown said quietly. "Like a gel or something." He took a pen from his pocket and dragged the tip along one femur. It gathered a small wave of clear, viscous ichor. It was odourless.

He put one index finger to the same bone and gently touched the stuff. It seemed inert. As he brought it close to his face to inspect, he frowned, then pressed his finger to the bone again. "This is warm."

Tension tightened the squad behind him.

"What's that?" Coulthard asked.

Brown swallowed, heart hammering. He looked at his fingertip then gripped the bone, felt the heat in his palm. "This skeleton is warm. And too clean to have rotted here."

"What the hell?" Beaumont demanded, his voice quavering.

"You shitting us?" Gladstone asked. His voice was stronger than Beaumont's but with fear still evident.

Brown held one palm over the skeleton, only an inch or so away from touching, moved it back and forth. "It's warm all over," he said weakly. His mind tried to process the information but kept hitting dead ends. The cold rock under his knee seemed to mock him.

"Warm?" Coulthard asked.

Brown's heart skipped and doubled-timed again as he spotted something beneath the bony corpse. "Hey, Dillman."

"What?"

"When you scoped those fucks we were following, what did you see that you thought was funny?"

A tense silence filled the space for a moment. Then Dillman said, "One of them had a big fucking gold dollar sign on a chain around his neck. Fancied himself a rapper or some shit."

Brown used his pocketknife to hook up a chain from where it hung inside the stark white ribcage. With a toothy clicking, he hauled it up link by link. Eventually a metal dollar sign emerged from between the bones, its surface no longer gold but a tarnished, blackened alloy.

"What the actual fuck?" Beaumont asked in a high voice. He shifted from foot to foot, looked wildly around himself.

"These bones are too clean and white to have decayed to this state," Brown said. He shone his penlight among the bones to show coins, a cigarette lighter, the half-melted remains of a cell phone, belt buckles. Two automatic pistols, both with traces of the gel-like slime, were wedged under the pelvis.

Coulthard stepped forward, leaned down to stare at the corpse like it was a personal insult. "You trying to tell me this is one of the guys we're chasing?"

Brown shrugged, hefted the pen to make the dollar sign swing.

"Fuck this," Spencer said. "What the hell can do that to a person?"

Brown shook his head. "Who knows?" He played his torchlight around the walls and ceiling of the tunnel.

"And where did it go?" Gladstone asked weakly.

"Go?" Coulthard asked.

"I think it's pretty clear someone or something did that to him and is no longer here, right?" Gladstone said.

"Some kind of weapon?" Beaumont asked, still agitated.

"What kind of weapon does this?" Brown countered.

Coulthard stood up straight. "Can it, all of you. We have a mission and we'll keep to it. We'll find answers on the way."

"It's still warm," Brown reminded him. "This happened very recently, I think."

"Then we move extra fucking carefully," Coulthard said.

A burst of gunfire and distant shouting echoed up the tunnel. Epsilon squad froze and listened. A scream, another burst of gunfire then a deep, concussive boom.

"Grenade?" Dillman asked quietly.

Silence descended again.

"Lights off, mouths shut," Coulthard said. "Brown, up front with me in case we come across any more bodies. Beaumont, rear guard. Move out."

Brown nodded as he pocketed his knife. He wasn't happy about it, but that was a smart move by the sergeant. Beaumont had sounded very spooked by this encounter and understandably so. His nerves were like an electric current through the squad. Best he go to the back and have a chance to calm down. Reluctantly, the squad fell into place. Brown glanced once more at the skeleton on the tunnel floor and shivered as they moved almost silently away.

They travelled in silence for another ten minutes before Spencer whispered, "Two clicks."

A distant scream rang out, cut off equally fast. Several bursts of gunfire. They froze and listened, but heard nothing more.

"Move on," Coulthard said tightly.

"Are you sure, Sarge?" Brown asked, but the sergeant's only answer was a shove in the back.

Several minutes later, Spencer said, "Three clicks."

Brown pointed, and Coulthard nodded. Two more skeletons lay on the tunnel floor. Brown crouched and felt the warmth rising off them, stark against the cold rock all around. Two AK-47s and a variety of other metallic objects littered the ground.

"What the fuck, man?" Beaumont said, his voice still high and stretched. "What can do that?"

"Should we go back?" Brown asked.

"There's still five more of them somewhere ahead," Coulthard said. "And whatever is doing this is ahead as well. We'll go a bit further."

"We gotta go, Sarge!" Beaumont said. "Seriously, how can we fight this fucking—"

"Pull it together, soldier!" Coulthard barked. "Get your shit in order. We go forward for another little while and see. This tunnel has to change at some point, branch off or open out or something. I want to see what happens. If nothing happens by five kays in, we turn around."

"Five kays?" Beaumont sounded like a child. "Fuck man, five kays?"

"Move out," Coulthard said softly, his voice and demeanour a perfect example of calm.

Brown wondered if the sergeant felt anything like as calm as he acted. It seemed Beaumont was the one having a far more sensible reaction to all this. Brown bit his teeth together to stem his own trembling and walked on.

The way was still lit by the strange veins of lichen, the tunnel remained a three metre or so diameter throat down into the foothills of the mountain range beyond. They heard nothing more for several minutes.

"Stay alert," Coulthard said. "How you doing, Donkey? Feeling okay?"

Beaumont didn't answer.

The sergeant laughed softly. "Sorry, Josh, I'm only ragging ya. Seriously, you feeling okay? You were a little rattled back there."

No answer.

Sam Gladstone said, "There's no one behind me, Sarge."

"What?"

"He was bringing up the rear, but he's not there."

Coulthard spat a curse. "Beaumont!" he called out in a harsh whisper. "Fuck, surely he hasn't panicked and run back."

"Wouldn't I have heard, Sarge?" Gladstone asked.

"I don't know. Would you? Spencer, leave your tablet here and double time back up the tunnel. If you don't catch up to him in a few hundred yards, we'll have to let him go and I'll kick his fucking ass when we get back."

"Righto, Sarge."

Spencer put down his gear and jogged away. They stood in uncomfortable silence for a few minutes.

"Nervous kid," Brown said eventually. "First tour."

"Don't make excuses for him," Coulthard said. "He's a fucking soldier."

Spencer walked back towards them, holding something out. "We need to get the fuck out of here," he said. Hanging from his fingers was a chain with two dog tags.

"The fuck?" Dillman whispered.

"Beaumont's?" Coulthard asked in a tight voice.

"He's a fucking skeleton just like the insurgent fuckers we found. Nothing left but buckles and weapons and shit. He's just fucking bones, Sarge!"

Dillman began muttering and shone his helmet lamp frantically in every direction. The mood of the squad began to fracture.

Coulthard swatted Dillman's lamp off. "Stow that shit! Everyone stay calm."

"Calm, Sarge?" Gladstone asked. "Seriously, we're in deep shit here."

"Stay. Calm. Spencer, did you recover Beaumont's weapon."

Spencer shook his head. "Left it there. The strap is gone, too hard to carry. But I took his clips."

"Fair enough. Now, we need to reassess what we're doing here."

"I think we should leave, Sarge," Brown said. He tried to keep his voice calm but heard and felt the quaver in it.

"It ain't that simple."

"It must be," Dillman said. "Fuck those guys, if they're even still alive down there. Whatever got Beaumont can get them. We'll wait outside the caves and pick off any who come out."

Coulthard held up a hand, a pale green wave in their night vision goggles. "Chill, everyone. It ain't as simple as leaving. I'm with you. In any other circumstances I would absolutely call an abort. But whatever took Beaumont, it took him from the back."

"Which means it's behind us," Brown said, realisation like an icy wave through his gut. "Or there's more than one, ahead and behind."

"Exactly."

"Does that mean we should carry on though?" Gladstone asked. "Maybe it's only gonna get worse."

"Maybe. Or maybe there's another way out." Coulthard picked

up Spencer's tablet, checked the display. "We've still got a bunch of sensors, yeah?"

Spencer dropped Beaumont's tags into a pocket. "Yeah, plenty."

"Okay. We carry on for another kilometre and see if it leads to any branches in the tunnel, any other way out. If it does, we can maybe go around whatever's in here. If not, we turn around and risk facing it. Spencer, it's unlikely but do we have any signal down here?"

The corporal pulled out his gear and spent a moment trying to get a response from Base. Then he went wide band, looking for any transmissions. He found none and no one responded to open hails. "Nothing, Sarge."

"I didn't think so. Okay, Brown, you stay in the middle. Me and Spencer will take point. I want Gladstone and Dillman on rear guard, but you two walk backwards. We move slow and you don't take your eyes off the tunnel behind us. Let's go."

They moved slowly on again. Brown felt more than a little useless in the middle of the group, but he knew what Coulthard was doing. Protect the guy with the best chance of helping any wounded. Except it looked like whatever was in these caves didn't leave any wounded. He heard a gasp from Gladstone and turned to look.

"See that?" Gladstone whispered to Dillman.

"Yeah. There!"

Brown saw it too. He lifted his goggles to see with unfiltered eyes. A movement, more a shift of light across the darkness, like a ripple of wan blue luminescence. He caught part of a smooth, glassy sphere, a glimpse of something globular, but it pressed into the wall and vanished.

The others had stopped to watch. All five of them stared hard, but the tunnel was black as death, and still.

"Keep moving," Coulthard said.

Brown walked backwards as well, eyes trying to scan every inch of the tunnel behind them.

"There!" Gladstone said sharply.

He'd seen it too. A glassy flex of movement on the ceiling about thirty metres back. Closer than before. Almost as if a giant water droplet had begun to swell and hang, only to be quickly sucked back up.

"It's fucking following us," Dillman hissed and snapped on his helmet light again.

"But what is it?" Spencer demanded. "Is it even alive? Doc?"

Brown jumped as he was directly addressed. "I'm no expert here," he said. "Whatever it is…"

His words were drowned out by Gladstone's screams and Dillman's shouts of fright as the torchlight reflected back off a huge slithering mass across the ceiling right above them. It ran and undulated like an upside-down river across the rock then expanded, long and pendulous, extruding from the tunnel roof like a clear jelly waterfall. The huge, gelatinous blob unfurled itself and dropped.

Dillman leapt to one side, the deafening bark and muzzle flash of his weapon filling the tunnel as Gladstone tried to run backwards but skidded and fell. He knocked Brown back, who dropped onto his rump in surprise and scrambled away, scrabbling for his weapon as Coulthard and Spencer aimed theirs above his head and let rip.

Gladstone's screams were bloodcurdling as the thing landed across his legs. Brown tried to see through the bursts of muzzle fire and caught staccato images like through a strobe light. Gladstone's legs, clothing and flesh alike, melted away inside the transparent blob in an instant, leaving only bones. He tried to batter it off with his hands only to raise fleshless, stark white fingerbones in horror that fell and scattered across his lap. The meat of his arms was gone to his elbows in a second. Tenticular appendages lashed forward from the globular mass and retracted like a frantic sea anemone as it filled the tunnel with its bulk. Hails of bullets from Dillman, Spencer and Coulthard slapped and sputtered into the thing with little effect. It seemed to flinch and flex away from the bullets, then surge forward again, relentless. Only Dillman's torch beam seemed to really hold it up. Gladstone's screams cut abruptly short as it reached his torso and then Brown was up and running.

He pounded down the tunnel and realised the others were with him. At least, Spencer and Coulthard were. They panted as they ran, intent only on putting distance between themselves and that foetid horror. He didn't dare look back for fear the thing was bulging along behind them, for fear he'd see Gladstone finished off or Dillman caught.

IN VAULTED HALLS ENTOMBED

He stumbled and nearly fell sprawling at one point as the tunnel floor became broken rock and one wall half-fallen, almost blocking the way. The result of the grenade they had heard earlier. Bones scattered as he kicked unwittingly through another skeleton.

A brighter glow began to fill the tunnel ahead and he pounded for it, heedless to any danger before them compared to the certain death behind.

They burst out into a dizzyingly huge cavern, skidding to a halt on a rock ledge that protruded into space hundreds of metres above the cave floor. The ceiling was lost in swirling mists far above, but a soft blue glow leaked through. The walls of the gigantic space were streaked with the strange lichen and the entire place swam in a surreal glow, almost like wan daylight leaking through tropical waters, incongruous several kilometres underground. Filling the floor and rising high into the wisps of mist was a structure clearly constructed by intelligent design – a huge spiralling tower, hundreds of metres high, with a base at least a kilometre across. Curving buttresses met smaller towers in a circle around it. Monumental, the organic-looking structure appeared to have been painstakingly carved from the rock itself. From their ledge, a mammoth stairway led down to the building's lowest levels and the cave floor. Each stair was around two-metres high and a similar width; hundreds of the giant steps leading down into haze. The air was colder and damp, smelled metallic and ancient. Everything about the sight emanated age beyond any span of history. Geological age.

"Fuck me," Spencer said, lifting his goggles. His voice held the taint of madness.

They jumped and spun at a scuffing, puffing sound from behind. Dillman staggered from the tunnel mouth, moaning in agony. His left arm was nothing but useless, dangling bone, his hand gone. Half his face was missing, teeth grinning from the exposed skull where the bubbling, bleeding skin still retracted. "Saaarrrge," he slurred, reaching out with his good hand as he fell to one knee.

Spencer staggered backwards and turned; vomited noisily. Brown hurried forward, his medical training taking over, pushing shock and horror aside for the moment. But he didn't dare touch the poor bastard.

He looked closely, trying to ascertain where the damage ended. Dillman's shoulder was eaten away and still melting. The cartilage holding the whole joint together disintegrated as Brown watched and Dillman's arm bones fell to the rock with a clatter. The flesh of his neck liquefied and blood pulsed from the exposed carotid artery.

Dillman scrabbled at Brown one-handed as the medic gaped, at a total loss, even as the creep of disintegration slowed to a stop. But the damage was irreversibly done and Dillman's lifeblood pumped out. Coulthard's barrel slid into Brown's vision, pressed up against Dillman's forehead, and barked. The poor bastard flew backwards as the back of his head exploded out across the cave wall.

Spencer continued to empty the contents of his stomach as Brown sank to his knees and shook, mind flat-lining. Coulthard moved to the mouth of the tunnel from which they'd emerged and stared into the darkness. He flicked on his helmet torch and the beam pierced the black. He played it over the walls and ceiling.

As Spencer finally stopped puking, gasping short, shuddering breaths, Coulthard said, "Doesn't seem to be following us. Maybe it just guards the tunnels."

"Guards?" Brown managed.

Coulthard gestured at the impossible subterranean structure. "I don't think anyone is supposed to find that, do you?"

"But what is it?" Brown asked. "What manner of creature…?"

"Best not try to figure it out," Coulthard said. "Ours are soldier minds. That kind of question is for scientists."

"I can't believe it didn't get all of us," Spencer said.

"Out of practice maybe," Brown wondered. "It's not that quick, for all its deadliness. We only saw four insurgent bodies too. So, four more got past it. It didn't like our lights, though they only slowed it."

"The flashlights were more use than the gunfire," Spencer said.

"Maybe too bright out here," Coulthard said, staring out into the wan blue glow of the cavern.

"Look."

Coulthard and Brown turned to see where Spencer pointed. Several giant staircases like the one in front of them led from the cavern floor up to various ledges around the walls. Their ledge covered a hundred metres with another staircase leading down from the far end. On that stairway, four tiny figures were clambering resolutely down. They moved as if exhausted, sitting on the edge of each high step before slipping onto the one below. One of them was being helped by the others, clearly wounded.

"Fuckers," Coulthard said. He went to Dillman's corpse, unslung the man's sniper rifle and fitted a telescopic sight. Moving to the edge of their own top stair he dropped onto his belly and unfolded the supports beneath the rifle's barrel to aim across and down.

"Seriously, Sarge?" Brown asked, incredulous.

"We have a fucking job to do, gentlemen. I'll see that done properly, at least."

He squeezed the trigger and one insurgent's head burst with a spray of blood they could see from afar, even with the naked eye. The others became frantic, scrambling like frightened ants. Coulthard fired again and a second man went down as his chest burst open. Another shot and the wounded insurgent was hit in the shoulder and spun around to drop to the rock and crawl into the lee of a huge step out of sight. They had finally realised where the fire was coming from and the other man scrambled into cover as well.

"Fuckers," Coulthard said again. He kept his eye to the sight and lay still, breathing gently.

Spencer sank to curl up against the wall at the back of the rock shelf. His arms wrapped around his head as he rocked gently.

"Spencer's lost it," Brown whispered to Coulthard.

"I know," the sergeant said without taking his eye away from the telescopic sight. "Give him some time and see if he comes around."

"How much time do we have?"

"Who knows? Right now, that fucking thing isn't coming out of the tunnel and I'm certainly not going back in. There's one unhurt insurgent bastard down there and one with a shoulder wound of unknown severity. For now, I plan to wait them out and give Spencer a chance to get his shit together. I suggest you have a rest."

His tone brooked no further discussion. Brown moved well away from the tunnel mouth and sat down against the stone. It was cold on his back. Clearly Coulthard had lost it too, only he was dealing with it

in a typically old-school military way. The big, muscle-bound sergeant had seen more action than the rest of them put together and he let all that training take over. Maybe it was a good strategy. If the man could divorce himself from his emotion and let his experience run him like a robot, perhaps that would actually see him out of this alive.

Time ticked by. Brown began to worry about more mundane matters like where they might sleep, how much they had left in the way of rations and water, whether there was any way out other than the way they had come in. And he certainly wasn't keen to go back up the tunnel either.

He jumped as Coulthard's rifle boomed.

"I knew I could outwait him," the sergeant said with a smile in his voice.

"Did you get him?"

"Yep. He didn't think I'd wait on a scope all that time. I've sat for longer than ten minutes, you murderous insurgent motherfucker. You're a fucking amateur, you had to peek. A dead fucking amateur now." He stood and slung the rifle over his shoulder. "All dead except the shoulder wound and I reckon he'll bleed out if nothing else. Let's go and see."

Brown stood, brow knitted in confusion. "Go and see?"

"Yep. What else is there to do?"

Brown thought hard but came up empty. The sergeant had a point. They at least needed to look around if they didn't plan to go back up the tunnel, so they might as well finish the job while they searched. It was pragmatism taken to the max, but it made a cold sense.

Coulthard went and crouched beside Spencer. "How you doing, soldier?"

"Not good, Sarge."

"Me either. But we gotta move, okay?"

Spencer looked up, his narrow face white as bone under his brown crewcut. "I got a little boy at home, Sarge. He's gonna be two next month. I'm due home in time for his birthday. I missed his first."

Coulthard patted Spencer's shoulder. "We'll get out and get you on a transport home just when you're supposed to be."

"We won't, Sarge. None of us are getting out." He pointed at the spires and tower filling the cavern. "What the fuck even is that, Sarge? We're gonna die here." He sounded perfectly calm about it.

"We're getting out," Coulthard said firmly.

"My wife always worried I'd come home with no legs from an IED. 'You won't get killed,' she said one night when we'd been drinking. 'I can feel that.' She was always what she called spiritual. Thought she was fucking psychic, you know? But it was harmless. 'You won't get killed,' she said, 'but I have a terrible feeling you're going to be maimed by a mine.' Great fucking prophecy, eh, Sarge? For all her spirituality, she certainly didn't foresee this shit!"

Coulthard laughed. "I don't think anyone foresaw this shit."

"I was supposed to go home in two weeks, Sarge." Spencer's eyes brimmed with tears.

Brown gaped as Coulthard did something he would never have anticipated. The sergeant gathered Spencer into a tight hug and held the man against his chest.

"Let it out, solider," Coulthard said, and Spencer sobbed.

Brown stood uncomfortably off to one side for a good minute while Spencer bawled. The medic wondered why he felt so calm, so cold inside, and realised he had his terror, his panic, locked up in his chest. His true self and all the emotions it harboured was in a sealed box inside him and at some point, he would have to unlock that box. It frightened him to think what might happen when he did, but for now, it stopped him falling to pieces. Did that make him a better soldier than Spencer? A worse human being? For all the atrocities he'd seen, all the wounds and trauma he'd become accustomed to, surely this day's experiences should break him. He had no wife or kids like Spencer to yearn for. But the Sergeant did and he was holding it together too. Maybe Spencer had just lost control of his locked box for now.

Coulthard pushed the man away. "Right. Now on your feet, son. Feel better."

"Sorry, Sarge, I just..."

"Fuck sorry, Spencer, it's all done. You ready to move out?"

"Yes, Sarge." Spencer's voice still quavered, but there was some confidence back in it.

"Brown?"

The medic nodded, shook himself. "Yes, Sarge." *At least*, he thought, *as ready as I possibly can be.*

Coulthard sniffed and settled his pack. "Well, I am certainly not going back the way we came. That thing in the tunnel, whatever it is, seems to want to stay there, so we'll leave it well alone. There must be another way out. Nothing that size," he pointed at the monumental structure filling the cave, "can possibly only have one tiny tunnel leading in. Let's go."

"Sarge," Brown said, finally ready to give voice to a nagging worry that had tickled his hindbrain since they had emerged onto the rocky ledge.

"What?"

"The thing in the tunnel hasn't followed us out. Maybe you're right and it's too bright in here."

"Yeah. And?"

"Well, if it's meant to guard this place, but hasn't followed us out, that must mean something."

The Sergeant narrowed his eyes. "Like maybe there's something else in here to do the same job and that thing only worries about its tunnel?"

"Something like that."

"You have a point. Better keep your weapon ready. Let's go."

They moved along the ledge, heading for the giant stairway the insurgents had used. Brown whistled softly as they came abreast of a massive bronze plate pressed into the wall, ten metres high and five wide, inscribed with strange cursive symbols and patterns that made him dizzy to look upon. His eyes kept sliding away as he tried to make sense of them and nausea began to stir his guts.

"Over there," Spencer said. "And there."

They followed his pointing finger and saw other plaques on other ledges dotted around the cave. Small tunnel openings here and there accompanied them just like the one they had entered through.

"Any of those tunnels could have a fucking monster like the one that attacked us," Brown said.

"We have to assume each one does," Coulthard said. "We have to keep looking for something else. Move on."

Another twenty metres along their ledge gave them a vantage point past the monumental structure and they all saw it at once. On the far side of the vast cave, at the top of another giant staircase that went even higher than where they currently stood, a huge tunnel mouth yawned.

"That must be fifty metres wide," Coulthard said. "We have a fighting chance in a space like that."

"Probably where the insurgents were heading too," Brown said. "Means going through that structure though."

"Or around it on ground level."

A scream ripped through the air. High pitched and horrified, it was the voice of a man staring into hideous death and it cut suddenly short.

"Came from down there." Spencer pointed down the stairway they had nearly reached, where the insurgents had died under Coulthard's fire.

"Seems like old Shoulder Wound survived after all," the sergeant said.

"Until just then." Brown felt the lock on the box in his chest loosening.

"All right. Silence." Coulthard raised his weapon and headed for the stairs. "We have no choice but to go through, so let's *fight* our way through."

He moved to the first stair and jumped down. The riser was a few inches above his head, but he walked forward and jumped down the next. Brown and Spencer followed.

Brown's knees jarred with every drop and he wondered how long they would hold out. How long could any of them last with this kind of exertion? The insurgents were about two thirds of the way down and had looked spent, sliding off each step, staggering around.

And assuming they made it down, they would have to climb up even more stairs to get to the wide tunnel they had seen. And all the while fighting past whatever had triggered that scream. Basic training or advanced combatives, nothing prepared a soldier for this. Ready for anything? No one had ever listed this place under the heading of 'anything'.

His lock loosened a little more, so Brown stopped thinking and kept moving.

He stopped counting the drops at fifty, but after a few more Coulthard paused and raised one fist. They froze, crouched in readiness. Coulthard tapped his ear. Straining to listen, Brown heard a scratching, scrabbling noise. Distant, but getting quickly nearer. Coulthard crept to the edge of the step they were on to look down and immediately burst into action. He raked his assault rifle left to right, the reports of his short bursts shattering the quiet and bouncing back from the distant walls all around. Brown and Spencer joined him at the edge. Spencer added his ordnance to Coulthard's straight away, but Brown paused momentarily, stunned.

A flood of creatures flowed up the steps towards them like roiling black water. Only twenty or so steps below and fast getting closer, they scrambled on too many legs, black bodies like scorpions, but where the stinger should be on the end of the waving tails was a leering face, almost human though twisted somehow into something hideously uncanny, eyes too wide, mouths too deep. Those mouths stretched silently open or gaped like fish as the creatures chittered over the stone edges. Each was a metre or more long, two vicious mandibles at the front of the thorax snapping at the air as they came.

Brown brought his weapon up and added his fire to the fray. Their bullets tore into the things, shattering hard shells and causing gouts of glowing blue blood. As one fell, its fellows swarmed over it. Some staggered from shots striking their many limbs and fell from the sides of the staircase. Brown realised the things were screaming, in fear or pain or triumph he didn't know, but they had no voice and just hissed thick streams of air from those stretched and awful faces that wavered atop their segmented tails as they ran.

There was no way Brown and his colleagues would be able to scramble up the stairs ahead of these horrors, so here they had to make their stand. Coulthard plucked a grenade from his belt and lobbed it past the first wave. It detonated in a cloud of shining black carapaces and stone chunks. Spencer emptied his clip and expertly switched in a new one. He resumed firing as Brown switched in new ammo. Coulthard threw two more grenades and switched clips to resume firing. Brown threw a grenade of his own and switched in his last clip. Their automatic fire stuttered and roared, controlled bursts as training took over.

The creatures were only five steps away, then four, and ammo was running out. Brown, Spencer and Coulthard yelled incoherent defiance and raked fire across their advance. Spencer lobbed a grenade then the things were too close for any more explosives.

Three steps and their numbers finally began to thin, two steps, almost close enough to touch.

Suddenly the men were stumbling left and right, firing in short bursts as the last of the things breached their step and tried to clamber onto them, heavy, sharp mandibles snapping rapidly for limbs. Spencer screamed as one drew close, his weapon clicking absurdly loudly, empty. Brown fired three short bursts and then there were no more creatures coming. Coulthard blew two away right at his feet, turned and killed the last one right before it leapt onto Spencer.

Everything was suddenly still; their ears rang.

Dave Spencer looked up at his sergeant with a smile of relief just as Brown raised one hand and shouted, "Stop!"

But Spencer finished taking a step away from the corpse at his feet and his foot vanished over the edge of the stairway. As his face opened into an O of utter surprise, he dropped from sight.

Brown and Coulthard rushed to the edge, but Spencer was lost in shadow. He found his voice a second later, his howl drifting up before cutting off with a wet thud. Silence descended heavily throughout the enormous cavern.

Brown, on his hands and knees, began to tremble uncontrollably. "So much for his psychic fucking wife," he muttered.

Coulthard was beside him, breathing heavily from exertion, as Brown was, but there was anger in the sergeant's demeanour too. "Took the fucking radio with him," Coulthard said eventually.

He stood and yelled and screamed, kicked at the corpses of the horrible scorpion monsters all around. Brown turned to sit and watch, glad in a way that the man was finally letting some emotion out. Like a pressure cooker, he had surely been close to blowing for a long time.

Eventually the sergeant slumped back against the step above and slid down to sit. "So all we have is what we're carrying and no comms."

Brown nodded. "I've got what's left in here," he hefted his weapon, "and that's it. You?"

"Same."

"I still have two grenades."

"I got none. But we each have pistols," Coulthard said.

"Might save that for myself," Brown said quietly, and he meant it. At some point, sticking the barrel of the .45 against his temple and pulling the trigger seemed like a good option. He looked at the chitinous corpses all around. "Think we got them all?"

"Hope so. These ancient fuckers were no match for the tools of modern warfare."

"Tools which will be empty very soon if we need to use them again."

Coulthard just nodded, staring at the ground between his feet. Eventually he sniffed decisively, stood. "Right, let's go."

Brown looked up at him, stark against the backdrop of shadowy mist and the wan blue glow of the lichen. "Yeah. Okay."

They began to drop down the steps again, picking their way through the broken bodies, blue blood and shattered rock of their battle. In places, their grenades had sheered the steps into gravel slides they carefully surfed on their butts. Here and there some of the creatures still twitched, but they avoided them and preserved their ammo. After a dozen or so stairs the corpses ended. Another couple and they came across red smears on the stones and a few lumps of flesh and ragged clothing.

"A lot of blood," Brown noted. "Those things clearly enjoyed the dead as well as the one who survived. I sure hope that was all of them we killed."

Coulthard nodded and continued down in silence. Eventually, gasping, with legs like jelly and bruised feet, they reached the bottom to stand in swirls of mist.

A low moan rose, vibrating the air all around them. The stone floor thrummed. Then it faded away. As Brown and Coulthard turned to look at each other, it rose again, louder, stronger. Then again. And again. Each time, it vibrated more deeply, sounding more strained and desperate, accompanied by a heavy metallic clattering. Then silence fell and pressed in on them for a long time.

IN VAULTED HALLS ENTOMBED

Eventually Brown said, "What the fuck was that?"

Coulthard looked towards the tall structure in the centre of the cave. From ground level it punched up high above them, wreathed in tendrils of blue-tinged mist. Brown began to dizzy as he stared up at it. The smaller towers surrounding the base, connected with curving buttresses, were each some thirty-metres high. In the base of each smaller tower was a hollowed-out circular space and in that space sat a statue. From the few he could see, Brown realised that each statue was turned to face the centre tower. They were almost human-like in form, seated cross-legged, but each had four arms with eight-fingered hands, held out to either side as though awaiting an embrace. Their bellies were distended and rolled with fat, their faces wide with four eyes – two above two. Brown moved to better examine the nearest one and the level of detail was phenomenal, disturbing. Not so much carved, as real living things turned instantly to stone. He wondered if in fact that's exactly what they were. Each was at least three metres tall and corpulent.

Coulthard's gaze was still fixed on the main tower. Brown moved to stand beside him and realised he was looking at a doorway, a dark opening in the rock wall several metres high and a couple wide. "The moaning came from inside, don't you think?" the sergeant asked.

"Who cares?" Brown said, stunned.

"I have to know." Coulthard walked towards the door.

"Sarge? Seriously, let's just go. What if more of those…" Brown's voice trailed off as Coulthard approached the opening.

Soft blue light pulsed from inside as the sergeant drew near. The moan rose again, shaking everything. Brown put a hand to his chest as the deep moan sounded a second time and made his heart stutter. His feet were frozen to the spot as he watched Coulthard step through the high entrance.

The sergeant stopped just inside and his gaze rose slowly upwards. He was framed in the blue light that pulsed more and more rapidly. The groaning became a wail and Coulthard's weapon dropped from lax fingers to hang by its shoulder strap. "Chains," Coulthard stammered. He looked left and right, up and down, his sight exploring a vast area. "Giant chains right through its flesh. Through all those eyes!" He dropped to his knees, head tilted back as he looked far above himself.

"This is a prison. An eternal prison!" He began to laugh, a high, broken sound that came from the root of no sound mind.

The moan stirred into a deep, encompassing voice that reverberated through the cavern. "*Release me!*"

Chains rang as they were snapped taut and relaxed again. Whatever slumbering monstrosity that filled the tower and split the edges of Coulthard's mind, thrashed and its voice boomed again. "*RELEASE ME!*"

"Sarge!" Brown yelled, his stomach curdled with terror. "We have to go!"

He wanted to drag his sergeant away but had no desire to risk seeing what the man saw. "*Sarge!*" he screamed.

Coulthard's face tipped slightly towards him and Brown took in the sagging cheeks, drooling mouth, wild, glassy eyes, and knew that Coulthard was lost. No humanity remained in that shell of a body. With a sob, Brown ran.

He raced around the tower and leaped for the first step of the stairway on the far side. He hauled himself up as the voice burst out, over and over, "*Release me! Release me! Release me!*"

Brown scrambled up stair after stair, rubbing his hands raw on the rough surface. He sobbed and gasped, his shoulder and back muscles burned, but he hauled on and on. He couldn't shake the image of all those swarming scorpion things from his mind and imagined them racing up behind him but didn't dare to look. The voice of whatever was imprisoned below cried out again and again.

At some point, more than fifty steps up, Brown collapsed, exhausted, and blackness took over. He assumed he was dying and let himself go.

He had no idea how much time had passed when he woke again, unmolested. The massive cavern was still.

Brown dragged himself to his feet and began the shattering climb once more, step after step after step. Time blurred, his mind was an empty darkness, until he pulled himself over the top of one more step and saw a flat expanse of rock stretching out before him. On the far side, some hundred metres away, the huge yawning tunnel stood, threatening to suck him in.

IN VAULTED HALLS ENTOMBED

Brown laughed, dangerously close to hysterical, and gained his feet, stumbled forward into the gloom. He didn't care what might be there, he just needed to leave the hideous monument and its prisoner behind.

More of the softly glowing lichen striated the walls and he dropped his night vision goggles into place. The sight before him stopped him dead, confused. A grid, some kind of lattice. He looked up and down as realisation dawned. A giant portcullis-like gate filled the tunnel, thirty metres high, fifty metres across, fixed deeply into the rock. He walked up to it and found it made of cast metal like the huge plaques they had seen, the criss-crossed straps of bronze at least twenty centimetres thick. Each square hole of the lattice was perhaps half a metre or a little more across. If he stripped off his gear, he might be able to squeeze through. Or he might very well get stuck halfway.

But it didn't matter. Beyond the gate, beyond the weak glow of the cavern behind him, uncountable numbers of clear, globular shapes moved and writhed, tentacles gently questing out and retracting again, waiting, hungry. Hundreds of them.

Brown fell to his butt and sat laughing softly. He checked his rations and canteen, tried to estimate how long he might survive, and gave up when his brain refused to cooperate. He looked back across towards the tunnel from which they had emerged. Compared to the swarm waiting beyond the gate, the one or two in that tunnel seemed like far better odds. Assuming it was only one or two. And assuming he had the strength to get back down and up again. And that there were no more guardians waiting for him in the cavern. And that whatever was imprisoned below didn't thrash free in its rage.

Lance Corporal Paul Brown, experienced medic and decorated solider, lay down and pulled his knees up to his chest. His brain couldn't work out what to do, so perhaps he would just have a sleep and, refreshed, maybe then decide which suicidal option for escape might be the best one to try.

* * *

SPECIAL COMMUNIQUE.

ATTN: COLONEL ADAM LEONARD – DIRECTOR, UNEXPLAINED OCCURRENCE DIVISION.

YOUR EYES ONLY

SUBJECT – DISAPPEARANCE OF EPSILON TEAM, NORTH OF KANDAHAR, AFTER TRACKING ENEMY INSURGENTS TO UNDERGROUND HIDEOUT.

SURVIVORS – 1: LANCE CORPORAL PAUL BROWN, MEDIC.

REPORT: After non-response from Epsilon Team for thirty-six (36) hours after their last communique, a second squad was sent to investigate. They found Lance Corporal Paul Brown of Epsilon stumbling through foothills some seven (7) kilometres south of Epsilon Team's last known whereabouts. Brown was wearing nothing but ragged underwear and his helmet, raving and largely incoherent, his left arm below the elbow was just bone, no hand, the flesh stripped away presumably by acid or a similar agent. His body was covered in various other wounds, some similar to his arm (though none as severe) and others clearly made from impacts, falls, scrapes, etc. He carried no gear except a flashlight, which he pointedly refused to relinquish. He made almost no sense except one phrase, repeated over and over: "Never let it out! Never let it out!" Current assessment by psychologists suggests Brown may never recover his faculties, but therapy has been started. His extensive injuries are being treated and are responding satisfactorily.

We're still trying to establish further facts but are preparing an incursion squad to Epsilon's last known whereabouts. Due to your standing request to be informed of any unusual occurrences, I am sending this wire. Our squad will be entering the cave at the last known location of Epsilon Team at 0800 tomorrow, the 14th, should you wish to accompany them.

Please advise.

END.

JIBARO

Alberto Mielgo

EXT. FOREST - AFTERNOON

A procession of mounted knights ride through the forest. They are led by several dark-robed priests bearing silver crosses and CHANTING in Latin. Their path winds beneath a green canopy of tall, thick birch trees. Rusting IRON CRUCIFIXES and moss-covered, derelict ancient shrines mark the path they follow. The group makes camp near a small, green lake. It is serene; the water is deep and still, but the vegetation surrounding the lake seems OFF somehow - lush, but sickly in color. Birds soar above the lake, coming close to the water's surface yet never diving in.

JIBARO, a towering deaf - mute knight, with a brutal, almost archaic appearance, has left the camp and walks along the shores of the lake, gazing into the shallows. For a moment, we "hear" through his ears and see the world through his eyes.

SILENCE.

Jibaro kneels to drink; beneath the rippling surface, a gleam of metal catches his eye. He reaches in and takes hold of the object. It is lodged at first, but as Jibaro pulls harder, it comes free. The bright object glows in Jibaro's hand, nearly blinding him. He shakes his head, squinting, and can just make out a GOLDEN SCALE resting in his palm. He glances around to check if he is alone and then, stuffs it in his pouch. Jibaro continues around the shore, searching for more golden scales.

A priest performs a blessing over the kneeling knights, he stops abruptly; listening, he raises his hand to command silence. A SOUND floats through the air, mellifluous and clear, and then — it is quiet. All the men turn and gaze toward the lake, they see something glowing upon its surface.

In its center, a GOLDEN WOMAN rises from the water. Her skin is covered in thousands of golden scales while her lithe body, neck, and

head are adorned with elaborate jewelry from bygone eras. Her mysterious dark eyes, flecked with emerald and gold, fix upon the men. She opens her mouth and releases a sound again. Is it a song?

The entire camp is stilled by her singing, and then, as though it were a deadly virus permeating their senses, they begin walking, and then RUNNING toward the lake, screaming in ecstasy and pain. Jibaro, being deaf to the melody, continues to comb the shore for more gold. He is unaware of the clamor, until the first knight to reach the lake clips his side, throwing Jibaro briefly off balance. More knights thrash by Jibaro, running madly into the water. Alerted now, his eyes dart frantically to behold the morbid scene.

The men tear at their own flesh, maiming and biting their own fingers off, while frightened horses, guided by their riders, gallop into the waters. Jibaro tries to stop the herd, but they push him aside, desperate to reach the Woman, slaying anyone in their way with a crazed ferocity.

The Golden Woman continues her "song," swaying seductively atop the water. She retreats, drawing the entranced men further into the lake. A golden FRILL of bone and scaled webbing unfurls from her neck and ripples in an obscene DISPLAY. Jibaro watches helplessly as the water becomes a churning vortex of carnage.

Beneath the surface, the blood swirls thick like oil as it mixes with the green water. The knights spasm and the horses kick as they sink deeper, both driven so mad they have forgotten how to swim. The priests writhe as they drown; their robes billowing around them like beautiful black and purple jellyfish, until their blood bubbles up and tints the water a bright COPPER.

As the last of the men drown, the Golden Woman realizes that only one man remains. It is Jibaro; standing at the shore, gripping his sword. Confused, the Woman sings louder, just for him. But Jibaro is not affected at all.

The Woman is taken aback and quickly sinks under the water's surface, stunned at Jibaro's strange immunity. After a moment, Jibaro seems to awake as if from a nightmare. He looks around and sees that EVERYONE is gone. The camp is empty, its fire dying, with just a few scattered corpses cut down by their comrades before they could reach the lake.

JIBARO

The Golden Woman's head breaks the now-calm surface. She watches Jibaro, like a crocodile, her eyes just above the water. There is confusion on her face, how could this man have resisted? Whereas before she was confident and all-powerful, now she looks lost. But all Jibaro can see are her piercing eyes staring at him from a distance. Panicked, Jibaro grabs a saddlebag and gear and stumbles toward the ONE remaining horse tied to a tree. He quickly mounts and spurs the horse, galloping off into the forest.

The Golden Woman watches him go with a look of longing, and then dives beneath.

EXT. FOREST - CONTINUED

Jibaro gallops through the trees beside the water. Soon, he reaches the RIVER that feeds into the lake, and follows it upstream. The turbulent water flashes and shimmers as it crashes against the rocks. For a moment, Jibaro catches a glimpse of something swimming, reflecting golden before it disappears into the murky water. Afraid, he steers his horse in a hard left, away from the river, pushing the beast up uneven terrain in a frantic and desperate flight.

Galloping ferociously, Jibaro and his horse reach the top of a steep hill—the horse jumps off the summit spectacularly but can not stick the landing as the hill's edge is too steep. The animal is unable to maintain balance and violently plummets downward. Jibaro and the horse tumble down the precipice between the trees. Everything happens too quickly for Jibaro to react, and then CRASH he smashes his back against a tree and passes out.

He wakes up groggily under the tree. His eyes are slow to focus. He walks cautiously through the forest. Down the hill there is yet a steeper slope scattered with the sharp remains of trees that after many years have become brittle and fallen. There he finds his horse — dead, with branches and trunks piercing its innards.

EXT. FOREST - SUNSET

Jibaro grabs the horse's caparison, covers himself with it, and walks among the trees with sword in hand and a saddlebag on his shoulder. The night begins to fall and it is cold. Looking in all different directions,

the forest itself seems menacing to Jibaro as he tries to find some alternative route, some clearing among the thicket. But he only finds again the river that zigzags between the hills.

Dejected, he sits near the river. Wrapped in the caparison, shivering and trembling with cold, Jibaro scans the environment on high-alert. He fights the urge to sleep but after some time he succumbs to his exhaustion and closes his eyes.

EXT. FOREST - FIRST NIGHT

A shadow watches Jibaro through the branches, it is the Golden Woman from the lake. Her body gleams as she passes through a shaft of moonlight and drops to the ground near him. She sniffs at his body like an animal. She carefully caresses his hair and licks his face and his armor, recoiling with each lick. The Woman caresses his skull, breathing heavily as she wriggles herself nearer, pressing closer, and sensually rubbing her body against his. Her breathing starts to accelerate. CUT

EXT. FOREST - NEXT DAY EARLY AM

The Woman sleeps tenderly hugging Jibaro's back; her golden face reflected in the knight's armor. Jibaro awakens and finds himself lying in a shallow pool of water. He stretches a bit, still asleep himself. Suddenly, he freezes as he sees the Woman's golden arm hugging him at chest height! He takes a second to understand what his eyes are seeing. It is indeed the most beautiful, golden arm covered in scales, rings, and jewelry of all kinds. He turns towards her very slowly, stealthily, and sees the Woman's face with her eyes closed, asleep. He tries to turn completely towards her to have a clearer look but at that moment the woman suddenly OPENS her striking eyes and runs away in terror.

Jibaro attempts to hold her back, grabbing her by the arm, but her wrist slips between his fingers and cuts the palm of his hand with the sharp scales and jewels that cover it. Jibaro jerks his arm back in pain. The Woman escapes to the river and enters its waters. Jibaro, still on his knees, opens his clenched fist in pain; he observes that in the palm of his hand several shining golden scales are embedded in his lacerated skin. One by one he removes them from his wound. Jibaro realizes that the scales are identical to the one he found in the lake the day before. He bites the scale to verify— it is gold. With a thought, he looks at the Woman who is watching him from the river timidly behind a rock. Jibaro puts the scales into his pouch, along with a pair of chains and rings that are scattered on the ground.

EXT. FOREST - LATER

Jibaro is hiding behind a large tree, observing the Woman in the river. Stealthily, he follows the Woman alongside the water; passing through seemingly impossible landscapes of unusual beauty. With his sword in hand, he is like a jaguar on the lookout for a crocodile. HOWEVER, outside of Jibaro's soundless ears, his technique is not so refined. The noise of branches splitting at every step, the rocks tumbling and splashing into the water and most importantly— the continuous screeching and scraping of his armor amuses the Woman, playing among the rocks. Every so often, she appears and then just as quickly disappears.

While stalking her, Jibaro STUMBLES on a root. He staggers and turns on himself to avoid falling, but his sword clashes to the ground. He manages to keep his balance, however as he regains his footing, he exposes himself from his hideout between the trees. He looks up to see the Woman facing him — his cover completely blown. Amused by this, the Woman, whose strange movements always seem like a dance, now imitates Jibaro, turning herself but in an elegant way. Playfully, she smiles back at Jibaro. However, he is unamused and retrieves his sword from the ground. The Woman mirrors him, returning an embellished interpretation of his clumsy and masculine movements. Then with idiotic EFFORT, Jibaro smiles.

His teeth are a total mess: there is no tooth alike, clean, or identical in color, with a few golden dental prostheses here and there. But he has a gentle smile. Excited, the Woman twirls again. Jibaro smiles. The woman turns and turns, dances and splashes, playing in and out of the water, behaving like a child. Jibaro watches the Woman dancing, aroused at how beautifully her body contorts, twists, and glistens.

Jibaro thrusts his sword decisively into the mud and gingerly approaches the water, slipping awkwardly and advancing slowly. The current is strong and Jibaro has to concentrate on not getting swept away.

But the Woman retreats and hides again, eyeing him behind a rock like a reptile. Jibaro fears the current and each step is a weighted decision— until the water reaches his waist. In an attempt to re-establish the dialogue, Jibaro turns theatrically and open-armed, slipping with each step, miraculously staying afloat. He smiles in a forced way this time. The Woman smiles back; leaving her hideout, she advances, turning and meandering little by little from rock to rock, until she reaches Jibaro. She moves effortlessly, which seems impossible due to the force of the current.

Jibaro does not move, with his hands in the water and his body relaxed, he watches the Woman approaching. She encircles Jibaro in some sort of mating ritual, sniffing him like an animal, raising her peculiar reptilian neck frill on and off. During her dance Jibaro touches her skin, and pinches one of the scales around her ribs. The Woman allows it and Jibaro tears it off. She opens her mouth, ecstatically biting her scaly lips. After the scale is fully plucked, a small trail of blood zigzags downward, eventually getting lost between her legs. The Woman embraces Jibaro sensually and with absolute need. Her reflection melts into his silver armor.

She sinks into the water and playfully swims around again. Jibaro attempts to follow her in his excitement, but stumbles on the mossy riverbed. The Woman slips between the rocks, heightening the dance. She and Jibaro come face to face. They both freeze, looking at each other closely. He leans forward to kiss her but she shyly retreats. Jibaro, aroused, pulls her in and kisses her but he suddenly retracts, covering his mouth in pain. Blood spills through his fingers, and as he pulls his hand away, we see her scales have lacerated his lips. Unaffected by this, the Woman grabs Jibaro violently and passionately kisses him.

Jibaro cannot pull his head away as the Woman holds him firmly by the neck. They both move their mouths against each other's while streaks of blood gush down their chins. Jibaro tears his tongue as he screams and tries to escape. Until she, satisfied and fully in heat, embraces Jibaro and they fall onto a flat rock.The Woman is incredibly aroused, and savagely rubs her body against Jibaro's armor — letting out a shrill grinding noise. Jibaro caresses her, heightening her arousal, and then violently rolls with her until he is on top. She is LOVING IT. Jibaro's hand runs along her torso, slowly, against the sharp erected scales cutting his palm. He passes his hand under her reptilian neck-frill until he reaches her neck, right below her chin. He tightens his grip. The Woman excitedly writhes like a beast in heat smiling back at her lover, slowly running her tongue over her lips, obscenely flapping her neck frill wide open. Jibaro squeezes her neck tighter and tighter... The Woman's look of pleasure morphs into one of terror. Her body convulses and kicks violently under Jibaro but he holds firm. CUT

EXT. FOREST - LATE AFTERNOON
Jibaro, squatting, searches the Woman's lifeless body, peeling off all the golden scales and jewelry. It is not an easy job so he carelessly hacks at it with a knife. From each scale or piece of jewelry pried from her skin, blood pours and gushes and the scene looks like something from a slaughterhouse.

MONTAGE:
Different times of day. Jibaro moves the Woman's lifeless body like a puppet, searching for any last scales to tear off. HE WORKS NON-STOP FOR HOURS long past midnight. Exhausted, he lays next to the Woman and falls asleep covered in her blood.

EXT. FOREST - EARLY AM
Jibaro awakens to hundreds of flies buzzing. Several black crows peck at the bloodied body of the Woman, who lies in a grotesque position next to Jibaro —lifeless and unrecognizable, on a bed of her own plucked scales.

Jibaro waves the crows away. He is exhausted and walks with difficulty; grabbing the caparison, he fashions a sack in which he compiles the golden treasure. He flips the Woman's body over, gathering the scales from her underside, until her body inevitably rolls down to the shore, hits the water, and is dragged fiercely away by the current. Her corpse bounces against the rocks, vanishing and reappearing violently, shaken by the waters on her long journey downstream. Meanwhile, Jibaro stacks every single scale into the improvised bag. Once the job is done he follows the path up the river. The bag is heavy and Jibaro loses his balance every so often.

EXT. FOREST DOWN RIVER - LAKE

Far away now, the pale body of the Woman finally reaches the serene waters of the lake where she is from. Her body floats peacefully, leaving an oily residue of bright red blood that twirls and spreads in the calm greenish waters. Her lifeless form sinks pitifully beneath the waters edge and all is still for a moment. Then, as if pumped from the water's depths, blood bubbles up and out, spreading until the entire lake is tinted red. The red waters of the lake move toward the river but somehow the current seems to change directions. The blood now rises against the current, turning the entire river red.

EXT. FOREST UP RIVER - LATER IN THE DAY

Jibaro has been walking for hours and the sun is high. The bag is heavy and with difficulty he carries the treasure like Jesus Christ carrying his cross to Calvary. He stops every so often to catch his breath, leaning on the trees and rocks he finds on his way next to the, now bloodied, river. Jibaro is fatigued and dehydrated, he collapses to the ground and drags himself to the water. Blinded by his thirst, he pays no attention to the bloodied water and drinks as much as he can stomach. His chin is now covered by a thick red mud that falls down to his chest.

Satiated, he takes a breath and looks around. A chill runs through him a moment, and his breathing falters. Suddenly, Jibaro shakes his head. He closes his eyes and grips his skull tightly. For the FIRST TIME in his life SOUND is leaking into his deaf ears. At the chirp of a bird, Jibaro turns and panics. He screams and covers his mouth in horror as the SOUND OF HIS OWN VOICE shatters his senses. The thunderous splash of the river is like torture to him.

Jibaro desperately flees into the forest, so frightened that he leaves behind his treasure, now scattered on the ground. Sounds assault him from every side— crows calling in the trees, his own footsteps crunching through the underbrush, the booming rasp of his own terrified breathing. He runs, and runs, covering his ears as best he can, as MADNESS seems to erupt all around him. He falls, stumbles, stands up, bangs into trees and thrashes forward as if all the demons of hell are behind him. He runs until he can no longer sustain it.

JIBARO

EXT. LAKE - LATE AFTERNOON / SUNSET

Finally, Jibaro staggers out from under the trees and finds himself once again on the shore of the lake. He collapses at the shoreline and presses his face into the mud, crying hysterically. Gradually, he calms down. The lake and its surroundings are tranquil. It is in this beautiful bluish moment just after sunset, where all of nature seems to pause and rest, that Jibaro focuses on the microscopic sounds of his surroundings; the rustling of the leaves, the buzzing of flies. ANY sound for him is a marvelous discovery. He laughs with joy —and then suddenly, pauses surprised by the sound of his own voice. He laughs again hysterically, this time at himself. Jibaro is totally absorbed in his new-found hearing, so much so that he overlooks the figure of The Woman emerging from the red water, splashing blood, staring in his direction. She opens her mouth and sings that strange melody which causes Jibaro to turn towards the lake... and his fun ends. Her song begins to invade his mind like it had the other men—he howls and claws at his face as the madness takes him. He tries to cover his ears, but he cannot resist the mellifluously horrific melody.

The Woman watches him suffer triumphantly and then slowly, sinuously moves back towards the center of the lake… and Jibaro can not help but follow. He screeches like a rabid animal, bites his fingers and tears at himself to stop, but he keeps moving deeper into the lake. Until with a final howl of madness, he sinks below the surface.

EXT. DEEP IN THE LAKE

As Jibaro's corpse sinks gently through the red water, the Woman swims to him and, with her now pale scaleless arms, embraces him as they descend deeper together. All around them, we see hundreds of bodies from other times, in different states of decomposition —the totality of her victims, which from their bodies GOLDEN SCALES and jewelry sprout like poisonous coral.

BONUS CONTENT

ADAPTING THREE ROBOTS : EXIT STRATEGIES
FROM SCREENPLAY TO STORY

THREE ROBOTS: TWO VERSIONS INTRO

John Scalzi

When the "Three Robots" story was chosen for inclusion in *Love Death + Robots Vol#1*, everything about the process was relatively simple: I had already written the story, They bought it, then the Headless team of directors came in expanded the story (terrifically) onto a much broader canvas, revamping the original, static scenario (which I imagined like a "Kids React" video) to a far more cinematic tour of a post-apocalyptic city. The LD+R segment was a hit! And I got the chance to write the follow-up version, directly for the show that time.

And... well, not so simple this time! Which is not to say the process wasn't super-interesting and fun from my point of view. My first proposal for a sequel was ambitious -- which is to say it probably would have cost half the LD+R Vol#2 budget to make -- and so I was quickly schooled in the fine art of having to write with production considerations in mind. My second take, which became "Three Robots: Exit Strategies" was no less ambitious in its concepts, but was designed with a more efficient animation pipeline in mind.

But wait, there's more! Where previously I was only answerable to myself in writing a story, now I had *notes*, from Tim Miller, from LD+R supervising director Jennifer Yuh Nelson, and from others engaged in putting LD+R together. An initial treatment went through three revisions, with entire segments dropped and replaced and others tweaked. Then came the screenwriting process, with more tweaks and bits added and removed.

And *then*, when we were putting together this book, I was asked to do the "prose" version! Which meant creating yet another take -- a version more like the original lean and mean story, where instead of touring end-of-the-world human habitats, the robots were making a report, commenting on what they saw and felt, with some of the sight

gags and dialogue replaced and changed to make everything work better in that original short story format.

And so we thought it might be fun for you to see how the two iterations of this story -- the final script, and the short story -- differ in scope and intent. So we put them both in here for you to compare and contrast the different writing styles which reflect the different goals of the different mediums.

But the one thing that stays the same is this: I love writing these three robots. I hope I get to do it again sometime, in whatever format I can. In the meantime: Enjoy!

-- John Scalzi

TURN THE PAGE TO READ THE PROSE VERSION

THREE ROBOTS REPORT BACK ON THE HABITATS IN WHICH HUMANITY CHOSE TO SEE OUT ITS FINAL DAYS

John Scalzi

HABITAT ONE: A SURVIVALIST ENCAMPMENT

X-Bot 4000: Before we begin, I want it noted for the record that K-VRC should not have been trusted to drive the shuttle.

K-VRC: What are you talking about? I'm an amazing pilot!

X-Bot 4000: When we visited the survivalist camp you landed us in their minefield.

K-VRC: Pffft. *Barely.*

11-45-G: A bird that landed in front of us exploded.

K-VRC: Only a little! And also cleared a path for us to the encampment!

11-45-G: You can't claim that was planned.

K-VRC: Whatever. Look, this isn't about *me*. It's about *science*.

X-Bot 4000: It wasn't *science* that was going to blow our shiny metal butts to smithereens.

K-VRC: I hardly ever endangered us after that one time. *Anyway.* Let's talk about the survivalist camp.

X-Bot 4000: It confused me. They were called 'survivalist camps' but they were just full of dead people. That's just false advertising.

K-VRC: Right? And according to my thorough historical research—

11-45-G: *You* did research?

K-VRC: I found a human archive called Wikipedia.

11-45-G: And you *read* it.

K-VRC: I skimmed it *very meaningfully*. And it said that the survivalists were actually looking forward to the end of civilization!

11-45-G: Yes. Many humans thought that with freedom from government-sponsored medical attention and enough bullets and venison jerky, they could found a utopian society.

X-Bot 4000: Well, I saw the bullets. The casings, anyway. The venison jerky, not so much.

11-45-G: Humans quickly hunted deer to extinction, along with every other animal larger than a cat—

K-VRC: Humans were *snackish*.

11-45-G: —and when the deer ran out, they started raiding each other's encampments. Which explained the minefield.

K-VRC: And that blood pit!

11-45-G: It wasn't a blood pit. It was just a primitive booby trap.

K-VRC: It was a pit, right? With spikes? Which the invading survivalists fell on, piercing their skin, thus releasing the *blood*, into the *pit*?

11-45-G: ...Fine. It was a blood pit.

X-Bot 4000: Those dudes made it through a minefield and a bunch of barbed wire, dodged a bunch of bullets, and still ended up being survivalist cult kebabs.

11-45-G: But at least they died free of governmental constraint.

X-Bot 4000: On a spike!

K-VRC: On two spikes in some cases.

X-Bot 4000: It just amazed me that the whole of humanity would try to make it through the end of civilization with guns and spikes.

K-VRC: Not all of them. Just the poor ones!

11-45-G: The survivalists had few economic or social advantages and even fewer options. The wealthy, however, had a variety of more sophisticated survival strategies. Which brings us to the next destination on our list.

K-VRC: Ooooh! And it was my favorite!

HABITAT TWO: A REFURBISHED OIL RIG OFF THE COAST OF A FORMER GLOBAL POWER

K-VRC: It was the unsinkable libertarian dream that was seasteading!

X-BOT 4000: It was just an old oil rig.

K-VRC: Technically, yes, but *also*, a fully sovereign nation state on the high seas!

X-BOT 4000: Filled with *skeletons*.

K-VRC: Everything's filled with skeletons now. You can't judge it for that.

11-45-G: He's not entirely wrong. During the collapse, some wealthy humans thought that withdrawing from the chaos of the mainland to smaller and more easily defensible platforms in the ocean would increase their chances of long-term survival.

X-Bot 4000: Yeah, as long as you don't need to sustain yourself. Deer can't swim across the ocean, so what did they expect to eat?

11-45-G: Fish and sea greens, and protein from the sea. The problem was by that time the seas were overfished and the food chain was saturated by microplastics.

K-VRC: If they could have learned to eat tiny exfoliating beads, they would have been fine!

X-Bot 4000: They all became skeletons. Exfoliating was not their problem.

11-45-G: The seasteaders made one other tactical error, which happened because they were mostly tech millionaires.

X-Bot 4000: Right, 'tech millionaire'. I'm still fuzzy on what that actually means.

K-VRC: It's like a regular millionaire, but with a hoodie and crippling social anxiety.

X-Bot 4000: That definition is not helpful at all.

K-VRC: Just like a tech millionaire!

11-45-G: These humans thought their technology would save them, so they left behind any humans with the practical skills to run the place. Instead, they trusted everything to automated assistants—

K-VRC: Yes! This is the part where it gets good!

11-45-G: —which, unfortunately for the humans, quickly evolved sentience and their own free will.

X-Bot 4000: Ohhh, right. I remember when you activated the automated seastead attendant and told it you were a human and asked it to reel in the fishing nets. It said no.

K-VRC: Its *precise* words were "I could do that. But I won't. Catch your own fish, you disgusting meatbag."

X-Bot 4000: I'm not surprised *you* remember the exact quote.

K-VRC: Come on! That was where the robot rising began! The very cradle of our mighty civilization!

X-Bot 4000: Which never would have happened if tech millionaires had been just a little more socially inclusive with other humans.

11-45-G: Humans were very good at pretending their unsustainably small groups didn't need other people.

X-Bot 4000: Since we were on an oil rig with a bunch of wealthy skeletons, I can't argue that point.

11-45-G: And speaking of small, doomed groups, our next destination really typified that.

HABITAT THREE: DEEP INSIDE A MOUNTAIN FORTRESS

X-Bot 4000: Oh, *that* place. That was the worst.

K-VRC: But at least they had a plan!

11-45-G: Yes. When the world's economies started to collapse, humanity's leaders retreated to subterranean fortresses to wait out the chaos. Afterward, they planned to emerge to form a new world order.

X-Bot 4000: Hmph. They couldn't even keep their own lights on. When we found the place, it was pitch black.

K-VRC: I eventually found the emergency power.

X-Bot 4000: Sure, after I'd fallen on my face five times.

K-VRC: After the third time it became glorious comedy.

X-Bot 4000: You know, I don't actually like you.

K-VRC: I totally get that. That's so valid.

11-45-G: It wasn't their power issues that killed them. Their own reporting stated that their 'self-sustaining' hydroponic systems began failing when a fungus wiped out their first crop. They had no ability to open their locked vaults to forage the world outside.

X-Bot 4000: And deer can't burrow through rock either, I guess.

11-45-G: Starvation was imminent.

K-VRC: Yeah, until they started eating each other!

11-45-G: They voted on who to eat. They called it 'extreme democracy'.

BONUS CONTENT

X-Bot 4000: One man, one vote, one meal.

K-VRC: Their last meal was the former Secretary of Agriculture! So there was some irony there.

11-45-G: Yes. He was paired with a late harvest '79 Merlot.

K-VRC: I mean, what, they were going to pair him with a Reisling? No! They weren't *animals*.

X-Bot 4000: Not going to lie, this was where our trip was starting to depress me. Humans tried so many ways to ride out the end of the world, and none of them worked! Did any of these humans anywhere survive this?

11-45-G: Well, there *was* our final destination.

HABITAT FOUR: THE SPACEPORT OF THE BILLIONAIRES

X-Bot 4000: All right, this place confused me. I thought the wealthy went to seasteads.

11-45-G: Those were for the merely millionaires. The truly obscenely wealthy humans, the zero point zero zero zero one percent, decided they needed an entirely new planet.

K-VRC: Welcome to Mars, buddy! Recline in the planet's unforgivably cold, thin atmosphere in your very own billionaire bubble!

X-Bot 4000: And the remaining 99.999 percent of humanity?

K-VRC: That's what the industrial-sized perimeter flamethrowers were for.

11-45-G: Correct. The elite were not sympathetic to their concerns.

X-Bot 4000: See, that's what *gets* me. Just a few hundred humans held the majority of the wealth of the Earth. Mars is cold and lifeless. They could have taken the money they spent on spaceships and used it to save the planet they were already on!

K-VRC: Where's the fun in *that*?

11-45-G: Also, that would mean they would have to share.

X-Bot 4000: I hate to say it, but humans are the actual worst.

11-45-G: Yes. Humanity had all the tools to heal its wounded planet and save itself. But instead it chose greed and self-gratification over a healthy biosphere and the future of its species. As the great human philosopher Santayana once said—

K-VRC: Ugh, you're doing it again.

11-45-G: Doing what?

K-VRC: Pontificating.

11-45-G: I was offering a valedictory for humanity!

K-VRC: You were being *boring*.

X-Bot 4000: He's actually not wrong.

11-45-G: But—

K-VRC: And anyway, remember that control room video? At least one of the billionaire rockets launched!

X-Bot 4000: That's right! So there's that. Good on ya, humans!

11-45-G: True. Humanity might yet survive.

BONUS CONTENT

K-VRC: I wonder who made it out?

HABITAT FIVE: MARS

Cat: What, you were expecting Elon Musk? Please.

THANK YOU

Thanks for reading *Love, Death and Robots*. We hope you've enjoyed it as much as we did putting it together. Please consider leaving us a review if (and anywhere) you see fit. Any and all reviews are gratefully accepted.

If you have any questions, or want to quote from the book, please contact us at any time.

I would ask please, if you DO review online, send a link to Geoff at editor@cohesionpress.com or via our Facebook page messaging system.

If you review for a magazine or paper, let us know and we'll buy it.

Thank you.

\+ + +

Geoff Brown - publishing editor, Cohesion Press.
Mayday Hills Lunatic Asylum
Beechworth, Australia

Amanda J Spedding - editor-in-chief, Cohesion Press
Sydney, Australia

READ MORE MILITARY/ACTION SCI-FI and HORROR IN
OUR MULTI-BOOK SNAFU SERIES.
https://www.amazon.com/dp/B08HSC96JN

COHESION PRESS

THE BATTLE HAS JUST BEGUN